THE GREAT WASH

by

GERALD KERSH

I0636941

VALANCOURT BOOKS

Dedication: For Freda Court

Copyright © 1953 by Gerald Kersh

First published in Great Britain by Heinemann, January 1953.
First published in the U.S. by Ballantine Books in June 1953 under the
title *The Secret Masters*.
A condensed form of the novel appeared in *The Saturday Evening Post* in
1952 under the title *The Mystery of the Third Compartment*.
First Valancourt Books edition 2015

Published by Valancourt Books, Richmond, Virginia
http://www.valancourtbooks.com

All Valancourt Books publications are printed on acid free paper that
meets all ANSI standards for archival quality paper.

ISBN 978-1-941147-65-8 (*trade paper*)
Also available as an electronic book.

Cover design by Lorenzo Princi/lorenzoprinci.com
Set in Bembo Book MT Pro 10.5/12.4

Part One

There was no escape. Some mysterious instinct must have warned him that I was coming, and guided him to the right doorway in which to lie in wait for me; so that just as I crossed Poppin's Court in Fleet Street, he darted out of the doorway of the Red Lion and caught me by the arm. "Albert Kemp," he said, "I want a word with you."

"Hello, Conker," I said. "What's up?"

"Where is George Oaks?" he asked.

I knew where George Oaks was, because I was on my way to meet him, but I said: "Isn't he in the Red Lion?"

"No," said the man we called Conker. "Nor in the Bell, the Cogers, the Punch, the Falstaff, the Irish House, nor the Cheshire Cheese."

"Have you tried the Clachan, or the Falcon, or the George?" I asked.

"Well, try the Black Swan, or the Press Club," I said, knowing that George Oaks was waiting for me in another part of the town; and gave him a ten-shilling note, which he snatched and squeezed small, and poked into a waistcoat pocket.

Then he said: "I don't want your dirty money, I want George Oaks," and tugged from the unsavoury hinterland of his coat a copy of the last *Sunday Special*, folded back at a prominently displayed feature article on page two entitled GEORGE OAKS PROBES MYSTERY OF MISSING SCIENTISTS. Conker had annotated and underscored this article with pencils of various colours. I read "Unmitigated Bosh!" in blue, "What Drivel!" in green, and "Hypocritical Eyewash!" in red. In plain black he had added a big H to the author's surname.

"Hoax! Hoax!" he cried, pointing with a long, stained fore-finger. "Where is he? You're his friend—Damon and Pythias, David and Jonathan!—tell me where he is, and I'll have it out with him! I'll thrash it out with George Oaks if I have to hand-cuff myself to the office railings!"

He would have done that, too. In 1916 he had handcuffed himself to the railings of No. 10 Downing Street in order that Mr. Lloyd George might be forced to do something about the adulteration of milk. On another occasion he had got into trouble for hurling into the King's lap some incomprehensible petition, a hundred and twelve pages long, when His Majesty was driving to open Parliament. He was one of those combative but harmless madmen for which London, of all the cities in the world, is most remarkable. Indeed, we are proud of them—or rather, proud of our sublime capacity to ignore them. There is, for example, a retired Korean acrobat who, for the past thirty years, has been parading the streets of the city dressed in a gold bowler hat, yellow bolero, violet waistcoat, cretonne shirt, scarlet silk pants, and aluminium shoes, and carrying a silver-painted umbrella: no true Englishman has ever turned his head to look at him, for fear of embarrassing him.

So it was with old Conker. He ranted and he roared; he rushed up and down Whitehall screaming; he dashed his hat to the pavement outside Buckingham Palace, and invited H.R.H. the Duke of Gloucester (as the tallest member of the Royal Family) to come out and put up his dukes and have it out like a man. The police simply moved him on: he was a character.

Everyone knew that eccentric, seedy old man whose desperate gasping voice was so like the last spluttering whisper of an exhausted soda-water siphon. A famous cartoonist had made a type of him—Roger the Reformer—the crossed eyes between the blown-up bladder of his glabrous forehead and the pricked bladder of his collapsed, toothless face were irresistible. We tolerated him in Fleet Street, because he had been a friend of old Austin Crabbe who, in his day, had been one of us, and one of the best of us, before he, in his turn, had achieved madness or had it thrust upon him.

Generally, a half-crown sufficed—not to pacify Conker, but to drive him away. But now he was having what we called "one of his funny turns", and nothing but bolts and bars could keep him from getting at George Oaks. "Oaks the hoax!" said Conker. "Oaks the sycophant, Oaks the lackey of the press barons, and the lick-spittle of the gutter press! Oaks the coward!

I'll turn your filthy Fleet Street inside out like a dirty sock, but I'll find him, I'll find him!"

Now, my affection for George Oaks was something so deep that I could hear nothing said against him, even by the likes of Conker that are not accountable for what they say, so that at this I forgot to make the customary non-committal placatory grimace, and said: "Conker, George Oaks has been a good friend to you, if you had the sense to appreciate it. One of these days you'll go too far. Get out of my way!" And I brushed him aside, and crossed the street, and got into a taxi.

Then I began to laugh. Conker had slandered, individually and collectively, every member of the Royal Family since Queen Victoria, together with Their Majesties' several Privy Councils; and this was a laughing matter. He had hurled abuse of the most scurrilous kind at every idol in living memory; and three generations had smiled at him, tapping their foreheads. Now he had called George Oaks by a few bad names; and I had lost my temper with him. *Well*, I said to myself, forgiving myself, *I, too, am in an unhealthy state of nerves—for which very reason I have come up from the country for the pleasure of Oaks's company* . . . and resolved that next time I would give old Conker a pound. And so I came to our appointed meeting-place, the Hop Pole, near Bow Street.

The Hop Pole, as a public-house, caters for a strange and fascinating variety of customers. It is one of the Covent Garden market pubs: that is to say, it is open from six until nine o'clock on week-day mornings for the refreshment of bona fide workers in the fruit, vegetable, and flower market. At that time of the day its electric lights are half blind under cataracts of smoke, and the bar is somehow bleary, querulous, and only half awake. At nine in the morning it retires for a wash and brush-up, a gargle, a spit and a polish; gets the smoke out of its eyes and the fur off its tongue; and opens again spruce and shiny, at eleven-thirty. Then visitors accompanied by lawyers' clerks drop in to wait for friends who are detained at Bow Street Police Court round the corner. They are joined, eventually, by these friends, who always look considerably the worse for wear, and take their first drink in one feverish gulp. By this time the newspapermen have come in from the offices across the way, together with potato salesmen, importers of pineapples or peaches or hyacinth bulbs. Riveted rather than buttoned into dark suits that might be cut out of sheet metal, detectives turn up for a short beer and a long look. The landlord, an ex-prizefighter who has a noticeable tendency to shake his head and shuffle his feet and tuck his chin into his shoulder whenever the cash register rings, keeps up a gallant appearance of running the place against fearful odds, under the eye of his wife who manages him, his father-in-law who handles him, and his brother who seconds him and, occasionally, slips him the wherewithal to moisten his lumpy lips. The Hop Pole is closed again from three until half-past five in the evening. From then until eleven trade is steady but quiet. A great peace has fallen over Covent Garden, the market men having gone home. The newspapermen linger for an hour or so, and then give place to Tom, Dick, and Harry.

The saloon bar was almost empty when I came in. An itinerant fishmonger had just startled the landlord into a defensive crouch by uncovering a basket, saying: " 'Ere, y'are, Bombardier. Lovely cock-lobsters, all alive-o."

The Bombardier mumbled: "Shut that brasted brasket, wi'ya? I 'ate the sight o' bruddy wobsters—they lives on dead men's bobbies."

"So does grass live orf dead men's bodies," said the fishmonger.

"Srimps, yes. Wobsters, I bar. Shut that brasted brasket."

A little horsy-looking man put in: "Go on, Bombardier, 'ave a lobster. You eat 'am, doncher? My cousin 'ad a pig wot eta baby. Now then!"

George Oaks was sitting at a table in the corner, in conversation with ex-Chief Inspector Billy Sparrow, sometime of the Big Five, the confidence-trick and forgery expert, who, having retired, was working for one of the great insurance companies. Sparrow was saying: ". . . . To my mind, written by three different hands, though, of course, chronic arthritis can to an extent change the character of a man's handwriting."

I knew then that they were discussing for the hundredth time the question of the authenticity of Shakespeare's signatures.

George Oaks's hard little hand snapped like a rat-trap at the detective's sleeve, and held it fast, as he said: "Listen. You must know that in 1599 Edmund Spenser was buried near Chaucer in Westminster Abbey. I daresay you remember, Sparrow, that among others who cast manuscript poems of adulation into Spenser's grave was Mr. William Shakespeare, then aged thirty-five. Thus, in 1938—only the Foreign Situation drove it into a six-line par at the foot of column five—Edmund Spenser's grave was officially opened, but nothing was found. So it was presumed that they had opened the wrong grave. Ah, *but had they*, eh? Eh, Sparrow?"

George Oaks waved me to the third chair and although I had not yet spoken said: "Be quiet just a minute, Albert, old friend, will you? . . . But had they opened the wrong grave, Sparrow? That business was very much hushed-up. What if they had opened the *right* grave, and found nothing whatsoever? Isn't it conceivable, Sparrow, that someone had got there first, and rifled it, manuscripts, coffin, bones of Edmund Spenser, and all? . . . Go on, laugh. If an eccentric Californian billionaire can spend millions to buy a rotting castle, and have it transported crumb by crumb, and re-erected five thousand miles away, why shouldn't he—or another billionaire who wanted to go one better—have stolen and transported the remains of the author of *The Faerie Queene*? Or of Shakespeare himself, for that matter? I needn't tell you, Sparrow, what you can do if you have the will to do it, the skill to pick your helpers, and money enough to pay 'em. Wasn't da Vinci's Mona Lisa pinched from the Louvre itself under the eyes of guards? Aren't living men spirited away in broad daylight with the whole world looking on? Wasn't——"

Sparrow said: "——Tell it to Mr. Kemp, George; he writes mystery stories . . . George is off again, Mr. Kemp. Ever since they printed that article of his last Sunday, he's got Missing Persons on the brain. There's no keeping him off it. Half an hour ago a fellow comes in and says: 'I wonder what's become of Harry?' You know, Honest Harry, the tic-tac man. And you should have heard old George! He's got it on the brain, I tell you. He half talked me into believing that Honest Harry had been spirited away behind the Iron Curtain, and I know for a fact that he was nabbed in Bristol in connection with wrist-watches. We sit down to have a quiet talk about handwriting, and, believe it or not, he twists the subject round to missing bodies!"

George Oaks, returning with drinks, said: "Eh, Albert, eh? To these stuffed owls nothing is ever missing—it is only mislaid, improperly filed."

"Oh, come off it, George," said Sparrow. "A joke is a joke; don't work it to death. I know you're trying to get my goat, and you know my goat can't be got. I came in here for a quiet drink of beer and a pleasant chat. Change the subject, can't you?"

George Oaks said to me: "How's Sussex, Albert, old friend?"

"Beautiful as ever," I said, "only one gets lonely."

"I'll come and keep you company, perhaps," said Oaks.

"I wish to God you would!"

Sparrow said: "That's better. Let's talk about something nice for a change. Let George once lay hold of a subject, and he'll worry it like a terrier. . . . Missing Persons! You know as well as I do, George, there's a thousand things we know that we daren't act upon for lack of sufficient evidence. I could name you half a dozen men walking the streets today whom I'd have in the dock like that——" he snapped his fingers, "—given a case that'd hold water. Knowing is not enough. If you could hang a man purely on the evidence of your common sense, justice would be dust and ashes. Knowledge, without evidence, is guesswork; any trained questioner can tear it to ribbons. Even given evidence to back what you know, you've still got to make your case watertight before it'll stand up to the Law, right or wrong. Look at Galileo."

"You see, Albert," said George Oaks. "I rib them, I needle them, I goad them into eloquence! This Sparrow, you remember, wanted to change the subject."

"So I did," said Sparrow. "Only you don't play fair. You lead off on a subject; you drop it and you come back to it; you let it go and catch it again, like a cat with a mouse——"

"—I was a terrier just before; now I'm a cat," said George Oaks. "Department of Mixed Similes, eh, Albert?"

"I thought we'd agreed to change the subject," said Sparrow.

"Once and for all," said George Oaks. "Enough is enough! . . . We were talking, Albert, about Missing Scientists in general, and Kurt Brevis in particular. It all came out of my article in the *Special*. The greatest nuclear physicist in the world disappears in America. 'Iron Curtain', says Sparrow. 'Which Iron Curtain?' I ask. 'Why, how many Iron Curtains are there?' asks Sparrow. 'More than one, for all you know,' I tell him—and so the fight starts."

Sparrow said: "George gets carried away. He starts on his facts all right, but his imagination runs away with him, and he gets into your line of work, Mr. Kemp: he sees a mystery story in everything——"

"—As if there were not a mystery story in everything!" said George Oaks. "But no, I beg your pardon. In Scotland Yard, there are no mysteries: they are filed as 'Incomplete'. Now, they have a beautiful filing section; they call it 'Iron Curtain'. . . . All I was saying, my dear Albert, is simply this: that there are two Behinds to every Iron Curtain; Russia is behind our side of the Iron Curtain, and we are behind Russia's side of that same Iron Curtain——"

"—Don't start him off again, Mr. Kemp," said Sparrow.

George Oaks said: "Be quiet, Sparrow . . . I was pointing out, Albert, that *while key men have disappeared, as it were, from our side of this Curtain, so key men have similarly disappeared from the Russian side*. Now, where have those men gone? One must assume—I speak, for Sparrow's benefit, in terms of filing cabinets—one must assume that there must be some neglected or carefully camouflaged Third Compartment between Two Iron Curtains, and that in this Third Compartment some of the most formidable brains in the world are being filed away. By whom? For what purpose? . . . That's all I want to know."

A shadow fell between us. The Bombardier was standing over us. He whispered: "George, cop a garo at the lofty geezer wi' the wofferty ogle, gammin wi' the rakli—should I put the block on?"

This, translated from mongrel Romany and old thieves' slang, means: *Pray glance at the tall gentleman with a cast in his eye talking to the young lady—shall I ask him to leave?*

I copped a garo, and so did George Oaks. The lofty geezer with the wofferty ogle was old Conker, talking to the barmaid thirty feet away. I said: "Conker's gunning for you——" but the warning came too late.

Conker was at our table, and hissed into George Oaks's face: "I am asking you civilly, for the last time, you cowardly gutter-snipe—will you, you lick-spittle, will you, you hired assassin —will you tell the Truth?"

"Get it over and done with, Conker," said George Oaks.

Conker dashed to the floor that colourfully annotated article, and jumped upon it. "Muck hound!" he said. "Who murdered Austin Crabbe?"

"Not I. . . . Leave him alone, Bombardier. . . . Not I, Conker."

There must have been something about him, perhaps in his voice, that soothed poor Conker; for, as soon as he spoke, the frenzy went out of the old man, and he said: "Austin Crabbe didn't do away with himself, Mr. Oaks—Lord Kadmeel killed him. He was my only friend, sir, and Lord Kadmeel murdered him. You tell them, Mr. Oaks—they won't listen to me . . ." Then white rage took hold of him again, and he cried: "But they shall not silence me until I've choked the last lies in Kad-meel's throat!"

"Here is Chief Inspector Sparrow, who is anxious to talk to you about it," said George Oaks.

I avoided Sparrow's eye as I ran out of the Hop Pole, with Oaks at my heels. We walked very fast until we reached the Strand, and stopped for a drink at the Wellington.

"Poor old Conker," said George Oaks. ". . . Right or wrong, they don't know how to start, or which direction to take, or when to stop . . ."

I asked: "What do you mean by 'right or wrong' and who do you mean by 'they'?"

He said: "Skip it. Look, Dr. Monacelli was due in from New York this afternoon: he's stopping at the Savoy, Nicks told me. I must go and say hello to him, after all these years. Come with me, for half an hour, and after that we'll make a night of it."

"Monacelli, the philosopher?" I asked.

"Yes, the great Monacelli. It will do you good to meet him," said George Oaks.

The lobby of the hotel was crowded, and somewhat noisy. George Oaks had to repeat the name of Monacelli twice before the man at the desk, begging his pardon, called a room number, and said: "He says he will be right down, sir."

"That's odd," said George Oaks. "I thought he couldn't walk. Are you sure he said that?"

"That is what he said, sir," said the clerk.

I observed then that the clerk's right ear was discreetly tamped with cotton-wool. And so it comes to pass that I am alive to tell my story, and you are alive to read it, because a clerk at a desk in the Savoy Hotel in London happened to have something wrong with his right ear. Therefore, instead of calling Dr. Monacelli after whom George Oaks was inquiring, he rang a Mr. Monty Cello. . . .

Upon such things hang our destinies: some tiny current of cold air, or some blob of wax that made necessary a plug of wadding in the ear-hole of a reception clerk—that draught, that pinch of cotton, saved the world. If it had not come between us and that young man's tympanum, the three hundred and sixty-five bones of your body would by now be scattered to the thirty-two points of the compass, and everything you ever loved would be washed away! One mote of dust, in its proper place, can shatter a cosmos. The scent of a rosebud can stop a clock. . . . Now where the devil did I pick that up? George Oaks must have said it.

If you love and admire a man you find that after a while you talk as he talks. And God knows, I loved and admired George Oaks. "The God knows," Oaks would say: he is very particular about this.

Then a lift stopped and opened, and several men came out and went away. Only one passenger remained, standing by the gate.

"Look at that one," said George Oaks. "What the devil is he afraid of, in the Savoy Hotel, at this hour of the day? He looks just like a man I saw—was it twenty years ago?—in the lobby of the Ambassador Hotel in Atlantic City, in the small hours of the morning, just before Mike Duffy was shot in bed. . . . It can't possibly be the same man, but he has exactly the same air. He's waiting for something, that one. He's expecting something. I bet you an even pound note that if someone fired a pistol in the grill room he wouldn't budge an inch—whereas if that lift-man touched him in the back with a fingertip, his hands would come slowly out of his pockets and go up empty to shoulder level."

"Why wouldn't he budge an inch?" I asked.

"He'd be all primed and ready for the *bang-bang-bang*, don't you see? But the touch between the shoulder-blades would be the last thing in the world he'd be expecting, because everything would have been planned and arranged for him. His objective, Albert, would be that open door, outside which there'd be a car. He would be one of those pathetic little fellows who pin their faith in an Unseen Fixer who can get them away with bloody murder, Albert. He would have had his orders, exact: to cover such-and-such a number of yards from the gate of the lift to the gutter where the car would be waiting. Strong in his faith in his Unseen Fixer, he would turn his back on everything that lay behind him, and fix his eyes on the gutter and the night . . . on the dark streets, Albert, guarded for him by officers bought and sold. No doubt he'd keep his courage up with a sniff of white powder. Still, I tell you, one gentle prod in the back—like *this* —and I tell you that poor little man's blood would turn to ice."

"Keep your damned fingers out of my ribs, will you?"

"I beg pardon, Albert. Watch his eyes, watch his eyes while he fiddles with that cigar—trying to be unostentatious—playing for time while he takes a good look around. Oh, there is a very frightened fellow!"

"Unostentatious in those clothes, George?"

"Only clothes he ever learned to wear, you silly cow. Imagine you could disguise that one in a bowler hat and a rolled umbrella?"

The man by the lift was dressed in a light camel's-hair jacket without lapels, dark tan trousers, and tan and white buckskin shoes. His shirt was ruddy brown, heavily hand-stitched in yellow about the collar, and in place of a tie he had knotted about his throat with a deliberate nonchalance (that must have taken a good half-hour of his time) a yellow silk scarf. But it was not his dress that drew your attention to him. For the past fifteen years every gents' outfitter in the Charing Cross Road and Shaftesbury Avenue had been selling Genuine Hollywood-Styled Men's Wear—Humphrey Bogart hats, Pat O'Brien suspenders, Lloyd Nolan socks, Victor Mature dressing-gowns, and so forth. Even George Oaks, as I was to observe later, was wearing a pair of underpants printed with crimson stags as worn by Richard Widmark or somebody.

No, it took more than outlandish clothes to catch the eye even in the lobby of a first-rate West End hotel like the Savoy. (From where I was standing I could see a Sikh in a rose-coloured turban, and a portly man in a ten-gallon hat and Texas boots, the trousers of whose sober black suit were cut so that the waistline fitted a good six inches below his middle.) No, it was the face that made that man.

Now how is it possible to tell of such a face? Considered feature by feature, it was nondescript; neither long nor round, neither fat nor thin, neither fair nor dark—a difficult face to describe in, say, a police bulletin, for it was quite devoid of what they call "distinguishing marks and characteristics." You could draw it on paper with a letter "O" filled in with a few punctuation marks: eyes like full stops, eyebrows like commas, nostrils like the dots of a diæresis, a smudge, as if you had drawn the mouth in the wrong place and imperfectly erased it: call that a moustache. It was so much like a child's scribble on scrap paper that as he moved the cigar in his mouth you almost expected the whole face to disappear with a crackle into the folds of a crumpled ball.

Ah, yes—that was it—that queer, crumpled-papery texture of the skin: his was, as you might say, a child's rough copy of a face, retrieved from the nursery waste-basket as an afterthought, and painstakingly smoothed out with a grubby fist. And when he came towards us with slow, short, measured steps, with an outstretched hand, I could almost see a long gallery of barred cells, and, under that right hand, the shoulder of the convict in front. I knew then in what dress that man would be comfortably inconspicuous—grey denim stencilled with a number, topped off by a peaked cotton cap. For the man had a jailbird's face; he was distinguishable from free men by a certain air, which old, experienced criminals call *The Smell of the Bucket*.

He said: "I'm Monty Cello. You fellows looking for me?"

"There's some mistake," I said. "We asked for Dr. Monacelli. He was due here from Southampton this afternoon."

"Excuse me," said Oaks, turning to the desk. I heard his voice spelling out the name of Monacelli in polite inquiry, while Monty Cello was saying:

"Is that right? Well, what d'you know? I got in five days ago on the *Queen Annie*. Monacelli, eh? I heard about him. Didn't I read a piece——"

"—It's that idiot Nicks again, Albert. . . . One of our lesser mines of misinformation, Mr. Cello. . . . Monacelli was on the passenger list, Albert, but at the last moment couldn't make the boat: secretary cabled hotel cancelling reservation. . . . All the same, Mr. Cello, this is a happy accident since it gives us the pleasure of your acquaintance. Let me introduce myself. My name is George Oaks, of the *Sunday Special*. This is Albert Kemp, the author."

"Glad to know you."

"Why not join us in a drink?" Oaks suggested.

Monty Cello said: "Be glad to—lemme buy it——" He got between us and led us to the cocktail lounge, talking eagerly, nervously, like a man who is hungry for conversation but does not know what to say. "Sure am glad to see you fellows. Say, what d'you *do* in London? Five days I been here. Who d'you *talk* to? I mean, where d'you *go*? Well, I sure am glad that fellow got the name wrong, I mean the clerk. Only you call it 'clark'. Isn't that so? '*Clark*!' . . ."

So he ran on. When we were seated in one of the big settees facing the door, Monty Cello relaxed a little. "I just come from Hollywood," he said. "I was with Sam Feinlight—you heard of him? Sam Feinlight?——"

"—Born: Mlava, Poland, 1878. Brought to America, 1890. Went to work for furrier, 1891. Formed partnership, 1900, with Goldfarb. 1905, bankrupt. 1911, head of Feinlight Films. Multi-millionaire. Present salary, $600,000 a year. His private address I forget. What were you doing with Feinlight, Mr. Cello?" said George Oaks.

"Say, I wish you'd call me Monty."

"Monty. Call me George. You were on the production side?"

". . . Look, your glasses are empty. Hey there! Fill 'em up, willya? . . . Come on, Albert. It's a funny thing I noticed, how they never put ice in their drinks in England. If you want ice, you gotta say '*Ice!*' I wonder what's the cause of that."

"The production side?" asked Oaks.

"Ah, it's swell finding a coupla guys like you to talk to. Par'me, what was you saying?"

"Or were you directing?"

"Uh? Hell, no. I was . . . well, connected with the writing side. Yes, the writing side. And say, d'you know what? You'd 'a laughed. I was there two years at six hundred bucks a week, brother, and I never did a lick o' work."

"*Cher collègue!*" cried George Oaks, gripping Monty's hand, "you are a man after my own heart."

As Oaks tightened his grip, Monty's face twitched, and I saw his mouth close and elongate—he was sucking in his lips and clamping them shut between his teeth. What was wrong with this picture? It lacked a glaring light overhead and a relay of perspiring detectives with lengths of rubber hose. At last the mouth loosened, and Monty said: "You gotta grip like a man I knew called Lefty the Monk."

"Not Monk Eastman?" Oaks asked, as one who inquired after a lost friend.

"No, not Monk Eastman. This fellow, Lefty the Monk, came from Tacoma. Monk Eastman was before his time. We called him Lefty the Monk because he was left-handed, and he hadda grip on him like a left-handed monkey wrench. Do they have monkey wrenches here?"

"Here to stay, Monty, until the real thing comes along. What did they ask you to write in the first place? What—if you will excuse my asking, as craftsman to fellow craftsman—was your literary background, so to speak?"

"First things first, George: lemme finish. Lefty the Monk could turn a key from the outside of the door—an old-fashioned iron key, see?—with his fingers. Ever hear of anything like that, Albert?"

Oaks did not let me speak. He said: "Of course he did, Monty. Our own Charles Peace was supposed to be able to do that—a very cunning and desperate burglar in the 1880s. We hanged him for a very stupid murder. He was game to the last, old Charley Peace. His trial was a perfect treat: even in the condemned cell he argued it out, with the utmost calm, with the warders and the chaplain. Couldn't scare Charley Peace. Gave no quarter and asked for none. Game to the last——"

"—So was Lefty the Monk," said Monty Cello, nodding.

"—Game *to* the last," said Oaks, "but *at* the last? Aha! The world waited eagerly for a few defiant last words. And what were Charles Peace's last words to the hangman? 'Please don't hurt me!' So ends the criminal world, not with a bang but a whimper, Monty. . . . Touching the matter of your friend, Lefty the Monk: he would have worked the brownstone houses in New York between the Seventies and Morningside Heights, around West End Avenue and Riverside Drive, about 1917, I believe——"

"—You heard all about Lefty the Monk, eh, Georgie?" said Monty Cello.

"No! You just told me all about him. It wasn't until after the First War that the genteel old brownstone houses on West End and Riverside became blocks of flats, apartment houses for every Tom, Dick and Harry. When you take an apartment in a house full of strangers, naturally you want a lock and key of your own, so you put in a Yale lock, which requires quite a different sort of technique when it comes to illegal entry. Your Lefty the Monk couldn't have been up to the innovations called for by the Yale lock—for instance, that trick with a sheet of thick celluloid. . . . Therefore, Lefty the Monk's theatre of operations in the brownstones would have become more and more circumscribed, until he found himself in a very narrow ring. He must have left his autograph on every job, so that it took only one honest detective to pinch him just about the time when you were whistling 'K-K-K-Katy' instead of 'Over There'———"

"You're right. It was a cop they called Seagreen Dooley that got Lefty the Monk," said Monty Cello. "They called him Sea-green———"

"—Because he was incorruptible. 'Seagreen incorruptible' was still in use in America then. A little later he might have been called 'Honest Mike' or 'Clean Dooley'. . . . Lefty the Monk shot it out with the police, didn't he?"

"I thought you said you never heard of the guy."

"Calm! Calm, Monty. You don't die for burglary. If Lefty the Monk died, it must have been for murder. He must have shot somebody, probably a policeman. Again, he was your boy-hood hero. What boy of your generation around—say, Sullivan Street—would make a hero of a thief who consented to be led away to imprisonment for life? Or even the Chair? No, a boy's hero has to die in battle."

"Where'd you get that 'Sullivan Street'?"

"Your parents were hungry New York Italians, weren't they? Where would they have lived if not among their own people, in or near Sullivan Street?"

"Well, we lived on Prince."

"—Which is just off Sullivan. The same thing, only more so. . . . Excuse me," said Oaks, getting up, "I must telephone."

Monty Cello was quiet for a few moments, then he said: "Is that guy psychic? What gets me is this—how did he know us kids was singing 'K-K-K-Katy' then? Tell you something —I'll never forget that number. I used to stutter a little bit, myself, when I was a kid, and every time somebody sung 'K-K-K-Katy' I got so mad I'd———" He stopped. My friend was coming back, making signs to the waiter in passing. When he was seated, Monty Cello said: "Honest to God, it beats me how you know———"

"—You talk too much, Monty; you don't let a man get a word in edgeways."

"Say, listen———"

"—Never mind your Lefty the Monk. Forget him for a minute. You and your Lefty the Monk! You call him tough? He would not have lasted five minutes with Scott in the Antarctic.

Tell me instead how you came from the Carnival business down to Hollywood."

At this Monty Cello sucked in his lips and chewed them again. "What Carnival business?" he said. "Who said I was in Carny?"

"You did. You do nothing but chatter and chatter about yourself. 'In Carny'—the way you said it! Anyway, your accent."

"What accent? I never had much education but——"

"No accent—that's the point, man! And who said anything about education? Accent and education! Why, one of my best friends was a Doctor of Philosophy of Oxford, Monty, and for such a degree I can assure you that you have to do something more than clip a coupon out of *NAUGHTY STORIES* and rush it with five cents in stamps to Box P X, Sardanapolis Post Office, Delaware, to cover the cost of postage and packing of a free prospectus and one trial lesson. You cannot do it through the mails, as you can learn horse-breaking in the U.S. You cannot get an Oxford doctorate by playing Rounders—of which your baseball is a primitive form—on an athletic scholarship. You must read for it. This friend of mine did so, proposing to devote himself to ornithology, or the study of birds. He was all set for a Chair in a northern university, when he fell madly in love with a girl who did an Oriental snake dance in a beaver-board booth in 'Lord' Baron Rivers's Fun Fair.

"He visited the Fair, Monty—eh, Albert?—when it was performing in Durham City, having heard that one of the side-shows was exhibiting what was called the Beast of *Revelations*: a stuffed calf to which some clever taxidermist had added the wings of a condor and a leopard's teeth. Between the gramini-vorous hoofs, the carnivorous teeth, and the nonexistent wing-musculature, my friend tore this fake freak to pieces. Old Man Rivers prevailed upon the snake dancer to woo him into keeping his mouth shut. My friend fell in love with her, tossed aside a most respectable career, and followed her from pitch to pitch all over England, working for the Fun Fair. Doing what? Lecturing on the Beast of *Revelations*, proving that it was a hundred per cent genuine. It was something like Emil Jannings and Marlene Dietrich in *The Blue Angel*: only my friend's end was happier; he died in a zoo in Buenos Aires, or Rio, as keeper of the bird house."

"We had a Professor——" Monty Cello began.

George Oaks gave him a look. "——Only one word, Monty!"

"——Par'me, George."

"Granted, Monty; thank you. This friend of mine, originally, and by habit, spoke Oxford English. After ten years of life in the Fun Fair, his accent became indefinable; don't you see? He was what is popularly known as a 'spieler', but more accurately classed as a 'talker'. Apart from the Beast of *Revelations* he was remarkable on Worms——"

"——That means snakes," Monty Cello said to me.

"——Just so," said Oaks, "but he could have talked about anything that had ribs—even of one or two creatures that had none, like octopi (or Pussies, as they are sometimes called, as distinct from Cats). He was very hot, again, on some piddling North American flying fox painted phosphorescent, and billed as Dracula the Vampire Bat. He talked always like the scholar and gentleman that he was, making his arguments, influencing his audiences. To him, everyone in front of him was a potential student—just as to every sideshow spieler (or barker or talker) everyone who has ears to hear is a possible mark.

"The best talker is the one who believes wholeheartedly in his show, because belief begets belief. Believing wholeheartedly in what he is trying to sell, he will stop at nothing to sell it: the means will justify the end. He will, therefore, in spite of himself, adjust himself on the surface to those upon whom he hopes to make his impression. First of all, he will adjust his voice to their ears, and his manner to their habits: first and foremost, he has got to get in their ears! So, whether he likes it or not, he tries to talk to his mark in the style to which the mark is accustomed—if he knows his business. Hence, after long and painful experience with listeners from the north, the south, the east and the west, he learns to talk the basic language of the nation without any accent at all. To the northerner he is a northerner, to the southerner he is a southerner—his manner of speaking is universal.

"The intonation he can never lose: but the accent is mutable, and arranges itself. So; the King of England speaks in the accent of all England; and the President of the United States similarly avoids localisation by touching some point between the twangs and the burrs of the north and the south. The great Franklin D. Roosevelt, for instance, deliberately dropped his Harvard accent and cultivated something like the accent of San Francisco, which is all American accents in one. So it is with the talker in Carny, my dear Monty. He acquires an imitative faculty; he takes his tone from his surroundings. In Maine he would say 'Yes' like this: *Eeaw*, reluctantly, grudging the very sound of the word; in Georgia he says *Yassum*—willing to say the word, but too lazy to shape it. So, between the *Eeaw* and the *Yassum*, he develops an indefinable 'Yes' that might be almost anything. How would a Sullivan Street boy who never got beyond the fifth grade get himself an indefinable accent except in Carny?"

"I got to the sixth grade," said Monty Cello. "Otherwise you're right. I was in Carny for seven years. I was talker for the fight shows. Then I quit. You're smart, George. You're all right."

"I wish I were, Monty, I wish I were. But I'm not. I'm like you, a fool, a wanderer . . . always roaming with a hungry heart, Monty . . . and, like you, much have I seen and known; cities of men, and manners, climates, governments . . ."

George Oaks closed his eyes and talked on dreamily: ". . . I know something of the Americas, too, both North and South. I also ran away from school, Monty, to be ship's boy on the *Olaf Trygvesson*, a windjammer. Youth! Oh, dear me, dear me! These fingers have been frozen to a topsail off the Horn. The mate was a man-breaker, one of the old school, Bucko Keate, an old Black Ball sailor with a golden ear-ring. He was supposed to be the original 'Kicking Jack Williams' in the song. He broke my nose. He taught me the stars. . . . And Ole Larsen showed me how to knot stockings. All gone, Monty; and in the furrow that the ploughman makes, a stampless penny, a tale, a dream. . . . In Los Angeles, did you work for Buggsy Siegel?" he asked suddenly, opening his eyes.

"I met Buggsy," said Monty Cello.

I said: "I take it you're over here for a holiday?"

"Yeah, a vacation, that's right. Kind of seeing Europe, looking around, taking a rest. I gotta hernia," said Monty Cello. "Only what the hell d'you *do* in London?"

Then George Oaks nudged me under the table and said: "If it's a rest you want, why don't you come with us to Sussex for a few days? We'd be delighted to have you, wouldn't we, Albert?"

"Of course," I said, "only too delighted."

Then a boy sang "Mis-ter Mon-ty Cel-lo . . . Mis-ter Mon-ty Cel-lo . . ."

Monty sprang out of his seat, shouting: "Okay, okay!" and fumbling in his pockets for a small coin.

"Wanted on the telephone, sir."

"Okay . . . par'me for a minute."

"And what the devil was the idea of that?" I asked, after Monty Cello had disappeared.

George Oaks said: "Albert, as soon as I saw that man, I felt a pricking in my thumbs. Carny man, mobsman . . . but Hollywood writer, my foot! In Los Angeles he was probably carrying a gun for Buggsy Siegel. . . . And now, on the run, Albert; hot, hotter than hell; and scared, scared of his own shadow. He is a story, Albert, a story worth reading———"

"———Will you keep your fingers out of my ribs!"

"———Never mind your ribs. This is more important. When John Stuart Mill's servant girl used the manuscript of Thomas Carlyle's *French Revolution* to light the fire—she said that since the paper was all written on she assumed that it was no good any more; an Irish girl, of course—Carlyle sat down and read the light novels of Captain Marryat. Read Monty Cello, Albert, read Monty Cello—he will do you good. Besides, something tells me that there is a tragic destiny hanging over that unhappy man. Clasp him to your bosom, squeeze out his refreshing juice!"

"You said *us*. Are you coming too?"

"If I may. May I?"

"May you! Don't be a fool. But will you come, even if this Cello fellow doesn't?"

"Of course I will, old friend," said George Oaks, patting my knee, "I'll come and keep you company. No one shall hurt you while I'm around, not even yourself. For God's sake, let us sit upon the ground and tell sad stories of the deaths of kings—eh? We will show Monty the abbey at Battle, where the last of the Saxon kings went down with a Norman arrow in his eye eight hundred and eighty-four years ago at Senlac Fight. And he will sit upon a stool and tell sad stories of the deaths of Dion O'Banion, Hymie Weiss, the Amberg Brothers, and Dutch Schultz."

George Oaks rubbed his hands and beckoned to the waiter. "I hope he comes; I think he will. . . . Aha, here he is now, Albert, like one who on a lonesome road doth walk with fear and dread, and having once looked round, walks on and turns no more his head, because he knows a frightful fiend doth close behind him tread—eh, Albert? Woe, but he's frightened! I wish I could have listened in to that call."

Monty Cello's face was white now, and when he released his lips from between his teeth they quivered. He said something that sounded like *Ji-Ji-Ji-Ji*—as he picked up his glass in an unsteady hand and made one great gulp of its contents; wiped his face and his dark glasses with a silk handkerchief, and pressed his hands against his thighs to steady them. At last he said: "Jeez—Jeez, it's hotter'n hell in them telephone booths!" and began to chew his lips again.

"Good man!" said Oaks to the waiter, who had arrived with fresh drinks. ". . . What's the matter, bad news?"

"Nothing. Forget it." Monty Cello poked thoughtfully at the ice in his glass. "Where is this place, Sussex? Anywhere near Liverpool? I knew a guy married a girl from Liverpool when he was in the army. Her father was a farmer in Liverpool—made a hell of a lot of money. This guy said he had a nine-thousand-acre ranch in Texas. Well, so he had for a fact; but half of it was desert—and the other half, it took twenty acres to feed one cow. Tex hadda hustle for a living in New York—couldn't go back home, anyway, on account he busted a parole and was hotter'n hell. His marriage broke up. Girl said she didn't like his friends. Nine thousand acres sounds like a hell of a lot to an English farmer; don't it?"

"Whereas, on Sullivan Street nine thousand acres is a mere window-box," said Oaks. "Do you know, once, between Sullivan and Prince on a clear day I saw the sun coming up ninety-three million miles away? Oh, for the great open spaces!"

"Now you're kidding me," said Monty Cello. "I didn't mean anything; no reason to get sore. . . . Only England's, well, so little; isn't that so?" He said this with a pathetic kind of despair, drying his wet palms on his trousers, while his uneasy eyes flickered left and right.

"No State lines: only one Law instead of forty-eight plus Federal; and if you tried to bribe a magistrate you'd probably be sent for an inquiry into your mental condition. . . . Out of date, Monty, backward. Albert's house, for example, has been standing five hundred years—it doesn't know enough to fall down. No, joking aside, Monty, I know how you feel: hemmed in, surrounded by sea; nowhere to hide—is that it?"

Monty Cello said: "This place, Sussex, is it far?"

"Fifty or sixty miles," I said. "You could get there comfortably in a couple of hours or so, by car."

"I could make it in less," said Monty Cello. "I gotta car. I paid six hundred pounds for it—got it right away because I paid in dollars. Were you serious when you said I could come?"

George Oaks answered: "We were never more serious in our lives, Monty—were we, Albert?"

I said: "Come any time you like."

"Thanks a lot, Al! How about tonight?" asked Monty Cello, eagerly. "I can get packed and check outta here in twenty minutes. Fifteen minutes. I only unpacked one suitcase. I gotta car. Show me the way, and I'll drive you there. What d'ya say?"

Before I could say anything, George Oaks said: "Excellent, Monty, excellent! Give me a man who can make a quick decision every time! Order another drink and then nip upstairs and pack."

"Okay," said Monty Cello, and some of the fear went out of his face. "I'll be ready in ten minutes. Let's get the hell outta here. And thanks again, I appreciate this. You're sure it's okay for me to come—no kidding?"

"Oh, pack, Monty, pack!" said Oaks, and "Yes, pack," said I.

"I'll check out right away, then," said Monty Cello, "and the hell with London. Meaning no offence, but it's kind of . . ." He paused, rummaging in his muddled mind for a word.

"Crowded?" I said; and simultaneously Oaks said: "Lonely?"

Monty Cello stuttered again: "Kik-kik-kik-kik . . . come upstairs with me while I pipack. I want to gigive you giguys a hand-pipainted tie."

He was afraid now even to go to his room alone.

So he paid his bill, tipping indiscriminately but with extreme moderation. I remember that Oaks stopped him in the act of offering a two-shilling piece to a moustachioed officer of the Royal Marines, and whispered that eighteenpence was not enough for the porter—whereupon Monty Cello pulled out a fistful of money and thrust it into my hands, saying: "Be a pal, do it for me—let's get outta here."

At this point he stopped abruptly, chewed his lips, and, quick as a lizard, darted to the place where the telephone booths are. We followed him. He was sweating again.

"Listen," he whispered, "kikikind of cocover me, fellows. There's a gig——" he gulped, "—a guy at the desk I don't wantta see. A stringbibean, a skinny fellow with a little tiny bibeard. Cocover me, willya?"

"Of course, we will," said Oaks. "Eh, Albert? We will engage him in conversation while you slip out to your car." He nudged me with a sharp elbow. "Wait a few seconds, Albert, and then, when you see me talking to a tall thin man with a little beard, walk towards me slowly, covering Monty. You, Monty, when Albert draws this thin man's attention, make a quick dash for it through the grill room, out at the side entrance, and into your car. We'll join you in one minute."

Part Two

We did as Oaks said. But when I saw the tall, thin man whom Monty Cello was so anxious to avoid I started with unpleasant surprise, for he was Major Chatterton. I hated that man. And, indeed, I never met anyone worth talking to who had a good word to say for Major Chatterton, yet nothing specifically evil was known of him. His manners were excellent; his manner charming. In spite of his appearance of emaciation he was, in a way, handsome, especially as he was dressed now, in evening clothes—in which he was handsome from behind like a perfect beetle, and handsome in front like a black bird with a glossy white breast—handsome bird, handsome insect, collector's specimen of anything but Man.

His eyes were very bright, but quite devoid of warmth. An instinct warns one to beware of cold light in a human being; one asks oneself: *Where does it go, that heat which ought to be radiant? To what secret power station does it feed itself?* No, nobody ever liked Major Chatterton. His energy was inexhaustible: one admired this as one admires the tirelessness of the black ant, while failing to see to what it tends. His ingenuity was remarkable, like the blind cleverness of the chimney-swift that has the knack of building its nest against the apparently impossibly vertical interior of your home chimney, sticking the twigs together with its own saliva, which is peculiarly glutinous . . . but where in the world does it go in the winter? Nobody knows.

And where did Major Chatterton go in the winter? Nobody knew. What did we know of him? Little enough. He had left the Indian Army to become equerry to a Prince; and so, having access to high places, became an important man on the shadowy side of Public Relations. Therefore, since his business took him in and out of Fleet Street, we all knew him to speak to. We knew that after the disgrace and subsequent suicide of poor Austin Crabbe, Major Chatterton had taken his place as Personal Assistant (whatever that might be) to Lord Kadmeel, who, as it was generally agreed, was next-door but one to certifiably insane with delusions of grandeur, which is by way of being an occupational disease of press barons.

The point was, what had Major Chatterton to do with Monty Cello? And why was our Carny-man and gangster afraid of him?

"—I wish I had time to offer you a drink, George, old fellow," the Major was saying, "but I've got to see a man . . . Why, Albert, how are you, my dear fellow?"

"Anyone I know?" asked Oaks.

"I doubt it," said Major Chatterton, offering his cold, dry hand. "I'll be seeing you, I hope? . . ."

Oaks and I left the hotel.

"This is distinctly rum," he said. "Albert, what do you make of it?"

"Nothing," I said. "What do you?"

"Nothing, as yet. But patience, patience, Albert! Calm, calm! It is like a *pointilliste* painting—we are too close to it; we can't see the picture for the dots. We must wait and see."

The engine of Monty Cello's car was running. He was huddled over the wheel, his hat pulled down over his eyes. "Thank Gig-Gig——" he said, and got it out, "—God! Giget in quick!"

And a minute later we were in the Strand.

Monty Cello was one of those drivers under whose hands an engine seems to throb with something like love and understanding. Little was said until we were on the open road.

Then Monty Cello said: "I hate to drive at night. One time, driving at night, I got a buckshot in my shoulder. I was pushing a load of beer. . . . Well, all at once I see a crate ahead go wibble-wobble, wibble-wobble, zig-zag, right in the middle of the road, so I gotta brake sudden. Then these guys cut loose with sawed-off shotguns, and I got one buckshot in the shoulder. I couldn't afford a good croaker; I was just a punk then. You know something? That buckshot's still there, and it gives me hell every time it rains. I should hate to've got the whole load—it would have blown me apart."

I said: "There isn't any buckshot in Sussex."

The road behind us was empty. Monty Cello relaxed. He

stopped the car to light a cigar, and said, very sincerely: "I appreciate this, George. Al, you don't know what this means to me . . . I hope you liked the ties."

"They're worth framing," said Oaks; and I made an ecstatic noise.

"They cost seventy-five bucks apiece," said Monty Cello, not stuttering now. With his hands on the wheel, he was happy. "Real artists hand-painted them ties: Jake Joy pays 'em up to fifteen, twenty bucks just for painting on the picture. He gave Julie Romeo a dozen for a present, Christmas before last, and Julie—he gave me six! . . . Julie used to be kind of in the men's clothing game: he took care of manufacturers' welfare, sort of insured 'em against damage by fire, acid, and all that . . . you know? . . . I got one tie painted with a picture of Our Lord like it is on Saint Veronica's handkerchief—while you look at it, the eyes open! I only wear it on Easter. . . . I wouldn't give a tie like that away to anybody, not never. I've gotta gold medal of Saint Christopher, too, with diamonds for the halo. Wearing it round my neck, right now. . . . He's the Saint that watches over travellers, and I can tell you for a fact I've needed Saint Christopher's intervention on *my* travels!" He touched his breast where the medal hung. ". . . I want you guys should wear them ties in good health."

I never wore mine. It is of rich black satin upon which some amorous dreamer has painted a nubile nude in a provocative attitude; but I keep it in memory of Monty Cello, enemy of society and unwitting servant of humanity.

We were passing through Obham, when Monty Cello suggested that we pull in at a pub called the Game Chicken because he wanted to eat a sandwich and—as he put it—powder his nose.

"Chicken," he said, looking up at the old swinging sign, upon which some unknown genius had painted a fighting cock, murderously spurred, standing triumphantly over the corpse of another cock, which lay on its back with uplifted claws. Crude though the painting was, it was vividly alive, because the artist had put his heart into it: you never saw a chicken like that undefeated game-chicken on the board, yet you could almost hear his crow of victory.

Monty Cello, driving in, said again: "Chicken . . . I was in the business one time, only they was kosher chickens. With Jews, see, so their chickens gotta get their throats cut. It's in their religion, and I respect it. With a Jew, if a chicken meets up with an accident, it's no more kosher; it brings less than half the kosher price. We insured them Joosh chickens against accident. . . . It was the same with flowers, you know, like gladioli; perishable commodities—if your glads don't hit north before the buds open, it's a glad thrown away. Also they gotta be picked in time, and in the south them Dutchmen that plant glads have labour problems. And there again. . . . Chicken! Say, I wish this was Mross the Chickenman's! He made you an individual chicken with soup in a pot; vegetables, noodles; ninety cents. . . . Boy! Chicken! Did you ever taste Furio's chicken cacciatore? No, you never did. Say, that sauce was something! Only it stained: it was the red pepper and tomatoes that did it. Never will I forget a summer suit, kind of check like the Prince of Wales used to wear—set me back a hundred sixty bucks. Got Furio's cacciatore sauce all over it—dame slung it at me—and I'll tell you something: no cleaner in Chicago ever got out the stain of Furio's cacciatore sauce. Boy, could that man fix a chicken! . . ."

As we got out of the car and went into the Game Chicken, Monty Cello said: "I'm funny that way. A stained suit I'll wear over my dead body! Over my dead body I'll wear a stained suit!"

When we asked the landlord what we could have to eat, he said, out of force of habit: "Anything you like, gentlemen, anything you like!"—adding, in a much smaller voice: "Cheese . . ." So we ordered bread and cheese, and beer.

Monty Cello, winking at us, asked the way to the "powder room". The landlord took him upstairs, and he came down again in a minute, laughing: it seems that the Game Chicken has, on the second floor, a powder closet—a kind of cupboard in which ladies and gentlemen dusted their wigs with flour two or three hundred years ago. The landlord redirected Monty Cello to a place out in the yard, and busied himself with a waxy slab of vividly yellow cheese, saying: "Oy'm sorry, gentlemen; this is the best Oy can do. Toime was when we kept a Cheshire

cheese on this bar, and help yourself gratis. . . Haven't laid eyes
on a good cheese getting on for nine or ten years. . . . Cheddar,
Cheshire, Wensleydale, Stilton—there's cheese!—Where *are*
they all? This muck is like soap, only it don't lather. But a good
pickled walnut, now that Oy *can* give you."

He laughed. "That's a funny 'un, the other gentleman—Oy
showed him the old powder closet, and he called me 'Toots'.
He'll be a Yank, Oy dessay? Gets himself up to look like one,
but nowadays you never can tell . . ."

And I was saying to Oaks: "George, I'm all for having this
little fellow around. To tell you the truth, in a kind of way I
like him. But honestly, now: do you take him seriously? That
gangster business! No, joking aside, what real mobsman talks
like that—if he talks at all, George?"

George Oaks said, with a certain disdain: "Albert, you have
been reading too many tough gangster stories. You have been
stuffing your fat head with too many romances. Come, come,
now, you know better than that. For God's sake—since you
have taken to writing fiction you have got around to believing such nonsense as, for example, that gangsters never squeal,
and that gentlemen never talk about their wives. Don't be silly!
There comes a time when any man talks, hardened gangster or
gentleman of the blood. Mark my words, the more a man has
to keep locked up inside himself, the more imperative must be
his urge to unlock his heart and spill it, under the seal of confession or of professional confidence. So your Irish and Italian
gangsters go to the priest, and the others to the psychiatrist—to
'get themselves straightened out'—in other words, to talk shop
out of school with confidence.

"Idiot, there never yet was an admitted criminal who was not
a talker. What have these wretches to live by, but their vanity?
This being the case, how can they fulfil themselves, or justify
themselves, except by saying something like: 'I am the man
who threw the pineapple into that car-load of Cohen's kosher
chickens' . . . ? But generally they say it to a priest. When they
start chattering outside, then their nerves are gone, and so are
they: for example, Shotgun George Ziegler, who couldn't stop
talking about the Saint Valentine's Day massacre. A man *must*

talk to someone, sometime. And when he feels that compulsion overtaking him . . . better for him that he had put himself in a barrel of concrete and cast himself into the depths of the East River."

"All right, all right," I said.

"No . . . Monty Cello is genuine," said Oaks. "He'll talk, Albert: his nerves are chewed up, sucked out; pale white fibres! What interests me now, first and foremost, is this: why, all of a sudden, does he run out of the Savoy; and for what reason is he anxious to avoid, of all people, Major Chatterton? There's no twopenny-halfpenny gangster business here. Here, Albert, here is dark stuff. . . . Peace, brother, say no more; and now I will unfold a secret book and to your quick-conceiving discontent I'll read you matters deep and dangerous. . . . Eh?"

"Hotspur in *Henry IV, Part I*," I said.

"That's right. . . . Send danger from the east unto the west, so honour cross it from the north to the south, and let them grapple! . . . Eh?" said Oaks.

"You'll get no honour or danger out of this spiv, George," I said.

"Hold hard, Albert, hold hard! Ask yourself: 'What does Chatterton want with Monty Cello? Why does the sight of Chatterton make Monty drip grey like a candle? Of what is Monty Cello so very much afraid, especially in connection with Chatterton?' I say, hold hard!"

"All right, all right," I said, "there's nothing to lose, and God knows the poor little fellow is welcome. He's quite an engaging little spiv, although I don't believe a word he says. There's plenty of room."

George Oaks said: "And another thing; only don't tell Monty —don't breathe a word, or he'll be gone like a shot. I wouldn't miss this for the world!"

"You wouldn't miss what?" I asked.

"Why, a Situation. . . . Who is your landlord?"

I replied: "I haven't got one. I bought my house and three acres freehold from Sir Peter Oversmith. You know I did, George —I told you all about it at the time. Why?"

"Well, you know what I meant by landlord. You are on old

Oversmith's land. Oversmith and Chatterton are old pals, thick as thieves. I bet you five pounds to four, Major Chatterton will call on Monty Cello at your house by the week-end."

I said: "No bet. If Chatterton was looking for Cello, and wanted him that badly, he could easily find out that he'd left with you and me after having checked out. Knowing where I live—which, God knows, is easy enough to find out around Fleet Street—he'd simply come to visit Oversmith, and casually drop in on me. . . . I hope he doesn't, George. George, I give you my word of honour, I dislike that man as . . . as it might be a spider."

"Yes, he's a bad 'un," said George Oaks. "Bad, bad! . . . But where the devil is Monty Cello?"

I said: "No, but damn it all, George—I don't feel well about this. It puts me in a false position. The man is my guest, George —your guest too, in a way, since my house is yours. I don't know why this Monty Cello man is frightened to death at the sight of Chatterton. I don't care. But it occurs to me now that if I take this little fellow home I'm simply delivering him to Chatterton, and I'll see Chatterton in hell first!"

"Calm, calm!" said George Oaks, as one who talks to soothe a nervous horse. "Take it easy, Albert. If Chatterton really wants to find Monty Cello, there isn't a rat-hole in England deep enough and dark enough to hide him. Don't you see, Albert, that the safest place for Monty Cello, in that case, is in the home of a famous man like yourself? I don't know why Chatterton wants Cello, or why Cello doesn't want Chatterton. But there's no harm in trying to find out and, incidentally, in doing Monty a good turn at the same time, if you like. Because if he's in trouble, Albert, where in the world could he be safer than in your hands and mine, eh?"

"It's probably something to do with some dirty deal in American dollars," I said.

"Something a good deal deeper than that, I'll lay you thirteen to six," said Oaks. "But where is he?"

Just then a sturdy man in leggings came into the bar, armed with a shotgun. He said to the landlord: " 'Evening, Tom; looks like rain."

"Don't say that," said the landlord, drawing a pint of old ale. "You're out late, Ralph."

"The gyppos are camped in Ballantyne's Hollow, d'ye see," said the man with the shotgun. "I've got my duty to do, and Lord Jimmy's pheasants to keep an eye on, if it takes me twenty-five hours a day. And even so, there's not a man-jack of them gyppos that won't be eating his 'chicken' for breakfast, damn 'em! A liddle bit o' poaching is neither here nor there, in moderation. But gyppos—gyppos are beyond all reason."

"Oy won't have 'em in my house," said the landlord. "Oy mind when they used to go about poisoning pigs, in my father's toime."

George Oaks said to me: "That was called *drabbing the baulor*. Poison the pig, and get the carcass for the price of the hide. A full-grown pig, of course: a young pig you simply steal—grab him by the snout and tuck him under your arm. It takes skill, because pigs bite; and when a pig bites, he bites for keeps. But tougher yet is an indignant goose. . . . Isn't that so? You're a gamekeeper, you should know." He turned to the man called Ralph.

"You're as wise as I am, sir," said he. "Would that be your car outside, by any chance?"

"Well, we're riding in it," said Oaks. "Why do you ask?"

"Well," said the gamekeeper, "no offence, sir. . . . A kind of foreign-looking man, got up to represent a Yank—would he be with you, by any chance?"

"Wearing a yellow choker?" asked the landlord.

"That's right. Foreign-looking man. As I come in, he nipped into the Ladies' place. Being a foreigner, I dare say he can't read right . . ."

We caught Monty Cello in the act of starting his car. "Hold hard, Monty," said Oaks.

Monty stuttered again: "There's a gigig—with a shishi——"

"A guy with a shotgun? Calm, calm, and come and eat your cheese. He's only a gamekeeper, Monty. A kind of warden. Come on in. No one will hurt you while we are around."

Monty Cello said: "One thing I can't stand—a shotgun. I got a bibuckshot in my shishoulder . . ." (But I have not the heart to laugh at Monty Cello, funny as he was; for we all owe him some gratitude, as you will see.) ". . . I'm funny that way; when I saw that guy with that shotgun I got scared. A rod I don't mind. But two things throw the fifear of Gig—into me: a shishotgun and a shishiv. And rats, too. Par'me, my nerves ain't too good."

"Come and eat your bread and cheese, and let's get along," I said.

When we returned to the bar I saw the landlord putting out of sight a newspaper parcel from which protruded a long, feathery tail. The gamekeeper said, presumably for our benefit: "Yes, Tom, the poor old cock broke his wing, so I wrung his neck to put him out of his misery . . ."

There was a powdery smear of whitewash between Monty Cello's shoulder-blades, where he had had his back to the lava-tory wall. He begged Oaks to brush it off, saying: "I'd hate to get this coat dirtied up. This is my favourite coat. I never had anything but good luck in this coat." And he felt under his handstitched shirt for the medal of Saint Christopher, who protects wanderers in the dark.

"It's a pretty coat," I said. "Had it long?"

"Two months. Handmade—over a hundred stitches to the inch—English fabric, guaranteed to last a lifetime. I got another one in blue. I'll give it to George—it'll be too small for you, Al; but I'll give you a hand-tooled leather belt. Or say, wait a minute—I gotta snake-skin belt, if you like it, with a Mexican silver buckle. It's a matter of opinion: some folks say a snake is lucky. Lucky Luciano always wore a gold snake-ring with big emerald eyes, with its tail in its mouth; and he had luck all right. On the other hand, some folks say a soipent is a symbol of sin. But you couldn't get a belt like that for forty bucks. It's yours, Al, soon as I unpack; and George gets the blue coat. I can't tell you how I appreciate your hospitality. . . . But *this* coat? No sir!" He smoothed the breast of it. "This is a lucky coat. But lucky or unlucky, I hate filth. Lucky or unlucky, I won't wear a messed-up coat. Over my dead body!"

He laughed, almost at his ease again. "If you fellows had seen some sights I saw, you wouldn't laugh at me because I don't like shotguns," he said. ". . . If there's one thing I hate, it's a mess. . . . A forty-five is bad enough, especially in the head, but a shotgun —hell, there's nothing to show you used to be a human being any more . . . and you kind of see yourself as others see you, if you get what I mean . . ." He might have been talking on a psychiatrist's couch.

George Oaks nudged me gently, and asked: "Which kind of gun *did* you favour, Monty?"

"Who, me? A thirty-two revolver on a thirty-eight frame," said Monty Cello.

"You went in for accuracy, I see, Monty."

"I read it in a magazine, George—how a gunmaker can mount a thirty-two-calibre revolver barrel and action on a thirty-eight-calibre frame. It was something I read about in a book, some man's magazine. Forget it."

We were riding down the road that runs through Brimble Wood, not far from my house, when a grey-white ghostly thing with shining golden eyes rushed out of the night towards us. I distinctly felt a soft, unpleasant jolt as it struck the radiator of the light little car, and then there was a high screaming of tortured steel as Monty Cello threw on the brakes, so suddenly that our three heads came together like billiard balls in a cannon-shot on the cushion. Indeed, having in my eyes a vision of green turf, vivid under glaring headlights as we swerved towards the side of the road, I thought of the game of billiards at the moment of impact.

George Oaks cried: "It's only an owl, you fool!" But Monty Cello crouched, trembling, over the wheel. Oaks got out, took the corpse of the owl from the radiator, and held it up by the wings, saying: "An owl, man! Pull yourself together!"

Half incoherent for stuttering, wiping his face with the yellow silk handkerchief that was still wet with the sweat of his earlier terrors, Monty Cello said: "Throw it away, I don't wantta see it—throw it away—an owl is a sign of death."

"For mice," said Oaks, "not for men."

"Throw it away, for God's sake," said Monty Cello. "And one of you guys drive, willya? Like I told you, I hate to drive at night. . . . I can't stand owls. Or bats. They're a bad sign."

I took the wheel then, and so we got home.

My old house was very beautiful in the moonlight.

When we were comfortably seated, with full glasses in our hands, I laughed and said: "You and your owls! It's lucky for you your name isn't Jack."

He chewed his lips before replying: "Now I wonder what makes you say that!"

"Well, the landlord of my local, the Piebald Horse, has a pet raven that talks. He comes up to you and croaks 'Hello, Jack,' and if your name happens to be Jack it's quite startling, first time."

"A raven, that's a black bird like a crow. And he says 'Hello, Jack,' does he?"

"Only that and nothing more . . ." I said.

"Oh, hell!" said Monty Cello. "A black crow—crows are un-lucky. You know something? A crow is a sign of death. When they found Potatoes Hoffmann's body in the marshes near Hoboken it was the crows that led them to it; they'd pecked out Potatoes' eyes and eaten most of his face . . . I read about it."

George Oaks said: "Monty, you keep telling us things you've read about. A good book is the precious life-blood of a master spirit, but why not tell us something about yourself?"

"I wouldn't have a crow around the place," said Monty Cello. "But I used to keep pigeons, once, when I was a kid."

"Monty," said Oaks, "you know as well as I do that you're alone and in trouble——"

"—Who said I was in trouble?"

"Alone and in trouble, Monty. In plenty of trouble, as I guess, if you run for your life in fear of Major Chatterton."

Monty Cello chewed his lips, and then, having got a firm grip on them, became deathly still. Feeling that it was my turn to say something, I said: "You know, George Oaks and I are not bad friends to have if you're alone and in trouble—especially in trouble with Chatterton."

Still Monty Cello said nothing. George Oaks went on: "No-body will hurt you while I am around, Monty, especially under Albert's roof. Better be frank with us. You know, if Chatterton wants you, he has the means of finding you anywhere in the world. By 'he' I mean, of course, his employer, Lord Kadmeel. He could, for example, get at you through official sources, simply by informing the proper authorities that a man who calls himself Monty Cello is in England on a faked passport——"

"—Faked passport? You're crazy!"

"Faked passport," said Oaks firmly. "It stands to reason; it couldn't be otherwise. Under your true identity you could never have got beyond Southampton. It must be years since you signed your real name, old fellow."

Monty Cello said, evenly: "You're drunk. I got a genuine passport and I can prove it."

"Genuine, maybe, for Monty Cello—wherever he may be —but not genuine for you, whoever you may be, Monty. Want to bet? I lay a hundred to six in fivers—Albert, lend me thirty pounds—that you wouldn't, of your own free will, give me one clear thumb-print to take to Scotland Yard. Bet?"

"What the hell do you guys want?" asked Monty Cello; and his voice now was thin, flat, and dangerous.

"Calm, calm, calm! We are neither coppers nor robbers, Monty: we only want to know for the sake of knowing . . . to follow knowledge like a sinking star beyond the utmost bounds of human thought . . . we want to *know*, Monty. It is as simple as that. What the hell did Leuwenhoek want when he poked his home-made microscope at a drop of dirty water? Simply to know. We are made that way, you see; the same as Galileo who aimed the first telescope at the stars. . . . So felt I as some watcher of the skies when a new planet swims into his ken. You have swum into our ken, Monty, and we want to know. Eh, Albert?"

I said: "That's it. The idea is, that George and I already know so much about you that we can't rest until we know some more. But what really started us off was that comic opera business with Major Chatterton at the Savoy. Let me freshen your glass."

Monty Cello covered his glass with an outstretched hand, shaking his head.

George Oaks said: "Just so, Albert. . . . If you consider our conversation of this evening, you will see how much we know of you already. Now, among other things, but first and fore-most, we want to know just why you are so terrified of Major Chatterton, and what your connection is with him, and there-fore the Lord Kadmeel. Be sensible, Monty, and talk. For all you know, Albert and I may be the very ones you came to Eng-land to contact——"

"—I told you, I came for a vacation——"

"—Apart from your pal in London who slipped you the word that Chatterton was in town. Eh? I mean, the one who phoned you at the Savoy and threw you into such a sweat that you were out of the place in ten minutes."

"I don't know what you're talking about," said Monty Cello, through his teeth. Then his voice changed. "Lay offa me, George, for God's sake, willya?"

"If you won't tell us, Monty, we'll have to guess," said Oaks. "You came to England *en route* for some other destination in Europe, and stayed in London to make contact with some other friends, because you believed that Major Chatterton was looking for you elsewhere. You wanted to avoid Chatterton until such time as you could make some deal with Lord Kadmeel through him—some time when he would gain nothing by hurting you. Now my guess is this: (One) what you have got, and Chatterton wants, is in the form of papers——"

"—Who says so?"

"Must be; Kadmeel is too big to send Chatterton chasing after mere money, or money's worth. Obvious as a punch in the mouth . . . (Two) you have those papers on your person. Why? Because if you had had an opportunity to dispose of them safely as you had planned, you would already have done so, and therefore have met Chatterton man to man, and made your deal. Eh?"

"Go on," said Monty Cello.

"(Three) these papers were of such a nature that you dared not entrust them to a bank vault, to which, in certain circum-stances, the police might have access. And to which you, if you were strictly on the run, would not dare to go. Eh?"

Monty Cello was silent. Oaks patted him encouragingly on the knee and proceeded: "I'll bet you, furthermore, that you were expecting your London contacts this very evening; because you thought that no one else in England knew that a certain party going by the name of Monty Cello was to be found at the Savoy (as for Chatterton's appearance on the scene —as I guess it, the man who sold you your passport squealed for a consideration). . . . Poor old Monty," said George Oaks, dreamily. ". . . I can see you waiting in that room, tense as a banjo string, with your eyes on your wrist where you wear that three-hundred-and-fifty-dollar chronometer watch that tells the barometric pressure, the date, the hour, and the split second —ears cocked at the telephone—eating your lips, wishing you had a sniff of the stuff they cured you of taking in Joliet——"

"—I was not in Joliet!"

"—Then ting-a-ling!—gentlemen to see Mr. Monty Cello. Oh, joy! Your nerves are shot. Obviously you have never before met the party, or parties, you are expecting. You look over the visitors at the desk, take a chance, come forward. *If these are wrong guys*, you reason, *I'm a gone goose anyway*. Case of mistaken identity. Disappointment is mixed with relief and, by the very preponderance of relief, Monty, it is demonstrated that you are lonely and frightened. So you drink with the two strangers, of all the ten million strangers in London, who happen to be Albert Kemp and George Oaks. The God is just, Monty. For all you know, we might be the two that were sent to help you. Now be calm. In any case, don't you see, we have you by the short hairs. In effect, you are situated like Gilliatt in *The Toilers of the Sea*: to go is impossible, to stay is madness. If you go, I'll have you collared in three-quarters of an hour. If you stay, you must trust yourself to us; in other words, talk a little. Whichever way you jump, Monty, I catch you. But here's a consideration for you: upon my word of honour, Albert and I are not friends of Major Chatterton, and we hate Lord Kadmeel."

"George never said a truer word," I said. "Friends! Very far from it, Monty. As for Kadmeel's New Movement, Sciocracy, we'd fight it to the last ditch—wouldn't we, George? So you see, if Chatterton is against you, we are for you . . . to that extent, at least. So why not talk to us?"

"You will talk eventually to someone, Monty," said Oaks,

"mark my words, you will. If you've fallen foul of Crazy Kadmeel and his Sciocrats, you're in a devil of a hole, in one way or another. Better tell us what's on your mind while there's time."

Monty Cello snapped his fingers and drew a deep breath which he held for quite ten seconds before he let it out—that was the longest sigh I ever heard. Then he said: "If you guys play ball with me I can get you a million bucks. What do you say?"

Oaks replied: "We say nothing, Monty. It is you who must do the saying. Tell us about your connection with Lord Kadmeel and the Sciocrats."

"About that I don't know from nothing. I never saw this Lord Kadmeel. I don't think I ever even saw his picture in the papers."

"No, he never liked to have his picture printed—afraid of being recognised in public, and assassinated," said George Oaks. "He had me thrown out of the Kadmeel Building, and blacklisted on all his papers, for riding in his private elevator: fear of assassination again—it frequently goes with megalomania. An uncouth, gross, horrid man, Monty. Imagine the Emperor Nero modelled in cream cheese, with a dark moustache. An unprepossessing figurehead for the Sciocrats, who propose, through the application of unadulterated Reason, to rule the world. But go on."

Monty Cello said: "Money rules the world. Senators rule the world, and if you got the dough, can't you buy off Senators? Sciocrats, hell! Money rules the world, you take it from me. I know. I learned it before I could walk. I never saw this Kadmeel, and I don't want to."

"But you did see Major Chatterton?"

"I guess I've gotta trust you," said Monty Cello sadly. "Yes, you're right. Like I said, I was in Hollywood at the time, drawing six hundred bucks a week from Sam Feinlight, but not for writing. It was part of—kind of insurance Sam Feinlight was paying in case of any labour problems coming up, if you know what I mean."

"I know what you mean," said Oaks, "and a very dirty racket you were in."

"Well, like fruit and flowers, film is a perishable commodity——"

"—Like men?" I said.

"Oh, all right then—it's a dirty racket? Okay. So that makes me a dirty racketeer? Okay. If I didn't do it, somebody else would, wouldn't they? It's either that, or be a sucker. My father wasn't a dirty racketeer, he was a bricklayer; so he got killed when a building fell down before it was finished on accountta the concrete was no good. The crook that sold that concrete to the city left seven and a half million dollars, and his daughter married a Bulgarian Prince. So I'm a racketeer. All right, I'm a racketeer. Governor Ferguson of Texas went to jail for being a crook—admitted it in the papers, like it was a good joke—came out, and got himself elected again. So I'm a crook. Ah, you make me tired! In all my life I never knocked off more than six guys, always strictly for business. So I'm a murderer! The contractor that put up that building murders forty-two men in five seconds. So he dies rich, in a penthouse on Park Avenue. The guys he murdered were mostly honest men. . . . Four of 'em died slow—it was three days before they could dig 'em out. Anyone I knocked off was a dirty racketeer, like what you'd call me; an enemy of society, and good riddance. And anyone I killed, I killed quick and clean—I saw my father when they dragged him out; I hate mess. And if I hadn't done it, somebody else would've. The State, maybe. And if I had to choose, believe me, I'd rather get shot than burned in the Chair, or hung up with a rope, or choked in a gas chamber. But what's the use of talking?"

Monty Cello paused and leaned back, looking up at the great black oak beams. Looking, he grew tense again, and said: "Say, there's a bad crack in that middle beam up there"—and shifted uneasily in the deep chair.

"Calm, calm, Monty," said George Oaks; "that timber was felled when Richard Plantagenet was a pup, and shaped when Henry VIII was a twinkle in his father's eye. It rests on solid stone; it'll last out our time; it'll stand, please the God, when you and I are gone and forgotten. Go on, Monty, go on."

". . . Five hundred years, eh?" said Monty Cello, shaking his head. "Can you imagine that? I can't. I don't know that I want to. You build a house to stand up five hundred years. So then you die. So where does it get you?"

"Major Chatterton?" said George Oaks. "You were going to say . . ."

"As I was saying, this Major Chatterton contacted me on the Coast, in Hollywood. First of all, I couldn't figure what he wanted me for. Even if I was a real writer, this Major Chatterton wouldn't go out of his way to ask somebody in my bracket to come to his suite at the Ambassador for a quiet drink. But I got nothing to lose, so I go over; and this Major Chatterton treats me like a Prince. He tells me he's heard a lot about me, and he's interested in my life story. Well, I could show you a dozen grifters that get twenty-five grand and more for a lot of hooey that they called their 'life stories'. I mean, it's found money; you pay some poor bum a thousand, fifteen hundred bucks, to build it up around a few clippings from the newspapers, and he writes it up; and all you do is write your name on the top. There's nothing to it. Naturally, in a case like that, you sing like a canary, but, strictly speaking, you say nothing that everybody didn't read already, and forgot. Because, take it from me, the truth pays no dividends. Well, this Major Chatterton, he's got a few clippings on me about three-four raps I beat; one in Portland, the Riggio killing in Detroit, the McTeague Massacre in Gary, and how One-Eye Regan got knocked off in broad daylight in a telephone booth in Philadelphia . . . stuff like that. Nothing. It was in all the papers. I never kept my clippings; that's a mug's game; but it's all there for anybody to read. Open and above-board, if you get what I mean; because they got nothing on me. Apart from punk stuff, like when they sent me to reform school when I was sixteen for carrying a concealed weapon, and a couple of raps I took for income tax, and for being in possession of narcotics. This Major Chatterton looked like easy money, see? It doesn't worry me even when he tells me my real name."

Monty Cello paused, and I asked: "Which is——?"

"Jack Orsini. Otherwise 'Lippy' Orsini, on account of an impipediment in my speech; also because I used to be a talker in Carny. You know something? Talk in a Carny talker's singsong, and you'll never stutter."

George Oaks said: "True. The orator Cicero found that out two thousand years ago."

"Cicero?"

"A sad-looking suburb, even for Chicago, isn't it? But go on, Monty, go on."

"Well," said Monty Cello, "I wasn't known as Jack Orsini for a hell of a long time. But that don't matter; it's on the records for anybody to look up. All the same, I begin to wonder what's on this Major Chatterton's mind, if he goes to all this trouble to find out about me, when there's plenty of big shots he could contact without any trouble at all. And even while I'm wondering, this Major Chatterton kind of smiles at me, and this smile puts the fear of God into me. Yes, like I said, my nerves ain't too good; still, I don't scare easy. All the same, this Major Chatterton, all of a sudden, scares the hell out of me." The man who called himself Monty Cello moistened his lips. "He says: 'All this is very interesting, Mr. Cello; but you haven't told me about the little affair of Casimir Pulacki, otherwise known as "Loopy the Polack", in Saratoga, in 1948. What about that, Mr. Cello? Surely, you remember when Pulacki was shot down in the lobby of the Hotel Alexander Hamilton, and the unidentified killer, making his getaway, murdered State Trooper Laugherty near the Pike?' he says . . .

"Well, only one other man in the world could know about that, and he's supposed to be dead; but, dead or alive, this was one guy in the world I could trust. If he squealed, this is one rap I would never beat . . . Pulacki had it coming to him, and with the cop, I fired in self-defence; according to plan, the cop had no business to be there at that time. That was either a slip-up somewhere or a double-cross. But it's too late to argue. This Major Chatterton has got me cold; he makes it clear—I got to do like he says, or I burn 'on information received.' . . . Conklin *must* have squealed, somehow. I hate to think what they did to him, to make *him* talk! But that's how it was: this Major Chatterton don't want my life *story*—he wants my *life;* he knows the story already. It's obey, or burn. Put yourself in my place."

He stopped to take a mouthful from his glass, and George

Oaks made a non-committal sympathetic noise. But I, feeling myself called upon to say something, right or wrong, murmured: "There, but for the grace of God, go I."

At this Monty Cello turned, quick as a snake, positively hissing with hate: "*Aaah!* There but for the grace of God goes you —says you! And who the hell are you? Ain't *I* entitled to the grace of God as well as you? Oh, shut up! Don't give me that stuff! I once heard a Governor talk like that—those very same words—and he'd got greased by every grifter in the state. One of the boys went to the Chair: and there but for the grace of God went *him!* . . . I'm sorry, Al. Forget it. . . . As I was saying; put yourself in my place. You're me, see? And this Major Chatterton puts it to you like this: 'My friend, I have only to drop a certain word in a certain quarter to fry you like an egg. I will not drop that word if you do exactly what I tell you to do. If you do what I am going to tell you to do, I guarantee your safety, and will see to it that you are heavily paid for your work. If you don't . . . well . . .' What do you say to that?"

George Oaks said: "First of all, I say—'Major Chatterton, what's the job?' "

"Okay," said Monty Cello. "And then what if I say to you: 'Say Yes or No, Mister; but if you say No, you burn . . .' What do you say then, George?"

"Why," said George Oaks, "putting myself in your shoes, Monty, that's easy. I say: 'Major Chatterton, first I must know the inwardness of what you want me to do. I am a great sinner, sir, and may burn in Sing-Sing for my crimes to date. But, as I am taught, beyond the hot squat there is a place where our 'fires are not quenched.' "

Monty Cello began: "Ah, you're full of . . ." Then he felt under his shirt, and changed his tone. "Leave my religion out of it, will you, George? This Major Chatterton, he never asked me to do anything wrong. It was like this: there was a guy, strictly legit, but crazy. See? This guy had actually been in a nut-house, somewhere in Pennsylvania, but they got him out. It was a neat break, smoothly organised. Major Chatterton, and his set-up, were hiding this nut under cover in Canada."

"Who was this so-called nut?" George Oaks asked.

"A scientist, but he'd gone crazy, so the Government locked him up."

"He had been working for the Government, then?"

"That's right. And the F.B.I. was watching him—but close! All the same, Chatterton's set-up got him loose—it must have cost them plenty—and hid him out, in Canada. They must be worth all the dough in the world. Well, after a little while this crazy scientist broke loose—he couldn't have been so crazy, to get past Chatterton's mob—slipped back over the border, and disappeared, like *that*." Monty Cello snapped his fingers. "Chatterton's mob traced him as far as Kansas City, and then lost track of him. He just evaporated—*psst!*—like spit on a hot-plate. The F.B.I. were looking for him, too; but they didn't have a chance in hell of catching up with him, unless he gave himself up of his own free will."

"How was that?"

"Well, as soon as Chatterton's set-up got him to Canada they operated on him, and changed his face. See? And I don't mean just altered his nose, like with Dillinger. They did a real job on that guy's face, like you couldn't get done for ten grand in a legitimate hospital—built up a new chin with plastics, pulled his hair-line down a good inch, made skin grafts, and everything; even tattooed a genuine social security number on his arm. So you can see, this Major Chatterton and his set-up must have wanted him pretty bad; they must have spent a fortune on this guy. Well, what I had to do was this: find this guy, wherever he was, and bring him back to Chatterton all in one piece, safe and sound. That's all." Monty Cello laughed bitterly.

"And how were you to recognise him?"

"They took pictures of him after his face was healed, full-face and profile, just like police photographs, in case of emergency. Those guys, I tell you, they give you the creeps. Well, so this Major Chatterton gave me ten grand in advance, and there was another twenty grand coming when I delivered. You can guess what this guy must have been worth to Chatterton, eh? And this Major Chatterton says: 'And don't imagine for a moment, my friend, that you'll get away with any monkey tricks. Find this man Rheingold and bring him back, and you have thirty thousand dollars and perfect security. Fail, and you die. Now be off.'"

"Rheingold?"

"That was the name of the guy that had the social security number they tattooed on him. His right name was———"

"———Dr. Kurt Brevis?" said George Oaks.

"That's right," said Monty Cello. "There's only one atom-bomb scientist that was certified crazy, locked up in an institution, made a getaway, and disappeared. Dr. Kurt Brevis."

"But what could Kadmeel want with Kurt Brevis?" I asked, with excitement.

"Calm! That's one of the things we are going to find out, Albert. The point is, Monty, did you find Kurt Brevis?"

"Yes, I did," said Monty Cello.

"You did? Where is he?" I asked.

Rigid-faced, speaking in the monotone of a prisoner under cross-examination who has to choose between a commitment for contempt of court or a possible charge of perjury, Monty Cello said: "I'm afraid I can't answer that question."

George Oaks asked: "Did you bring him back alive?"

"No sir, I did not."

"Did you bring him back dead, then?" I asked.

"No, I did not," said Monty Cello.

George Oaks said: "You found Kurt Brevis. You didn't deliver him alive; you didn't deliver him dead. Is that correct, Monty?"

"That's correct."

"Is he still at large, then?"

"No, he is not," said Monty Cello. Then he started, chewed his lips, shook himself, laughed uneasily, and said: "What the hell! Is this the D.A.'s office? I've got to trust you guys. Listen. I'll tell you . . ."

Part Three

Given time, and a strong magnet, anyone may find a needle in a haystack. With patience, and a Geiger counter, it is not difficult to pick out a milligram of radium in the mixed detritus of a city dump. But how, unassisted, do you find a missing man in a continent—a shrewd, a cunning man, with keen senses and an unnoticeable face?

This man, standing up, straddle-legged and at his ease, will occupy about nine square feet of ground; one square yard. The United States of America covers something like one and a half trillion square yards of the world. From square yard to square yard of this vast area, a hundred and fifty million people perpetually shift; and every one of these people is so inconstant that it is impossible even for a serious investigator of man's mind to squeeze one sixth of the whole truth out of him. . . . In effect: every one of these one and a half trillion squares is the surface —the impermanent, fluctuating surface—of something like a self-playing chessboard with all its incalculable permutations and combinations.

And even this is an over-simplification, since (if you accept this analogy) you must assume every man to contain within himself the whole game and play of chess in all its imagined and unimagined intricacies, played on as many planes as may exist inside a mysterious cube of black and white cubical blocks strangely inter-blending and inter-penetrable . . . and these very planes are fluid!

No, no! Your mind baulks at this infinity, so that you must get out of this world, into a dream of Another Dimension . . . in which case you go mad, like that same Kurt Brevis whom Monty Cello was sent to find.

I believe that, according to human standards, even a man like Einstein must be mad, since he has made an exact science of that which is not, yet. (For "mad" read "precocious".) He should have been born hereafter. His Dæmon gave him his Theory, as

48

an overdriven nursemaid, for the sake of five minutes of peace and privacy, might give a delicate clock to a wilful and inquisitive child who, properly curious to know what makes it tick, carefully takes it to pieces . . . and so squats weeping in the debris of that which he cannot reassemble, crying for the steady ticking of recorded time, which he has interrupted.

I draw no comparison, here, between Albert Einstein and Kurt Brevis. I see Einstein now as a sort of prodigious baby, weeping into the wheels of that unpredictably complicated clock, mourning the irretrievable loss of that balance which he will never re-establish, and never should have disturbed . . . a sad man who is sorry for what he did in good faith. He feels now something of the anguish a child feels who confides a dream to someone who looms large, smells of cigars, and inspires confidence in a cosy corner, only to betray him.

Kurt Brevis, while he was far enough out of this world to transubstantiate his mathematics, was far enough in this world to ask: *What is in it for Kurt Brevis?*

Einstein desired only to seek and to find: his giving of what he sought and found was, in a cloudy way, an act of faith. Kurt Brevis, who was comparable with Einstein as a mathematician, but who, being a more fleshly man, was of weaker fibre, hungered after glory and all that goes with it.

I don't know what Kurt Brevis hoped for when he offered his services to the U.S. Government. He might have known—surely he must have known—that he who files a key to unlock any of the oubliettes of imprisoned energy must himself be locked up. This much is certain: instead of fame, Kurt Brevis found organised obscurity. Instead of liberty, or licence, for which he must have hungered, he found himself in a kind of comfortable jail. Instead of the wealth that he had led himself to expect, he found himself comparatively poor on a salary of eight thousand dollars a year. Dollar for dollar, an executive in an advertising company selling deodorants could have bought him out before breakfast.

He belonged to two worlds. Torn between two dreams, his mind split. Suddenly he began to discover "truths" that made no sense. By degrees, but with extraordinary rapidity, he became certifiably insane—incurably so, as the psychiatrists said —and therefore he was put away in what Monty Cello called an "Institution", closely watched by a strong guard. There was no sense to be got out of Kurt Brevis; but with a man like Kurt Brevis, asleep or awake, one takes no chances.

In the later stages of his mental breakdown, which the doctors agreed was incurable, he talked constantly of Russia, where a man of his calibre would live like a Prince, served by slaves who would indulge his every whim. He babbled of bullet-proof limousines and sable topcoats; and orgies in the Russian style, saturnalia at which a man might purge, and therefore clarify, his soul by throwing off all the inhibitions that cloud the Christian mind. There was nothing like "getting it out of your system", he maintained. The viler the sin, the more sincere the repentance, said Kurt Brevis; provided one sinned deliberately, and in cold blood. As a case in point, he observed: Consider a man with the hangover of a seven-day debauch—who could be more unquestionably penitent and therefore closer to God? He took to drinking absolute alcohol diluted with distilled water; raved, laughed, wept, scribbled equations without rhyme or reason. Even if he had toyed with the idea of trafficking with foreign powers—which could not be proved—the doctors certified that Brevis could not be called to account in any court of law because he was no longer responsible for his actions. Even if he might be held responsible, he could do little harm because somewhere in the weird convolutions of that semi-detached brain something had gone wrong. The man who could solve, in his head, in five seconds, the trickiest problem in calculus could not now work out a simple sum without counting on his fingers.

He wandered in the walled gardens of the institution where he was confined, sometimes silent for days on end, sometimes making up imbecilic rhymes which, he insisted, were of the profoundest significance. For example:

> Bloo bloo
> Oranges moo
> Thistles whistles

But gladioli
Lie, lie, lie!

This, he asserted, was greater than Hamlet, for the Prince of
Denmark was an ignoramus; Ophelia, who covered herself with
flowers and in drowning displaced her own volume in water
—ah, she knew her botany and her physics. . . . Sometimes he
played the match game with his attendants, but, since he insisted
that 2 was 3, and that 1 was 2, he invariably won. He played for
ten million dollars a game, but was idiotically satisfied to accept
in settlement a daisy or a fallen leaf. He stored his winnings in
a cache under a tree. Later, after Kurt Brevis's escape, everyone
swore he had warned everyone else that Brevis had been putting
on an act; that his imbecility was too good to be true. Wise
after the event, the doctors talked of the fabulous subtlety of
the schizophrenic and of the tortuous cunning of the paranoiac.
But the fact remained that Kurt Brevis had disappeared, as completely as if he had evaporated—*psst!* like spit on a hot-plate, as
Monty Cello put it—and the cleverest detectives of two continents had failed to find any trace of him.

Yet Monty Cello found him.

". . . And having found Kurt Brevis, to what address were
you supposed to deliver him?" George Oaks asked.

"I don't know," said Monty Cello. "As soon as I found him, I
had to cable Major Chatterton, Hotel Henry Morgan, Barbados,
giving my whereabouts. I was to hold this Rheingold (as he was
called), but hold him tight; and wait for further instructions.
See?"

"But you didn't? Why not?"

"Well, in the first place, I was kind of curious. I wanted
to find out what this guy had got that was worth that much
dough. Because if I played my cards right, well, there might be a
chance to make myself a better deal. See? That wouldn't be easy,
and it'd be dangerous as hell. But what the hell? By the time I
caught up with him, I had a feeling that things were going my
way. I felt lucky, see? I felt I couldn't go wrong. Because up to
then I'd had all the breaks—all the luck in the world, and I felt

good, I felt strong. The dice were rolling for me, I couldn't lose. In the first place, the way I got on the trail of this guy, that was a chance in a million. It was like drawing four cards to an ace, and picking up a royal flush—it could happen, maybe, once in a lifetime. Listen . . ."

Even if I had the time to tell Monty Cello's story word for word, I could never convey to you the manner in which he told it, in the recitative sing-song voice of the Carny talker, chopping it up *staccato;* instinctively avoiding *B-* and *D-* and *K-* and *P-* and *T-* sounds on account of his stutter, so that he spoke with a certain insistent sibilance, pausing only to light fresh cigarettes . . .

. . . He set out with a certain trepidation, for his chances of success were slight and the consequences of failure would be terrible. He travelled by car, stopping at every town between Detroit and Kansas City, sniffing after the broken trail of Kurt Brevis, hoping against hope for some stroke of luck that might lead him to some clue, some scent that Chatterton's bloodhounds had failed to pick up. He had the criminal's faith in his luck; the gambler's love of long odds and last chances. As it happened, his luck held. Yet it was not entirely by chance that Monty Cello picked up the trail of the missing man.

He reasoned, somewhat as follows: *Here is a guy strictly on the lam. He's got to hide out someplace until it's safe for him to move again. But he's got no dough, so he's got to find some. How? He can't get work on a farm—he hasn't got the strength. He's a scientist; well then, he might get work dispensing in a drug-store; only even if he had the right diplomas and all that, he wouldn't dare to produce them because if he lets on he's Kurt Brevis the F.B.I. pick him up in five minutes, and back he goes to the looney bin. . . . Obviously, he's got something in mind— someplace he wants to go by himself, to play a lone hand—otherwise he might make a deal with the F.B.I. by telling them all about this Major Chatterton set-up, which must be pretty big, and strictly Opposition. No, this guy has got to get someplace by himself. But to get there, he's got to eat. He can't ride the rails, because he doesn't know how, and he daren't risk being picked up by a railroad dick. He daren't try to bum his way farther south—which is the way he's been going steadily—because they'd have him on a chain gang for vagrancy in no time at all. He might*

get a job in a book store, or something, but that would be pretty dangerous.
He couldn't get work on a boat, because he's not fit for it in the first place,
and in the second place he's got no papers, and no dough to buy them with.
What is the poor guy to do, then? . . . Steal? He's inexperienced, but,
crazy or not crazy, damn smart; otherwise he wouldn't have slipped away
from Chatterton's set-up the way he did. Steal, maybe . . . but what?
And then, they could change his face, but not his finger-prints—one little
pinch, and here's the F.B.I. again. . . . Well, no harm trying. . . .

So, in Kansas City, Monty Cello went to see a man who ran a
flourishing used-car business under the name of Noodnick, but
who was otherwise known as Nick the Fence—a formidable
power in the not-inconsiderable underworld of the city. Nick
the Fence said: "Say, who *is* this character, for God's sake? A
couple guys were asking for him eight—ten weeks ago. Big
Hymie and another one I don't know: offered two grand for
the tip-off on where this little fellow's holing up. Where the
hell would Big Hymie get that kind of dough?"

"No idea," said Monty Cello.

"Sorry I can't help. You know I would if I could, don't you.
. . . I'll be seeing you." As an afterthought he said: "—There's
only one stranger in town that I know of, and he's keeping the
books for Plato the Greek. You might try there."

"Keeping the books, eh? For Plato the Greek, eh? Maybe I'll
try there," said Monty Cello.

He told us that then and there he had a feeling that he was
on the beam. Plato the Greek operated a numbers game over
his Hyades Restaurant, and was an old companion of Monty
Cello, who went there forthwith. In any case, he was hungry,
and liked pilaff. Plato the Greek had kindly remembrances of
Monty Cello; invited him to have whatever he liked on the
house—pilaff, shishkebab, wine, anything—anything at all.
Monty Cello did not say No, but asked as a personal favour
to be allowed to take a quick glance at the new book-keeper
upstairs, making it clear that this was a private matter and that
the book-keeper was in no circumstances to be informed that
anyone had been inquiring after him. The Greek laughed richly,
opening a bottle of Mavrodaphne, and said that it was necessary
only to sit down at such-and-such a table and take it easy; the

book-keeper would be coming down to lunch in a few minutes: a harmless old man, "but with the figures, a whiz"—he kissed his hand in ecstasy.

But the man who came downstairs was not Kurt Brevis, but a pale pink, pop-eyed, boiled shrimp of a man, awkwardly bent and inquisitively bewhiskered like a shrimp. He walked painfully with the aid of two sticks. Monty Cello knew him well. This was the "Professor" to whom he had referred when George Oaks talked of his vagabond ornithologist in the Savoy Hotel. The Professor, whose professional name was Nemo Memo, the Human Calculating Machine, had earned his living for forty years by his freakish photographic memory. One of his tricks was to glance for a second at any printed page which might be held up to him and then, blindfold, to repeat the contents line for line and comma for comma. He had no more intellect than a camera or a wire recorder, but he never failed to astound you: led in by a practised talker, you paid twenty-five cents to see him perform and, before you left his booth in the Carnival, paid another fifty cents for his *Complete Guide to Memory Training*, with his photograph on the paper cover. He performed in a cowled black robe, and painted his face dark brown. It was given out that he came from Lhassa, the Forbidden City in Thibet; actually his name was MacNabb and he was born in Seattle.

Monty Cello said: "Hello, Professor. Long time no see." His hopes were dashed; he was already trying to think of some fresh angle from which he might approach the problem of the missing scientist. In the meantime he had to eat, and, having always a nostalgia for the old carefree days on the road, he invited the old man to join him at lunch. "Quit Carny, Professor?" he asked.

The Professor replied: "I'm sorry to say I have. The machine breaks down, son. I'm not long for this world, I fear."

"What, losing your memory, Professor?"

"No, son, not that, thank the Lord. Arthritis, rheumatoid arthritis." He held up his hands, which might have been red rubber gloves stuffed with walnuts. "A terrible affliction. Yes, the old life got to be too much for me. I couldn't stand the jolting of the cars any longer. The pain kept me awake night after night, so that I got sleepy on the job. Kansas City was my last stand. For the first time in forty years, son, I had to pay out a twenty-dollar prize—here, in Kansas City, of all the places on God's green earth!"

"So you quit, eh?" said Monty Cello. "I'm sorry, Professor," and he took out fifty dollars.

But the old man waved the money aside, saying: "Bless you, son, you always had a heart of gold; thanks all the same, but I have enough for my modest needs. My grouch-bag was never empty. I have something put by, enough to live on. Besides, Plato pays me fifty dollars a week for my services, and in addition to that there is still something coming in from the old act."

"How come, Professor?"

"Why, there was an Act of Providence, son. The finger of Fate pointed a way, and I took the hint. Losing that twenty dollars would have decided me, anyway. Gather ye rosebuds while ye may, son, for you can't stay young for ever . . . Put your trust in Providence and keep your grouch-bag dry. . . . It happened on our last day in Kansas City. What with pain and tiredness, I was just about all in. I'd made up my mind to finish the day, and then quit once and for all. But my mind was clear—never clearer in all my life. My talker went through the routine, and the marks came crowding in——"

"—Who was your talker? Johnny Hopkins?"

"No, another one, Charley Brooks; you wouldn't know him. Charley gave them the old business—twenty dollars to any man woman or child if Nemo Memo fails to name any date in history which he she or it sees fit to ask! Twenty dollars in cash money to any man woman or child who can put to Nemo Memo the Human Calculating Machine any problem in arithmetic, geometry, trigonometry, or algebra which he cannot solve without the aid of pencil and paper in thirty seconds! Four brand-new five-dollar notes. . . . You know, you remember . . ."

"Sure I remember, Professor, and I still don't know how the hell you do it."

"Neither do I, son. I was born that way. I could do it when I was twelve years old. . . . To proceed: up pops the regular bunch of marks that have been waiting all year, ransacking the public library for difficult questions, including that same old crackpot who always comes out with squaring the circle. But then there stands up a mark, the like of which I have never encountered in all my professional experience, and he floored me. I didn't think anybody could have done it, son; in the line of business —you've got to be prepared for anything, and twenty dollars is a lot of money—I've even memorized Einstein, not that I understand a word he says. But this mark was something extra special, I assure you. Charley tried to cut it short and laugh him off, but I gave him the sign to pay the man off after the rest had gone. We sold eighteen books. I wanted to talk to this stranger alone, because I had an idea. The long and the short of it was, I paid him his twenty and suggested that he take over the act on a fifty-fifty basis. He was to use my professional name, my props, my talker, my stock of books which are my copyright— everything. In return, weekly, he was to forward me one-half of the net take after Charley and the overhead had been paid."

"Go on," said Monty Cello, very tense.

"Of course, as you know, I have a reputation as Nemo Memo, of which I have some right to be proud," said the old man, "so I started to give him a test. He ended by testing me. Oh, it was the finger of Fate all right, son—he demoralised me; I knew I had met my master. So we went with Charley to Quarto's Bar and made the deal."

Monty Cello asked: "What did you say the guy's name was?"

"When I asked him in Quarto's, he said: 'John Pabst.' I should add that we were drinking beer at the time: I suspect he adopted the name on the spur of the moment. But that's all one to me, son. He fulfils his obligation like an honourable gentle- man. I trust him implicitly, and I can trust Charley to keep an eye on him. In due course, human nature being what it is, they will combine to double-cross me. Meanwhile, the money comes in like clockwork. Last week he sent one hundred dollars, in cash, by registered mail. He must be taking in well over three hundred dollars a week. . . . But you're not eating."

"Tell you the truth, I'm not hungry, Professor," said Monty Cello. "This guy Pabst: would he happen to be a little fellow, kind of small-boned, with a big head, little eyes, little ears, forehead like a monkey? About this much between his eyebrows and his front hair?"—Monty Cello measured an inch and a half between a thumb and a forefinger. "—With a chin like one of these Boston bulldogs?"

"Exactly. Why, do you know him?"

"I don't know," said Monty Cello. "I might. Where would he be now?"

"Wherever the show is, of course. My last remittance was postmarked Atlanta, Georgia. My next—the last until next spring—should come from Tampa. Why? Are you going down that way? If so——"

"—No, I've got business in St. Louis. Better take that fifty just for luck, Professor."

The old man put the note in his pocket. "Well, since you are so pressing—many thanks. . . . And how do you happen to know this man Pabst, son?"

"I think I ran across him in Philadelphia. He used to work in a bank, or something," said Monte Cello, carelessly.

"What a perfect set-up!" the Professor murmured. "He simply wraps himself in my garment, assumes my identity, and has the run of the country, perfectly safe as Nemo Memo who has been nationally famous for forty years. . . . I wonder how much he embezzled. Do you know, son, I fancy I've been a little too generous with that man?"

"Well," said Monty Cello, cursing himself for having talked too much, "I should say it's a perfect set-up for a shake-down, like you say——"

"—Nothing of the sort entered my mind. How could you think that of me, son?"

"But if I were you, I'd let him get good and settled before I put the bite on him. Otherwise, the guy gets scared, takes a powder, and then where are you?"

"True . . . Still . . ."

"Well, I better get going. It's a long way from here to Saint Lou—— So long, Professor."

He drove like a cold demon and, much as he hated driving by night, stopped in St. Louis only to eat and stretch his legs. In McCarthy's place, back of a cigar store, he idly dropped a quarter into a slot machine and won the jackpot—there was no doubt about it, his luck was in. But a certain glint he had seen brightening the Professor's protuberant black eyes had made him uneasy. He rushed on through the darkness, following the route of Sultan Watson and King Alfonso Johnson's Combined Shows—a route which he knew almost by instinct. He did not rest until the following evening in Nashville, Tennessee, where he slept four hours, starting out again before dawn. His purpose was to get to Tampa ahead of the carnival, and wait there for his man to come to him, while he spied out the land, figured angles, made a plan. He took a room in the Tampa Terrace because he liked their charming practice of sending newly arrived guests a pretty little basket of kumquats, tangerines, and oranges, free of charge with the manager's compliments; looked up some friends in the Cuban quarter of the town and won three thousand dollars in a crap game. No use talking, he could do no wrong; it was scarcely necessary even to talk to the dice.

And when the Sultan Watson and King Alfonso Johnson's Combined Shows came into town, his heart beat strong and high. But when he sought out Nemo Memo, he was directed to a big, happy-looking young man playing blackjack with two midgets and a human skeleton, and drinking rum and Coca Cola. This young man was the talker, Cheerful Charley Brooks.

"Where's the Professor?" asked Monty Cello.

"Oh, he went right on to pick up a part-time job for the winter. I got me one, too, on a snake farm, showing the marks around, you know, and picking up the rattlers, cottonmouths, moccasins, and all that. The pay is good, the pickings are easy —what more can a man want?"

"You're a Worm Man?" asked Monty Cello, speaking casually but chewing his lips with impatience.

"Me? I don't know. I never handled a snake in my life, but there's no harm trying. What did you want to see the Professor about?"

"I got a message for him from the other Professor—you know, MacNabb, in Kansas City. He knew I'd be passing through here, so he asked me to give Mr. Pabst this personal message, see?"

"How is the old man? I wish I had half his money."

"He's got arthritis, but he's all right. Where can I find Pabst?"

"You've been in Carny yourself, haven't you?"

"I used to be talker for Barney Bull; before your time, I guess. I know the old man from then. About this Pabst . . ."

"Crazy as a coot, a bundle of nerves. You'll find him at the Pompano Hotel on Narragut Key, seventy-eighty miles south from here in Pompano County, on the Gulf. The old man used to rest up there and paid his expenses keeping the books. I saw no reason why Pabst shouldn't take over. My God, I thought the old man had a head for figures until this one came along; but compared to Pabst, old MacNabb was still in the first grade. He's okay, though. Where'd he come from? He was never in Carny before."

"He was a college professor. He got into trouble on account of some frill. Pompano Hotel, Narragut Key, you say? Thanks a lot, Charley."

"You're welcome. Have a drink; coke isn't too bad if you dilute it with rum. Pompano Hotel, you can't miss it—it's the only hotel on the key. A crummy place—lives off its trailer camp and grocery store, mostly. Bar trade, mainly beer. Customers, mostly farmers from up north; they come south on a shoestring to get away from the snow, and spend a fortune in nickels playing 'I'm Dreaming of a White Christmas' on the juke-box. Or 'Jingle Bells'. I'm here to tell you, it's a lot of hooey—it's no fun at all to ride in a one-horse open sleigh, especially in New Hampshire——"

"—Well, thanks a lot, Charley," said Monty Cello again.

"You bet!" said Cheerful Charley, and went back to his game singing "The Song of the Wild Goose". Monty Cello told us that he had never in all his life met such a happy man: he hoped Charley made out all right with the snakes . . . to some people snakes were lucky.

He drove slowly, now, to Narragut Key. It seemed to him that things could not be better. If he had found Kurt Brevis in Tampa he would have been faced with the problem of getting him to some out-of-the-way place like Narragut Key. Everything was going his way.

He curbed his impatience, reasoning with himself as he had reasoned with the Professor in Kansas City: that Kurt Brevis, confident that he had thoroughly covered his tracks, would relax a little; settle down to restore himself in peace and quiet, hatching fresh schemes. In the last analysis, it came down again to money. Kurt Brevis would lie still until he had the where-withal to leave the country: this much was evident. *Let him feel safe and comfortable; then spring your trap:* so Monty Cello advised himself. Therefore, he spent a quiet day in Sarasota, where the Ringling and Barnum & Bailey Shows rest for the winter; then he crawled on at twenty-five miles an hour through Manatee, where the traffic policemen are supposed always to be on the look-out for marks travelling at a speed exceeding forty miles an hour. Thus, supremely confident in his luck, he pulled up at the Pompano Hotel and booked a room for a week. And there he met Kurt Brevis, who kept the accounts for his keep, and slept in a kind of closet behind the store-room.

Monty Cello watched him for several days. Kurt Brevis rose at six o'clock, and, comfortable in sandals, slacks, and one of those little shirts that hang over the trousers, walked medita-tively on the beach, pausing occasionally to pick up a curious shell or a bit of stone licked into some strange shape by the water. One morning Monty Cello made it his business to be up and about by five o'clock. He walked half a mile up the key to Narragut Point, and strolled back over the sand towards the hotel. As usual, the quiet little book-keeper was there, trying to match coquina shells, and toying with the empty carapace of a horse-shoe crab which the tide had washed up.

"Kind of ugly-looking thing, isn't it?" said Monty Cello.

The little man shrugged, and said: "Do you think so? I wonder why. It could not hurt you one-tenth as much as the lobster for which you pay through the nose A La Newburg or Thermidor. No doubt, sir, you read the pulp magazines, and have studied the illustrations which are supposed to represent the horrors out of this world. No?"

Monty Cello admitted that, while he had little time for read-ing, he did occasionally curl up with a copy of *Astounding Stories*.

"Yes," said the little man, idly throwing away his handful of coquina shells. "Yes. They are people of limited imagination, these illustrators in black-and-white of these stories, what? To them, the *ultima thule* of the Terrible is, an over-blown crab, or some exaggeration of a jellyfish. Even if they knew, poor fellows, that the most terrible things—if destruction, as such, is terrible—must be forces that cannot be seen, felt, or foreseen. Fools!" And he spurned the crab-shell with a scornful foot: it turned over on its back, rocking like a cradle, whereupon a swarm of green iridescent flies came out of nowhere and settled in the noisome crevices of its joints.

Monty Cello said: "Well, after all, how do you expect a fellow to draw something he never saw?" The other man laughed, and with the tip of one sandal described a circle in the loose sand.

He said: "O, for example: that is the symbol by which we are enabled to visualise Oxygen, without which life as you know it would cease to exist on this planet. O: a line, which actually has no dimensions, enclosing an empty space. In other words, Nothing; and, as Zero, symbolic of nothing . . . and two Nothings, conjoined, as in a pretzel, in mathematics symbolise Infinity. . . . Crabs? Bah!" He smiled.

Now this smile, Monty Cello saw, was the smile of a man with an ace in the hole—the indefinable, uncontrollable smirk of a bad poker player. Such smiles cannot be simulated; they come, as it were, from the roots of one's being seemingly through the skin. Evidently, Kurt Brevis too felt that everything was going his way. Therefore, this was the time to shake him. Monty Cello said: "Well, I'm glad to know you, Dr. Kurt Brevis."

Now you must imagine a sack of rice suddenly slashed open. All that the skin of Kurt Brevis enclosed appeared to rush away in a gasp; he seemed to fold, buckle, and crumple as he went down in a sitting position on the sand. Monty Cello sat, too, saying: "Better take it easy, Doc. Have a cigarette."

At least a minute passed before Kurt Brevis spoke. He said: "My name is not Kurt Brevis. My name——"

"——I know. I know! Your name's John Pabst. That's the name you picked off a beer ad to give Old Man MacNabb. The name Major Chatterton gave you is Rheingold. You want me to give you the social security number tattooed on the upper part of your right arm? Mind if I feel your chin where they built it up around that plastic stuff? Your real name's Kurt Brevis. Why argue?"

"You are out of your mind!"

"Haven't you got it the wrong way around, Doc? No? You know best who you are, but for my money you're Kurt Brevis. And if you don't believe me I'll call the F.B.I. to prove it. You escaped from the looney bin, Doc, not me."

". . . Who are you? What do you want of me?" asked Kurt Brevis. "Why are you talking to me like this?" His voice was bewildered, but his eyes were watchful.

"Chatterton sent me to bring you home," said Monty Cello. "Doc, you haven't got a chance."

Monty Cello told us that, in talking like this, he was playing a hunch, a tremendous hunch and a dangerous one, for upon this hunch he was staking his life. He had decided on his plan of action: having located Kurt Brevis, he had intended simply to send that cable to Barbados, and keep the little man in sight until Chatterton acted on it. He had no doubt that Chatterton would move swiftly, decisively, and with deadly precision: he guessed that within forty-eight hours, two men, faultlessly disguised as federal officers and armed with perfect forgeries of the requisite papers, backed by a hoodwinked local sheriff, would come to the hotel in a big black car and carry the bookkeeper away to a destination unknown. (This, he said, was how he would have done it, given Chatterton's set-up.) Then Monty Cello would have nothing to do but collect twenty thousand dollars and go to the devil his own way. Monty Cello, you see, was trying to put himself in Major Chatterton's shoes. It may be, therefore, that he said to himself: *If I was this Major Chatterton I'd ask myself: "This Monty Cello—doesn't he know a little bit too much? He won't call copper, because he's got nothing to gain that way. But if he was smart enough and lucky enough to trail this Kurt Brevis from Kansas City to Narragut Key, he might be smart and lucky enough to trail him back from Narragut Key to wherever-it-is, and put the bite on me good. Better rub Monty out." And I'd rub Monty out. . . .* Be this as it may, it is certain that Monty Cello found himself in the grip of a passion that is stronger than the fear of death—curiosity. If it cost him his life, he would get a little nearer to the dark heart of this affair.

He dealt with Kurt Brevis as George Oaks, later, was to deal with Monty Cello, saying something like this: ". . . Now listen, Doc, why not be reasonable? Take whichever side you like, you're in the middle. This Major Chatterton wants you, but bad. The F.B.I. wants you too. You don't want to go back to that looney bin, do you? No. And you don't want to go back to this Major Chatterton either—otherwise, why make a break like you did? The F.B.I. couldn't find you. The Chatterton set-up, with all its connections, couldn't find you because you fell into the most perfect layout in the world when you took over the Professor's pitch in Kansas City. All the same, I caught up with you in two-three days. See? You can duck the F.B.I., you can even duck this Major Chatterton—but me you can't duck. Now wait a minute, Doc, take it easy; listen. I don't like the F.B.I., and I don't like Chatterton, I don't like anybody. As a general rule I operate strictly alone. I'm not one of Chatterton's mob—I was called in to locate you for the simple reason nobody else could find you. You haven't got a hope but one in hell of getting loose again. But one; that is, cut me in on whatever it is you're trying to do. What your game is I don't know, but I want to know; and believe me, Doc, I'll find out. Listen: all I've got to do is pick up that hotel telephone and send a ten-word telegram to get twenty grand. Then why am I wasting time talking to you? Because you and me might make a deal."

Kurt Brevis smoked a cigarette in silence, then said: "I have no alternative but to confide in you. You want money?"

"I got dough, Doc, but I could use a whole lot more."

"You are shrewd, yes? You are of the underworld, is that so? You could help me, hide me, protect me? You have your friends; you could find me passports, papers? . . . Then listen to me. If you will do this for me I promise you, I swear to you, that you shall have one million dollars, and freedom to spend them as you please."

Monty Cello smiled with half a mouth as he told us all this. He said: "It looks like history repeats itself. The Doc offers me a million bucks because I've got him in a corner, and I offer you guys a million bucks because you've got me out on a limb. Well, what comes, comes; that's life. . . . All right. So I tell the Doc to sing—just like you told me to sing—because if we're going to work together he's got to trust me, there mustn't be any holding out on either side. I tell him, we can't double-cross each other, because his life is in my hands, and my life is in his hands. We're both of us bucking the F.B.I. on one side, and Chatterton's mob on the other. So he sings. He tells me he's made a terrific discovery. This Dr. Kurt Brevis has worked out the secret of something that makes the atom-bomb plant at Oak Ridge in Tennessee look like two cents. And anybody who's got this secret, and enough dough to go to work on it, can be boss of the whole world."

I said: "Madness!" But George Oaks silenced me with a gesture, and Monty Cello went on.

He said that in many ways Kurt Brevis was crazy all right. Because, in the first place, he didn't believe in Good and Evil. Monty Cello had done one or two wicked things in his time, but he was always sorry afterwards and never failed to make a firm purpose of amendment, like Little Hymie Weiss who, having got his death-wounds coming out of church, was pretty sure to get to Heaven in due course; give or take a season in Purgatory, which, no doubt, he could take. . . .

But Kurt Brevis had come to believe that he was God. The trouble was that ape-men, human-all-too-human, had fettered him to be their servant. So he had gone over to the small but immensely wealthy Sciocrats, who believed that it was necessary to cleanse the world for the occupation of its rightful rulers, the super-aristocrats who pretended to have purged themselves of all the passions and most of the instincts that motivate ordinary men, and who believed that any means justified the end they had in view. "—Like Hitler? Or this Stalin?" asked Monty Cello. Kurt Brevis told him not to be a fool. Hitler and Stalin were mere demagogues, rabble-rousers, utterly dependent upon the goodwill of huge masses of hysterical idiots and compelled, therefore, to waste good time talking, even appealing, to them with promises of bountiful meals and comfortable beds. Musso-lini, Stalin, Hitler—they had some glimmering of the right idea, but in the final analysis they were no better than swineherds, hog-callers.

The true aristocrat, the Sciocrat, should not demean himself in demagoguery or diplomacy. Mankind should come crawling to the feet of the Sciocrat, imploring: "Master, allow me to live. Suffer me to survive in order that I may serve you, head, heart, and hand. Do with me, Master, as you will!"

Monty Cello said that he had seen, in a cartoon by Ripley, or somewhere, that there were more than two billion people in the world. As he figured it, that was a hell of a lot of people. You could take over a town, yes; even a country, like Stalin. But even then you had to watch your step.

Kurt Brevis said: "My friend, you must have the right stuff in you; otherwise how could you, alone, have survived so long in opposition to organised Law and Order? Still, you are a child in the dark. Yes, there are two billion people on this earth (theoretically it would be possible to pack them all into the space of one cubic mile) but who wants two billion people? What are they to you, my friend? Can you name me ten people whose deaths would seriously affect you—that is to say, one two-hundred-millionth part of the world's population? Can you name me five? No, and neither could most other men. If you read in your paper tomorrow that some sudden pestilence had wiped out the entire population of Asia, would that take your mind off the sports page? No. I tell you that the cataclysmic destruction of all the cities of Europe could cause you less consternation than a crick in the neck of Joe DiMaggio. Similarly, a devastating flood in Ohio would trouble you far less than a sharp shower on the race-track at Saratoga. In other words, you are concerned with the well-being only of those who can serve you as an individual, or amuse you for a few minutes. Admit it."

Monty Cello could not deny it. "The Sciocrats," said Kurt Brevis, "apply pure Reason to that which you know in your soul. As you say, there are two billion people in the world, only an infinitesimal proportion of whom are other than nonentities. Such a crass mass is, as you indicate, awkward and unwieldy —a suffocating mass of sweaty, greedy, bestial little men who, when you balance the joys against the miseries of their lives,

would be better unborn. This mass is not necessary. It poisons
and exhausts the earth. It is incapable of putting back into
the earth that which it takes out. Seven-eighths of the earth
would be better washed away, since, after all, it is nothing but
a breeding- and feeding-ground for this species of two-legged
vermin that leave it as soon as they can walk to infest the centres
of civilisation. There are too many people, in short, and there is
too much habitable ground. The time has come when the world
must be washed and aired for those who are fit to occupy it! So
say the Sciocrats; and they are right. But . . ."

But what? Having escaped from the sanatorium, Kurt Brevis
found himself caught in a still tighter trap. He was like the hero
of an old romance who, unjustly imprisoned, laboriously cuts
a tunnel with a spoon, concealing the dirt he has displaced by
swallowing it; but he has made an error in his calculations so that
when he pushes out the last stone, he finds himself in a deeper,
darker dungeon. The Sciocrats altered his face so that he might
be recognisable to none but themselves, and held him tight.
They gave him every facility for work, and did not deny him
the means to relax. He could have anything to eat that he chose
to order. He was waited on by exquisitely courteous servants
who were humanoid rather than human in their efficiency. He
was allowed wine and liqueurs—but they were measured. If he
expressed a desire for female company, it was provided; but the
girls, like the other servants of the Sciocrats, were mechanically
courteous and absolutely obedient—no more, no less—they
said and did precisely what was expected of them, never what
was hoped of them. And in amorous expectation one hopes for
the unexpected, the fulfilment of the hope beyond hope.

It occurred to Kurt Brevis that he was a slave among slaves,
and in danger, too: the Law of Nations had had him in its grip
before, but the Sciocrats were above all laws. If you displeased
them, even if you gave them cause to question your usefulness
to them, they "disposed" of you; they saw to it that you were
efficiently and inexorably put to death, without fuss or drama.
Kurt Brevis perceived that he had escaped from obscurity only
to find nonentity. But he concealed his seething resentment and
pretended to involve himself wholeheartedly in the Sciocratic

scheme. It must be understood that he thoroughly approved of their programme; only he would not have it applied to himself. So he played the part of a man who is happily absorbed in his work, and bided his time.

"And where, exactly, was he?" asked George Oaks.

Monty Cello said: "I don't know exactly, but it seems that this Lord Kadmeel owns a hell of a lot of forests in Canada. And this place was in one of these forests. You could find out easy enough, because they got a great big industrial research plant up there, the idea being to make some newer kind of nylon or something out of woodpulp. This might give you a lead: when the Doc got away this second time it took him fourteen days to get to a place called Rimouski."

George Oaks said: "Why, then, that's easy. Rimouski? That places it in the Province of Quebec. Kadmeel owns a dozen big forests there, but only one industrial research place, very hush-hush, in the high woods up in the Gaspe Peninsula—top industrial secret stuff, Albert, like all the synthetic fibre plants of that interlocking world cartel—Britain's Courtauld, America's du Pont, the Swiss Celanese, and the German Bemberg. . . . This gets better and better. Tell us more, Monty; I almost begin to like Kurt Brevis."

"You know, that's the way I felt," said Monty Cello. "He wasn't much to look at, but, believe me, he must have been a hell of a hard guy to hold. He had guts, the Doc—enough guts to supply a sausage factory. Listen how he got away . . ."

Kurt Brevis made only one complaint, and that was about the cigarettes. He preferred Papagos Egyptian, gold-tipped, Imperial size. They could procure him only Dimitrinos Dragoons. Grumbling, he contented himself with these, and sent in a promising report about work in progress. He was playing poker, as Monty Cello put it. Then, coming out of an esoteric-mathematical trance, he became aware of life in the forest, and asked permission to go hunting. With true Sciocratic detachment he said that he had no desire to go after moose, because he was not hungry; he desired simply to shoot a squirrel or two, or a rabbit, because it pleased him to know that he could put a chemically-propelled lead pellet where he pleased.

They let him go into the woods, armed with a good .22 rifle but accompanied by a "guide" who carried a shotgun loaded with ball in the right-hand barrel and buckshot in the left . . . in case of a stray bear or a lynx. Kurt Brevis and his guard went into the woods and returned a dozen times. The guide, or guard, habitually carried a length of rope tied about his waist. Kurt Brevis picked up something of the craft of the woodsman. So there came a whispering evening when he did not return. In brief: he shot the guide in the back of the head. How did he dispose of the body? He hauled it on the rope to one of the lower boughs of a maple tree, and lashed it there. Who, seeking a corpse, looks upward? So this indomitable little madman slid away, knowing that he was safe at least from the police, with whom the Sciocrats would never dare to lay information. Having no money, how did he live? He sold the shotgun and the rifle to a farmer for only eighteen dollars and a bag of bread and bacon, it being understood that this was a transaction best forgotten. Without doubt, that farmer kept his mouth shut. Kurt Brevis got to Rimouski; and thence down the great river, begging and borrowing and stealing his way to Montreal; and so over the border into the United States, where there are a hundred and fifty million people to cover a man or betray him.

Part Four

One may imagine how Monty Cello made a mystery of his man-hunt out of Kansas City; Kurt Brevis was deeply impressed. He, too, felt that his luck was in.

"But where do we peddle this stuff?" asked Monty Cello.

Kurt Brevis told him that only one avenue was open to them. That avenue led to Russia. The U.S.S.R., he swore, would pay millions for the formulæ he had to sell, and guarantee protection into the bargain. He had arrived at the conclusion that, while they were far from perfect, the Russians had the right idea—theirs was something like a true aristocracy, an aristocracy of scientists, warriors, and ruthless men. . . .

"Okay by me," said Monty Cello. "But where do we go from here?"

Here, said Kurt Brevis, was where Monty Cello came in. The only Russian contacts upon which he might rely were to be made in London, England, where agents of Stalin had got in touch with him when he was in transit from Germany to the United States. It was necessary to get to London, first of all; after that, one had only to send a letter-card to Regent Lambert, Poste Restante, Charing Cross Post-office, saying: *Staying Such-and-such Hotel*, signed, any name in which you were registered. In due course someone would call on you and give you further directions. Most likely the pay-off would come in Vienna, in the Russian Zone.

Monty Cello said: "Wait a minute, Doc. These Russians, what I mean, they got people here, same as in Europe. What's the matter with sending your postcard from here, and have this Lambert contact you on this side?"

"That would be fatal," said Kurt Brevis. "In times like these, when all men are enemies, a transatlantic communication to an accommodation address would inevitably be suspect. In any case, we are in a delicate position in the United States of America, you and I, and are, therefore, at anybody's mercy. No, our only shield is the Iron Curtain proper. You must find us papers and the wherewithal to travel to Europe like prosperous Americans on vacation. Can you do this?"

Monty Cello said: "I got dough, Doc, and as for papers, I can get us both fixed up. But this secret stuff of yours—where is it? If I trust you, you got to trust me. Where's the dope?"

"It is in my head. I could write it down on four sheets of foolscap paper," said Kurt Brevis, "but you could not understand it. I do not believe that there are six men in the world who could understand it."

"Write it out for me, then, Doc," said Monty Cello. "If we're partners, we're partners. Don't forget, you can't move an inch without me, and I can't move an inch without you. Well?"

"Very well," said Kurt Brevis, meekly. "I will write you the formulæ." But Monty Cello noticed that as he spoke the little man, wide-eyed with simulated sincerity, pressed his hand not over his heart but over his abdomen.

"Wait a minute!" cried Monty Cello, and snatched at the waistband of Kurt Brevis's trousers. A button flew away, a zipper buzzed open; before Kurt Brevis could protest, Monty Cello had torn from about his waist a kind of crude body-belt made of a doubly-folded hand-towel filched from some washroom and held in position with adhesive tape. In the folds of the towelling Monty Cello could feel something that rustled dryly. "Why, you double-crossing bastard!" said Monty Cello.

Those were the last words Kurt Brevis ever heard. They were spoken in a whisper, in the playroom on the second floor of the Pompano Hotel three days after their first meeting. The little mathematician leaped at Monty Cello, but seemed to stop in mid-leap. He staggered, reached for his heart, made a half turn, and fell forward, knocking over a ping-pong table covered with neatly stacked bingo cards. Then he lay still. Monty Cello stuffed the body-belt under his shirt, and shouted for help. A doctor came and pronounced Kurt Brevis dead of a heart attack.

"A thrombosis, no doubt," said George Oaks.

"That's what they called it," said Monty Cello. "They were going to bury him under the name of Pabst, but his social security number said he was a toolmaker named Rheingold. No next of kin. He had five hundred and seventy-five dollars cash money, so they used that to bury him with, in the Holy Grace Cemetery. And there he lies. I waited two-three days—I didn't want to make myself conspicuous, scramming too soon—and lit out west. From Laredo, down on the border, I cabled Chatterton: *WIRE TWO THOUSAND DOLLARS CARE WELLS FARGO MEXICO CITY*—rode like hell all the way to Dallas, sold the car, and hopped a plane to New York. I mean, if there's two grand waiting for you in Mexico City, you go to Mexico City. Get me? . . . Well, in New York I went to Pen Quillan, and got myself fixed up with a passport in the name of Monty Cello: I paid him fifteen hundred bucks. Then I get aboard the *Queen Annie*. I never been on the ocean before. Believe me, it's over-rated. I won eighteen hundred bucks in the ship's lottery. I tell you, things were going my way. . . . I send this letter-card to this Regent Lambert, just like the Doc says, and I sit tight. Only all of a sudden I get nerves, and I'll tell you something; I am never gladder in all my life to see anybody like I was to see you two guys tonight. No, last night. Look, it's daylight. Pretty, ain't it? . . . And the rest you know."

"And where are Kurt Brevis's papers?" asked George Oaks.

Monty Cello loosened his trousers, pulled out his shirt, and unbuckled a chamois leather money-belt. "Right here," he said, throwing the belt to Oaks. It contained a wad of thin copy paper. We looked at the uppermost sheet. It was covered with figures and algebraic formulas with here and there a chemical symbol.

"You got a safe place, Al?" asked Monty Cello.

George Oaks pointed to the great fireplace, where, on massive andirons, lay three long birch logs over a pile of waste paper and scientifically arranged twigs. My housekeeper insisted on keeping the fire laid ". . . in case it turns chilly; anyway, to take away all that empty space," as she said. Oaks rolled Kurt Brevis's notes in the day before yesterday's *Times*, twisted the paper cylinder into something like a tight skein, and tossed it to the back of the fireplace, where it became one with a mess of empty cigarette packets and torn-up envelopes. "There," he said.

"Now wait a minute——" Monty Cello began.

"—Calm, calm, Monty, calm! *The Times*, even in an open sheet, will not burn. Try it and see—put a match to it—it will flicker blue, and smoulder out. It is a special quality of paper: many an Englishman has eaten a cold breakfast because of the fireproof Thunderer of Printing House Square. Letters have been written to the press about it. And even if this were not so, a hard twist of paper is a devilishly difficult thing to burn. And even if it were not, and somebody set light to this fire, it would take three good hours for the heat to reach the back . . ." He yawned voluptuously. ". . . 'God help me, Brother Latimer, I cannot burn'—'Be of good cheer, Brother Ridley, we have this day in England lighted such a candle as, by God's grace, shall not easily be put out.' Calm, Monty, calm! Breakfast and a little sleep."

"Al," said Monty Cello, "I'm not yellow, but my nerves are all shot. I got a certain feeling I've run out of my streak of luck. George, I've told you everything I know. I could use breakfast, and some sleep. I'm all in. Guess I've been smoking too much. . . . My mouth tastes like . . . Oh, what the hell! Where do I sleep?"

"Eat first," I said; so Monty Cello ate fried eggs. He liked his eggs fried on both sides: he hated the yolky ooze of eggs fried with their eyes open. He was very tired, now. When I showed him his room and wished him pleasant dreams, he said: "A million bibucks, Al? That's my idea of real dough. Free of tax. You could bibuy a yacht. I never had no nerves until I started thinking in mimillions. Honest to God, Al, I'd hate to have anything happen to me now. My luck's been running so good. . . ."

Shotguns were beginning to sound in the distance. I drew the curtains to keep out the rising sun. "Nothing's going to happen to you. Get some sleep," I said, and went downstairs.

George Oaks was in the kitchen, eating the carcass of a cold pheasant. "Well," I said, "and what do you make of all this?" He took me by the sleeve—the marks of his greasy fingers are there to this day—and said: "Albert, I told you as soon as I saw Monty Cello that I felt a pricking in my thumbs. This is the best night's work you ever did in your life. The God willing, you shall have a story to tell your grandchildren such as no man will ever have told before. Go and rest now, Albert. I'll sleep a bit down here."

"Why not go to bed, George?"

"For the present I think I'll take the couch by the fireplace. More later. First rest, rest!"

Mrs. Rose, the housekeeper, came in at eight o'clock. I heard her voice, as from an immense distance, saying: "Why, *Mis*-ter *Oaks!* What are *you* doing on the set-*tee*?"

"Composing my beating mind," said George Oaks.

"Well, you seem to be doing all right at it. Give me them chicken bones, there's a good soul. Why don't you go to bed properly?"

"Because I am in travail with my skeleton. Here I am, and here I remain. If you wish to sweep, sweep around me, and tread softly, because you tread on my dream. Mr. Kemp will sleep late, and so will the other gentleman from Hollywood, so you had better be careful. Away, thistledown. For lunch, bake us a pie."

Mrs. Rose giggled. In my mind a picture formed, of George Oaks guarding the fireplace. Then I slid into a dreamless sleep.

The bell of St. Wilfred's was striking one o'clock when I was awakened by a rhythmic tremulous squealing of rickety wood-work, and I knew that the electric motor which was supposed to pump water into the house had broken down again, and that someone was drawing from the old well. I went downstairs in my dressing-gown. George Oaks was offering Mrs. Rose a dead snail which he had just fished out of a full water-bucket, saying: "The French eat snails. Come on, frou-frou, have a bite. Snails are good for the chest, they help to cut the phlegm. Applied to the small of the back, they are guaranteed to make you shimmy like a Cairo dancing girl. And you can use the shell for an eye-bath when empty; or put it to your ear and hear the mysterious voice of the sea! And how much am I asking for this valuable snail? One guinea? No! Half a guinea? No! Three-and-sixpence, including stamp? No! One kiss, fifi, one butterfly kiss, my little pomegranate, in exchange for this medicinal snail, rich, ripe and rare!" Mrs. Rose, shaking with laughter, struck him on the head with a little aluminium saucepan. "You will have to marry me now, my proud beauty," said George Oaks.

"Oh, stop your nonsense. Now be a dear, do 'a done, Mr. Oaks," said Mrs. Rose, who weighed two hundred pounds, and had nine grandchildren.

Then he saw me and said: "Albert, the pump is *kaput*, the motor is burned out. Meanwhile it takes manpower. And if I were you, I'd do something about this well. The water is too low, and it's getting foul. Water level must be a good thirty-five feet down."

"And the rope's all wore out," said Mrs. Rose. "Shall I bring your coffee to the summer-house, Mr. Kemp?"

"Yes, please do," I said, "and take some up to the gentleman in the front bedroom."

When we were seated in the summer-house, I asked: "Well, George—what about it?"

"You mean, what about Monty Cello?"

"Among other things . . ."

"I've been thinking about him. I'm afraid Monty has had it. He's bitten off far more than he can chew, the silly little cow. If he were just an ordinary gangster on the run I'd say 'Albert, let him go and take his chance'. But what he has got himself mixed up in has made him extraordinary. As things stand now, he'd be comparatively safe in the hands of the police: he'd have at least a fighting chance for his life; which he certainly wouldn't have if Chatterton laid hands on him. So I'm afraid, Albert, that you'll have to violate the laws of hospitality and turn Monty over to the police. Later on I'll ring Chief Inspector Halfacre, and get him to send a couple of men down. As matters stand, I think Monty is too big a bird to trust to old Constable Hobson. I'm sorry, Albert, but you have no alternative."

"Oh, look here!" I said. "I don't like this one little bit. Couldn't we just send him on his way and let him chance his luck? The police would be certain to catch up with him eventually, especially if he got as far as Vienna. They're pretty hot on forged passports over there, in times like these, I understand. I should feel an absolute swine if I turned my house into a police trap."

"Brother Albert, you must assume that England is still at war, and that you happen to find a very dangerous enemy under your roof. It is necessary for you to waive the rules so that Britannia may rule the waves, old fellow. You must hand Monty Cello over to the police, and at once."

"But, George," I said, "is Monty Cello an enemy now? He's placed himself at our mercy. As I see it, Chatterton and Kadmeel are the real enemy now, and Monty Cello is on our side."

"All the more reason, then, why Monty Cello must be put in safekeeping, don't you see? All the more reason why we daren't risk letting him fall into Chatterton's hands. It's a dead cert that Chatterton knows he is here—as I told you last night, the porter will have told him that Monty left in a hurry with you and me. And it's a horse to a hen that he'll be down tomorrow for a long week-end with Sir Peter Oversmith. He'll drop over to say hello, and mark my words, he'll find some way of getting Monty alone—I can see him hypnotising that unhappy hoodlum as a snake hypnotises a rabbit—he'll simply paralyse him with fright. And then there'll be all kinds of threats and promises, especially promises, until Chatterton gets those papers back. After which, Monty will disappear, this time for good. No, we had better explain all this to poor little Monty and tell him that we'll do our best to help him . . . we'll cook up a story about his having given up those papers of his own free will in England, being in bodily fear of Chatterton's agents on the one hand, and the Law on the other hand in America. Whatever we decide to do, Monty must be locked up safely, and Kurt Brevis's papers must go to the proper authorities."

"Seriously, George, do you really think that those papers are of any value? It was pretty clearly established that Kurt Brevis actually was off his rocker, wasn't it?"

"No, it wasn't. Mark my words, Albert, no man is easier to fool than a psychiatrist. He can no more predict a pattern of human behaviour than you or I can predict the patterns that will form in a kaleidoscope. It isn't a science, yet. But in order to proceed scientifically, your psychiatrist must take for granted as scientific truths a whole lot of theories, generalisations and half truths—must convince himself that shadow is substance. That's why so many psychiatrists have nervous breakdowns, and have to put themselves in the hands of other psychiatrists, who in their turn go mad. It is quite easy for a man with a little more than average cunning to convince a whole Board of psychiatrists that he is schizophrenic, paranoiac, or anything you like. And Kurt Brevis was a very clever, a very cunning man, Albert. His every move was motivated by hard reason. Simply: we didn't give him what he wanted, so he went to Kadmeel; Kadmeel didn't give him what he wanted, so he made tracks for Russia—always against incredible odds. If that man was mad, he wasn't mad in any ordinary sense of the term. He was no more mad than Benedict Arnold. He simply wanted to be valued in hard cash, according to his own valuation of himself."

I said: "But what the devil does Kadmeel want with atomic energy scientists in that plant of his in Canada?"

"I don't quite know," said George Oaks, gnawing at a thumbnail. "It might be that he needs some kind of atomic energy for some purely industrial process. I say, it *might* be."

"Oh come now!" I said. "Are you going to tell me that a man like Kadmeel would organise a whole underworld of killers and kidnappers just for that? Come off it, George!"

George Oaks looked up at the sky and said: "Oh Lord, listen to him! And this man writes thrillers—makes fortunes out of them! . . . Listen, donkey, I ask you to consider your multi-millionaire—any multi-millionaire. How does he get to be a multi-millionaire, starting from nothing? By subtle planning and bold and ruthless execution of deep-laid schemes. He must be a man with an absolute disregard for his fellow-men. By the time he has made his first ten million he must have arrived at a condition of mind in which humanity in general is nothing but a kind of blurred mass which, from time to time, makes a plaintive noise against which he must stop his ears. He must lock himself away from the common man if he is to know an hour's peace. He doesn't dare walk in the street without a bodyguard to stand between him and the common man, who might upset his peace of mind by asking him for the price of a cup of coffee, or by throwing a bomb at him. If he wants to take the air, he must do so on a walled estate, or a private beach; a harassed, ulcerated, disenchanted old misery; his own guard and his own prisoner, a one-man concentration camp. What is it to him if his executives employ spies to steal secrets, lawyers to swindle inventors, or gangsters as private policemen? Your multi-millionaire has to manufacture for himself a special, personalised conscience. Otherwise, he couldn't possibly get to be a multi-millionaire, could he? . . . And Kadmeel is a very special kind of multi-millionaire—a multi-millionaire of the third generation, a very dangerous man. Money means very little to the Third Viscount Kadmeel. He wants Power for its own sake."

"Look," I said, "try just for a minute to keep to the point. You start talking about his wanting to use atomic energy for some kind of industrial process, and then——"

"—Calm, calm, Albert! I only said that that was what he *might* have wanted Kurt Brevis for. I don't imagine for one moment that Kadmeel had any such reason in mind when he got him out of that sanatorium."

"Then to come back to my point—exactly what *is* Kadmeel after?" I asked.

George Oaks said: "My guess is so wild, Albert, so unbelievably fantastic, that I'm not going to tell you until I've thought it over a little more, after we've found out what Kurt Brevis's papers are all about. Meanwhile, go and put some trousers on and we'll walk up the road to the Piebald Horse and buy some beer for lunch. I'll make my phone call from there, I think; I'd just as soon not call from the house. Better hurry, it's nearly closing time."

"No hurry," I said. "They'll let me have the beer any time, if I go round the back way."

The tone of my voice must have expressed something of my discomfort, for George Oaks patted my knee and said: "On my honour, Albert, I believe it's the only thing to do."

Then Mrs. Rose came out, chuckling, with our coffee. She said: "I took some breakfast up to the gentleman, Mr. Kemp. He said: 'Hello *Baby*' . . . He said I was to tell you he never slept better in years. He said he'd be right down. . . . Baby! Me! The cheek of it!"

"Oh God!" I said.

"Calm, Albert, calm."

Monty Cello came down a few minutes later, wearing a yellow silk dressing-gown over burnt-tangerine pyjamas. His thick white toes protruded from brown morocco sandals. I could not bring myself to look at his face. "Say, this is good air you got out here," he said, breathing deeply. ". . . Say, where d'you get those roses? Jeez, they smell good!" I borrowed Oaks's pocket knife, cut a red rose, and gave it to him. He said: "Thanks a lot, Al," and inhaled voluptuously. "This is the life! What would a place like this cost? When I get kind of straightened out, I'd like to have a place like this. . . . Fifty, sixty thousand bucks, maybe?"

"Something like that," I said.

Monty Cello stopped suddenly, and pointed. "Do my eyes deceive me?" he asked. I followed his finger: he had noticed the ruins of an ancient, scandalous-looking out-house, the door of which, pierced with a diamond-shaped aperture, hung askew on one broken hinge. "A genuine Chic Sale!" he said. For some reason, this delighted him.

George Oaks said: "Make Albert an offer. He'll sell. You can have it taken to pieces and shipped home, like Hearst does——"

"——Oh, shut up!" I said. "It isn't on my land, anyway."

"What's the matter, Al? Don't you feel so good?" asked Monty Cello.

"He's like this in the morning," said George Oaks; for the first time since I had known him, he seemed to have nothing much to say. ". . . Mrs. Rose is baking a pie, Monty, a steak-and-kidney pie, and Albert and I are going over to the Piebald Horse for a gallon of old ale. You go and get dressed, Albert, and Monty and I will have a drink out here while we're waiting."

I dressed very slowly. My hands were shaking. It was quarter past two when I went downstairs again. Monty Cello and Oaks were making conversation over glasses of whisky and soda. The raven had flown over from the public-house and Oaks, teasing it with a bright new sixpence, was saying: "That bird has more money put by than I'll ever have. Here, Monty, throw it to him, and see what he does with it." Monty Cello took the coin and threw it to the raven, who snapped it up and flapped away.

"Even a bird'll take a pay-off," he said, laughing comfortably.

"Gee, I feel good today. . . . George, you're all right. You too, Al. Thanks a whole lot. Everything'll come out right, won't it, George?"

"In the end," said Oaks, emptying his glass. "Well, Albert and I'll be off now. Make yourself comfortable, and we'll be back in half an hour."

"Take your time, I'm happy here," said Monty Cello. "I'll finish this drink and go get dressed."

"You didn't tell him, then," I said, when Oaks and I were on the road.

"Albert, I'm ashamed to say, I didn't. I was leading up to it, when that damned bird came over and said 'Hello Jack'. He gave it a bit of toast, Albert. In broad daylight, it amused him; but how frightened he would have been last night, eh?"

"In short, George, you didn't have the nerve to tell him?"

George Oaks waved this question aside, and said: "The hell of it is, he looked so happy. He's got it into his head that you and I are the salt of the earth. 'All right'—that means trustworthy, true . . . I'd been telling him about Mrs. Rose's steak-and-kidney pies, and how well they go down with a glass of old ale. . . . Somehow I couldn't bring myself to spoil his lunch, Albert. Halfacre's men can't possibly get here before five o'clock, unless he deals with the business through the police station at Bright-haven, which I don't think he will, seeing that it's I who call him. He knows me, Albert—he knows I don't make trunk-calls to the Yard for nothing. And you ought to know me too, by now. On my honour, if I don't tell you everything that's in my mind at the moment, it's only because it's not properly crystallised. I don't like this any more than you do, but we have no alternative, Albert. So, calm!".

Not without bitterness, I said: "You started all this. Who's going to finish it? So now you want to spring it on Monty Cello as a big surprise. A killer, a desperate gunman: you propose to hand him over to a couple of unarmed plain-clothes men in my house. Well, if he pulls a gun and lets you and me have it first, I shan't blame him."

"He won't pull any guns, I promise you."

Mr. Titmouse, the landlord of the Piebald Horse, let us in

by the back door, laying a thick forefinger against his lips, and beckoned us into the little Snuggery that used to be a highway-man's hiding-place. To this day Titmouse keeps in working order a little sliding shutter that conceals a spy-hole through which anyone in the Snuggery may watch, unseen, the comings and goings in the Saloon Bar, the Private Bar, and the Public Bar. There is also a trap-door, through which one may jump into the cellar; and in the cellar another door opening on a flight of stairs that leads to an upper room where a secret panel covers a sinister closet, cunningly ventilated. Here, in old Tit-mouse's grandfather's time, a landlady of the Piebald Horse hid the smuggler Jem Voles from the King's excisemen, while, in a secret stable, her stepson disguised the smuggler's bay mare by painting white stockings on her forelegs and white splashes on her muzzle and breast. But the landlady's husband, who was bed-ridden with the gout, became jealous of Jem Voles, and peached on him, so that there was pistol-play on the narrow stairs, and the smuggler, hotly pursued, and being more of a seaman than a horseman, fell at the Stumbling Stones in Scratcher's Meadow and broke his back. The landlady was transported for life; her husband was found dead in his bed with a cut throat. He is still supposed to thrash about with a lolling head after midnight on the fourteenth of March; but Titmouse, who sleeps in the same old bedroom with the secret closet, sleeps sound. He too, in his way, fights the good fight against H. M. Customs and Excise, and the Inland Revenue.

He said: "I put a gallon of the Special Old just outside the lavatory door, Mr. Kemp. Good afternoon to you, Mr. Oaks, sir. I put aside a little drop o' whisky against you come."

"Bring it, bring it, brother Titmouse," said George Oaks. "In the meantime, can I go upstairs and use your telephone?"

"Surely, Mr. Oaks. You know where it is. . . . Mr. Oaks, you're a knowledgeable man: tell me something. Liddle Childs reckons the telephone interferes with the television. Do it, now? If so I'll 'ave it cut off—I never use the telephone much 'cept to phone in a few bets."

"It doesn't interfere," said Oaks, going upstairs.

Thoroughly miserable now, I sat and stared at a steel engraving of Belshazzar's Feast until Titmouse came back with a bottle, a siphon, and glasses. He said: "That's a vallyble picture, Mr. Kemp. The man on the left in the nightshirt-like, he's the Prophet Dan'l, the one they took and cast into the lion's den. Did you hear the one about the Prophet Dan'l, sir? Well, the King of Babylon threw'm into the lion's den, you see, and left 'm there all night. Next morning the King comes downstairs after breakfast and there's Dan'l standing there just like 'e was the evening before. So the King says: 'What, you still here, Dan'l?' Dan'l says: 'Why yes, Your Majesty. I been here all night.' The King says: 'Well, Dan'l, I hope you had a nice restful night of it.' 'Why, no,' says Dan'l, 'I don't like to complain, sir, but to tell you the honest truth, I was a bit bothered wi' these here lions.' So the King says: 'I'm sorry to hear that, Dan'l, but you must ha' brought 'em wi' you.'"

Titmouse shook with laughter, and poured three large drinks. "You can have the bottle at the shop-price, seeing it's you and Mr. Oaks, Mr. Kemp," he said.

I took my drink neat, in one gulp, and replenished my glass. "I *say*," said Titmouse, "you're a thirsty gentleman today!"

Then George Oaks came in and said: "Everything's all right, Albert. They'll be along about tea-time."

"Visitors?" asked Titmouse. "I hear you got a gentleman staying with you, Mr. Kemp, with a posh liddle brand-new M. G. motor-car."

George Oaks said: "Just an overnight visitor, Titmouse. Some friends are coming to pick him up about tea-time."

"Well, I'll leave you gentlemen to it," said Titmouse. "I better get down the cellar to put the beer on. If you leave before I'm back, pull the back door to, won't you, now? My best respects, gentlemen." Titmouse swallowed his drink, touched the place where his forelock used to be, and left us.

"So that's that," I said heavily.

"That's that, I'm afraid," said George Oaks. "Try and look at it objectively, Albert. The man may be your guest, in a manner of speaking, but, after all, he is a dangerous criminal. Have another drink."

"I know that," I said, "and I daresay he deserves to be hanged a dozen times over. But I mean to say . . . under my own roof!"

"Oh, you and your roof! You've been reading too many of your own silly stories about Arab sheiks, or something. Say it had been Rudolph Hess. Would you have felt called upon to keep him in hiding for the duration of the war? Be reasonable."

"There's something in that, I suppose. Still . . ."

"Still what? And again: let Monty go now, and you put him on the defensive. In the first place, he'd want his papers back, and then there'd be ructions, and you or I would have to knock him down. If he got away, and found the police after him, he'd try the last resort—shooting his way out—and then there'd be bloodshed, and he'd hang for sure. He may not look it, but that little fellow can be deadly, Albert; a man who favours a .32 revolver on a .38 frame is a one-shot killer, take it from me."

"What guarantee have we that he hasn't made copies of those papers?" I asked.

"What for? Monty Cello was working strictly alone. If he did photostat those papers, with whom would he trust them?"

"He might hide them somewhere, so that if Chatterton caught up with him he'd still be in a position to make a deal."

"No. He wouldn't be so stupid as to hope that Chatterton wouldn't double-cross him, or find some nasty means of making him talk. No, no, Monty Cello is dreeing his weird alone, Albert."

"Then who phoned him at the Savoy?" I asked.

"My guess is this: Chatterton knew that someone calling himself Monty Cello was somewhere in London. He reasoned that Monty wouldn't go to some little out-of-the-way *pension* where he'd stick out like a punch in the mouth; he'd go to some great hotel where all kinds of foreigners are constantly coming and going. Furthermore, Albert, Chatterton was working on the assumption that his man was quite sure that no one except Pen Quillan, who forged his passport, knew his pseudonym. What Chatterton did was this, therefore: he telephoned all the first-class London hotels, to begin with, asking if there was a Mr. Monty Cello registered there. Almost certainly, the operator at the Savoy said: 'Who is calling, please?' 'Oh, just a friend,' said

Chatterton. 'Hold the line a moment, please,' said the operator, and paged Monty Cello. He, thinking that this call was from Regent Lambert, dashed to the telephone, and then Chatterton was probably indiscreet enough to say 'Hello' or something. Monty Cello recognised the voice; or perhaps he asked: 'Are you the man I wrote to?'—whereupon Chatterton says: 'That's right.' Then Monty Cello, always suspicious, asks: 'What's your name?'—and Chatterton can't answer this. So Monty Cello takes fright and clears out. . . . No, I don't believe poor Monty has a friend in London, or in the whole world for that matter. Courage, Albert. The troubles of our proud and angry dust are from eternity and cannot fail. Bear them we can, and if we can we must. Shoulder the sky, my lad, and drink your ale. One more drink, then home. It's a quarter past three, and the pie will be baked."

"Well, let's face it," I said. "Only I wish he hadn't given me that hand-painted tie . . . and as for sitting at table with him and helping him to pie, well! To complete the picture, I feel I ought to kiss him first, and later on take thirty shillings blood-money, and then go and hang myself on the Judas tree in St. Wilfred's churchyard."

"Come on," said George Oaks.

We left by the tortuous path that leads from the back garden of the "Piebald Horse" through a thicket to the road, Oaks carrying the beer-jar. We had walked no more than a hundred yards towards the house, when Mrs. Rose came panting round Little Dene Corner. When she saw us, she screamed: "Mis-ter Kemp! Oh sir, quick! The gentleman's in the well!"

Oaks and I ran then. The milkman passed us in his cart, lashing his old horse into a gallop. I heard him shout: "Man down the well—going get ropes!" Then we were in my garden. I saw Barnes, the gardener, dragging a clothes-line to which were pegged several pairs of socks. A little group of men were gathered about the well. One of them was yelling: "Tread water, tread water, man! Empty the bucket and hold it topside up— it'll keep you afloat! Tread water! Tread water! Help's coming!" I did not recognise the voice, it reverberated so. But when the man straightened himself to look about him, I saw that he was

Sir Peter Oversmith, wearing an old leather-patched shooting jacket and a canvas fishing hat. Beside him, elegant in green Donegal tweeds, stood Major Chatterton, with a 12-bore shot-gun under his arm.

"Rope! Rope! Rope! Rope! Rope!" cried Sir Peter—he sounded like a mastiff barking, but with his great bristling griz-zled head, with its red eyes, snouted face, brutal jowls, and huge upturned white moustaches, he looked like an old wild boar. He leaned over to shout: "Can you hear me down there?"

There was no answer. Barnes, paying out the clothes-line, bellowed: "Catch 'old o' this, sir, and we'll 'ave you out in a jiffy." But the line hung limp. He said to me: "I'm afraid 'e 'it 'is 'ead, sir, when 'e went over. I'll swear I 'eard it crack on the brick."

Sir Peter shouted: "Bloody hell, where's that scamp with the confounded rope?"

Major Chatterton, who appeared unperturbed, said: "Some of you get sheets from the house and knot them together. Hurry!" But then, the milkman returned with a coil of stout rope, followed by a couple of sturdy timber-fellers and an excited Airedale dog. Barnes shook his head. "I don't like this, sir, damned if I do," he said. " 'E's been down there nigh on ten minutes, and not a sound."

George Oaks was undressing. He had thrown off his coat and kicked off his shoes; now, as he wriggled free of his trousers I saw that he was wearing those preposterous underpants with the pattern of crimson stags. He knotted one end of the rope about his chest, under the armpits. "I'll go down and have a look," he said. "Take the rope, Albert. Now, the rest of you. And you over there"—he pointed to one of the timber-fellers who was the heaviest man in the village tug-of-war team "—you be anchor man. So! Pay her out steady, Albert, and when I give the word, haul with a will!" (He was remembering his old days aboard the *Olaf Trygvesson*.) Then he was over the edge, and lost in the darkness of the well. We paid out the rope foot by foot. After a few seconds I heard an echoing splash, and the rope went slack. I shouted over my shoulder: "Hold on, you fellows, for God's sake!" and then, after what seemed a very long time, George

Oaks's voice came booming hollowly: "Haul up there, haul up, now—with a will. Now! Not tomorrow!"

We pulled with all our might against a ponderous dead weight, and at last George Oaks appeared, carrying the limp body of Monty Cello over his shoulder. We dragged them out, and on to the path. Oaks's shirt was torn, and the china-white skin of his breast was torn and bleeding where the rope had bitten in; but Monty Cello's face was horribly distorted and hideously smeared with a mixture of blood and slime.

"Better get to work on him quick," Oaks gasped. "He was head-down, knocked out cold. Get a doctor, hurry!"

Barnes ran to the telephone, while we laid Monty face-down on the lawn, with his forehead resting on the backs of his hands. Then George Oaks went to work on his back, above the kidneys, rhythmically squeezing the water out of his lungs. Major Chatterton said: "Hadn't we better get that money-belt off him? Isn't it in the way?"

"How did this happen?" I asked.

"Haven't the foggiest," said Chatterton, but Sir Peter Over-smith grunted:

"Extr'ordin'ry thing! Chatterton 'n I out shooting this morning——"

"—I arrived late last night," said Major Chatterton. "Dropped in on the way back to the house to say hello to you."

"Exactly," said Sir Peter. "Brought you a brace of damned fine birds. Got more than I know what to do with." He pointed to a game-bag, which he had dropped, with his gun, on the threshold of the back door. "Opened the gate. Said 'How-d'ye-do.' And damme if this fellow didn't jump down the bloody well!"

"That's right, Mr. Kemp," said Mrs. Rose. "I came out to draw some water, and the poor gentleman was talking to Jim Barnes on this very spot where I stand. Wasn't you, Jim?"

"Doctor's coming," said Barnes, coming out of the house. "Yes, Nancy; that's right, sir. The gentleman was asking me about roses—about how did you grow 'em and what did it cost, and all that. When Nancy came out to draw a pail o' water the gentleman said: 'I'll do that'——"

"—He called me 'Momma'!" said Mrs. Rose. "When I took him his breakfast he called me 'Baby'!" and she began to cry, wringing her big brown hands.

Barnes said: "'E said: 'I never 'andled one o' these things before,' and sent down the bucket, pleased as Punch, like a kiddie wi' a toy. Then Sir Peter and this other gentleman come in at the gate, and this other gentleman says 'Good afternoon' and that poor gentleman jumps like 'e's been stung, spins around, steps back sudden-like, and stumbles over backwards. I tried to grab 'im, but I was just too late. 'E grabbed the rope and caught it too, but the rope broke and that rotten old woodwork snapped, and down 'e went. I 'eard 'im catch 'is 'ead a crack and then 'e was gone. Oh dear me!"

At this point the doctor arrived. He looked at Monty Cello's eyes, put a stethoscope to his chest, and said: "I'm afraid he's dead."

A bloated bluebottle settled on a sticky red patch above his left ear. I covered his face with my handkerchief and, on an impulse, straightened his coat. He had dressed himself in his handmade jacket of English fabric, guaranteed to last a lifetime. It was pitifully soiled now. ". . . Over my dead body," he had said. And there it was, a messed-up coat, over his dead body.

The men took off their hats. Barnes said: "If you don't mind my saying so, doctor, I reckon the poor gentleman 'ad a 'eart attack. The instant afore 'e fell 'e clapped 'is 'and over 'is poor 'eart like 'e'd been stung there."

(When they undressed Monty Cello, they found that he was wearing an empty holster at his left armpit; and later, workmen cleaning the well brought up a .32 revolver on a .38 frame, and a diamond-studded medallion of St. Christopher on a broken golden chain.)

A sharp smell of burnt flesh came to us through the open window of the kitchen. "Oh Lord, my pie!" cried Mrs. Rose, and ran indoors, still weeping, wiping her eyes on her apron. Then we carried the corpse of Monty Cello into the little back room on the ground floor, laid him on an old leather sofa, and covered him with a sheet. Hobson, the constable, arrived at last, bicycle-clipped at the ankles, brandishing a notebook, and was sent to the kitchen to take down the witnesses' statements, while Major Chatterton and Sir Peter came with Oaks and me for a whisky and soda in the sitting-room.

"Most extr'ordin'ry thing," said Sir Peter, wiping his moustaches with a red bandanna. "Say 'Good afternoon' to a man, and he jumps down a confounded well!"

Major Chatterton said: "I'm frightfully sorry, Kemp, but really! . . . Who was he, if I may ask?"

"An American tourist," I said. "Fellow by the name of Cello. I scarcely knew him. Met him for the first time last night, as a matter of fact, in the Savoy."

"Can't be too careful who you pick up nowadays—only goes to show," said Sir Peter. "Chance acquaintances, eh, Chatterton?"

Then George Oaks astonished me by saying, with admirably over-acted off-handedness: "Well, he wasn't exactly a *chance* acquaintance, you know."

"Oh, you knew him, George?" Chatterton asked.

"In a manner of speaking, we were what you might call 'pen pals'," said Oaks, "Cello and I. He was quite a character, Cello. He knew all about circuses, and so forth. We'd hoped to have some interesting talks with old Cello, didn't we, Albert?"

"It's a damned shame," I said. "You must have frightened him, Chatterton, coming up behind him like that."

It was not difficult to visualise that death-scene. "Good afternoon" says the beautifully modulated, faintly sneering, hateful voice of the Major; and Monty Cello turns to face the corpse-man and the wild-boar-man, and their shotguns. I could almost feel the last wild leap of the dead man's heart.

Chatterton said, earnestly: "I give you my word, George, that I didn't know Monty Cello from Adam."

"That's right, his name *was* Monty!" cried Oaks. "I never mentioned it. How did you guess?"

Another man would have hesitated before replying: not Chatterton. He said: "Cello isn't a common name, and I seem to recollect having read something or other about somebody called Monty Cello in one of those Hollywood rags when I was last in California. A name like that sticks in your head, you know. If you'd said the man's name was Durante, or Crosby, I'd most likely have christened him Jimmy or Bing. . . . *Monty Cello*, you say? He must have been quite well known, then?"

"I don't think so," said Oaks. "I read a bit about him in a Hollywood sheet, the same as you did, I daresay, and dropped him a line. He was working, at that time, for Sam Feinlight, wasn't he?"

Chatterton shrugged: "I wouldn't know. I couldn't possibly remember. It's odd about names, isn't it? I remember once when I was looking for the telephone number of a chap named Opfer, I happened upon the name Op de Beek, and, d'you know, I couldn't get that name out of my head for years. I still wonder who and what Mr. Op de Beek is or was. Curious, what? . . . Anyhow, it's an awful bore for you, Kemp. I suppose you'll have to fuss about with his papers and things, and send all his stuff back to his relatives, and so on and so forth."

"Oh, the police will deal with all that, I suppose," I said, taking my cue from Oaks and speaking with exaggerated carelessness. "What do you think, George?"

"Oh, just so, just so, Albert . . . By the bye, Chatterton, you mentioned something about poor Cello's money-belt. I think we'd better take it off, and get his papers out of his pockets before they get spoiled."

"That's what I was thinking," I said.

Oaks rose, grotesque in one of my dressing-gowns. "I'll come with you if you like," said Chatterton.

"Oh, that's all right, I can manage alone," said Oaks. Nevertheless, Chatterton followed him into the little back room. When they returned, in a minute or two, Oaks was carrying Monty Cello's body-belt, wallet, and passport. He said: "The passport's pretty wet, but the belt doesn't seem to have taken much harm—it's one of those tricky affairs with an oilskin lining. You are the master here, Albert. Shall we open it?" His lips framed a silent *No*.

I said: "It's probably stuffed with dollars. I wouldn't want to take the responsibility. If it's money, water won't hurt it. Any letters or other loose papers inside the wallet or passport, George?"

"Not a thing, Albert. Better dry this stuff off, though. And look here—I can still feel the chill of that damned well; it went right through me. Be a good fellow, Albert, and put a match to that fire, will you?"

"Wouldn't you rather warm yourself out in the sun?" I asked. "Mrs. Rose'll raise hell about fires in August."

"To hell with hell! Give me a match, will you? And let's have another drink. I don't feel too bright all of a sudden." He took my lighter and touched the flame to the loose paper in the fireplace. It caught immediately and burned brightly. The twigs began to crackle and I caught a whiff of sweet, pungent smoke. "Now we can dry poor Monty Cello's stuff off here, and you can lock it in your desk until the police take charge of it."

The constable came out of the kitchen, closing his notebook and brushing cake crumbs off his moustache. "Well, sir," he said to me, "that'll be all, for the present. The ambulance is here from the Cottage Hospital to take the deceased away, if that's all right with you, Mr. Kemp."

"The sooner the better," I said.

"In fact, it gives me the creeps," said George Oaks, shivering so that his glass rattled against his teeth; and I noticed that his face was wet with sweat. "I must be getting old, Albert. I can't take it the way I used to. I've half a mind to spend the night over at the Hither Valley Hotel, if you don't mind."

"If you do, I'll come with you," I said. "George, you don't look well."

"It's nothing, it'll pass," said he. "But what about the belt, and all Monty's other stuff? . . . Constable, we've got our friend's money-belt, wallet and papers here. I believe there's a considerable sum of money in the belt. Will you assume responsibility for it, or shall I ask Mr. Syd at the Hither Valley to lock it in his safe for the night?"

"I think that would be just as well," said the constable. "I'll run it over there on my bike now, if you like. You can't be too careful now that the gyppos are in. They got three of Mrs. Chinn's pullets last night. I'll do that, then, sir."

"Cello's car will be safe enough in my garage, and his bags will be all right locked in his room until tomorrow," I said.

"Right you are, sir," said the constable. "Good day, gentlemen." He took the belt, the wallet, and the passport, and strode out.

Chatterton said: "These things can be upsetting, can't they? If you feel like a change of atmosphere for the night, I'm sure Oversmith could put you up. Eh, Oversmith?"

"Why, yes, of course I could," said Sir Peter, but when Oaks said that he couldn't dream of it, the old man grunted: "Well, all right, see you at the Inquest, I daresay. Plain case of accidental death. Say 'Good afternoon' to a fellow, and he falls headlong down the blasted well. Cut-and-dried case of Death by Misadventure. 'Bye."

"So long, and thanks ever so much for the drinks," said Major Chatterton. "Be seeing you." When I had seen them out, I rushed to the fireplace.

"Calm, calm," said George Oaks, "as I guessed, the twigs have burnt out, and our stuff's safe. Now, send the old lady home and tell her to take the day off tomorrow. Tell her we'll be with Mr. Syd down at the Hither Valley."

I said: "All right. But tell me, are you out of your mind? What the devil was the idea of putting on that act for Chatterton? If there's a grain of truth in Monty Cello's story, don't you see what you've done?"

"Yes. I've put Chatterton on our trail, that's what I've done, Albert."

"But *why*?"

George Oaks chanted: "For I ha'e dreamed a dreary dream, beyond the Isle of Skye . . . I ha'e seen a dead man win a fight, and I think that man was I . . ."

"George, I'm tired of playing this game in the dark. Tell me what's in your mind."

"I will, tomorrow, I promise," said Oaks. "Patience, and shuffle the cards!"

"Why not put the papers into the proper hands, and have done with it?"

"Because I can't tell you what I have in mind until I know something of the contents of those papers, don't you see? And if I so much as hint at what I believe to Scotland Yard, they'll tell me to go and get my head examined. Bear with me, Albert, my heart is in the well there, with Monty Cello, and I must pause 'till it comes back to me." He passed a hand over his forehead, and drew it away dripping wet.

"George, for God's sake, what's the matter?"

"To tell you the truth, Albert, I'm afraid. Horribly afraid!"

"I don't believe you," I said; for George Oaks and Fear were incompatible. Yet there was something in his face that froze the blood in my heart.

"Believe me, Albert—horribly afraid!"

"Of Chatterton? Of atom-bombs?" I asked. "Oh, come, my dear George!"

"No, Albert, I am afraid of something beyond reason and out of this world. Let's get out into the open air, and I'll tell you something."

Part Five

Now what could there be, in or out of this world, that had the power to make George Oaks afraid? Life? No; as he once said to me: "I used to be passionately in love with Life when I was young and foolish, Albert, and then I was terribly jealous of her, and frightened to death of losing her. But after I had lived with her and given her everything I had—worn myself out trying to keep her—and she threatened to leave me, I found myself indifferent to her. Whereupon she grew jealous of me and clung to me, complaining that I'd die without her. She was trying to come it over me with pity, you understand. So I gave her a good smack in the face and told her that, much as I loved her, I'd see myself dead and damned before I let her humiliate me. So she blinked in a shocked kind of way, smiled again as she used to smile in the old days—only with more restraint, showing fewer teeth—and told me that without George Oaks she would be nothing at all, a mere wandering itch without direction. So we agreed to be faithful to each other until our dying day.

"As for Death, I have yet to be confronted with convincing evidence of his existence," said George Oaks; and went on to quote A. E. Housman: ". . . Every mother's son travails with a skeleton," and John Donne's *Death Be Not Proud*. "Calm, calm, Albert; I have been dead and buried and resurrected, and I can tell you for a fact: Fear is hollow in the centre and around it is Nothing, as they say in Slovenia."

He had come out of the First World War with a Military Cross, a D.S.O., and something like a post-dated death certificate, having been grievously wounded and burnt in the lungs with mustard gas: the doctors gave him six months to live in 1918. Referring to this, I have heard him say: "Yes, they more or less said to me, 'Captain Oaks, if, before the end of the year, the office-boy comes in and tells you that there is an Old Gentleman, wearing no flesh on his bones and carrying a sharp scythe, who insists on seeing you immediately, do not be a bit surprised.' It struck me then that the time had come to make a little money and have a good time, so I bought some cylinders of cyanide gas from the Government and went into the rat extermination business in the seaports. And here I am, right as rain." He laughed the Old Gentleman out of countenance. He would not say for what acts of valour he had been decorated. "In war, heroes are two a penny—in fact, if you are not a hero, you are nothing but a dirty dog," he said.

Outside of lunatic asylums there were not many un-disenchanted romantics left among the survivors of the First World War. George Oaks was one. For him, even in the black night of No Man's Land, stars came out. When the debunkers, in their very just wrath, were unburdening their overloaded hearts in shocking reminiscence, George Oaks, with a rapt smile that must have been maddeningly irritating at the time, was telling the world how, breaking the awful silence before the Guards came up the road to die in Nieppe Forest, one lonely thrush began to sing; and how, when we were preparing to join battle with the enemy at Agincourt, Oaks glanced in his diary and saw that it was St. Crispin's Day—whereupon he knew that we must win the day, and so we did. . . .

And now he said that he was afraid.

George Oaks crouched rather than sat in the summer-house, clasping his hands to keep them still, and a long, strong shudder stirred the loose fabric of the dressing-gown between his shoulders and his hips.

"Albert," he said, "it's the oldest fear in the world. I knew I had it, first, over thirty years ago, when I was a boy in Flanders. Until then I'd believed that nothing could make me afraid. I was sure of that, as I was sure that nothing could make me steal a penny from a blind man. Fear was mean, Fear was a coward and a thief, Fear was a liar and a sneak, Fear was a secret poisoner. It wasn't in me to be afraid. Remember, I was young and foolish then, Albert. I became as old and as wise as I am ever likely to be, overnight. My hair didn't go grey in that awful night—it fell out. I know that my face went grey, because as soon as I came out of that nightmare, as soon as I woke up, I called for a mirror. You remember Paphnutius—he had become so ugly that, passing his hand over his face, he could feel his own hideousness? So it was with me. I reached out of the dark to touch myself, and touched something that was not me. . . . Then the good Sister had my bed moved into the garden of the hospital, because I began to cry. When I found myself out in the sunlight, I chattered and laughed—I could not stop talking and talking, I was so happy to see the sky. The Sister called me *pauvre garçon*, and said: 'There, see now, the sun is shining.' And so it was, Albert, so it was. But I never could forget the horror of that night of mine, which was timeless and without space."

"George, you never told me about this," I said.

"No, I never did, Albert, because it's best for a man to keep his secret terrors to himself, especially in times like these, when . . ."

"When what?"

"Never mind. I can tell you this—every man has a secret fear which, properly played upon, will frighten him out of his wits, if he has not the courage to hold on to his reason until he dies of fright. You know that pain brings its own anodyne, if you can bear enough of it. In the same way, fear brings its own antidote, if only you can hold on to yourself long enough. But there are some fears, Albert, that frighten the realm of Chaos and Old Night . . .

"It happened in 1917. I told you, I believe, that I transferred from the Hussars to the Engineers, Special Branch. When Jerry started using gas, the W.O. asked for men with scientific education, which I had. So I went into Gas, and I got gassed. That didn't worry me. Incidentally, in a pretty little wood—I have not forgotten the birch trees, Albert; there was a dead squirrel—I was cut open through the belly by a shell splinter, and sat up against a tree-trunk, holding myself together with my knees, for two days and two nights, hanging on to my revolver and swearing to shoot the first man that touched me. When in doubt, Albert, keep still and hold your guts together. In any case, your men come first; that stands to reason. . . . However, this was nothing. Pain is not real for long . . . Death sends the lovely soul to wander under the sky, Death opens unknown doors. . . . It is most grand to die, Albert. Anyway, nothing to make a fuss about; there is always Beethoven, eh? Soon even the flies didn't bother me. When Jerry stopped firing, the trees whispered cheek-to-cheek—all except one great old birch split by the shell that had knocked me down, and he was groaning. And upon my soul, Albert, there were bees! . . . What was I saying? That was nothing. Have you ever noticed that pain has no power to stick in your mind? Ask any honest woman—I say *honest*, mark you—who has borne half a dozen children. Pain is the *Phenomenon*, here and gone from moment to moment; the Soul is the *Noumenon*, eternal. If pain were durable, Man would be devoid of soul. . . . No, pain can't hurt. You remember nothing but the anticipation of it. But Fear, Albert, Fear—which is Nothing—oh dear me, that can be real!

"It happened in Flanders. I was in charge of six Livens Projectors. You know what they are? Immense steel tubes buried in the ground, crammed with high explosives, designed to throw one colossal shell, only once. These projectors were fired six at a time by an electric spark. Some responsible person had to stay behind to fire them, with one of those old detonating machines that worked with a plunger that had a stirrup-shaped handle. Our lines had fallen back, Albert, and in that wilderness of sodden dirt I waited all alone under the barrage, in the dark, behind my projectors, keeping an eye on my luminous watch— which was synchronised with the others of my line—counting the seconds to Zero Hour. From time to time I tugged gently at the electric wire to be sure that it was still connected. About five minutes before Zero Hour, the wire went dead, Albert. So I crawled out and followed that wire, knowing that it must have been cut by a shell. It was pitch dark, Albert. The fingers of my left hand were on the wire. On the way, I put my right hand into a dead man's mouth. Still I was not afraid. At last I came to the broken end of my wire and groped about for the other end. Then a shell burst in the mud not twenty yards away, and I went over, not badly wounded, but stunned. And still I laughed, Albert! My left shoulder-blade was torn loose, so I groped with my right hand and found a wire. Somehow I managed, with one hand, to twist together two raw ends. Then I followed the wire back to the place I had come from, as I thought. My watch said thirty seconds to Zero Hour. I hurried. As I calculated, I was only twenty seconds away. Albert, my heart sang! I did not realise that I was following the wrong thread; that, in the confusion, I had taken hold of the wrong wire.

"So, exactly, at Zero Hour, I found myself right under six projectors that were not mine at the very instant when they exploded. They went off a few inches over my head . . . And then I found myself lying on my back, fully conscious although my head was singing and spinning like a top; staring up at two stars which shone through the smoke—but paralysed, unable to move. And still I was not afraid, and there I lay until the stars went out and the sun came up.

"Albert, I was quite happy. My body was dead, but my mind, Albert, had never been more alert and alive . . . although, when the guns jarred behind me—I think it must have been behind me; I no longer knew my back from my front—that sky seemed to jerk and quiver, like it did when the *Olaf Trygvesson* was shipping it green off the Horn, and I was clinging like a monkey to a frozen rope a hundred feet above the deck. Imagine a tempestuous sea overhead, and a cold black cloud at your back . . . the dolphin-torn, the gong-tormented sea; eh, Albert? When in doubt, look straight ahead. I looked at the clouds. By the God, Albert, I have always loved the sky! How happy I was! . . . Then someone said: 'Here's a dead 'un, Alex,' and an ambulance man started to go through my pockets for papers. When I heard this, I said: 'Hold hard there, you—I'm alive.' But I couldn't move my lips; no sound came out of me; I wasn't breathing. One of them picked me up by the head, and another took my feet. My eyes were fixed in their sockets; I could see nothing but the sky. Then a voice said 'Hup' and I was being carried.

"It was then, Albert, that I knew of what I was afraid. I was afraid of being buried alive. But I lay all day long, unable to move. A man came who recognised me. His name was Ted Margery, an Essex boy. We'd shared a dug-out once. He dropped a tear right on the tip of my nose, Albert, and I wanted to sneeze, but I couldn't move. 'I'm not dead, you silly cow,' I wanted to say; but he closed my eyes for me. Everything was black then, and then I really was afraid.

"We were burying our dead in a hurry then. I know that they carried me to the edge of a common grave, and rolled me over. Albert, I fell as you fall in a nightmare and landed on something wet and soft. The fall jolted my eyes open, and I saw that I was lying with my head on the chest of a dead soldier. He had only half a face—the lower half, set in a kind of whistling expression. Something hit me with a great moist smack—a shovelful of mud. And at that moment, by the grace of the God, I found the strength to scream, just as another shovelful of mud took me in the face. My eyes were full of mud . . . and oh, Christ, that darkness! And that fear! Sight and sound went away, and there was nothing but me in the grave.

"And so I woke up, crying, six months later, in the hospital garden. I touched my head, and it was bald. I felt my face, and it was not my face, but an old man's face, the face of a frightened old man. And when I called for a mirror, I didn't recognise what I saw in it—only my eyes, Albert, when I forced myself to stare my reflection out of countenance and told it to go away. When in doubt, stare your reflection out of countenance, turn the mirror face-down, and think of great music. Then shall be brought to pass that which is written: Death is swallowed up in Victory. Death, where is thy sting? Grave, where is thy victory? . . .

"So I came back. After the war was over, in 1919, I went to the Palladium to see George Robey, that great comedian, Albert. He was doing that monologue— you remember?—'He told me my society was superfluous. . . . In other words, buzz off.' And then, in the middle of a laugh, Albert, the proscenium arch seemed to come down, and narrow, and pout out to suck at me . . . and George Robey with his funny little hat was light-years away, and the auditorium turned upside down so that the galleries were so many tiers of the dead, and the clapping applause was a spattering of shovelled mud . . . and the walls fell in . . . and there was a terrible darkness. I found myself in Great Marlboro' Street, telling a policeman please, not to bury me —I wasn't dead, and calling him Margery. He had been an Old Contemptible—he understood. George Robey came out by the stage-door, and I felt myself called upon to apologise to him. I shall never forget the weariness of that funny puffy face of his when he smiled at me and wished me well . . . for he must have seen that I was sick with a very old fear, Albert.

"Claustrophobia. That dread of being buried alive. I thought I had cured myself. But when I found myself spinning down and down to meet the dead in that horrible, slimy, cold well . . . when that little disc of daylight seemed so far away, and your shadows fell across it and I was down there in the dark . . . everything came back, and for a few seconds I was struck senseless with black fear.

"And so now you know why I was afraid, Albert, and of what. And upon this I set the seal of confession. It is a very bad thing, I tell you, to let such a thing be known. I wouldn't have told you, even, if some little voice didn't whisper that it might be good for us to share this secret. For I feel in my bones, Albert, that you and I are going to find ourselves alone in the dark pretty soon—I feel it in my bones. . . . Confidence for confidence, Albert; tell me, what is your great fear?"

I said: "George, I swear to you, I don't know! I'm afraid of everything as it comes. I'm equally afraid of so many things that I can't put my finger on one thing in particular. I'm a bundle of worry—I'm afraid of everything and everybody, so to speak."

"Which should mean to say that, in the last analysis, you are actually afraid of nothing," said George Oaks. "Lucky man, Albert, lucky man! You yield to everything and to nothing, like rubber. I yield to nothing and to everything, like cast iron with a flaw in it."

"Yet you went down into that well after Monty Cello," I said. "Went down without hesitation, George."

"I know. In the first place, I am the lightest weight and (yourself excepted) strongest in the arms. In the second place, which is more important, Chatterton was watching, don't you see—and, as I told you, this is not the time to give Chatterton the advantage of knowing where to find the flaw in the iron."

"George," I said, "once and for all; will you or will you not, as man to man, give me some little clue as to what is in your mind concerning Chatterton and Kadmeel?"

He sighed, and said: "All right, old friend. I wanted to find out what was in Kurt Brevis's papers first, as I told you. But fair's fair, Albert; I'll tell you on one condition—that you don't laugh at me, and you don't write me off as crazy if by some chance I prove to be wrong. For my part, if I am not right, you may spit in my face and call me horse. Is that fair?"

"Go on," I said.

And then Mrs. Rose came out, equipped for her journey home, wearing a man's straw boater painted black and held in place by a great hat-pin decorated at the head with a papier mâché plum, and carrying a canvas shopping bag which was never quite full but never empty. She said: "Gentleman by the name of Halfacre to see you, Mr. Oaks."

"It'll have to wait, I'm afraid, Albert," said George Oaks. "Show him out here, Moon of my Delight."

"Oh, damn, damn it all!" I said.

"Calm, calm," said George Oaks, as Chief Inspector Halfacre, accompanied by a bigger man in ginger Harris tweeds, came crunching down the path to the summer-house.

Writers of crime fiction may have led you to assume that any detective worthy of the name must look like something else: he must live in dressing-gowns, be slender, have a nose for fine tobacco and a palate for good wine, know the difference between a drypoint and a mezzotint, have eccentricities, talk superior, and be able to distinguish a Dionysian tetra-drachm by touch in the dark. If he happens to be a gluttonous orchid-fancier, a jaw-bopping three-bottle-of-rye man, a violin-playing cocaine addict, a marasmic dandy who clips his English and rolls his own cigarettes with Bull Durham which he carries loose in his waistcoat pocket—so much the better. It is just as well if he happens to be a Belgian with funny moustaches, or a pimpish Greek with a temperamental wife, or a satanic blond man who has a superhuman capacity for bourbon and bullets and is reluctantly compelled to knock somebody's teeth down his throat in every other chapter. He may also be afflicted with locomotor ataxia, and play with bits of string in tea shops; or he may be a priest, a stupid-looking priest with dull grey eyes, of course, and a gampish umbrella. In peacetime, he may even be a Japanese who will clap the *Nami-Juji* on a felon five times his size before you could say "Jack Diamond", or an obese Chinaman who quotes Confucius. Anything quaint, anything out of character, anything but a policeman! (I find myself paraphrasing Oaks again. I echoed his howl of delight when Mr. S. S. Van Dyne, having been appointed honorary chief of police of a small town, had to call in Ellis Parker to solve a perfectly obvious murder-problem.)

In point of fact, a detective carries with him the stigmata of his profession, the same as a soldier, a doctor, or a barrister. Remember; he must have spent his formative years in uniform, obedient to ineluctable discipline. He is moulded to a certain habit of carriage and of speech. He must be cautious—he may leap at anything but a conclusion—he may be thrown out of any place but a court of law—he must be educated in extreme circumspection, so that his case will withstand the siege of a Birkett, a Liebowitz, or a de Moro-Giafferi. As for kimonos, etchings, vintage wines, and what-not; he can't afford them. He has to answer for every penny that he lays out on his expense account—and he must prove himself worthy before he is trusted with five shillings. He very properly despises the Old Man In The Corner, who can tell a good story but can't make evidence in a report.

Chief Inspector Halfacre was a big, stiff-backed man who must have been quite handsome before he took to boxing thirty years previous, when he was runner-up for the heavyweight championship of the Metropolitan Police. Now he had a nose like half a banana, and a thickened ear, for heavyweight policemen fight rough, especially when they fight for fun and let themselves go. These little deformities lent distinction to a face which, without them, would have been nondescript. He still carried himself as if he might have felt more comfortable in a tight silver-buttoned tunic—something like an old soldier on leave—so that the tail of his austerely-cut, well-worn flannel jacket crept up over his prominent backside. In spite of the heat of the afternoon he wore a high, starched collar and a heavy-looking brown homburg. His companion in the ginger tweeds must have weighed two hundred and fifty pounds. He was one of those rotund, tight-packed, Mongolian-looking men that always appear to be a little too big for their skins. Halfacre introduced him gruffly as Sergeant Bollard, and then said: "Well, George, what's it all about?"

"You're a couple of hours too late, I'm afraid," said Oaks. "Did you ever hear of 'Lippy' Orsini?"

"Yank gangster, isn't he? What about him?"

"We had him here, that's why I called you. He was in the country on a fake passport under the name of Monty Cello."

"Well?"

"Well, I'm sorry to say he's dead," said George Oaks. "Accidentally. He fell down the well."

Sergeant Bollard had a notebook on his knee, and I could see by the jumping and jerking of his ball-point pen that he was writing in shorthand. "Well?" said the Chief Inspector.

"That's right," said George Oaks. "Well."

"Don't be funny, George; I'm not in the mood. Why didn't you get in touch with the police at Brighthaven? This was supposed to be my day off."

"I'm sorry, Halfacre. How's the garden? How are those Japanese azaleas I gave you?"

"Very nice, thank you. Well?"

"I didn't get in touch with the local police, Halfacre, because this fellow was big stuff and he was behaving as if his life was in danger."

" 'Lippy' Orsini, eh? Fake passport under the name of Monty Cello, you say. How do you know?"

"He told us."

"Just like that, eh? How long had you known him?"

"A few hours only."

"How did you meet him?"

George Oaks said: "Be a good fellow and bring out the beer, Albert."

When I came back with the jar and four glasses, the Chief Inspector was saying: "If I didn't know you, George, I'd have a good mind to punch you right on top of the nose! You pick up this feller at the Savoy, he tells you he's a notorious gangster, carrying forged papers, and then he falls down a well. What was the idea, him telling you all this, eh George?"

"Halfacre, a drowning man clutches at a straw. As it happens,

I was that straw. I told you, Monty Cello was in fear of his life. He felt safe with Albert and me. There was no one else he dared to trust, and being at the end of his tether, he trusted us."

"Well, it *could* be. But why was this man in bodily fear, and of whom? Did he say?"

"Yes," said George Oaks. "You know Major Chatterton, Lord Kadmeel's man? Well, Monty Cello was afraid of him."

"And why?"

"It seems that Chatterton had in his possession evidence that could convict Monty Cello of a double murder in Saratoga, New York. Also, Monty Cello had possession of some papers that Chatterton very much wanted to get hold of. And shall I tell you to whom these papers belonged? To the mathematical physicist, Kurt Brevis."

"'You haven't been drinking, by any chance, George?"

"I have always been drinking, Halfacre, and propose to go on doing so. . . . Listen to this. Kurt Brevis, as you know, is missing. I can tell you where to find him. Get on the wire, and you'll find that a man named Rheingold was buried in the Holy Grace Cemetery near Narragut Key in Florida earlier this year. That man was Kurt Brevis. You'll find that his face was altered, built up with plastics. Most likely they embalmed him—he had a few hundred dollars, and the Yanks are pretty hot on embalming —and they'll find enough of his fingers to make a clear print or two, plenty to identify Kurt Brevis. What do you say to that?"

"Nothing. Now, where does Major Chatterton come into this?"

"Halfacre, that's something we've got to learn, don't you see. I can tell you this, upon my honour: in one way or another, Chatterton is in it deep, very deep. All you can do is, watch, Halfacre, watch like a cat. Albert and I will do what we can to help. I'll let you know anything we find out."

"Rheingold, you said. *Where* did he die?"

"He died of a thrombosis at the Pompano Hotel, Narragut Key, Florida, and is buried in the Holy Grace Cemetery nearby."

"This on information received from 'Lippy' Orsini, alias Monty Cello, in England on a snide passport . . . Got that, Bollard?" Sergeant Bollard nodded. "All right, George, Rheingold, you say, was an alias of Dr. Brevis, the atom-man; is that right?"

"Quite right, Halfacre. Check, and you'll find out. And you've got to check, you know."

"I know all about that," said the Chief Inspector, ungraciously. "Now you've got it into your head that Major Chatterton was after this man 'Lippy' Orsini, or Monty Cello, for some information which Orsini, or Cello, was in a position to give him. Is that it?"

"That's it," said George Oaks.

"This information, presumably, was got by the dead man from Dr. Brevis, I take it?"

"Just so, Halfacre."

"Any idea as to the nature of this information, George?"

"It had something to do with some researches Brevis had made into some new application of atomic energy, I believe."

"Any idea what for?"

"It might be for some new industrial process, seeing that Chatterton is employed by Lord Kadmeel. But to deal plainly with you, Halfacre, I only *think* I know what for, and I'm not going to tell you what I think. If I did, I might find myself in a padded cell. As I have indicated," said Oaks, "I'm giving you facts to work on, and nothing more. Because if I told you everything that is in my mind, and you happened to let your imagination get hooked by what I implied, you'd get yourself into trouble, and to no purpose. Therefore, I'm giving you nothing but demonstrable fact for the moment."

Chief Inspector Halfacre said: "Demonstrable fact, eh? Let's hope so. We'll soon find out. All right, then. Assuming 'Lippy' Orsini, or Monty Cello as you say he called himself, got information of a scientific nature from Dr. Brevis. It'd have to be in writing, wouldn't it? It stands to reason that it'd have to be some kind of facts and figures in black and white, I mean. In other words, if that were the case, there'd be papers."

"Must be," said George Oaks.

"You say you went over him," said Halfacre. "Well?"

"As I told you before, there was a money-belt, a wallet and a passport, which Constable Hobson gave to Mr. Syd at the

Hither Valley Hotel for safekeeping. While you're here, Half-acre, I suggest that you pick them up."

Chief Inspector Halfacre made a noise expressive of extreme exasperation and said: "Damn you, I wish you'd fall down dead! I'll have to do that through Brighthaven, you bloody nuisance, you!"

"Why? You have authority to act off your own bat in an affair of this nature, haven't you? A forged passport is reason enough, surely? . . . Oh, and I forgot to tell you that Monty Cello's papers were faked by Pen Quillan, of New York . . . Better get that down, Sergeant Bollard . . . Pen Quillan was got at by Chatterton, or one of Chatterton's agents. When your people contact the other side, I haven't the slightest doubt that Pen Quillan will be induced to talk a little, especially when he finds that he's involved himself up to the back teeth in the Kurt Brevis affair. There's another demonstrable fact for you. Simply come along to the Hither Valley, therefore, and show your card, and collect Monty Cello's passport, etcetera. Circumstances warrant it."

"Well, all right," said Chief Inspector Halfacre. "We'll have a look. Now what about the rest of this fellow's things?"

"They're upstairs in his room," I said. "Two suitcases and a smaller bag. Monty Cello travelled light."

"Might as well go through 'em while we're about it," said Halfacre.

George Oaks said: "I've a better idea than that. To give a man's luggage a thorough going-over takes time. I suggest that you sit tight and let somebody else do that for you."

"What do you mean?"

"Why, Monty Cello's luggage will be left unguarded in Albert's house tonight, and I'm willing to lay you any odds you like that somebody is going to break in and go through the deceased's effects with a fine-tooth comb. To be honest with you, Halfacre, I contrived it so that Albert and I would be staying with Mr. Syd for the night, just to give the interested parties a chance to show their hand. I pretended to be upset by the idea of a dem'd damp corpse in the house. We're in deep water, Halfacre." He looked in the direction of the well, and shivered a little.

"Well?" said Halfacre.

"Well," said George Oaks, "I suggest that you and the Sergeant here keep a close watch on Albert's house tonight while he and I create a diversion down at the Hither Valley. Sure as eggs, there'll be monkey business here, and if you play your cards right you're bound to get some kind of lead, don't you see?"

Chief Inspector Halfacre laughed shortly, and said: "You'd stake my professional reputation on that, eh George? Don't be silly. Do you seriously expect me and Bollard to stick around in Mr. Kemp's house all night on your absolutely unfounded suspicion of an attempted burglary by a person or persons unknown? Why don't you try and be your age, George? If you're so set on the idea, why don't you and Mr. Kemp double back to the house yourselves and keep your own watch, having tipped off the local police?"

"Because one thing is certain, that is, from now on Albert and I will be watched," said Oaks.

"If that's the case," said Halfacre, "what about Bollard and me? At least a dozen people watched us coming along from the station———"

"———I saw at least three peeping through curtains, sir," said Sergeant Bollard, without looking up from his notebook.

"———Added to which, there's the old lady that works here. Half the village will be buying her bottles of stout tonight, and she'll tell them everything down to the colour of my eyes. No, that won't wash, George. The best you might do would be to pass the tip to the local police and advise 'em to keep their eyes open."

"You know best," said George Oaks.

"Thank you. . . . Another little thing: what leads you to suspect that these papers, if at all, might be looked for in this party's luggage? You told me just now, when Mr. Kemp went to get the beer (I'll help myself to a little more, if I may), that Major Chatterton and Sir Peter Oversmith were present when you handed the money-belt, etcetera, to the constable. What leads you to assume that this man would keep papers of any importance in his suitcase, rather than on his person? His money, passport, and whatnot are in the safe at the Hither Valley Hotel, you say. Well then, why not recommend us first of all to keep an eye on the hotel? Well?"

George Oaks sighed and said: "Haven't I already suggested that you go to the Hither Valley Hotel and pick up Monty Cello's papers?"

"That's right," said Halfacre, "you did suggest that. But the way I look at it, George: it stands to reason that the likeliest place for a man on the run to keep documents is, next to his skin. Isn't it? . . . Well?"

"I think I indicated that Monty Cello was a very frightened man," said George Oaks. "He might, therefore, have hidden his papers almost anywhere, mightn't he? You ought to know something of how such minds operate, Halfacre. At a certain psychological moment, your crook may squeal; a little while later, especially after a few hours' sleep, he retracts everything he has said. It might have been like that with Monty Cello . . . *might* have been, I say."

"Did you actually see these papers?" asked the Chief Inspector, turning suddenly to me.

"Eh?" I said. "Are you speaking to me, Inspector? . . . Yes, Monty Cello showed us some papers, but what papers I haven't the faintest idea."

"When?"

"Why, last night, in the sitting-room," I said.

"Well, where did he have them, then, last night, in the sitting-room? In his pocket, for instance?"

"No," I said. "If I remember rightly, he took them out of his money-belt."

"If you remember rightly, this man took papers out of his money-belt. If you remember rightly," said Chief Inspector Halfacre; and his face twisted itself into an expression such as I have seen on the face of a certain famous musician when I came out of his bathroom still singing *The Last Round-up*.

"That's right," I said, clipping my words. "—Or do you want me simply to answer Yes or No."

"Oh, I'm not trying to cross-examine you," said Halfacre. "I'm just asking a civil question, Mr. Kemp. You dragged me into this business, remember——"

"—I did not!"

"—when I might just as well have spent the afternoon in my garden. You know that piece of poetry that begins 'A garden is a lovesome thing, God wot'? Do you know the rest of it, by the way? You and George are always spouting poetry—I'd meant to ask you. I thought of cutting it on a bit of stone and putting it up inside the gate. . . . About these papers. You saw them, I take it, Mr. Kemp? Beg pardon, of course you did; you just told me so. Get me on to poetry, and I run on and on. Could you give me any kind of description of these papers George keeps talking about?"

"They looked to me like cheap, thin copy-paper covered with algebra," I said. "They conveyed nothing to me at all."

"Did they convey anything to you, George?" asked Halfacre.

George Oaks said: "For crying out loud, Halfacre, don't be a silly cow! Haven't I already told you that Monty Cello was carrying some kind of information from Kurt Brevis, one of the most abstruse mathematical physicists on earth? If these bits of paper have any meaning in them at all, there can't be more than half a dozen men in the world who could begin to get a glimmering of it—and one of these is a woman, Lise Meisner."

"That goes without saying," said Chief Inspector Halfacre, turning back to me. "Well, you tell me you saw this man take these papers out of his money-belt, and he showed them to you, in your sitting-room. What did he do with them after that? Swallow them?"

"He gave them to George," I said.

"Right you are, sir. . . . Well, George?"

"I gave them back to him," said George Oaks. "I told him that they had better be kept safe. He put them back in his belt."

Then I became afraid; not because Oaks found it necessary to lie, but because he was lying clumsily. Something like despair took possession of me. I remember that I tried, without hope, to create a diversion by beating at a wasp with the Chief Inspector's hat. This wasp had been circling an inch or two above the back of Sergeant Bollard's neck. The Sergeant picked the maimed insect off his collar, put it on the table, and flicked it away with a forefinger that moved like a released spring—one could almost hear it twang. Chief Inspector Halfacre said: "When I was training for the Finals in my younger days, d'you know how I used to perfect my left jab? By catching flies in mid-air. . . . Now come off it, George, old boy. Man comes to you and says, substantially, as follows: 'George, between you and me, I am a notorious murderer, travelling with a snide passport, and in bodily fear of a certain party. I was in at the death of Dr. Brevis, who was badly wanted, all over the world. This Dr. Brevis was in possession of information which, in the hands of an unscrupulous person, might be worth hundreds of thousands. A certain party, or parties, who have got wise to my whereabouts, will stop at nothing to get hold of this information. In effect,' this man says, 'I might as well be walking about —like the anarchist that tried to blow up Greenwich Observatory—with a bottle of nitroglycerine strapped round my belly.' Well?"

"Well?" said Oaks.

"And you are sitting there and telling me that, knowing the character of this man and the nature of the information he was carrying, you let him put the stuff back in his belt, and left him alone in the house?"

"Who said I left him alone in the house?" asked Oaks.

"I do. The number you called from wasn't Mr. Kemp's number. It was Hither Valley 365, name of Titmouse, the Piebald Horse."

Replenishing our glasses from the jar, George Oaks said: "Quite right. Naturally you checked the call. You didn't think I'd be foolish enough to risk calling from the house, which resounds like the belly of an old violin, just when we'd lulled poor little Monty Cello into a feeling of security—did you, Halfacre?"

" 'Poor little Monty Cello', my foot! Bloody little murderer," said Halfacre.

"He was my guest," I said, "under my roof——"

"—Yes, sir. And he would have been the King's guest under His Majesty's roof, but that wouldn't have saved him. . . . Go on, George; you nipped across to the Piebald Horse by Titmouse, to buy some beer just after closing time. I mean, the call was received after two-thirty, you see. You hung about the 'Piebald Horse' after hours, half an hour or more. . . . All right, don't worry. I'm not after Mr. Titmouse's licence. . . . As I was saying, George: you didn't come back to the house here until after this man had tumbled down the well———"

"———In the presence of four witnesses, Halfacre—Mrs. Rose, Barnes the gardener, Sir Peter Oversmith, and Major Chatterton," said George Oaks. "In a manner of speaking, the very sight of Chatterton frightened him to death."

"Well, what then? . . . Why, George, you haul the body out of the well; and after that, if you please, believing that the dead man's money-belt contains papers of world-wide importance, and being convinced that there is some immediate danger of their being got hold of by hook or by crook right here in the neighbourhood, you simply give the stuff for safekeeping to the poor old local constable, just like that! That's your story, isn't it, George?"

"And what if it is?" said George Oaks.

The Chief Inspector said: "Why, just this—it isn't like you, George, that's all. And I know you, old man; it doesn't rhyme with you. If you genuinely believed that these here documents were in this dead man's money-belt, I don't see you letting that belt out of your sight. Now what I *can* see you doing, George, is this: deliberately letting that money-belt, etcetera, go, knowing full well that any important papers which it might have contained were safely stored elsewhere. I know you, old fellow; I know you of old."

"Very well, then," said George Oaks, "in that case, you might as well credit me with something like average intelligence, mightn't you, Halfacre? Put yourself in my place. Here is Major Chatterton and his friend, Sir Peter Oversmith. Chatterton is itching to open Monty Cello's belt. In two minutes he will have his way, because Sir Peter is a Justice of the Peace, and a pig-headed old fool to quarrel with. The constable happens to be on the premises, getting ready to leave. This being the case, what would you do, Halfacre?"

Halfacre said: "That's easy. Say I am you, eh? All right. I say to myself: 'I am a knowledgeable fellow, a Bachelor of Science, and all that. I have glanced at these papers, and they were so much Greek to me. What harm can there be, therefore, in letting Major Chatterton take a glance? I know that Chief Inspector Bob Halfacre is coming along around tea-time: therefore, if Sir Thingummybob, J.P., tries to come the acid, I can simply tell him that I refuse to relinquish the deceased's documents to any but the highest authorised official.' Well, George? . . ."

"Reasonable enough," said George Oaks. "But what if you, being me, took it into your head to act on intuition?"

Halfacre said: "No, thank you. Plain common sense is good enough for me, if you don't mind, George."

"Halfacre, there is common sense *and* common sense; and more often than not, in the last analysis, common sense is something esoteric. It involves something behind knowledge. That is why what you call common sense, in its most dazzling application, is unexplainable. Common sense involves the intuitive: that is to say, it relies upon that which it *senses* rather than sees, upon what it perceives rather than knows. Don't you start getting rational with me, Halfacre! Ask yourself what happens in your mind when you take one look at a man and say to yourself: 'There's a bad 'un.' Ask an experienced diagnostician how he chooses a specific disease from a mass of similar symptoms. Ask a Japanese expert to explain how he determines the sex of a new-hatched chick. Ask——"

"——If you don't mind, George, we'll save all that for some nice long winter evening, some time in the New Year. Come back to the point. About letting these so-called important documents out of your hands: where was the common sense in that?"

George Oaks said, slowly: "In the first place, Halfacre, I have at the back of my mind a suspicion so preposterous that I simply daren't give voice to it yet."

"All right, then, don't," said Halfacre. "But I'll tell you one thing, if you like. If you start making a case on that basis, the probability is that you'll argue yourself into going nuts, doolally, stone staring crackers. Don't do it."

"Just so. That is why I'm keeping my case to myself, Halfacre —so that, if I'm crazy, which I almost hope I am, I won't altogether discredit myself like old Austin Crabbe."

"God forbid," said Halfacre. "But what makes you bring up poor old Austin Crabbe at this point, George? He *was* off his rocker, you know."

"You think he was, do you?"

"Don't you, George?"

"No, I don't, Halfacre. Austin Crabbe was *on* his rocker. Simply; his rocker didn't happen to be your rocker. A monomaniac, I grant you; Austin Crabbe was that. But the fact that a man is a monomaniac doesn't necessarily mean that he's wrong, Halfacre. A fixed idea may turn out to be a very right idea, expressed before its time and without supporting evidence. You know that ironic Cockney saying: 'You ain't crazy, Bill—yer right, an' all the world's wrong'? That can be so. If it were not for monomaniacs, you'd still be swinging from a branch. You can heave it or sink it, leave it or drink it—I tell you that the time may yet come when you'll remember Austin Crabbe in your prayers," said George Oaks.

Halfacre said: "Austin was all right. He was one of the best until he went barmy, and went and gassed himself."

"Gassed himself. Shall I tell you something? Austin Crabbe did not gas himself. He was murdered in cold blood." Halfacre raised his eyebrows: George Oaks caught hold of his wrist and held his eyes with his keen, intent stare. "Austin Crabbe was foully murdered, Halfacre!"

"No need to break my arm, George. All right, then, Crabbe was murdered. By whom?"

"By Lord Kadmeel."

"With what motive?"

"Either he knew too much, or suspected too much."

"You mean, about Lord Kadmeel?"

"Yes. And as for his lulling himself—you and your common sense!—doesn't your common sense tell you that the very last thing a man like Austin Crabbe does is, kill himself? Crabbe was a man with a big hate, Halfacre. Such men will do anything but kill themselves. In hate or in love, you don't kill yourself—only in despair, when all desire ceases."

"Very well, then, George," said Chief Inspector Halfacre smoothly. "Austin Crabbe didn't kill himself; he was murdered.

Let's get back to the point. *Why did you let Dr. Kurt Brevis's papers off the premises and out of your sight?*"

George Oaks said: "Take certain facts in order. I think I know what I know. I know better than to tell you what I think I know, without first having convinced you, through material evidence, of the need for action. You couldn't properly act on my suspicions, which are out of this world. Therefore, don't you see, I create a situation in which you will be compelled to act."

"What situation?" asked the Chief Inspector. "You've told me that Monty Cello, deceased, is an alias of 'Lippy' Orsini; and you've told me that Dr. Kurt Brevis's body may be exhumed at such-and-such a place. Well, where's your situation?"

"Yet to come," said George Oaks calmly. "The proper authorities must pick up Monty Cello's things between now and tomorrow, mustn't they? As I see it, between now and then there is bound to be some attempt to burgle Albert's house, and probably to get at the safe in the Hither Valley Hotel. This being the case, considering information already received from me, you'll be bound to act, one way or another, won't you?"

"Right you are, George," said Halfacre, "I'll grant you that. Still, we haven't got back round to my original point. You know Austin Crabbe, you tell me, and you say that it wasn't in the nature of the man to kill himself: that was strong enough reason for you to come to a certain conclusion. All right, George, what's sauce for the goose is sauce for the gander. I know you, d'you know; and *I* say that it isn't in the nature of *you* to let Kurt Brevis's documents out of your sight. See? . . . Well?"

"Bait for a hook, Halfacre, bait for a hook!" cried George Oaks.

"Oh no," said the Chief Inspector. "I'm a bit of a fishing man myself, you know, in one way and another. . . . In the first place, there's bait that's much too heavy. You cast a fly to catch a trout; you don't cast a trout to catch a fly. In the second place, where the hell's your hook? Well?"

"In the first place," George Oaks replied, "this is a case of casting a trout to catch a whale. In the second place, you are the hook, Halfacre."

"That won't do, George. It's bad fishing. If it's whales you're after, your tackle's too light. And your boat's too small. Doesn't it say something in the Bible, somewhere, that you can't draw Leviathan out of the water with a hook in his jaw—Book of Job, I think? . . . Peter Piper went a-fishing for to catch a whale, and all the water he had got was in his mother's pail . . . speaking of literature. But you're not Peter Piper, George, and I happen to know that you're a cunning hand with a rod; so when you come around to damn silly comparisons of that nature, I get more and more suspicious of you every moment. I know you, don't forget, and I tell you, as sure as I sit here, you knew perfectly well that these documents of yours never left this house. Now then!"

"Very well," said George Oaks, "come to the Hither Valley and see."

"All right, so I will," said Chief Inspector Halfacre. "Bollard, you wait here, and see to it that not so much as a fly comes in or out of the house while I'm gone."

"Very good, sir," said Sergeant Bollard, closing his notebook.

"And I give you fair warning, George—if you've been withholding anything of any importance, I'd shop you if you were my own brother. Let's go."

When we were at the garden gate, Halfacre excused himself and went back into the house. "Bathroom my eye!" George Oaks muttered. "He's gone to tell Bollard to go over the house. No fool, Halfacre! And I like the look of Bollard too."

I answered bitterly: "No fool? He made you look like an absolute ass. Why not give him the papers and have done with it? As soon as he goes over Monty Cello's things at the Hither Valley, Halfacre's bound to come right back and shake the whole damned house through a sieve. And I can tell you this, George—before he does that I'll simply tell him where those papers are."

"I beg you, Albert, don't do that. I must admit that I underestimated Halfacre. Damn his eyes, he's harder to side-track than a bulldozer. . . . I must be getting old. . . . Please have faith in me just for the present, Albert, old friend, please do. Something tells me I *can't* be wrong, here."

Then Chief Inspector Halfacre rejoined us, whistling, and so we walked the long mile down the road to the Hither Valley Hotel. I remember that he bared his head, smiled at the sky, and, breathing deeply, swore that there was nothing so beautiful as the smell of hops mixed with wood-smoke. He paused once or twice to pick a few prematurely ripened blackberries, the largest of which he offered me; I took it and, in my angry preoccupation, put it in my trousers pocket.

Part Six

Mr. Syd must have been a fine figure of a man twenty years ago, and his face still has a certain delicacy of feature; but his powerful frame has taken on a little more weight than it can carry with perfect dignity, so that he tends to move like a man in a Christmas shopping rush balancing two armfuls of hastily wrapped parcels, the topmost of which, marked *Fragile*, is on the verge of overbalancing. I have seen him put out a Saturday night crowd at closing time simply by leaning against it. He is not given to the expression of strong emotion. For example: when Adolf Hitler shot Eva Braun and poisoned himself, and the countryside was buzzing with the news, all Syd said was: "Hitler never did have much sense of honour, did he?"

But now, when I introduced Chief Inspector Halfacre and said that he had come to pick up the dead man's property, Mr. Syd showed signs of helpless astonishment—just as if that *Fragile* parcel had at last toppled over to fall at his feet. He winced at the inaudible crash. "I don't quite understand this," he said. "You are from Scotland Yard, you say, sir?"

"Here are my credentials, Mr. Syd," said Halfacre. "I'll have a look at those things, if it's not too much trouble."

"I'm sorry," said Syd, "but it seems as if the Brighthaven police were here a bit ahead of you."

"What the devil d'you mean?" cried George Oaks.

"You shut up, George," said Halfacre. ". . . What *do* you mean, Mr. Syd? How do you mean, ahead of me?"

Syd took from his fob pocket a bit of paper, and handed it to the Chief Inspector, saying: "Naturally, I insisted on an official receipt. Here it is. The Constable Hobson came round, about half-past five or so, with a sergeant in uniform from Brighthaven and a detective in plain clothes, and asked me for the stuff old Hobson himself had left with me to be locked in my safe. Naturally, I handed it over. Of course, I asked to see some written authorisation."

Halfacre said: "Quite right. And they produced it? . . . I see. So you handed the stuff over, then."

"What else was I to do?"

"Nothing, Mr. Syd. I see that the signature on this receipt says *Noah Hobson*. That's the local constable, I take it. Happen to remember the names of the other two, by any chance?"

"The plain-clothes man's card said Bosworth. Old Hobson introduced the sergeant as Ayrton," said Syd.

"I see. Mind if I use your phone?"

"Not at all. And would you like me to try and find Hobson for you?"

"I'm sorry to trouble you, Mr. Syd, but I'd be much obliged if you'd do that."

Mr. Syd and Chief Inspector Halfacre left the dining-room in which we were sitting. As soon as the door was closed behind them George Oaks punched me in the chest, and whispered: "Albert, Albert, by the God, this is perfect! This is it!"

"What is *it*? What is what?"

"Breathing-space; wait and see!"

Nothing more was said until Halfacre came back. "Definitely peculiar," he said. "Brighthaven has got a Sergeant Ayrton, and a Detective Bosworth, but neither of them have left the town today. Brighthaven received Hobson's report by telephone, but have done nothing about it as yet. It seems there's an outbreak of crime in Brighthaven—bunch of roughs smashed up a tea dance at the Casino de Paris there. . . . Where the hell is that idiot Hobson, for God's sake?"

The constable came, at last, looking very severe; and then, when Halfacre went to work upon that perspiring, important old policeman, it was impossible not to be reminded of a callous little boy dismembering a fat blue fly. Halfacre now had all the quiet seriousness of a child at play . . . Was Hobson acquainted with the Brighthaven Police Force? Yes. Did he know Detective Bosworth and Sergeant Ayrton? . . . By name, yes; by sight, no . . . One wing was torn off and laid aside, and Hobson began to buzz, grounded, in wide circles. . . . He had received telephonic notification that these two men were to call, had he? Oh, he had. It had not occurred to him, at that point, to telephone the Inspector at Brighthaven for confirmation, had it? So that, therefore, all any Tom, Dick or Harry needed to do, to have the Law at his mercy, was, drop two pennies in a telephone box, eh? . . . Off came the other wing, and now Halfacre had him by a leg. Mr. Syd, his face creased with pity, brought tankards of bitter, and the tortured fly, looking in two hundred directions at once, moistened his agonised proboscis . . . Was Hobson aware that the two men he had brought to the Hither Valley were impostors? That they might be international crooks who, through his stupidity—his culpable incompetence, his inane ineptitude, practically with his connivance—had got away with a vast sum of money, in American dollars at that? . . . Did Hobson realise that he had acted like a blithering idiot and a pompous slob? Did it occur to Hobson that Halfacre could have his pension taken away for less than this? Could he, at least, give a detailed description of these two men? . . .

The sixth leg was out of its socket; Hobson could only writhe. Of course he couldn't describe the men who had said that they were police officers from Brighthaven; what policeman looks at another policeman with a view to identifying him—let alone a policeman wearing the stripes or carrying the card of authority?

It was Syd who came to the rescue, saying: "Mr. Hobson did mention that the Sergeant's tunic was much too tight across the shoulders, and a little bit short in the sleeves . . . Didn't you, Hobson?"

"That's right," said Hobson, brightening. "But it was a brand-new tunic, you see——"

"——So that he wouldn't have had time to get it fitted, and him a sergeant—is that what you're trying to tell me?" said Halfacre. "Don't make matters worse, Hobson. You've made a pretty nice mess already, for one day. . . . What else did you notice, Mr. Syd?"

"The plain-clothes man was wearing a single-breasted dark brown suit, obviously ready-made. His coat being unbuttoned, when he leaned forward, I couldn't help noticing his tie. That was when we were in my office bending over the safe; I had my glasses on. I noticed that the maker's label on the thin end of the tie said *Sulka*, and that struck me as being a bit out of the way, for a common or garden plain-clothes man. I hope you don't mind my saying so."

"I should hope not; lucky if we can afford to buy a tie at all. Go on, please. You'd recognise the man if you saw him again, I daresay?"

"Fresh-faced, presentable young man, not big-built, about three inches shorter than me, which would make him about five feet ten. Lightish-mousey hair; the sort of man that has bluey-grey eyes. The sergeant was shorter and broader, quite dark, and his hair grew low down on his forehead; he had big ears."

"Thanks. They come in a car?"

"They did, sir," said Hobson. "An Austin 12, colour dark blue." And he blinked hopefully.

"—Of which, of course, you didn't dream of taking the number?"

"On the assumption it was a bona fide police-car, with bona fide officers from Brighthaven . . ."

"—You're a bright spark, aren't you?"

"I assure you, sir, as a general rule, I make it a habit to notice number-plates, but under the circumstances——"

"—I'll give you circumstances," Halfacre muttered, through his teeth, and he proceeded to complete his destruction of Hobson, head, thorax, and abdomen.

But Syd said: "Everything was done so fast and smooth, you see, Inspector. They let Constable Hobson into the car first—"

"—And *that*, in itself, would have aroused the suspicion of a child of six!" growled Halfacre.

"—But I saw them off. By the way, when the plain-clothes man bent down to get in, I saw he had a pistol in his hip pocket. I'm accustomed to noticing these things, you see, because for several years I owned the Café de la Paix de Novembre Onze on the waterfront at Bordeaux, where it paid to keep your eyes open for that kind of nonsense. . . ." Halfacre looked at him with interest and approval. He went on: "I thought it was rather strange, especially in these parts, for a detective to be carrying a pistol. But then again, I'd seen his credentials, and he was backed up by the uniformed police, and he was carrying the pistol on his hip. If it had been under his arm, perhaps I might have given it a second thought. The bulge was flattish for a revolver, so I should say it was an automatic. However, I believe our police do carry automatics sometimes, don't they, Inspector? So that was that . . . Anyway, I did happen to notice the number of the car. It was T P Y 3141."

"I'll trouble you for the use of your phone again, if I may, Mr. Syd," said Halfacre. To Hobson he said: "That's all for now, you. Go about your business, and mind nobody steals your bicycle"—and went back to the telephone.

It was like a film run backwards: Hobson reassembled and rearticulated himself in a couple of seconds, and left with a ponderous "Good-evening, gentlemen" as if it were he who had sent the Chief Inspector about his business.

But we learned, later, that someone *had* stolen his bicycle —or rather, hidden it in the hen-house just for a lark. A pink-haired hoyden of bad reputation was accused of having done this thing, but she had an alibi—it was proven that she was in solitary confinement in her bedroom at that time, on suspicion of petty larceny in the matter of plum jam in her own mother's house, evidence of which was discovered in her ears. So that case fell through. I believe Hobson hushed it up. Rest assured, however, it made folklore. Hobson's blue shoulder was starred by a startled pullet. . . . Thus, he was made an Inspector, or something, because a hen ran off on his bicycle . . . A few years from now she will have laid a golden egg in his pocket. Anything for a good laugh at Law and Order. . . .

I wish this were a light-hearted tale; or, at least, that I could see it in long perspective. But I can't. I am too close to it, so that it still troubles my dreams; and if I laugh sometimes in telling it, it is that I may not weep.

Mr. Syd had returned to the bar long before Chief Inspector Halfacre came back. Evening was closing in. Looking at the western corner of the sky, into the half-closed inflamed eye of the afternoon, I could see that the Black Hope had the better of it again and waited for the raising of a bloody half-moon. George Oaks said nothing, and I had nothing to say. We sat in the darkening dining-room until Halfacre came in.

"Well? Begin to see what I mean?" said Oaks.

Halfacre licked his lips, and said: "All right, George. Now look here, friendship aside. If you're leading me any kind of a dance here, take my word for it, there'll be hell to pay. Is that clear?"

"Clear. There's going to be hell to pay anyway, Halfacre. But first things first, as poor old Monty said: do you begin to get my point? Do you begin to see that we're up against a certain something? Eh?"

Putting aside George Oaks's probing finger, Halfacre said: "So what? Now listen to me. I'm not going all over what I said before. I believe you *knew* these papers you were talking of were definitely *not* here among this man's effects. If there were any papers—and I believe you and Mr. Kemp when you say, on your honour, that you saw them—they must be either on your person or in Mr. Kemp's house. George, I'll deal honestly with you—and with you too, Mr. Kemp—I told Bollard to take a look around Mr. Kemp's house in our absence. I told him to go through everything, but that's a tall order. I know that, strictly speaking, I have no right to give any such instructions, but I know you and your tricks, George, and I was sure Mr. Kemp wouldn't mind——"

"In the circumstances," I said, "it's all the same if I do, isn't it?"

"——Don't be bitter, Mr. Kemp. George started all this. If I was supposed to take him seriously, which I'm sure you both intended, what else was I to do? Don't worry, Mr. Kemp, Bollard will have put everything back exactly where he found it, and nobody'll be a penny the worse—unless you happen to be concealing something; in which case I'll have to do my duty. . . . Now, George, and you, Mr. Kemp, give me an honest answer. On your honour, mind! Apart from baggage, etcetera; do you know of anything that was in the possession of this so-called Monty Cello, which is concealed on your persons or in Mr. Kemp's house?"

George Oaks said, without hesitation: "Halfacre, on my honour, I have concealed nothing."

"How about you, Mr. Kemp?"

I said: "For my part, I can swear to you that I have concealed nothing. I saw the papers to which George referred last night, before I went to bed. I haven't any idea what might have happened to them between that time and this. The last time I saw them, they were in George Oaks's hands, and if George gives his word of honour, for my part I accept it. I'm willing to be searched, if you like, and I daresay so is George." I looked at Oaks bitterly as I said this.

"Well, let's stroll back," said Halfacre. "I'll take your word, Mr. Kemp."

We walked back to the house. Sergeant Bollard was reading the *Dictionary of Slang and Unconventional English*, open to Page 305, FUB/FUG.

"Well, Bollard?" said Halfacre. "It's all right, speak up. The gentlemen know all about it."

Sergeant Bollard said: "I went over the house from top to bottom, sir, as thoroughly as I could in the time. I expected you to ring before you started back, as you said you would——"

"——wasn't necessary. The gentlemen know all about it."

"I turned over the pages of all the books, sir. There are 2,950 of them."

Then Chief Inspector Halfacre said: "Chimney in the man's room?"

"Nothing there, sir, as far as a broom would reach. . . . I'm sorry to say I accidentally got some soot on the rug."

"How about the fireplace down here?"

"Fireplace?" I said, and my voice must have sounded strange, because Halfacre looked twice at me before saying: "Fireplace. Last place anyone'd be likely to look . . . Well?"

"First place I looked," said Sergeant Bollard.

"Quite right, Bollard. . . . Old trick, Mr. Kemp. Some genius like yourself writes a detective story; a certain party has to hide a document. Where? Unlikeliest place for important document —unlaid fire. In the story, it fools everybody, especially the copper in the bowler hat. Fact of the matter is, even coppers have read Edgar Allan Poe's *Tales of Mystery and Imagination*. People take that for granted nowadays—assume the policeman, therefore, will go straight for the obvious. Therefore adds artistic touch—lights fire in August to draw attention to it, thereby making the obvious doubly obvious . . . you know? . . . You looked in that rubbish incinerator, of course? . . . Poked down the barrels of those old muskets, or whoever you call them? . . . *Did it occur to you to shake out the telephone directory?* . . . It did? Good. . . Very well, then, Bollard. Mr. Kemp and Mr. Oaks are stopping at the Hither Valley overnight. Mr. Kemp will give you his keys. Mr. Kemp and Mr. Oaks will see you and me off on the next train. I'll go on to London, but you'll get off where I change trains a couple of miles up the line, double back, let yourself in, show no light, and lie doggo until further orders, sleeping light if at all, standing by for monkey business. The rest is taken care of. Is that clear?"

"Yes sir," said Sergeant Bollard.

"Better put out something cold to eat and drink, with Mr. Kemp's permission, and do it now, because you won't be back till pitch dark. . . . Now, let's lock up behind us, gentlemen, and be off."

Halfacre and Bollard caught the last train. It seemed to me that the hedgerows were as full of eyes as the sky of stars. "Calm, calm," said George Oaks, punching me in the back, "let us stop at your place to pick up the papers, and then back to the Hither Valley."

I said: "George, you gave your word of honour, and I stood by you as near as I could this side of a dirty lie!"

"Albert, remember what I said, will you? I gave my word that the papers were not in your house, not on your person or mine, and not concealed, did I not?"

"Where are they, then?"

"It was always possible that Monty Cello might have changed his mind overnight, so after you were asleep I got up and put the papers somewhere else."

"But where?"

George Oaks began to laugh. "Dear old Halfacre and his 'obvious and doubly obvious'! Him and his Edgar Allan Poe, eh? I doubled back to the ludicrous. You remember Monty Cello noticed that old out-house just beyond your garden? Well, quite simply, I slipped out and spiked Kurt Brevis's papers on the nail there. So I told the truth; they aren't on your premises, they're on Oversmith's land; and since the door has fallen down they are not even concealed. So this is quite literally a case of the handwriting on the wall, eh? He reads Edgar Allan Poe, does he? Well, here's *The Purloined Letter* in all its sublime simplicity. To the out-house!"

"And what then?" I asked.

"To the hotel. Everything is going beautifully, Albert. By tomorrow we'll have the most unscrupulous and powerful gang of criminals in the world on our track, closely followed by the most terrible police force in the world. Good, eh?"

"So that, really and truly, you and I are nothing but decoy ducks, is that it?"

"Nothing of the sort. We are hunted buffaloes in the long grass, retreating in a perfect circle, sweetheart, our goal being our hunters' backside. Get it?"

"You really think, then, that there will be an attempt on the house tonight?"

"I think there must be, once Chatterton has found out there's nothing but money in that belt. . . . Don't worry about Bollard; as I guess, Halfacre will have somebody watching from the outside, tonight. Worry about yourself, Albert, because we're due for the works at any moment now. Well, I always said that you were one man I'd like to have with me on a wiring-party. Tomorrow, you and I are going to take Kurt Brevis's papers to my old friend, Ohm Robertson, and I lay you a horse to a hen, Albert, we'll be shadowed every inch of the way by coppers and robbers, cowboys and Indians, alike . . .

"This kind of game is good for the nerves, if you manage to survive it. One way or another, it takes you out of yourself."

So he took the papers off the nail in the disused out-house, and we walked back to the hotel down the twilit road.

Syd had allotted to us the Bridal Chamber, a large room furnished with two bright brass beds which, at the slightest touch, went off like the thousand twangling instruments in Caliban's dream, and were covered with plump dimpled pink eiderdowns. We locked ourselves in, after supper, with two tankards of Dog's Nose, and sat on our beds to talk. I was unaccountably happy, vividly alert. The Dog's Nose—like a happy life—was not too bitter and not too sweet. There was a whimsical kind of music in the plangent bedsprings, to which I listened with smiling satisfaction, while with the other ear I heard and enjoyed the noises in the Darts room below: old Mrs. Hawthorne, the matriarch of Cockney hop-pickers (I would know her voice in a million), was singing and dancing "Knees Up, Mother Brown" to the accompaniment of an abused piano that must have been strung with baling wire and lacked the middle C . . .

> *Knees Up, Mother Brown,*
> *Knees Up, Mother Brown,*
> *Under the table you must go,*
> *Eee – i – ee – i – ee – i – oh!*
> *If I catch you bending,*
> *I'll turn you upside down,*
> *So knees up, knees up,*
> *Don't get the breeze up,*
> *Knees Up, Mother Brown! . . .*
> (Piercing Scream)

. . . with a great thunder of boots on the sturdy, long-suffering floor. Somewhere in the background a man was trying to sing "Down Mexico Way", which had been popular when he was young and in his prime ten years before—I knew him, too; his name was Holiday; he lost a leg at Anzio.

This was one of those moments—how shall I put it?—one of those moments in which, looking away from the crushed husks of lives, you see the expressed wine, and, in a flash of sublime understanding, perceive the ultimate goodness of many little things. . . . I found a mothball under the eiderdown, and balanced it on my palm, and it caught the light and threw its own shadows in such a way that I might have been holding in my hand the full moon in all its mystery; so I kept very still, knowing that one false move would roll it away for ever beyond recapture. This mothball, poised in that moment, was something no one had seen before or would ever see again.

Suddenly—I started, and that nacreous, volcano-blistered globe turned a hundredth part of a degree and became a mean mothball again—George Oaks said: "About Austin Crabbe. You heard Halfacre humouring me when I said he was murdered. I suppose you think I'm mad. Well, I'm not, you know."

I flipped the mothball away with my thumb, so that it broke in two in the clean, blackened fireplace. The plane surfaces of the hemispheres, brilliantly crystalline, crazily rocking and spinning, caught the light again. One half of the ball staggered away into the shadow; the other half turned, scintillating. "No, George, you never could be mad," I heard myself saying. "George, I believe you. You are my only true friend, so I believe without seeing. I want no evidence, only your word. . . . Do you know, I felt something like ice in my heart when I thought you were lying after your word of honour in connection with those papers this evening? Silly, yes. But that is how I am. I can't give half my faith . . . Tell me about Austin Crabbe, George."

Half smiling at the ceiling, shaking his head with a kind of awe as one who finds himself tingling fingertip-to-fingertip with the Inapprehensible, George Oaks said: "Really, how beautifully everything fits together! . . . When I was a child, my mother gave me a jigsaw puzzle, mixed up the pieces, and left me alone to play with them—having, mark you, given me a glimpse of the picture of which they were the mixed-up fragments. There was some blue sky, green leaves, black tree-trunks, black shadows, a girl in red with a brown basket, and a grey beast. When the assembled puzzle was broken up, and its parts all mixed together, I went to work with confidence, having the picture in mind. Blue to blue, green to green, red to red, grey to grey, and black to black—that is what my instinct told me. So I put green to green and blue to blue, and so on, and found that, out of their proper juxtapositions, even identical colours and interlocking shapes didn't make sense. . . . The shiny shoe of the little girl was the wet nose of the grey beast, and somewhere between the trees and the sky there occurred a hairy paw with nails. You can't imagine, Albert, how I cried over it—I was only a child—until it occurred to me to transpose four identically-shaped pieces—shiny shoe to wet nose, and shadow between leaves to shadow in grass. After

that, everything seemed to fall into place of its own accord, and
there was Little Red Riding Hood with her basket, accosted by
the wicked wolf. And will you believe me when I tell you that my
soul soared up as if I had discovered some tremendous truth—
which, indeed, I had? Albert, all are but parts of one stupendous
whole. . . .

"Needless to say, once the spell was broken, the easiest bits to
piece together were the hopelessly complicated bits. The high
blue part, the open sky, that took longest of all; because every
little part of it was of the same colour and maddeningly similar
shape. But at last, with frenzy and patience, I found one bit that
fitted a certain dangerous corner, and so saw God's heaven.

"Well, so it has been with Kadmeel. But in his case, the picture
that I started, quite idly, to piece together was a mad montage, a
kind of evil dream in which it was horribly logical for the wrong
things to be in the right places. . . . You know, Albert, Austin
Crabbe was an old friend of mine. He was Lance-Bombardier
in the Artillery when I was Trooper in the Cavalry. He got a
D.C.M.; last man of his battery alive on the Dunes at Dunkirk
—in the First War, of course—still manning his gun, though
seriously wounded in the side. A common, pig-headed Geordie,
he was, from Durham City, and one of the best of the younger
men in Fleet Street at the time. Wrong-headed, cross-grained,
cantankerous—anything you like. Mean, if you like; brutal, if
you like; but honest, right or wrong, and a fighter first and foremost.

"In 1918 he came out very sad, very bitter, disillusioned. It
happened to a lot of the best of us, Albert—Richard Aldington,
Siegfried Sassoon, and so forth. I remember Crabbe threw his
medals into the Thames at Blackfriars. We all had reason to be
bitter then, Albert . . . Mr. Sicker, who sold the War Office
shoddy khaki serge, retired with three million of money . . .
Douglas Haig, for his military blunders, got an earldom and a
bronze statue in Whitehall . . . I caught the poet, Wilfred Owen,
when he fell with a bullet in his head—I am the enemy you killed,
my friend—do you remember? . . . And where was old England?
Oh yes, we were bitter then—especially against politicians. How
does it go? . . . I could not dig, I dared not rob, Therefore I liked

to please the mob—Kipling has a word for everything . . . What tale shall serve me there, among my angry and defrauded young? Eh?

"So: some of Austin Crabbe lived, but most of him died; *not* even as you and I, as it happens. He curdled, Albert, curdled with hate. Now, you must know, hate can be healthy, provided it isn't blind; like human love. Blind love is the father and mother of blind hate. Austin Crabbe loved England blindly, and hated her enemies blindly. After that war he transferred his hatred of Germany to cartels and combines and trusts; to Big Business in general.

"You remember, Albert? First of all it seemed that he was going over to the Bolsheviks. Then it looked as if he was with the Fascists. And finally—marvel of marvels!—he became the official spokesman for Lord Kadmeel's Sciocrats, and everybody said that Austin Crabbe was bought out. Albert, that was not so. Albert, it must have happened to you, as it has happened to all of us—hot and tired and desperate, with the bum-bailiffs on your doorstep, you went half-crying to your bank that has a certified capital of forty million pounds, and went on your knees for the loan of a fiver. They told you your account was fifteen shillings overdrawn, and turned to you a face of stone. You and your wife and children would be put out into the street tomorrow morning? Then it was: 'Very sorry, Mr. Kemp. We can't help. You should live within your means'—a bloody lecture, mind you, into the bargain! In that moment, didn't you pray from the bottom of your heart for a great bright fire fanned by a strong north wind to blast these pot-bellied, hollow-hearted, piggy-bankers off the face of the earth? You did, and rightly so; but you are a sane man, Albert; in your darkest hour there was nothing wrong in your head that eight hours of sound sleep and a cup of tea and a cigarette wouldn't cure. I mean, you live by recharging yourself with fresh hope in your sleep, as a sane man must.

"But Austin Crabbe lived in a state of permanent disgust, and the trouble was that this disgust of his was not without good reason, and the very intensity of it gave him a certain power. Kadmeel should have known better than to employ Austin Crabbe. There must always be something intensely personal about a very profound disgust . . . There is nothing so dreadfully lonely as a very great hate: it can't be touched, it bites indiscriminately, it must eat into that which is nearest to it . . . eat its way out, and burn and corrode until it has spent itself and forced everything that would combine with it to turn to salty dust. Austin Crabbe in a Movement! You might as well say, vitriol in a paper bag, or fluorine in a jampot.

"Austin Crabbe went over to Lord Kadmeel, not for the money, which was considerable, but because he really believed at the time that the Sciocrats were right—that the time had come for a colossal cleansing of the world, some stupendous clean sweep, some cataclysmic spring-cleaning . . . I imagine he wanted to scrape away the memories of a million years, the fool, and start from scratch again, nobler and stronger. (This, Albert, is by no means a rare yearning: why do you think two continents fell in love with Tarzan?)

"But the time came, as it was bound to come, when Austin Crabbe woke up one morning to realise that he and Kadmeel were, in fact, enemies. Dear old Austin Crabbe! In his heart he loved the good and the true and the beautiful . . . I mean, he loved what we, in our nostalgia, choose to remember of the past, which can't ever be brought back, Albert, except in travesty. He was an ageing man in search of his youth. Poor Austin—nothing goes quite so sour as boyhood or girlhood kept too long in the cask. To cut it short: Austin Crabbe began to hate and fear the crazy New World of the Sciocrats and, bitterly honest as he was, he said so. Therefore Kadmeel got rid of him.

"There's no doubt that if Chatterton had been Kadmeel's right-hand man at that time, Crabbe would have met with an accident there and then—something would have got into his last drink, perhaps, and he'd have been found drowned. As it was, Kadmeel had Austin Crabbe neatly framed on a charge of embezzlement and sent to jail for eighteen months. It wasn't a bad move, at that. Austin Crabbe went in like a roaring lion, and came out spluttering, completely discredited, a hopeless crank. On Sundays he used to address the crowds in Hyde Park; people came miles—to laugh at him. A regular group of hecklers turned up every week to bait him. 'Three cheers for Lord Kadmeel!'

they shouted, these bloody loafers, and Crabbe would literally dance and foam in a perfect ecstasy of rage. Once he went for the whole crowd single-handed with his bare fists, and knocked three men down before the police collared him. There was serious talk then of having him put away. But we got him loose, somehow, and after that he gave up public speaking and sat down in his frightful little furnished room in Blood Alley to compose a formidable pamphlet exposing Kadmeel and the Sciocrats. His idea was to force Kadmeel to have him up on a charge of criminal libel, pleading justification. . . .

"Oh, that room, that furnished room in Blood Alley! The house was run by an old hag called Mother Glory. It was lighted by gas. I don't believe that a window had been opened there for three hundred years. Crabbe's room was a kind of excrescence on the roof, which had been lit by a skylight, over which Crabbe had pasted brown paper for the blackout in 1939. He was very particular, you see, about running as few risks as possible—he didn't want to die with his work unfinished. Remember that, Albert. Crabbe told me so, in so many words, the night he died. It was in the Cheshire Cheese. He was weary rather than drunk, but cheerful, for him—he had been commissioned (the irony of it, eh, Albert?) to ghost-write the life story of some bucket-shop keeper, and had fifty pounds advance to draw in Paternoster Row on the following day. Meanwhile, could I lend him a little something, because he was absolutely penniless? I lent him a pound note, and he went home.

"Next morning, he was found gassed in his bed. They had to break the door down—he had screwed on two great iron bolts, and a pair of gate hinges too. It seemed that anything but simple suicide was absolutely out of the question.

"But, Albert, listen: Crabbe's attic was lighted by gas, and so was the landing outside his door. One slot-meter on the landing served both gas jets. When they went over Crabbe's pockets, they found one pound note, no other money. And in the meter, which had been emptied only two days before, they found thirty-six pennies. I was there soon after the police. Old newspapers had been stuffed into the crack under the door. But who, smashing in the door of a gas-filled room, waits to see whether such caulking has been tamped home from the inside, or the outside? And I noticed, also, that in all that sordid old house there was only one clean thing—the one thing that, in any house, has a right to be dirty. That is, the tip of the gas jet on the landing. As sure as I sit here, what happened was this: somebody climbed those stairs after Austin Crabbe that night, waited until he had begun to snore, made sure of a good supply of gas by putting a handful of coppers in the meter, connected the gas jet on the landing with Crabbe's room by means of a length of rubber tubing, turned on the tap, and went away; returned at dawn, disconnected the tubing, turned off the tap, and there you are—a perfect murder. Objections: didn't the first man in Crabbe's room notice that the gas jet in there was turned off? Answer: the first thing you do when you've burst into a gas-filled room is to rush to the gas-tap and turn it, presumably, off; in the excitement of the moment it's a horse to a hen you won't notice which way you're turning that tap. Query: all this involved a certain amount of coming and going, surely? Reply: in Mother Glory's den, men and women of all sorts were constantly coming and going all night long. Conclusion: Deliberate, cold-blooded murder, unprovable.

"I had a look at Austin Crabbe's papers, of course. They were pretty numerous, but arranged in remarkably neat order. Most of them were notes, scrupulously compiled, concerning vast and intricate financial manipulations by Lord Kadmeel and his associates—complicated, mysterious manœuvres involving tens of millions of pounds, billions of dollars, all over the world. And, curiously enough, there were some crude scrawls that looked like a schoolboy's first attempts at map drawing—primitive, clumsy outlines of places I had never seen before, as if poor Austin Crabbe had been trying to soothe his exasperated mind by inventing new continents, or dreaming up Atlantis. . . . I remembered how, whenever I felt sad and lonely, as a boy, I used to comfort myself by drawing maps of places that were not—islands, always islands, Albert—and marking them full of jungles, swamps, pirates, cannibals; and so go on a dream-hunt for buried treasure. Somehow, there was always a golden-haired girl involved, who was the spitting image of Queen Alexandra, only she wore a dress

you could almost see through, but not quite! . . . And my heart
bled for Austin Crabbe.

"I wanted those papers, but they were sent to his next of
kin, his sister, a school teacher who had been sent with some
evacuated kids to Devon. I went down there, sorted her out,
and told her that if she had no use for her dead brother's notes,
it was possible that I might make something of them, so that I
wouldn't mind paying a few pounds for them, provided they had
no sentimental value. She asked how much I'd be prepared to
pay, and when I said about twenty pounds she sighed with relief,
and said: 'Oh, then I wasn't robbed, after all. I had no use for the
stuff—it was just lists and scribbles. So when poor Austin's friend
—Mr. Gaylord Taylor, I daresay you know him—offered me
fifty pounds for them, I let him have them. Gaylord Taylor, you
know, of the *London Evening Post*?' I didn't know, because there's
no such man as Gaylord Taylor on the *London Evening Post*. She
said he was a well-spoken young man; but as for particulars of
his appearance, really, she wasn't in the habit of looking at men
very closely. . . . But surely I must know him? He was just the
right height, somewhat taller than herself, but not too tall, and
of a sensible age—between forty and fifty. He had very good
teeth, dimples when he smiled, a profile 'like a Roman coin', was
tastefully dressed in nigger brown with a black tie in mourning
for Austin, and had capable-looking hands. He would not stay
for tea, but she had promised to send him some Devon junket
care of his office, and would I please give him her kind regards?
Then she sniffed a couple of times over her brother, said that the
trouble with him was that he drank, and chucked me out. And
that was that. Another dead end.

"Putting piece to piece in this puzzle, Albert, what had I
assembled? A monomaniac who wasn't bad, a murder without a
murderer, and a spot of light without source.

"Austin Crabbe couldn't have been crazy—he must have been
trying to make sense out of Kadmeel's schemes, which were so
fantastic that they came near to what men love to dream about
and blush to acknowledge as feasible. Old Crabbe, foaming on a
soap-box on Sunday afternoon in Hyde Park, was harmless. But
Austin Crabbe, holding his tongue and directing his venom in

fine filaments at the sharp point of a pen—Austin Crabbe in high concentration—*he* was dangerous; he had the power to force an issue and to expose matters that the Sciocrats couldn't try to explain away in open court without setting fire to certain trains of serious thought. So he was killed.

"Killed by whom? Obviously, by Kadmeel through his agents. Hence, even in dying, Austin Crabbe proved himself in the right. To whom did he prove this? Only to old Conker—only to me Trooper George Oaks, who knew the man Lance-Bombardier Crabbe, and understood him in his frenzy . . . And here, you may say, was an opportunity for me to raise Cain, arouse suspicions, and force official enquiry into the Open Verdict on the Death of Crabbe? Oh no! There were too many ways of discrediting me, even if I had managed to get hold of Crabbe's papers and sweat the rhyme and reason out of them. Even if the whole world has faith in you, it's dangerous to show unfinished work, Albert . . . and the greater the work, the remoter the end. . . .

"If in doubt, old friend, keep still. I kept still, reasoning like this, 'If I am right, which I feel I must be, the picture-puzzle of which I hold assembled only a few pieces *must* take shape somewhere around me, eventually. If I show my hand now, the design must be changed, so that what I hold can be proved meaningless. If I am patient, the God will send me a certain something more, and then I shall have in my hand a certain nucleus without which even a madman's dream cannot exist'. . . . Of my Base Metal may be filed a Key that shall unlock the Door he howls without. Eh, Albert?

"So. Then came this Monty Cello, and several more very tricky pieces of my puzzle slid into position . . . exceptionally tricky, because this puzzle is largely an affair of shadow and penumbra, in which light occurs only that it may let you see a twilight, and the twilight itself is only a device by means of which the designer cleverly emphasises a most mysterious darkness under the cover of which anything may hide.

"Don't you see, Albert, don't you see?" cried George Oaks, his eyes like stars, "don't you see that this Monty Cello affair—especially after the Yank authorities have exhumed the corpse of Kurt Brevis—starts a trail which Scotland Yard absolutely must follow? Don't you see that quite soon, now, I shall be in a position to *compel* the world to take seriously something I never dared to whisper before? For all his grunting and groaning, Halfacre is well and truly aroused now, so that even if you and I should happen to get our throats cut, it wouldn't matter a great deal. . . . In fact, it might be a very good thing if Chatterton cut our throats at this point, Albert, because then Halfacre would have a real blood-spoor to follow, and there's nothing that makes Halfacre more indignant than murder—especially of a friend. This is excellent, excellent!"

I was surprised to find myself laughing. "You don't think it will come to that, surely?" I asked.

"Not immediately," said George Oaks. "Most likely, as I guess, after he's had a go at your house tonight, Chatterton will try to get hold of you and me with a view to extracting information. Dead men can't talk, you know. So my bet is that he'll try to torture us a little first. Now you go and get some more Dog's Nose before Syd goes to bed, and we'll have another look at the Brevis papers." I took away the tankards, which Syd refilled, and when I came back to the bedroom, George Oaks had the papers spread out on his bed.

"Lock that bloody door," he said. "Albert, put those cans on the washing-stand and come here quick! What d'you make of this, I ask you? Look and see. By the God, Albert, Kurt Brevis drew some maps, too—maps of no countries in this world!"

Part Seven

If calligraphy is an art, then Kurt Brevis was an artist. I have never seen more fastidiously elegant penmanship than that with which four of the seven sheets of paper were closely covered. He had written, as it seemed, with a needle point in black ink, and while I stared with blank incomprehension at the massed figures and mathematical symbols I marvelled at the meticulosity of the hand that had outlined them. I saw then that it is possible to beautify an equation just by loving it. I could see—never ask me how—that these μ's and θ's, α's and π's, these delicately angled cube roots, these top righthand dots of infinite recurrence, were inexplicably but with marvellous certainty shaped and placed in some terribly significant design. I could see a closing-in in the brackets, and inexorably-closing scissors in every α. Perhaps I was over-excited, but I swear to you that, just then, I saw Kurt Brevis's notes as a kind of abstraction symbolising black Danger. Without meaning anything to me, it frightened me.

"Never mind that, never mind that!" said George Oaks. "Look at these, look at these!" and with a quick, nervous gesture, he indicated the other three sheets of paper. These were the "maps of no countries in this world" which Kurt Brevis had drawn— there was no mistaking that fine strong hand, even though the contours must have been sketched in haste; it was impossible for the man to be slovenly.

"Magic casements opening on the foam of perilous seas!" cried George Oaks. "Now look at this one. What is it? Where is it?"

"I don't know," I said. "It might be a group of islands, or a cluster of lakes. There's nothing to indicate which is land and which is water. As for its whereabouts, how can one guess when there's nothing to tell you north from south? This should be up your alley, George—you've told me often enough that you're supposed to be a bit of a navigator, or something."

"I ought to know my maps of the world, especially maps of out-of-the-way places. But these maps, I swear, don't look like any islands or lakes I ever saw in an atlas. The God guide me. First, Crabbe; now, Brevis!"

"Did Austin Crabbe's maps look anything like these?" I asked.

"I can't swear to that, but these look maddeningly familiar. They *must* be real places, Albert! Listen—as a boy, did you use to try and draw maps of imaginary places, as I did? Would you like to try now? I'll tell you something: however well you do it, it won't look real except in your dream. You can't invent a plausible continent, any more than you can invent a plausible animal, vegetable, or mineral. You may stick Popocatepetl in Kew Gardens, or put Cuba in the Irish Sea, just as you may hang wings on a lion or horns on a pig—but you can't make a new shape that looks real. You absolutely must draw on familiar things."

"I know all that," I said. "Well?"

"Well, look steadily at these maps, Albert, and you'll see that they're the real thing—outlines carved by some mysterious sea —shapes cut in the dark, inch by inch, through endless ages! You can see, somehow, that these can't be the outlines of little places. Isn't there something about them that conveys to you . . . something?"

There was, indeed, a certain elemental ragged majesty in those contours.

The largest of the islands (or lakes) in the first of the maps was a woman blown to smoke: I could see the curve of her back, the droop of her dragging leg, and the last supplicating gesture of her poor attenuated arms. Below her was balanced a kind of clown, throwing a great handful of tattered scraps into the wind, closely watched by something like a poodle dog; and at the clown's foot lay a great basking shark blindly waiting.

"I make nothing of this," said I. "Yet I could swear that I've been there!"

"And here?" said George Oaks, pointing to another map.

Here, again, were lakes (or islands) and again there came over me an eerie sense of familiarity. "Have I been here before?" I said. On the right a monstrous parrot with extended claws screamed at another struggling woman whose right hand reached for the invisible. Her high-heeled foot almost touched the crowned or crested head of a great gross creature with a dropsical right arm, who wagged an admonitory forefinger. From the lower right-hand corner of the map, the greedy conger eels were coming up for the killing: but from above a man with clasped hands was diving to the rescue from a jagged promontory.

The third map might have represented the gnawed remains of some colossal elk, or moose. There, on the left, lay the shattered bone of the lower jaw with its loosened teeth; and on the right, the splintered fragments of an antler. Such forms belong to living rock—thunder the mallet, lightning the chisel, time the abrasive.

"You see," said George Oaks, "if you invent a map, if you imagine a place, it must be a place all alone. Now, the God wills that there can be no such thing as a totally disconnected place on earth. A world is a complete and beautiful thing, Albert. A blind understanding guides you to recognise a natural shape. You are satisfied, let us say, with the shape of Australia because something tells you that it is as it should be—that it belongs in a certain universal pattern——"

"—No," I said. "I accept the shape of Australia, for example, because I'm familiar with it: I know it's there."

"Thanks to Captain Cook, who did not see but being blind believed . . . Albert, up to a point, I believe in the materialist conception of history. I do believe that the old explorers sought out new islands largely for profit—because there were fortunes to be made in pepper and cinnamon, elephant's teeth and black ivory (I mean, slaves), gold and jewels, and what not——"

I interrupted: "—Well, George, I'm ready to agree, if you like, that the old merchant speculators were motivated purely by a desire for dividends. But I don't see——"

"—You don't see a shrewd man like Columbus striking west-ward in a shell like the *Santa Maria* in which no sensible pas-senger nowadays would sail from London Bridge to Margate. Eh? Neither do I, Albert, neither do I. I'm telling you that even Columbus, who was greedy enough for money to gyp the look-out-man out of his reward for sighting the New World—even Christopher Columbus was a man with a vision. He absolutely *had* to be a man with an eye for the main chance—otherwise how could he have made his sales talk acceptable to the financiers? He had to talk with passion and conviction of that gold where the sun went down. It was necessary for Columbus to sell himself to himself in order to pay dividends . . . because what he wanted, really, was a ship. Remember he was a reader of ancient maps; in other words, a brooder over puzzles. He had to reach beyond the known horizons for lost pieces, once he saw the world as a ball. . . . In effect, Albert, he knew in his heart that the known world was of the wrong shape, and it was this knowledge that ate him up rather than greed."

"Very well, then," I said, "granting all that, where's your point? There aren't many square miles of this world left uncharted—certainly no great islands or inland seas, are there?"

"No. The only places of which we haven't got scale maps are largely jungles. But wait a bit, Albert. Hold hard! When you speak of The World, to what do you refer?"

"The land and the sea, of course," I said, "the whole surface of the world, which, you'll admit, the cartographers have been over with a fine comb."

"There you are, you see!" cried George Oaks. "Look at him, a writer of fantastic fiction, the great Albert Kemp, who's already convincing the suckers who read the shiny magazines that he is *au fait* with the mysteries of Time and Space, let alone the Cosmos! An interplanetary flight is a penny bus-ride to this one here, because his childish imagination has got hold of Rockets. Put him in a cigar-shaped container of Oojiam, the non-gravitational metal, and he is off to fight telepathic crocodiles in the liquid ammonia atmosphere of the planet Pluto—*psst!*—simple as all that! The earth is too tame for this passionate beast, eh? Furthermore, he knows that there is going to be an atomic war, and so he must take off from Terra with one blaster-pistol, one Rita Hayworth in a transparent nylon space-suit, and a ready-made man-child screaming: 'Aw gee, Pop, when'm I gonna get one of them Venusian green-feathered, five-dimensional, multi-lingual, seven-legged singing teddy bears to play with?' Whereupon Rita Hayworth, clinging to you like Scotch tape, gives you a kiss that sends a blast of super-heated steam down your gozzle and says: '*Nnnnnn*, hon, if Pop, who is president of Inter-Galactic Flights, Inc., knew we were here! Did you sabotage the Umbilicator? Lover, have you watered the jeep? . . . Gooksie, lover, super gooksie, let me feel your deltoids . . . By this time, of course, the earth is a dwindling speck—No?—and the galaxy a sparkling shower, like when Black Monty spat into the electric fan in O'Hanrahan's place on the Avenue of the Americas, Lima City, Neptune, what time Ivanovitch the Martian spy drugged your drink with Poptol which paralyses the will . . ."

I said: "Cut it out, will you, George?"

"You unmitigated fathead, you interplanetary great suckling! You child with a Buck Rogers pistol! Tell me something. How far into the sky has man flown, or even fired a projectile? Answer me."

"I believe that's a military secret," I said.

"I can tell you, without breaking it, that we've sent a projectile up to the very rim of the earth's atmosphere. Say, sixty miles. That is to say, about one four-thousandth part of the distance between here and the moon. Is that right?"

"Well?"

"Now—this being up *your* alley, Albert, you being so familiar with the world as to be contemptuous of it—tell me, how deep is the deepest excavation we have made into the earth, as from sea level? Shall we say about a mile? I believe that copper mine in Montana is about a mile deep. You tell me, Albert, you know the world—it's a dwindling speck to you . . . Say a mile, then. All right. Then, when you have finished firing your pop-guns at Sirius, will you pause to consider that man, even in favourable conditions and given the stimulus of heavy dividends, has succeeded in penetrating less than one four-thousandth part of the distance between Charing Cross station and the earth's core? Have you forgotten, Albert, that there are the Waters Under the Earth? Have you never stopped to think that beneath your feet, quite uncharted, lies a fantastic underworld of caverns, underground rivers, and ghostly islands floating in sunless lakes? Has no one ever told you that the land under London itself is nothing but a kind of lid that covers a subterranean sea? Did no one ever tell you that the land you know as England is nothing but a skin, only a mile or two thick, on top of another place? Eh, star-gazer?"

I said: "My God, George! What the devil are you trying to tell me? Be serious with me. You're not hinting, are you, that these maps here are charts of the waters under the earth?"

"I'm hinting nothing, Albert. I'm saying, simply, that we have explored and charted only the surface of this world, and that there is another world below the surface. I am saying that these maps of Kurt Brevis's are maps of real places, great places, that do not belong on the face of the earth as I know it. And, if you like, I'm saying this: *Every one of Kadmeel's later enterprises has been in the nature of an excavation, a digging-down. While the rest of the world has been watching the heavens, Lord Kadmeel has been burrowing deeper and deeper into the bowels of the earth.*"

"Couldn't it be that, anticipating an atom war, Kadmeel is digging underground factories?" I asked.

"Could be," said George Oaks, putting the papers under his pillow. "Pass the Dog's Nose, and let's go to sleep. Tomorrow we talk to Ohm Robertson."

So we switched off the lights. George Oaks fell asleep in the middle of a yawn. I teeter-tottered for a while between wide wakefulness and broken nightmares of black chasms rushing down to lightless bodies of bottomless water. . . . Somewhere under a dank dome something flapped wet, leathery wings, and a cold wind stinking of rotten fish fanned my face . . . The winged thing plunged. The broken water splashed phosphorescent so that I caught a glimpse of a toothed beak closing on a kind of slug with blind white eyes and tentacles . . . Behind me a beautifully modulated voice said: "Take it easy, now, Kemp, it's only a pterodactyl diving for a slug-fish," and I turned and saw Chatterton. "You want to look out for the mudworms, though—they're naughty; reproduce through their teeth, you know, three months of the year, and if they bite you they plant a whole bally colony in your flesh. Takes you half a year to die and, believe me, it isn't funny for the fellow concerned. We generally shoot you if you get bitten by a mudworm, for your own sake, you know. . . . You'll get used to it, old man . . . And, by the bye, if you see something like a sea anemone kind of hopping about on its stem, shine a light on it double-quick—that'll kill it. Its sting brings you out in ulcerated warts all over—unhealable, too, and with an absolutely putrid stink." Then Chatterton disappeared, leaving me alone in the dark, and something flabby

and cold coiled itself about me; a detestable bubbling voice snig-
gered: ". . . May I take your soul, sir?"—and something like a
wet rubber cap fastened itself between my shoulder-blades, and
I was sucked away in a spiral, down and down, so that I started
awake and was afraid to close my eyes for a while.

I thought of Monty Cello upside-down, dying in the well,
and I reproached myself for thinking: *At least I didn't have to meet
his eyes when Halfacre came* . . . Then it seemed to me quite logical
that Lord Kadmeel, digging and digging deeper and deeper in a
frenzy of fear, should indeed have come upon a watery world
under the earth's crust. . . . But surely, it would be a hot, steamy
place, rotten rich with mulch, dripping with the drained fertility
of the sunlit world above—cancerous with life run wild and ma-
lignant, dominated by monstrous creatures of corruption?

At last I fell asleep, thinking of Ohm Robertson, and wondering what he would say.

Oaks shook me awake at half-past six. "Breakfast," he said,
offering me a glass beer-mug full of black tea and a cold baby
chicken stuck on a carving fork. "Have a *petit poussin*, and when
that's gone call for more. An Annual Outing of the Froth
Blowers, or something, didn't turn up for dinner as scheduled
yesterday. There are thirty-seven little chickens in the ice-box,
stark naked, with their legs in the air—a veritable extermination
camp of young fowl. I've just eaten two . . . Eat up. Better let the
tea settle a bit; I couldn't find a strainer . . . Better hurry up and
come down, Albert. The police want a word with you."

"Who, me? What now?"

"Calm, calm, Albert; everything is all right, everything's perfect—couldn't be better. Just as I said, your house was broken into
about half-past three this morning. What is there to be excited
about? I foretold it, didn't I? And exactly as I guessed, Halfacre
had a couple of coppers from Brighthaven on the prowl outside.
It seems that the burglars were three-handed. Two of them got
into the house, and the third was posted as sentry. Those yobs
from Brighthaven—they're too slow to catch a cold, the thumb-
fingered chaw-bacons—let one of the inside men slip away, the
gawking fly-catchers; the most important of the three, you may

bet your life. They collared the outside man all right. Apparently
he mixed it and there was a bit of a bundle. One of them, apparently, was 'injured'—I suppose that means he was kicked on
the shin, or something. Anyway, their prisoner yelled bloody
murder. The idiots, they ought to have got up behind him and
throttled him; but I suppose they were afraid that might be un-
constitutional or something, the flat-footed fatheads. However,
they snaffled him, he calls *Cave*, and Bollard has no alternative
but to tangle single-handed with the other two in the upstairs
passage. They jump him, and he knocks one down; would've got
the other, only it's too dark to see straight, so he only grabs him
by the foot, whereupon the man kicks him in the stomach. Man
then kicks loose, leaving his shoe in Bollard's hands, jumps out of
the back bedroom window, slides down kitchen roof, and gets
away. Bollard might have stopped him but, rushing after him,
forgets that low beam in the passage—don't we all?—and hits
himself on the forehead and knocks himself groggy for a couple
of seconds, which is all the other fellow needs. Thus, when the
lights are switched on, what have we got? Two gypsies, a little
the worse for wear, and one gent's lightweight tan calf shoe with
a Goodrich rubber heel—no gyppo's shoe, no hop-picker's shoe,
but a well-preserved gentlemanly monk-shoe, that fastens with
a buckle, as made by Staples of Northampton for the American
Officers' P.X. in the 1940s. . . . In addition to Sergeant Bollard's
squeezed-out fingerprints, there must, of course, be some of
the owner's dabs on the shoe around the heel and the strap. I
reminded Bollard of this, but he had already taken it into consideration; had the shoe wrapped up in tissue paper—had the
insolence to tell *me* that a criminal might wipe possible dabs from
a pistol or a doorknob, but never from his own shoe, it being the
last thing on earth he'd expect to leave behind him . . . They read
too many detective stories, the dogs!"

"No doubt the man was wearing gloves," I said, buttoning
my trousers.

"Even so, it must occur even to you that he wouldn't put on
his gloves until after he had buckled his shoes, dopey. In burglary, gloves are a last-minute affair."

"The gyppos won't talk, of course," I said.

"No more than Chinamen," said George Oaks.

"But the shoe," I said, "the shoe, surely, must be a giveaway. A man can't get very far on half a pair of shoes, can he? It seems to me that this man must have had some kind of hideout close by—otherwise he'd have risked anything rather than leave that shoe behind. He'd even have taken a chance on tangling with Bollard, who, if I know the look of a man, must be like fifteen stone of hard rubber to tackle. He'd know that inside half an hour the whole countryside would be looking for a man with one shoe—and so would every policeman on every road for miles around. Am I right, George?"

"Of course, of course, Albert," said George Oaks, impatiently. "That's plain as print. . . . The gyppos they caught are a pair of brothers named Hearn, out of an encampment down in the dell on Oversmith's land. The police will have been down there hours ago: they'll meet with blank faces, of course; the Hearns are better known as the 'Black Brothers'———"

"—They've been in trouble before," I said.

"Oh, never mind about that! As for the man with the shoe, or without the shoe, I've advised Bollard to keep an eye on Sir Peter Oversmith's house."

I said: "A fat lot of good that'll do! Oversmith is a Justice of the Peace and the local Squire—you'd never get your nose inside his house unless you had a direct invitation except within the last letter of the law, and not then without the devil to pay."

"Albert, I know that. There will be the devil to pay. That's exactly what I want, don't you see? As far as I am concerned, all this fits in with the Design, as I see it. Like this—" George Oaks made a ring with thumb and forefinger. "Now, let's get the formalities over and done with, and catch the eight-fifteen train to Charing Cross . . . And when so sad thou canst not sadder, Cry, and upon thy so sore loss, Shall shine the traffic of Jacob's Ladder, Stretch'd between Heaven and Charing Cross, eh? Come now . . ."

In New York the garbage collectors ride about the city in dirty white trucks in which is embodied some toothy mechanism designed to chew up everything and spit it, masticated, into a dark tank. Irreparably smashed trunks, bean tins, chicken bones, rags, broken bottles, dead flowers, potato-salad cartons, bolts of stained ticking and kapok that once were mattresses, millions of cigarette ends, burnt stews, sprouting onions, dead cats, electric light bulbs, and the remains of demolished radios—all go into this elaborate dust cart which, at the touch of a dustman's hand on a lever, gives out a vibrant growling noise that gets into your bones and makes coherent thought impossible, while it licks and gnashes and gulps until the bewildering detritus of a hundred houses lies quiet and compact, dun-coloured and dense . . . It may go to fill in a swamp to build a viaduct, or level a runway from which huge winged machines may take off for the Spice Islands . . . You hope so. Your reasoning mind in abeyance, you wait until the noise has ceased, and then you take in your garbage pail and peel more potatoes. . . .

The insistent buzzing in my muddled head called to mind this image. "Come downstairs and let's get it over with," I said.

But apart from being officially informed of the breaking and entering at my place, there was nothing to be got over with, so we went back to the house. Hobson was on guard outside, keeping away a gang of dangerous-looking small boys armed with cap pistols, and led by the notorious girl with pink pigtails, who brandished a hockey stick and directed operations: they had tied up a fat boy and were putting him into a little truck preparatory to taking him for a ride. The parson's youngest son, a smooth-faced killer of eleven years (the girl was supposed to be his Moll), had one of those trick daggers with a disappearing blade, with which he repeatedly stabbed the fat boy in the abdomen, while he chewed a plug of liquorice and practised spitting brown at the same time.

"If they're like this before breakfast, can you imagine what they're like by teatime?" said Hobson, cringing as a white-headed ten-year-old threatened him with a broken flit-spray. ". . . Dicky Queen, you put that down—I've got my eye on you," he said, looking as if he was about to be violently sick, which meant to say that he intended to look fierce. ". . . They learn it in picture palaces, Mr. Kemp."

Meanwhile, four panting children, one of them wearing an Air Force cap, were rolling up a rusty oil drum, screaming: "We got an atom bomb!" and "Blow the bugger back to Japan!"

"Better get them to untie that boy," said George Oaks, "they'll probably soak him in petrol and set light to him; I wouldn't put it past them." He threw the girl half-a-crown. "Ransom money. Now hop to it."

She complained: "We haven't written a ransom note yet!" But then a woman appeared and carried her off, whereupon the mob dispersed.

Sergeant Bollard was in the sitting-room, drinking a cup of tea. He was wearing two black eyes with ineffable dignity; that beam must have caught him just over the bridge of the nose. One of his knuckles was bound round with sticking plaster; it was safe to assume that one of the Black Brothers must be gap-toothed this morning. He said: ". . . Nothing missing, sir, and no damage done. They forced the window-catch of the little spare room. If it hadn't been for that beam we'd have got the lot . . . My word, sir, they seasoned their oak pretty well in the olden days, didn't they?" He rubbed his head.

"Made inquiries at Oversmith Hall yet?" Oaks asked.

"Don't you worry about that, sir," said Bollard, smoothly. "I've been in touch with the Chief Inspector, and I have my instructions."

"Mr. Kemp and I are going to town for the day," said George Oaks. "I've got an article to finish. If you want me, you can get me through the office, or at my flat—Halfacre knows the address, 29 Chalcot Terrace, Earl's Court . . . That'll be my first port of call, I think. You know what? I want first and foremost to change all my clothes—I can still feel the slime of that well on me."

"All right, sir, I'll tell him that." Bollard looked at his watch. "I suppose you'll be catching the eight-fifteen, Mr. Kemp?"

"That's right," I said, "and if Halfacre wants me, I'll be with Mr. Oaks most of the time. In any case I'll be back here tonight. I can rely on you to lock the place up? You can leave the keys with Mr. Titmouse at the Piebald Horse, if you like."

"Definitely, Mr. Kemp," said Sergeant Bollard.

"Then, speaking of changing, George," I said, "I'll put on a fresh shirt, and we'll be off."

It struck me that this, somehow, was an occasion for dressing up. I put on a silk shirt and a sober blue flannel suit. The acoustics of these old houses are remarkable—George Oaks's stage-whisper seemed to hiss through every crack as he said: "Kemp keeps some Scotch in the linen press, under some spare blankets . . ." Bollard replied: "Yes, Mr. Oaks, and he also leaves his money lying about, too. Happy-go-lucky."

I remembered then a little cache of fifty new pound notes in my handkerchief drawer, left over from the bracing days of the blitzes, when anything might happen and it was not a bad idea to keep a little ready money about the house . . . when Silly Sussex became a forest of unlicensed shotguns, and farmers' wives kept extra kettles of water boiling to throw into the faces of the Enemy if he landed (in my neighbourhood, the only recorded case of the use of a kettle of boiling water against an invader was the case of old Mrs. Lupin *versus* the Luftwaffe: she caught a shot-down bomber pilot with a fractured thigh among her marigolds, and made him a cup of tea, and stood over him with the kettle until the Home Guard came) . . . when law-abiding day labourers displayed a mysterious knowledge of the countryside by night, and Mr. Shepard, the shepherd, who saw Kronje captured, came out with a suspiciously well-oiled Colt's Navy revolver. . . . The whole countryside seemed to whisper with the unsheathing of concealed weapons then. A certain respectable umbrella shop in Piccadilly filled its windows with life-preservers of all kinds, from oaken clubs studded with hob-nails and loaded with lead to neat little jaw-breakers designed to slip under a lady's garter. On my first forty-eight hours leave, I went into this shop and spent forty shillings on a most elegant cosh, or blackjack, of whale-bone weighted at both ends with lead and covered with plaited strips of kangaroo hide. The shopman politely assured me that this instrument, properly used, would shatter even a Nazi skull with a flick of the wrist. I settled for the cosh before he sold me a Toledo rapier concealed in a guardsman's ash-plant; and, having the thing, felt silly, and hid it under my civilian things.

Now I put it in my inside breast pocket with the money. "No sense of values; easy come, easy go . . . Say when," said George Oaks. Sergeant Bollard said: "Not for me, if you don't mind." And then I hurried downstairs.

On the way to the station, George Oaks said: "A horse to a hen, Bollard is on the phone now, so that someone'll be inconspicuously around to trail us from Charing Cross."

"You asked for it, didn't you?" I said.

"Yes, yes, Albert—but not just yet, not too soon! Therefore, we'll change lines at the Junction, so that instead of arriving at Charing Cross at ten-eight we'll presumably come into Victoria about twenty-five to eleven."

"The idea being to duck Halfacre, I take it," I said. "I thought you'd seen enough of the man by now not to underestimate his intelligence. He knows you're hiding something from him and want to keep out of his way for a bit. I ask you, George, won't he put himself in your shoes, and be all set to trail you from Victoria, therefore?"

"Albert, Halfacre goes in for the Double Obvious stuff. He will say to himself: 'George tells Bollard that he's catching the eight-fifteen to Charing Cross. Knowing full well that I don't want him out of my sight just yet. George knows I expect him to hop off and switch trains at the Junction so that I'll have someone keeping an eye out for him at Victoria. So I'll have a man at Charing Cross—because it would be just like George to double back again. And, knowing George as I do to be as tricky as a wagon-load of monkeys, why, to be on the safe side I'll have men posted at both Charing Cross and Victoria.' "

I said: "Then what's your idea?"

"Simply," said George Oaks, "we'll get off the train at the Junction and take a taxi."

"Make this clear," I said. "Forgive me, but I don't understand. Your whole aim has been to have Chatterton trail us, and Halfacre trail Chatterton. And now you go to the most ridiculous lengths to throw them both off the scent you've so carefully laid down! Where is the sense in all this?"

"Oh, you great baby!" said George Oaks. "You surely must know that if both Chatterton and Halfacre are looking for us, which they surely will be, it can't be more than a matter of hours before one or the other catches up with us? A matter of hours, Albert, hours—that's what I'm playing for, a matter of just a few hours alone with Ohm Robertson. Of all the men I dare approach in confidence, Ohm Robertson alone on God's green earth can tell us what we've simply got to know. See?"

"Will Ohm Robertson see us?"

"Yes, Albert, he will. We're old comrades. In 1915, when the War Office asked for men of science to help fight the German gas offensive, Ohm Robertson—the youngest professor ever to hold a Chair in an English university, offered himself. . . . Some apothecary's clerk who happened to be a lieutenant gave Ohm Robertson chlorine cylinders to carry. He was browned off, Albert, cheesed off. I cheered him up by——"

"—You poked him in the ribs and quoted Shakespeare, saying, 'This is more important,' I bet."

"As a matter of fact, I hummed him the first movement of Beethoven's Fifth, playing an obbligato on a plum-and-apple jam tin."

"Which cheered him up, no doubt?"

"It took his mind off things. We became good friends. We've met many times since, Albert. Ohm is a great scientist, and a good man; pure and simple—pure with the purity and simple with the simplicity of a wonder-child. He——"

"—Here comes Chatterton," I said.

A suave, sweet-running Lagonda pulled up abreast of us with no more noise than a billiard ball makes when it bounces off two cushions. The man at the wheel was young, with a pale, compressed face. He was dressed like an officer's servant in a high-buttoned single-breasted blue serge suit, a round-cornered stiff collar, a regimental tie, and a bowler hat. Major Chatterton, in the back seat, was elegant in pearl-grey. "Good-morning!" he said, leaning out. "Want a lift?"

"Catching a train," said George Oaks. "Going to London."

"Perfect bloody bore, isn't it? So am I. Want a ride?"

George Oaks said: "A nice day for it, but I'm in a bit of a hurry."

"Quicker by road," said Chatterton, patting the shiny black door of the car. "Care to try it and see? She's a beauty."

"Bet you an even fiver my train beats your bus to Charing Cross, starting even at eight-fifteen," said George Oaks.

"That's a bet. I'll be in the lounge of the Charing Cross Hotel at a quarter to ten. But I thought you'd come down for the week-end," said Chatterton.

"Who, me? I work for a living. I was under the impression that you were down here for a bit of shooting."

"So I was, George, but the Kad wants me, and I must be about my master's business. It's always like that. . . . I hear you had a bit more trouble at your place last night, Kemp."

"Bit of a burglary," I said.

"Oh, hard luck! They didn't take anything much, I hope?"

"They were only gyppos on the prowl," I said. "Police caught them. No harm done."

"Oh, good for you. Those gypsies are an infernal nuisance . . . Well, if you're sure you won't come, that's a bet, George. I'll be drinking a cup of coffee in the Charing Cross Hotel by the time you arrive." I could hear the train whistling in the distance. "So long, then. I'll see the train out, and then we'll start. Got that, Powell?" The chauffeur nodded. "Have your fiver ready, George!"

So we walked on to the platform. "Better yet, better yet," said George Oaks, prodding me. "This means that Chatterton will be at Charing Cross, and one or two of his men at Victoria. What do you think of that chauffeur-valet of his?"

"A gentleman's gentleman," I said.

"No, that one was brought up to be a gentleman, God save the mark! Name of Mungo-Mitchell, if you please; top-drawer, Albert, upper crust. His sister, Deborah, sold her favours (if you know what I mean) to the Free French for smuggled perfume which she sold on the black market. There's bad blood in that family. If you lifted up that fellow's shirt you'd see white scars on his back: in 1937 he got three years and eighteen strokes of the 'Cat' for robbery with violence—broke a jeweller's jaw with a knuckle-duster in Imperial Palace Court Hotel and nearly got away with ten thousand pounds' worth of diamonds. A wrong 'un, bad to the backbone, that one. He doesn't know me, but I know him; I was in Bow Street police court when he was charged. He'll end up one of these fine mornings with a nasty knot under his right ear, he will. A Mayfair man, a night-club man, a playboy *sans loy, sans foy, sans joy.* Oh, he'll dance, he'll

dance—on nothing, Albert, to the tolling of a big dark bell!
. . . Powell, he calls himself, does he? I lay you thirty-three to
one that he owes Bollard a shoe; and he'll pay, Albert, he'll pay.
Never turn your back to that one in a lonely street, old friend;
he's deadly poison. But it's excellent that this should be as it is;
Bollard will have his prints, and the Yard will have him up for
inquiry inside thirty-four hours."

"He's sure to have an alibi," I said.

"I daresay, and a good alibi, too—somebody stole his shoes,
very likely, and both Oversmith and Chatterton will swear to
that."

"Is Oversmith also involved, do you think?" I asked. "I mean
to say, Oversmith is such an unmitigated old idiot."

"I know he is. That is why he's involved, don't you see . . . Any
new movement, Albert, must in the last analysis fatten on unhap-
piness. I defy you to name any movement in history that didn't
get its first strength from the anger, the misery, the hunger, the
boredom, the hate, and the bitterness of its first followers. True
love doesn't move—it has arrived. Love knows no fear; it inspires
nothing but bliss which can't be communicated. Only discontent is easily communicable. The bitterest kind of discontent is
not the discontent of the man who has nothing but his chains to
lose and all the world to gain. The bitterest discontent is that of
the man who has something and fears to lose it—or who, having
had something and lost it, wants it back with interest. Oversmith
thinks he's lost something—his ancient feudal rights. He hates
the rigour of the laws that he upholds as Justice of the Peace. He
doesn't want justice, and he doesn't want peace—he wants to be a
bold bad baron, like his ancestors, and I tell you that the fact that
a ditch-digger can sue him for assault and battery keeps him in a
state of bloody rage. You know, I suppose, that he came peril-
ously near Brixton Prison in 1941 because of his Fascist tenden-
cies? Fascist, my foot! What does that wild pig know of anything
but Sir Peter Oversmith? All he wants is the right to rob a Jew,
flog a merchant, swindle a creditor, hang a peasant——"

"——Want some tickets, Mr. Kemp?" said the station-master,
who is also the ticket collector and porter.

"Two first class to London," I said, and he gave me two third-class tickets, saying, for the hundredth time: "No sense paying first class, sir. Have third class, and get in a first-class carriage. If the inspector comes round, you can always pay the difference, can't you? If it works once in ten times, it shows a profit, bless your heart. Old Mrs. Hawthorne has been travelling first class, bundles and all, for twenty years, and only once did the inspector demand excess—and she larruped him to rights."

"There speaks a man!" said George Oaks, digging him in the ribs, and then the train came in.

George Oaks telephoned Ohm Robertson from the Junction. He came out of the booth rubbing his hands, and said: "Just as I said. He greeted me like a twin brother. It's all right to come any time after half-past eleven, Ohm says—be delighted to see me. Now, there's one of those taxi services round the corner, as I remember. Let's go."

"You're not going home to change, then?"

"Afterwards."

"I suppose you really can trust Ohm Robertson, George?"

"With my life, Albert, with my life and with yours, too."

"All right, then," I said. So we found a decent old Austin at the car-hire place and were driven at a comfortable speed to Hampstead, where Ohm Robertson lived secluded in a pretty little house in a high-walled garden on the edge of the Heath.

He listened attentively while George Oaks talked. I have never seen a living man sit so still. With his folded hands, his closed eyes, and his pale lips slightly parted in a tiny smile, Ohm Robertson looked like a man who, having achieved perfection, has died in his sleep. At last he opened his eyes and, putting on a pair of rimless spectacles, began to study the Kurt Brevis papers, and we sat for a long while without speaking. There was something so intensely concentrated in that stillness that the buzzing of a bumble-bee that blundered into the room made me duck my head with a start, as if it had been a dive-bomber. This bee passed —almost roaring, it seemed—within half an inch of Ohm Robertson's thin white nose, but he did not stir. I heard two o'clock strike before he turned the fourth sheet.

Then he said: "This is most interesting, Oaks. I may say, profoundly interesting. I believe that these are papers of the most vital importance. Really, you know, you ought not to have taken them. And while I wouldn't, for any consideration, have missed this opportunity of glancing at Dr. Brevis's maps, I must say that you were awfully indiscreet to show them to me on trust like this. How are you to know that I am not a 'collaborator', as I believe they call it? What leads you to assume that I am not another Kurt Brevis? For all you know I may be that very same Regent Lambert with whom this American friend of yours was supposed to make contact?"

"But you're not," said George Oaks.

"No, I am not. But what right have you to take it for granted that I am not? Really, Oaks, in taking me into your confidence in this affair you put me in a false position, and it is too bad of you. Really too bad. You must see, of course, that it is my duty to place these papers in the proper hands?"

"Of course it is, Ohm; of course it's your duty, and mine too. But I simply must find out what those notes really imply, and what's their relation to those queer-looking maps, and how Kadmeel and his Sciocrats come into it. Because, don't you see, without a man like you to give it weight, my story will be dust and ashes."

"In other words, nothing but a story. You are trying, you mean, to accumulate sufficient evidence to make a Case. That is so, is it not?"

"Yes," said George Oaks.

"Without which evidence, your story must be dismissed as mere fantasy?"

"That's right. Ohm, you *must* help!"

"Oh, I'll help you, Oaks," said Ohm Robertson, with a smile of peculiar shy tenderness. "I haven't forgotten how you tied my puttees for me—it must be thirty-five years ago. I will do anything for you, Oaks, on condition that you promise not to sing to me, or beat tin cans with a bayonet."

George Oaks said: "I nearly gave you the Bach Toccata and Fugue in D."

"No friendship could have survived that. But to be serious, and this is very serious, I assure you: I will help you, yes, conditionally. Before I can make a positive statement as to the import of these notes I must study them very closely for several hours more. You must leave me alone to do this. If you wish, you may stay in the house, provided you keep perfectly quiet, and my housekeeper will put up a cold lunch. If you have other business, you can attend to it, and come back here in about four or five hours from now. Then I will be able to give you—roughly, of course—some idea of the meaning of these notes in relation to these maps."

"Reasonable enough," said George Oaks.

"Secondly, after I have told you as much as you can understand of what you want to know, you must not object if I insist on handing these papers, in your presence, to the proper authorities."

"I'm all for that," said George Oaks, "I'd have insisted on that myself. Only I must clarify my ideas first."

"Very good. Leave me alone now, and come back later, and I believe I'll have everything clear for you," said Ohm Robertson. "Now please excuse me."

As I closed the door of the study behind me, I saw him turning the papers with his left hand while his right hand groped for a pencil, and then we were on the gravelled drive again, walking back to the road. "Now we're getting somewhere," said George Oaks, with a sigh of pleasure.

"But where?"

"We'll know by tonight. Let's go to my place now, so I can change." We walked over the Heath towards the station. He led me by a tortuous little path to a copse of silver birches, where he stopped and pointed to a little hollow. "On this spot, nearly forty years ago, I fell in love," he said, "with a girl I met near The Spaniards. She was in service in that big red house right over there—dusky, vivid, Albert. She hung upon the cheek of night like a rich jewel in an Ethiop's ear. I peeled her an orange and quoted poetry. When I got around to 'Come into the garden, Maud' she said: '—Or shall I bring the garden in to you? No, thank you very much! Does your mother know you're out, you and your oranges?'—and so passed out of my life. I tried to explain that oranges were the Golden Apples of the Hesperides, but she asked me if I had swallowed a dictionary. I saw her walking along The Spaniards the following Sunday arm-in-arm with a Guardsman. I wrote a poem about it, the words of which I have completely forgotten. . . . Come on!"

We took the Underground to Earl's Court, where he occupied the top floor of a sad-looking villa. His sitting-room, at the best of times, was like a junk stall in the Caledonian Market. Now, it seemed, he had taken up hydroponics and was making a television set. Dense vegetation struggled for light out of an immense trough of sand into which some colourless liquid dripped through glass tubes connected to great bottles clamped on iron stands. In the heart of this little jungle I could see two or three ripening tomatoes. The television set was already six feet high and eight feet wide; he told me that it was scarcely started yet, and that when it was finished it would revolutionise the industry, provided it worked. He led me into the bedroom and made me sit in a deep arm-chair of odd design.

"Try it," he said, "it's a special kind of chair, an American idea. Old Waters of the *Chicago Post-Express* had it sent all the way from New York. Touch that lever at the side, and the chair adjusts itself exactly to your every movement, thus prolonging your life seven years at the very least. Waters only sat in it once, and it threw him and dislocated his shoulder. It's a perfectly good chair, provided you keep perfectly still and keep your hands away from the controls; otherwise it'll break your bloody neck." Thereupon I touched the lever and the chair became perfectly flat, like an operating table, so that I cried out in alarm. "You see? Have a drink, while I change my shirt."

He opened the door of his wardrobe with a jerk, and a French steel helmet fell from an upper shelf and clanged on the floor. "Winston Churchill tried this one on for size," he explained, brushing it with his sleeve before putting it back. He threw on to the bed a rakish-looking green shirt, which, he said, had belonged to Ernie Pyle. "I shall wear Monty Cello's tie for luck," he said, pulling it out of his pocket, and taking down a light-brown suit. "Now this suit of clothes, Albert, is something out of the ordinary. I designed it myself in 1941, when there was going to be an invasion, and you never could tell when a suit like this might come in handy. Bumfitte of Stratton Street broke down and cried like a child, practically, when he cut this coat according to my instructions. It's all pockets, like a conjurer's coat —you could hide anything in this, from a live rabbit to a portable radio transmitter. And every button, Albert, is a little receptacle, a tiny watertight box. A twist, and they open—a twist, and they close. Clever, eh?"

"Not so dazzling," I said; "the parachuters had tiny compasses and what not, disguised as fly-buttons."

"I know. I introduced the idea. I thought I told you. There's a compass just here," said George Oaks, buttoning his trousers, "and here, a piece of the finest spring steel converted into quite an efficient little hack-saw . . . and here, *en cas de soif*, a couple of cyanide pills——"

"—Good God!"

"Well, you never could tell, don't you see. If one got caught it would never have done to be in a position where one might be forced to give information . . . And *here*, right on top, is another little gadget. This isn't a button at all, strictly speaking. It's a capsule. I made it out of a bit of one of those rubbery plastic bottles. It contains a lump of metallic potassium sealed in kerosene."

"What on earth for?" I asked.

"Well, at the time, it occurred to me that it might come in handy as a delayed-action incendiary bomb. You know what potassium is. It decomposes water so fast that it catches fire while floating on the surface in a molten blob, and when it catches fire, Albert, it goes off with a hell of a crack. Burns with a bright violet flame. Deadly stuff, properly applied. Get the idea? Pull off the button, pierce the capsule, put it in a wet place, and get the hell out. The water gets in as the kerosene comes out, and whammy! . . . Oh, you can laugh, Albert, but I was in deadly earnest at the time."

"I wasn't laughing at that," I said, "only it seems so damned silly now, walking about with cyanide and incendiary bombs in your pants——" and then I remembered that deadly cosh in my inside breast pocket, and stopped abruptly.

He was quick to observe the involuntary movement of my hand. "What have you got there?" he asked, and pulled open my coat. "A handy little thing," he said, testing the spring of the cosh and balancing it. "But you want to rub a little oil into it now and again, to preserve the leather." Then he began to laugh at me, and I laughed with him. On the face of it, it really did seem absurd. But he became serious again in a few seconds, and unlocked a drawer. "Shall I . . . ?" he said, taking out a small automatic pistol. "Yes, I think I will." He looked to the magazine, snapped a cartridge into the breech, secured the safety-catch, and put the pistol in his hip pocket. "One never knows; it might turn out to be one of those nights. You need a gun just about once in a lifetime, and a certain pricking in my thumbs tells me this might be that once. Now let's enjoy a quiet drink. But first of all, get out of that chair. You make me nervous. I have the hang of the thing."

We changed seats. George Oaks sat, with easy grace—and the American chair jerked into a sprawling *W*. He kicked himself free and sat on a footstool. "Not four o'clock yet," he said. "Plenty of time for a little rest and a bit of a walk."

"I don't feel much like walking," I said.

"Neither do I, Albert, but we'll walk and like it. Why? Because it's a horse to a hen that both Halfacre and Chatterton will have been watching the house since this morning. We will walk, therefore, in order to be followed, and when we decide to ride we will take a bus."

"Are you sure we weren't followed this morning?"

"Positive. I know when I'm trailed, and I'm sure we weren't. And I'm equally sure that we will be this evening. So take it easy, and leave the rest to me . . . Oh yes—would you like to make a small bet? A pound to a penny, if and when the rough stuff starts you'll quite forget to use that cosh."

"It's a bet."

We left the flat at a quarter past five and walked languidly to the Robin Hood for sandwiches and beer. We stayed a quarter of an hour and then went on, more briskly. George Oaks set the pace. "Everything's in order," he muttered, "we're being followed, but by policemen only, I should say. Rather odd, that. But maybe Chatterton's men are following the policemen."

Part Eight

Ohm Robertson was resting in a great green leather easy-chair, drinking some pink-frothed, milky chocolate-coloured vitamin stuff out of a long tumbler—*Vitfu*, according to the label on the jar at his right hand—and a very old woman in black dress and a white apron was kneeling before him, coaxing his feet into wrinkled brown slippers. "Do stop it, Herbage," he said, and the old woman withdrew with a self-satisfied curtsey, saying: "Mind you drink it all up, Master Ohm."

"Herbage is a treasure," he said, when she was gone. "She was my nursemaid when she was only seventeen years old, about sixty years ago. She insists on my drinking this filthy concoction every evening. She read about it in *Tit-Bits* in 1899; *Vitfu* is short for 'Vital Food'—it is made of inferior powdered skim-milk, malt and cola nuts, to which she adds glucose, cream, and new-laid eggs. It tastes like glue, but I daren't refuse it. I shan't offer you any, but if you'd like something else to drink, look on that laboratory table in the corner, and you'll find a large blue fluted bottle with a red poison label: it contains cognac. I keep it like that because Herbage won't allow alcohol in the house, but she'd die rather than touch a bottle or a sheet of paper in my rooms. The Wurtz-flask on the stand with about two hundred c.c. of colourless liquid in it contains Hollands gin. Take a couple of beakers, and help yourselves. Have no fear; outside of Herbage's medicine chest, there has been nothing noxious in the house for forty years, to my certain knowledge . . . Only rinse the beakers when you have done with them and put them back in the rack or I shall never hear the end of it. . . . No, I won't join you; Herbage makes me take a glass of her Blackberry Cordial in the evening, and that is quite enough for me—it is strong enough to fell an ox, and she says it is good for the chest. . . . Now!"

He settled his feet more comfortably on the plump plush-covered pouffe. "Let us take these things in their proper order. First of all, these notes of Dr. Brevis."

"You checked them?" asked George Oaks.

"I did. A most extraordinary brain, Oaks, transcendentally brilliant. I have no hesitation in saying that even Fuchs must have deferred to Brevis as his master."

"You know Fuchs?" asked George Oaks.

"Oh yes, necessarily so. You see, if there are, say, only three men in the world who speak your language, you will tend to seek them out, impelled by an urge to make yourself understood— driven by loneliness, you might almost say. Fuchs corresponded with me out of loneliness."

George Oaks said: "And you, Ohm? You were never lonely?"

"No, I have always been a perfectly happy man. Apart from my work, everything else always seemed so silly. . . . But you want to know, first of all, the import of Brevis's notes.

"Briefly, he has worked out, in a series of equations, the mathematical possibilities of developing the most highly fissionable isotope—which he calls a megatope—of Silicon. And in the second set of equations he has developed the critical mass. Does this convey anything to you?"

I shook my head. George Oaks said: "In other words, Kurt Brevis has demonstrated that one can convert Si_{28} into Si_{32}— which is impossible!"

Ohm Robertson said: "It was hitherto undemonstrable, never impossible. Brevis has demonstrated that it *is* possible."

"Then God help us!" cried George Oaks.

Ohm Robertson shrugged loosely, pursing his thin lips and raising his eyebrows. Then he looked at me and, in the indulgent manner of a policeman giving a complicated street-direction to a bewildered foreigner in a great city, he said: "Mr. Kemp, you must know a little something of the nature of an atom. An atom consists of a nucleus around which travels a certain number of electrons. The nucleus and the electrons are kept in cohesion because the nucleus is charged with positive electricity and the electrons with negative electricity. One atom differs from another—and therefore substance differs from substance—in accordance with the number of electrons held to their orbits by the nucleus. The stability of a substance, therefore, is dependent upon the constancy of the electron to its orbit around its nucleus in every atom of that substance. Hence, to unbalance an atom is tantamount to unbalancing the whole of a tiny solar system. Imagine, for example, that the density of the sun were suddenly enormously increased—hundreds of worlds would come to an abrupt end, would they not? Now, what we call 'atomic energy' is dependent upon an increase of density of the nucleus of an atom, so that, in point of fact, an infinitesimal universe rushes in upon its centre and blasts itself back to pure Energy in a flash.

"Now, take a stable atom—a respectably balanced atom with a certain number of electrons, and out of this make another atom with the same number of electrons, but a different nucleus, and you have an isotope. This isotope is active, unstable—in other words, frightfully explosive, for Nature abhors unbalance, and will not for long permit a state of unbalance to exist. She will let it shatter itself to bits, tear itself to pieces, disintegrate. Do you see?"

I nodded, and I heard George Oaks whisper: "Shatter it to bits, and then remould it nearer to her heart's desire."

Ohm Robertson proceeded: "Your atomic energy scientists have evolved a method of making isotopes of thorium and uranium by giving the atoms of these metals heavier nuclei, thereby making them unstable. They have achieved this by means of particle accelerators—as, say, the Cyclotron, in which atoms are whirled about by magnetic force until they achieve an astronomical speed, whereupon, being released into an immense tube, they lose some of their electrons. The atoms, thus unbalanced, become unstable. Again, this has been done in the 'atomic pile', as it is called, by a chemical process. In this case, they distil from huge quantities of thorium- and uranium-bearing ore microscopic quantities of the active isotopes which, of course, are unstable.

"Microscopic quantities, you understand. An atomic bomb of any magnitude is not possible unless a certain considerable weight, or 'critical mass' of these fissionable isotopes, is brought together—in which case you have something like the bomb that was dropped on Hiroshima, and up to the present we have been able to demonstrate no means of making such a bomb without employing certain exceedingly rare metals which, in themselves, are extremely difficult to purify.

"Now, here is what Brevis has discovered—that it is possible —indeed, comparatively easy—to make an atomic bomb out of Silicon, or more properly Si_{28}. What is Silicon? It is the essential element found everywhere in sand, clay, the very mud off your boots! Brevis shows here how one may take Si_{28} and, by increasing the density of its nucleus in a Cyclotron or an atomic pile, thus produce Si_{32}—which must be at least as terrible for its purpose as Plutonium. This is what Brevis terms the 'megatope' of Silicon.

"And there you have the import of these papers: in a word, a heavy industrial plant with access to a sand dune or a clay pit may manufacture atomic bombs as easily as television sets. And, furthermore, Kurt Brevis clearly demonstrates that the critical mass, or war-head, of the Megatopic Silicon Bomb need weigh no more than 3.2 kilograms; about the weight of a volume of the Encyclopedia Britannica. . . . There, gentlemen."

"Which means," said George Oaks, "that one might easily turn out atom bombs at least two thousand times more deadly than the Hiroshima bomb."

"Quite that," said Ohm Robertson.

"And any totalitarian dictator could make them?" I asked. "Or any megalomaniac industrialist?"

"Of course," said Ohm Robertson, with another shrug and moué of complete indifference.

"Anyone who could harness atomic power would without question become master of all the world. But as affairs stand at present, and are likely to stand for very many years to come, it is quite out of the question that any government in the world could permit atomic energy to be used extra-government-ally."

"Which means to say that Kadmeel's aims are extra-govern-mental," said George Oaks.

"Distinctly so. . . . Still, according to what I am told, there are few ordinary humdrum citizens who do not break the law whenever they think they can do so without being detected. For example, who would not leap at an opportunity safely to defraud the Collectors of His Majesty's Inland Revenue, or cheat the Customs and Excise? . . ."

Ohm Robertson smiled faintly. "Law . . . I have so little time, and so little need, to fuddle my head with what is legal and what is illegal. And I do not like lawyers, whose primary function, when all's said and done, is to make a practical truth of that which isn't supposed to be, and vice versa. Yours is a remarkably sound intelligence, Oaks, in a scatter-brained way, and I'm sure you won't think me too wickedly amoral when I say that your Decalogue to me is a thing of the moment, and that my primary conscious obedience is to Laws that are eternal."

"Now you're talking like a Sciocrat, Ohm," said George Oaks, with a laugh.

"Am I? Perhaps I am. I don't know. Another thing you asked me about was the matter of those little maps."

"Yes! I guessed, vaguely, what you were going to say about the Brevis notes, Ohm, but tell me in what way they're connected with those unknown islands."

"Oh, really, it's perfectly simple, my dear Oaks. These are maps of places you must have travelled over a score of times. Surely, you must have been having a little game with me? See here——" He got up lazily and shuffled over the thick green carpet to the desk. There was a Chinese pot filled with carefully sharpened pencils. He selected one, and spread out Kurt Brevis's maps, saying: "It can't matter a bit if I mark these things, you know. They are mere tracings, quite valueless. Without some indication of the complementary land masses as they exist at present they are, I admit, momentarily confusing. You see, they are the outlines of sea-coasts that exist, at present, only in theory. See?"

He began to draw. "By the God!" cried George Oaks, striking himself on the forehead. "Idiot that I am!" For, with three swiftly-thrown lines in the waters of the first map, Ohm Robertson had pulled the contours of a familiar continent out of the sea. The Woman, the Clown, and the Shark, linked together, became North America. On the second map, the Woman, the Parrot, and the Diver became one with the continent of Europe, and the poor little crumbs in the north, now we saw, were the

The "Unknown Islands" (or Lakes) according to the
Maps of Dr. Kurt Brevis.

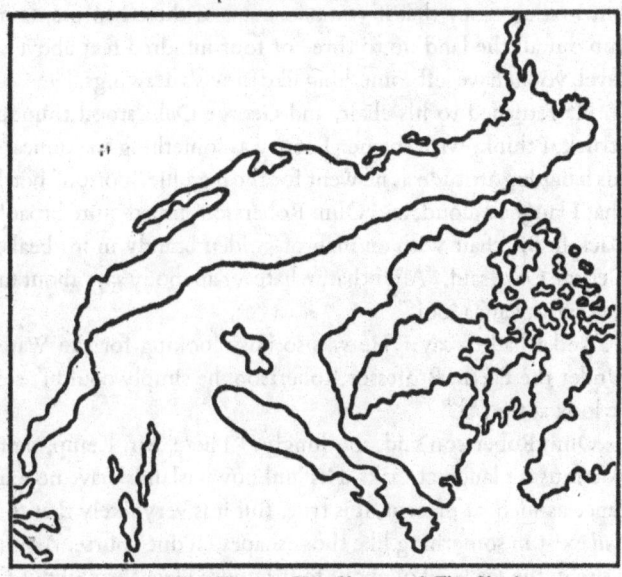

No. 1   The Woman, The Clown and The Shark

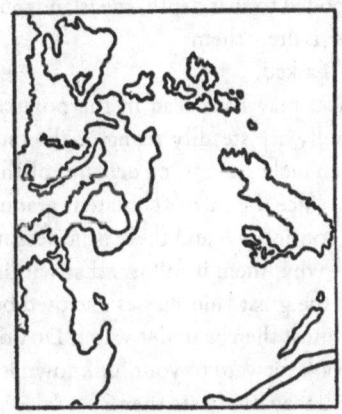

No. 2   The Woman, The Parrot
and The Diver

No. 3   The Gnawed Jaw
and The Antler

British Isles. Two scornfully scrawled lines on the third map,
and the Gnawed Jaw and the Antler became South America.

"In a word," said Ohm Robertson, "you were puzzled by

some simple sketches of the higher points of Europe, and of North and South America. I do not profess to be a geographer, but I rather fancy that if you take maps of these continents and rub out all the land up to three or four hundred feet above sea level, you'll have left something like Brevis's drawings."

He returned to his chair, and George Oaks stood thunderstruck, I think, with shame. There was something so comical in his hangdog attitude as he went for the big blue "poison" bottle, that I laughed aloud, and Ohm Robertson smiled quite broadly. Back in his chair with an inch of golden brandy in his beaker, George Oaks said. "After that, whatever anybody says about me, he's right. I am a fool."

And I had to say: "He was so busy looking for the Waters Under the Earth, Professor Robertson, he simply couldn't stop to look at the sea."

Ohm Robertson said, soothingly: "There, Mr. Kemp, there, you mustn't laugh at Oaks. His 'unknown islands' have no existence as such, at present, it is true. But it is very likely that they *will* exist in something like those shapes, in due course. Assume a rise in the sea level of about four hundred feet throughout the world, and, the land being flooded to that depth, the islands automatically stand much as Brevis drew them."

"Will exist in due course?" I asked.

"More than likely, yes. You may have read in the popular journals that sea levels generally are steadily rising at the rate of something like ten or eleven inches a year, on account of the melting of the polar ice-caps, since the earth's climate is gradually growing warmer. If this continues—and there is no reason why it should not continue—why, then, it follows that within five hundred years from now the great land masses enclosed by the outlines I have just drawn must then be under water. Do not be downcast, Oaks, you can look forward to your 'unknown islands'. And who knows but you may live to see them?"

"What d'you mean by that, Ohm?" said George Oaks, alert again.

"I do not mean, of course, that you may live five hundred years; only that it may not be necessary for you to live five hundred years in order to see these islands."

"You mean that this process of the rising of the waters might be hurried?"

"Why, yes."

"Naturally, or artificially, hurried?" asked George Oaks.

"It would have to be artificially hurried, Oaks, if you were to live to see it," said Ohm Robertson.

"By melting the polar ice-caps?"

"Of course. How else could you increase the volume of the seas?"

"Then the connection between Brevis's findings on the Silicon megatope and the maps he drew must be this—Kadmeel proposes to use Megatopic Silicon Bombs to melt the polar ice!" said George Oaks.

"It would seem so," said Ohm Robertson. "I don't know what was in Brevis's mind—apart from his figures, of course. But the conjunction of those figures with the drawings might indicate that Brevis was seriously considering the application of the Megatopic Silicon Bomb to some very substantial reduction of the polar ice and a consequent alteration of sea levels. Very likely, yes, Oaks."

"Do you know," said George Oaks, with a short laugh, "I had in mind a certain idea that Kadmeel's Sciocrats were going to make some serious attempt to take the world by assault, somehow, with atom bombs. That'd be crazy enough. But what you imply, Ohm, doesn't make sense!"

"What is Sense?" Ohm Robertson murmured.

"This, for example, is sense, old friend—that the most terrific atomic bombardment imaginable upon the polar ice caps couldn't conceivably melt more than a few cubic miles of the Eternal Ice!" cried George Oaks.

"Wait a bit," said Ohm Robertson, putting finger-tips to finger-tips and pressing together the heels of his hands so that he seemed to be making a kind of cage to protect something invisible. "One thing at a time. Who suggested a superficial bombardment of the polar ice-caps? Not I. And I am quite sure that Brevis could never have had any such thought in mind. As you say, it is indicated that the melting of the earth's ice-caps and the subsequent rising of the waters may be expedited by the use of bombs. But does this necessarily imply that your bombs must be dropped directly upon your frozen seas? Think carefully, now, Oaks. Think, now! I must refer you to your own work. In 1943 you wrote for your newspaper an emotional but well-informed 'story' of the bombing of the Ruhr Dams——"

"—Gibbo, Wing-Commander Gibson, V.C. . . . And the world shall end ere I forget," said George Oaks, under his breath.

"—Quite, quite. No doubt you remember, then. Your Wing-Commander, on that occasion, earned the Victoria Cross, and the adulation of the whole world, by cleverly and courageously placing a certain number of ordinary high-explosive bombs at certain points, so that a valley was flooded. The virtue of Wing-Commander Gibson's operation lay in the fact that he caused to occur in a matter of days an inundation infinitely more terrible than a million Gibsons armed with buckets could have poured out in five hundred years. Now, speaking in terms of the melting of the polar ice-caps—in other words, the flooding of the low-lands of the world; it is the same thing—assume that your polar ice-cap is kept in its place, that is to say, held solid, by a kind of Ruhr dam, the breaking of which will let loose upon it a steady flood of hot water."

"Yes?"

"Assume that in this case your Ruhr dam is a great barrier of living rock under the sea, and that your Wing-Commander is Commander of a submarine, armed with an unlimited supply of atomic bombs and exact information as to where they may most effectively be placed!"

George Oaks's corded hands were spliced rather than clasped together, and his voice was very quiet and evenly measured as he said: "I get what you're driving at, now. Go on, Ohm."

Ohm Robertson, parting his finger-tips and scrutinising his palms with something of the air of a fortune-teller, went on: "Why, then, it must be evident to you that these submarine dams which are to be pin-pointed with atomic bombs must be in the rocky barriers which extend under the sea between New-foundland and England in the Atlantic, and under the Bering Straits in the Pacific. This same rocky barrier, upon which the Atlantic cable is laid, is the barrier that diverts the warm waters of the Gulf Stream from the Arctic Circle. Smash this barrier, and countless billions of tons of comparatively hot water must rush north to the polar ice, which must inevitably melt, releasing in its turn an uncontrollable deluge smashing southward. Break down the barriers under the Bering Straits, and under the Atlantic, and you may force to come to pass in six months a cataclysm that in the course of nature would take five hundred years to mature."

"But that would be pointless——" I began.

"—To what end?" asked George Oaks, simultaneously. "That would mean the annihilation of the civilised world!"

"Of course it would," said Ohm Robertson, parting his hands and putting them down flat on the arms of his chair. "As you may see by the maps, most of the centres of civilisation (civilisations are born and thrive in valleys and on low-lying coasts, remember) would be drowned. Terrible tidal waves would rush inland, of course, from every point of the compass, together with typhoons, cyclones, and hurricanes of hitherto unimagined fury. The great mass of humanity would be as helpless as the Siberian mammoths and rhinoceroses were when the sudden frost of the First Ice Age froze them in their tracks. There would be, of course, a wild rush of people to the highlands and the mountains. There could be no time for a shifting of centres of government, or of industry—most certainly, no time for an uprooting and transplantation of farmers. In practically no time at all, primitive conditions would obtain. Man and beast, fighting tooth and nail for a hands breadth of purchase on the uplands, would be motivated only by the instinct to survive. It would be dog eat dog, until the rage of the elements subsided—which might take a few years; at the end of which time the sun would shine through a dripping mist upon a fresh, a scantily-populated world. And who would be the masters of this world?"

George Oaks said: "Obviously, those who'd planned the cataclysm, and, therefore, taken precautions against it. Those who had stored food and weapons—those who had established themselves in the high places of the earth. For example, Kadmeel!"

"For example," said Ohm Robertson, shrugging.

And at this, somehow, I felt as you might feel if, coming home after a brief absence, a cobweb brushed your face: one touch of the Unexpected, and a homely shadow becomes a lurking beast, and the light-switch is half a world away. . . . Something *wrong* has found its way in through some crack in the old place, and this wrong thing is lying in wait for you, filling the dark—you can feel the cold night curling about your ears as the Thing smiles, and you know that if you turn back to the outer door, cold and sticky filaments will fall across your eyes and turn you around and around until you are wound over and over and spun into a black cocoon . . . One loose thread makes horror in the house before the lights go on. . . . Do not ask me why I felt so cold just then. I only know that, suddenly, I was afraid, because something had touched me out of turn.

Perhaps George Oaks felt as I did, because his hand closed like tongs on my wrist as he said: "You take it coolly, Ohm."

Ohm Robertson said: "And why should I not?"

My nerves were strung high. I expected some little note of deprecation, at least; not another shrug, not another pursing of lips and elevation of eyebrows over the bridge of the nose while the tails of those eyebrows lingered lower down to tickle the tired wrinkles. George Oaks was right—Ohm Robertson was not of the world of common men, any more than a child is of this world of pity and passion. "Why should he not!" I would have tried to make him see the reason why not, only I was struck dumb by a sense of awful inadequacy—paralysed by the impotent rage of a man who knows that right is right and wrong is wrong but holds his tongue for fear that he may be asked why and wherefore.

So I shrugged my shoulders, too, and then I felt George Oaks's fingers pressing out an old familiar signal, dot-dot-dot-dash, dot-dot-dot-dash . . . the old *V* sign for Victory, while he said: "Now, Albert, now do you begin to see why I didn't dare talk before for fear of being earmarked crazy?"

"Oh, but you never were crazy, Oaks," said Ohm Robertson. "Emotional, I grant you. Never crazy. In your way, Oaks, a man of the highest perspicacity, a thoroughly honest man, one in many thousands."

"Well, Ohm," said George Oaks, "for example, I think I see

now why it was necessary for Kadmeel to murder Austin Crabbe. He also tried to draw some maps, as I told Albert, here, last night. Austin Crabbe's maps—the little I remember of the shapes of them—were somehow similar to and at the same time absolutely unlike Kurt Brevis's maps. (Oh, Designer Infinite!) *Seeing those scribbles of Austin Crabbe's in my mind's eye now, I recognise them as something like the areas that you blocked in!* Ohm—Albert—whereas Kurt Brevis mapped out the highlands that were to be left above water, Austin Crabbe tried to draw the lowlands that were to be flooded under. I can put the shapes together in my head and, by the God, they fit!"

"Good," said Ohm Robertson, nodding . . . and I had a vision of him, dryly kind and pityingly patient, counting the bubbles in the foam at the mouth of some bright young scholar at his university thirty-odd years ago. "Good, Oaks. Proceed . . ."

Now when he said *Proceed* in that tone of voice, I felt, again, a curious hollowness in the breast, because George Oaks, in his more arrogant moments, spoke just like that; and it occurred to me suddenly that this man was Oaks's master. "Go on, Oaks."

Stumbling over his words like a schoolboy, and looking at me as a schoolboy looks at his neighbour for moral support while he talks at his teacher in class, George Oaks said: "And Austin Crabbe's figures, I mean, the lists of figures he compiled and wrote down—among his papers that were stolen, that is to say, bought under false pretences by the man who represented himself as Gaylord Taylor from the *London Evening Post*—those figures applied to transactions and stock manipulations by Kadmeel and his associates. I remember some of the headings: Rocky Mountains, Appalachians, Apennines, Andes! Norway, Africa, India, China! All high places of the world, eh, Ohm?"

Ohm Robertson took out his watch, opened it, consulted it, listened to it, closed it, wound it, listened to it again, and put it back in his pocket before saying: "The greater part of these places would, indeed, stand above water in the event of such a cataclysm as we have been considering. Go on, Oaks. What are your conclusions?"

George Oaks said: "My first conclusion must be, that I have been an unmitigated ass in assuming that Kadmeel and his Sciocrats would look for a world either above or below the surface of the known world. If I hadn't dreamed myself into being more of a fool than God made me, I might have known that Kadmeel and his friends would go after a complete, open, arrogant conquest of a world which they at present partly rule. I might have known that it must hurt the Sciocratic pride to tamper with a legislature here, and finance a politician there, and fiddle with common bribery and corruption everywhere. Of course, of course—premising that the Sciocrats are mad—it is perfectly reasonable to assume that they'd want to make their present power openly absolute. . . . They hate all the laws that bind them, all the laws of the world, Ohm—all the laws begotten of hunger, love, and the fear of death."

"For me," said Ohm Robertson, "you're speaking entirely in unknown quantities. For my part I have never known hunger, love, or the fear of death. But I beg pardon—do go on, Oaks."

"You know, Albert, Ohm is telling the truth. In the first big show, Jerry was strafing hell out of us—Minnies, Jack Johnsons and all—Ohm simply plugged up his ears and read a book. He doesn't understand what fear is. I told you, Albert, he isn't of this world."

With another of those pale smiles, Ohm Robertson said: "A heavy bombardment was the only thing that could drown Oaks's voice, Mr. Kemp. I welcomed a shower of Minnenwerfer missiles, for the sake of peace and quiet, especially when Oaks decided to hum Sir Edward Elgar's 'Enigma Variations', with appropriate gestures, playing *pizzicato* with the lid of an empty herring tin. Apart from a jew's harp, I have never heard a more deplorable twanging than Oaks got out of that bit of tin. Upon my word, Mr. Kemp, I verily believe that if you enclosed that man in cotton wool, he would contrive some means of making a noise out of it."

"Why, yes," said George Oaks. "Being pretty strong in the fingers, I'd spin the cotton into strings of varying thicknesses, and, by the God, I bet you I'd make you a workable harp. Would you like to bet, Ohm? Give me a carton of cotton wool and a chair frame—especially one of those bentwood frames—and in two hours I'll play you 'Scheherezade'. Eh?"

I said: "Don't bet, sir. He'd do it, and then you'd have to listen to it. During the first blitz he made a one-string fiddle out of a soup plate, some twisted-up cellophane from cigarette packets, and an umbrella rib, and played 'Lily of Laguna'. Also, 'A Bicycle made for Two'."

"Yes," said Ohm Robertson, still smiling, but smiling to himself now, and not at me. "Oaks has a most remarkable gift—to get a certain joy, a certain merriment, out of anything and everything. And I really believe that he sincerely loves, in their fundamentals, the laws of the world that are begotten of hunger, love, and the fear of death!"

Now George Oaks was strangely still, and there was a look about him that made me uneasy. He glanced at me before replying, and I saw that his eyes were, at the same time, watchful and bewildered: they were the eyes of a man across whose consciousness has flashed a thought that ought to be unthinkable. But he said, immediately: "And so I do, by the God! Where would we be without them, Ohm? Without them, there'd be no Beethoven, no Shakespeare, nothing. Take away hunger and love, and the world becomes a castrated fat cat on a mat. There's no glory, Ohm, except in achievement, and there's no fun in achievement except through a clean fight. It must be so! If you're starving in a kennel, your instincts tell you that it must be so. If Winnie had said: 'I can offer you nothing but champagne, deodorant, and Chanel Number Five', whose blood would have stirred? Blood, sweat, tears—hunger, love, fear of death—Man lives by these things. He always must, if he is to keep on being Man. I subscribe to the laws begotten of hunger and love and the fear of death, I do!"

"Now I wonder why," said Ohm Robertson.

"Why? For the simple reason that men are men, or ought to be, and must bleed and sweat and weep their way."

"Their way where, Oaks?"

"Nobody knows, Ohm. He is born to struggle as a hammer is made for percussion, or a file is cut for friction. Otherwise, he wouldn't be a man. On my honour, old friend, nothing is born without healthy pain."

"You must correct me if I am wrong; I am no pathologist,"

said Ohm Robertson, "but I am informed that Pain is in the nature of a warning signal, a danger signal, indicative of the nearness of a state of affairs to be avoided."

"Yes," cried George Oaks, "but hold hard, there! There are two kinds of pain. There is good pain and bad pain. There is clean pain and dirty pain. Good pain is the pain you accept because you know that it leads to something beyond yourself—the pain of the woman in labour, the pain of the wheel on the road, the pain of the artist in travail. These pains you forget or forgive, because they don't hurt you—they make you stronger. But bad pains you never quite forget, and never forgive, because they are pain for pain's sake—destructive pains—the pangs of unnecessary death. Ohm, in the last analysis, the right to inflict Pain belongs to the God, Who can see the end of it. Not to Man——"

"—Hush, Oaks, hush. What can one gain by shouting? We are not deaf, I believe? . . . For my part, I believe that pain is unnecessary; that the human organism is all-too-human, and deucedly clumsily designed and inefficient in operation. I am by way of being a perfectionist, you know—theoretically, Oaks, necessarily theoretically, since after all I am a similar parcel of similarly-working parts. But I cannot find it in my heart to be out of sympathy with, say, your Kadmeels and your Kurt Brevises who find natural processes of evolution somewhat slow, who very properly desire to be alone and untrammelled and who find the maximum life-span too short."

And then Ohm Robertson looked again at the face of his watch, so that I said to George Oaks: "George, I think we are keeping Professor Ohm Robertson."

But Ohm Robertson put away his watch, saying: "Oh no, please, not at all. This is a great pleasure, I assure you. Don't go." And he got up and fetched the brandy bottle.

While his back was turned, Oaks looked at me with something like a grimace of agony: his mouth squared itself in a kind of *rictus*, and then narrowed under a ponderous frown, so that his expression said: *Calm, calm; above all, be calm and leave it to me!* "Thanks, Ohm," he said, taking the bottle, and pouring only a little brandy into my beaker and his, while the scientist settled himself again: ". . . Ah, Lord! If it were Albert talking and not

Ohm Robertson, I'd begin to look forward, now, to some non-sense about super-evolved thinking creatures, all brain and no body, all pure reason divorced from emotion . . . a kind of palpitating bladder of convoluted grey slime which it would be the function of leggy bipeds like me and Albert to feed and lubricate."

Ohm Robertson replied: "The romances of Mr. Wells apart, Oaks—seriously now; what is the man in the street to you as an individual, except a creature that makes your everyday life possible? In your heart, you must confess, you put yourself a cut above the cabby who drives a taxi, the barman who draws your beer, the waiter who fills your plate, the office-boy who brings your tea, the telephone operator who puts a plug into a socket to connect you with me through the wire. Don't you?"

Ohm Robertson's eyes were closed again. George Oaks gave me another keen, hard look as he said: "I suppose I do." His voice was low, and his tone indecisive, now: I did not know whether to hate him for his humility, or his old friend for his condescension.

"As a reasoning man, Oaks—which you are—you must see that these Sciocrats (an ugly and pretentious term, but one label is as good as another, given the content, as witness the bottle by your side), these Sciocrats, Oaks, although they may be mad, are not without reason. And they reason as follows: The world is too full of too many people. In the course of nature your Too-Many must reduce itself in ultimate combat, each to each, until a kind of manœuvrable mass of population is established. The resources of the earth are being rapidly exhausted. Food-producing soil is diminishing year by year, as are the sources of mechanical energy—I mean, fuel. A Lord Kadmeel, or whoever it may be, may accumulate in billions or in trillions, I grant you."

"But——?" said George Oaks.

"——But what your magnate amasses is a mere flea-bite compared with what is blindly consumed every day by the unseen swarms of utter nonentities that live simply for the sake of living. It is all very well to complain that your Fords and your Rockefellers accumulate more than they can possibly, as individuals, produce. But have you ever stopped to think of your

Superfluous Man—the man who, merely in the act of living, consumes something like one-sixtieth of his average weight in solids and liquids every twenty-four hours, constantly multiplying himself, and exhausting the world without replenishing it? Have you paused to consider, Oaks, that your Man of the People is by far a more ferocious glutton than your multi-millionaire? Now really, Oaks, you cannot reasonably deny that the majority of Mankind is unnecessary?"

"I do deny it," said George Oaks.

"If you consider the facts and the figures of the matter," said Ohm Robertson, as if he had not heard, "speaking quantitatively, even as manure, the Average Man comes expensive: as a mass, he must (speaking in figures) put back into the ground no more than about seventy per cent of himself in the next two hundred years. From the viewpoint of Humanity, therefore, he pays less than three-tenths of one per cent per annum. Your average inhabitant of the earth, then, though he be the humblest toiler in factory or field, accumulates where he does not produce. Hence, it may be argued that the rapidly multiplying population is superfluous and parasitic . . . this mass, by its very existence, is destroying itself. The process of its self-destruction must necessarily be bitter, painful, and prolonged: it must involve war upon war, famine upon famine, pestilence upon pestilence. And, in the end, what can remain to nibble the last few blades of grass and gnaw the last few thigh-bones and roots on the face of a vitiated earth? A reduced breed of bestial men, living by the laws of tooth and nail—a broken mass that, by the very exigencies of survival, must have climbed back to the tree-tops or slunk back into the caves. The figures say so, Oaks; it must be so. Figures don't lie; that is why I am devoted to them. Similarly, Oaks, I have a high regard for you, because you are a lover of the truth. In your emotional way, I believe that you are a realist."

"It depends what you mean by reality," George Oaks said. But Ohm Robertson smiled and waved this away.

"Your Sciocrat," he said, "or whatever you like to call him, proposes, if you like, to hurry things along. In the evolutionary sense, it is necessary to consider Mankind as something on the move—is it not? This being the case, why should not Mankind, on the move, move faster in its given direction towards its pre-ordained goal?"

I asked: "Who ordains the goal? Who dares to set the direction?" I said that because George Oaks was unaccountably silent, and I felt that this was what he would have said if he had spoken. Looking to him for approbation, I received a cold stare; and somewhere between his eyebrows I saw an inward-and-downward movement which said: *Shut up!*

"Well, then," said Ohm Robertson, making a little tent of his hands, and putting his nose into it, "your Sciocrat, or whatever you like to call him, proposes to do for Mankind, as a body on the move, no more than Watt and Stevenson proposed to do with vehicles: in effect, to convey him, as it might be from York to London, in less than one-tenth of the hitherto accepted time. Quite simply; your Sciocrat anticipates the Inevitable. He sees his destination, and takes steps to get there somewhat sooner. Life being short, your Sciocrat aims to achieve tomorrow a little in advance of the clock. Think, now, Oaks, and tell me—what is there in this to which a reasoning man may take exception?"

George Oaks said: "One has a prejudice, of course, against washing out three-quarters of the civilised world at one *swoosh*."

"Of course one has, Oaks, on the face of it. But on reflection, why should one have? In five hundred years, or less, quite two-thirds of the Unknown Superfluous must be eliminated more or less unpleasantly in the course of nature."

"Agreed, Ohm; but given five hundred years, they'd have a sporting chance," said George Oaks. "The God gives a sporting chance."

"I don't quite follow you," said Ohm Robertson. "The world, as its inhabitants knew it, has been changed overnight many times before now. Would you call the explosion of Krakatoa a sporting chance? Or the eruption of Vesuvius that buried Pompeii? Or the frost that froze the mammoths? Or your Hiroshima bomb? Since the Part is comprehended by the Whole, every act, surely, must ultimately be an Act of God?"

"I agree with you there," said George Oaks. "Ultimately, yes. Ultimately. But let's get back to the Kurt Brevis papers, and Lord Kadmeel's connection with them. As I see it, Kadmeel and his

Sciocrats propose to blow down the Atlantic and the Pacific barriers, and flood the world. Having established themselves, dug
themselves in, on the high places of the world, the Sciocrats propose to come out in broad daylight, and rule the earth under a
brand-new code. Like that!" He snapped his fingers.

Ohm Robertson, nodding, said: "That is about it, Oaks."

"Of course, the Sciocrats can't do this without Kurt Brevis's
Megatopic Silicon Bomb?"

"Without something of the sort, I believe, it would be out of
the question, Oaks."

"Just so, Ohm. Now correct me if I'm wrong: Lord Kadmeel and his associates have put an immense sum of money into
what the newspapers call the Bathyspheric Survey—that is to
say, Kadmeel has been watching and measuring the ocean bed
by means of the Hohenlohe Bathysphere between England and
Newfoundland. I put it to you that the end he has in view is,
a blasting of the barriers with Kurt Brevis's bomb—a releasing
of the hot sea-currents to the north, and the loosening of a new
deluge."

Ohm Robertson took out his watch again, and opened it. This
time he did not put it back, but kept on gazing at the face of it,
nervously scratching at the arm of his chair with the forefinger
of his free hand. "Yes," he said slowly, "I believe that to be the
case."

There used to be a form of torture called "The Cord"—they
twisted a knotted rope about a man's forehead until his eyes came
out. Looking at George Oaks's agonised face, which was watery
white now, like candle grease, and at his straining eyes, I knew
what the victim must have looked like when the torturer put on
the pressure. "An overdose of sanity can drive a man mad," he
muttered. "Too much Reason, taken neat, can induce delirium."

"I don't follow you," said Ohm Robertson.

"I mean that I've been thinking too hard, and I've given
myself a headache. Do you happen to have a couple of aspirins,
Ohm?"

"Certainly. I'll get them for you. I'd better not tell Herbage
—she'll think I want them for myself, and she'll make me go to
bed with a hot-water-bottle. Excuse me."

He left the room, and then George Oaks whispered: "My God, my God! The man is mad!" He caught up Kurt Brevis's papers and stuffed them into his pocket. "Let's get out of here, and get rid of this stuff, quick. Follow me close. If there's any rough stuff outside, hit to break bone, but not unless I give you the office. I think Halfacre's men will be on the watch outside. Above all, take your lead from me. Come on!"

But then Ohm Robertson returned with a bottle of aspirin tablets. He had the vacant look of a sleep-walker; I noticed that his watch, still open, was dangling at the end of its chain from his waistcoat. As he sat down, the watch rattled against his knees, whereupon, with a faint start, he took it up and consulted it again. "Ah yes," he said, closing it and putting it away. "Ah yes. Yes . . . Here are some aspirin tablets, Oaks. Take a couple with a little water. I don't think you ought to have any more brandy. In such quantities it really can't be good for you, you know. Sit down, sit down."

"We must go," said George Oaks. "I'm not well."

"All the more reason why you should rest a bit, surely? . . . Well, Oaks, I have helped you to the best of my ability, as I said I would, and in view of the significance of Brevis's papers, it remains only to hand them over to the proper authorities, as I told you it would be my bounden duty to do."

"Just so," said George Oaks.

"Just so," Ohm Robertson agreed. "I took the liberty of telephoning them shortly before you and Mr. Kemp arrived."

"You did?" cried George Oaks.

"Yes. You'll forgive me, Oaks. I know that you're an honest man, but in these muddle-headed times one cannot be too careful. A clever and honest man may be ideologically on the wrong path. For all I know, you might in all honesty have allowed yourself to become corrupted like Brevis. In such cases there is no way of telling, is there? Therefore——"

A bell rang. Herbage—I recognised her quick, firm footsteps —went to the front door.

"—This must be they. Sit down, sit down, Oaks—if your hands are clean in this matter, there can be nothing for you to fear, surely?"

Herbage tapped at the door, and opened it. "Three gentlemen to see you, Master Ohm."

"I'm expecting them, Herbage. Show the gentlemen in."

She held open the door. Three tall men came into the study.

The foremost of them was Major Chatterton. "Good evening!" he said.

Part Nine

Then I felt as one of those Siberian mammoths must have felt when that unimaginable ancient frost that struck like lightning deep-froze him quicker than a startled nerve can tell a muscle to jump. Or—speaking of lightning—as a condemned man in Sing-Sing must feel when the switch is thrown and the current courses through him. I believe that if I had been strapped tight to my arm-chair by trepidation, the shock would have sent me hurtling out of it. I am quite sure that my body convulsively, between shoulders and loins, made what wrestlers call an "arch", while something beyond sensation shot through the bore of my spine from brain to buttocks. . . . No, let us say that it was something like electrocution, because somehow I had been bracing myself for some shock from the moment when Ohm Robertson started to worry over his watch.

And then it was as if, the switch thrown back and the current cut off, I was miraculously alive in the electric chair, still strapped down, and tingling at the tip of every nerve and capillary . . . Or, again, as if, having survived a deep frostbite, I was thawing too fast. I looked first to George Oaks; he nodded to me and smiled, but one of his eyelids quivered in a wink, before he raised his head and said: "Oh hello, Chatterton."

"Ah, there, George! Hello, Kemp!" said Chatterton, grinning and posturing like the Dance of Death. "Sorry if I'm a little late, Robertson. Couldn't help it. Couldn't let poor Powell down. Ever so sorry."

"Powell?" said Ohm Robertson.

"My man Powell, you know. Devil's own job. He was arrested this afternoon. Perhaps Kemp told you his house was broken into last night. Bobby tore off one of the burglar's shoes. Shoe belonged to my man Powell—had his fingerprints on it, as it happened, and because once upon a time he was rather a naughty boy, I'm afraid Scotland Yard had his prints in their files. A mistake, of course—my man Powell had some shoes and some other

177

stuff stolen last evening. Sir Peter Oversmith knows all about it
—suspects gypsies, I believe; and will bear witness, of course.
Meanwhile, nothing much one can do about it, although naturally one does one's best to stand by . . . poor Powell. It'll all come
out in the wash, of course. Damn good man. Sorry to lose him.
Made a mistake when he was young and wild—haven't we all?
—but tried to go straight ever since."

George Oaks said, with a short laugh: "What, so you let them
pinch Mungo-Mitchell? Chatterton, my boy, if I know that
fellow, he'll owe you one for that. He'll get you, I fancy, if it takes
him twenty years, Chatterton, and what he'll do to you won't
be nice, you mark my words. You see, Albert," he said, turning
to me and winking again—for the life of me I could not inter-
pret the meaning of that wink—"you see how these people fall
down. Disappointed man puts himself at head of disappointed
men. Eh, Albert? Paranoiac directs paranoiac. Impotent ambition leads ambitious impotence. Blind leads blind. . . . My dear
Chatterton, who holds a wolf by the ears dare not let go. Mungo-
Mitchell, alias Powell, will tear your throat out for this. If you
had to have dealings with the underworld, why couldn't you deal
with common, simple-minded thugs like the couple behind you?
Why did you have to involve yourself with a Mungo-Mitchell,
who is your superior by birth and breeding? Chatterton, Chatterton, what a silly man you are!"

Now, when Oaks said "birth and breeding" Chatterton
flushed. Blood in his cheeks did not become him—it looked like
rouge. But he still smiled, saying: "I don't know what you are
talking about . . . Oh, I beg your pardon! Professor Ohm Robertson—Colonel Lalouette, and Mr. Oettle."

The darker of Chatterton's companions bowed, smiling; I decided that this must be Lalouette. The other, presumably Oettle,
nodded curtly; he looked dangerous. He was dressed, like his
companion, in sober blue serge, but no tailor could have cut a
coat to hang comfortably upon his grotesquely developed body.
From the points of his shoulders almost to the lobes of his ears
there swelled such hillocks of muscle that his torso was shaped
like an obus. His head appeared to grow straight out of his chest;
his heavy, out-thrust chin covered the knot of his neck-tie. It

was the chin of a Punch, and he had a nose to match it; but the Punch's grin on his face was reversed. I have never seen a grimmer mouth. *If there is to be a rough-house*, I thought, *here is the one I must take first, and fast, and sudden.*

I was thinking very rapidly, now, entirely in terms of hand-to-hand combat. If I could hold the big fellow, as I supposed I could, if only for a minute or so, Oaks might make a dash for the street, with the papers. This, I guessed, was what he had in mind, for as he talked he began to pace easily up and down, his hands loosely clasped behind him. I observed that the end of every turn took him a few inches closer to the curtained window at my left hand.

"Lalouette . . . Oettle . . ." he was saying. "The one that looks like the pork butcher will be Oettle, I suppose. How do you do, Oettle? Or should I say 'Heil Hitler'? When did you slip over the Swiss border? And what's your real name? A horse to a hen, there's a rope knotted for you . . . May I open the window, Ohm? The room stinks. I can smell Auschwitz and Maidenek." His hand was on the curtain.

"Leave the window alone, won't you?" said Chatterton. "And please keep still, George."

Standing now only a foot or so away from the window, George Oaks went on: "And the other one, Lalouette. What did you do before you took money from Abetz? There's a smell of the gigolo about him, somewhere, eh Albert? 'May I have the pleasure of the next dance, dear lady?' What unfortunate seam-stress took you out of the gutters of Montrouge, and how much did you get when you sent her to Buenos Aires? I shall call you 'Bubu'."

Chatterton must have trained his men well. They appeared not to have heard; only Oettle licked his lips, and Lalouette's smile became square at the corners. Chatterton said: "You will have your little joke, George, but I don't think you're wise to annoy Oettle, you know. There was a time, once upon a time, when he was called the 'Angel of Death'."

George Oaks chanted: "Then came the Lord and slew the Angel of Death who killed the Butcher that slaughtered the Ox that drank the Water that quenched the Fire that burned the

Stick that beat the Dog that bit the Cat that devoured the Kid that my Father bought for two pieces of silver. I spit on your 'Angel of Death'!"

"All this," said Chatterton, "is an awful waste of time, you know. You know, George, you've been awfully ill-advised—frightfully indiscreet. You too, Kemp. You must realise that you are very lucky fellows, both of you. Otherwise, we mightn't be chatting together as we are now——"

"—You mean that, if you hadn't wanted us alive, you'd have had us killed by now? Not on your life!" said George Oaks. "Too risky. More than you dare do. You could murder Austin Crabbe, but you daren't touch us. Firstly, you don't know how much we know, or to whom we may have told what we know. Secondly——"

"—Excuse me, never mind the 'secondly'. The 'firstly' will do, you know. We have a lot of questions to ask you and Kemp, George, in our good time and at a convenient place. . . . Meanwhile, Robertson, where are those Brevis papers?"

"Well, they were here, a few moments ago. I imagine either Oaks or Mr. Kemp has put them in his pocket."

George Oaks, who was idly rifling the pages of a heavy volume which he had picked up from the desk, slapped it shut, and said: "Right you are, gentlemen." Then he shouted: "Now, Albert!"—and hurled the book at the green-shaded lamp, which went down with a great clattering crash, while I threw myself upon Oettle. My head hit him in the pit of the stomach just as the light went out, so that for a split second I thought that I had miscalculated my distance and butted a heavy piece of furniture and knocked myself out—for that man might have been made of seasoned oak. I remember, also, in that same instant hearing a screech of brass curtain rings and a shattering of glass behind me, and I knew that George Oaks had jumped the window. Then one of Oettle's great fists came down on the back of my neck like a mallet, half stunning me, and driving my face down against a knee which came up to meet it.

"Lights! Lights!" cried Chatterton; but my head was blazing with a new-born galaxy as Oettle hit me again and again. I must have gone berserk then—found some of that madman's strength of which the weakest of us has sealed reserves. I shall never forget that queer metallic taste which came into my mouth—a taste as of verdigris on old copper coins, mingled with a kind of slaughter-house flavour from my broken nose—nor the strange, unholy joy that took possession of me then. If Oettle was an oak, then I would uproot it! I had him round the waist, under the ribs, my hands locked behind him. He must have weighed two hundred and fifty pounds, but I lifted him as easily as if he had been a hundredweight, and then, butting him in the face, brought up a knee into his belly. But I could not carry him on one leg, so I fell forward with Oettle underneath me, and I heard his head strike wood, which broke, and then he lay still. I suspected a trap, felt for his face in the dark, and hit him on the chin with all my might. He did not even sigh. Then I sprang to my feet, blind with blood and the night, and turned, wildly swinging. My right fist struck flesh; I thought I heard bone break, and laughed aloud. Somebody fell over a chair. I went after him, but stumbled in my turn, and heard the man I had struck scrambling away.

It was all over in two minutes. Then the central light was on. Chatterton was standing by the door, his left hand on the switch. In his right he held a short black pistol. Lalouette was leaning against the wall a few feet away from him. He too had a pistol, but his left hand was busy with a handkerchief with which he was trying to staunch the blood that was dripping from his mouth: at least I had spoiled his fine white smile for him. Oettle lay on the floor. In falling he had broken off a segment of a massive, round, mahogany coffee table with his head; I was appalled and delighted at the ruin I had made of his face. As I looked he stirred, groaning.

Chatterton said: "Now, I give you my word of honour; if you so much as move a finger, Lalouette and I will shoot. Not to kill, Lalouette—to cripple. In the knees."

Then a voice behind me muttered: "Slight miscalculation."

If Chatterton and Lalouette had been a pair of charging lions I could not have helped turning my head. I saw George Oaks sitting in a mess of broken glass, half covered by a torn-down curtain. As I stared, he struggled to his feet, wiping some blood from his forehead, and said: "My jump was perfect, Albert. But I might have guessed that at lighting-up time Herbage would have put up the shutters."

"She always does," said Ohm Robertson, climbing out from under the desk and settling himself again in his chair.

"Cover them, Lalouette," said Chatterton, advancing. "And if they move, remember—not to kill, only to cripple." He came forward, and Lalouette followed him.

My berserker spell had passed, and I felt weak and spent, though still exhilarated by my victory over Oettle. He was struggling to his feet now; still on his hands and knees, he started towards me, red and wet about the neck and shoulders like a wounded bull.

But Chatterton said to him: "Not now, Oettle. Later, perhaps. Simply keep him covered." So Oettle drew a Luger from his hip and stood, looking steadily at me out of his right eye, for I had closed the left. Chatterton thrust his hand into Oaks's breast pocket and drew out the Kurt Brevis notes.

"Is this right?" he asked, handing them to Ohm Robertson.

"Yes, Chatterton, these are they," said the old man, handing them back, and Chatterton in his turn pocketed them.

"You fellows really have been rather naughty," he said, "but I bear you no malice." His eyes, however, said otherwise. "I'm quite sure that when everything is explained you will see that you've behaved rather unreasonably, and that all this bother is quite unnecessary. And now, I'm afraid, I'm going to have to ask you to take a little trip with us. Sit down on that sofa, both of you, and stretch your legs out straight in front of you, and for goodness sake don't make any sudden movements. . . . Lalouette, go into the bathroom, please, and dip a couple of big towels in cold water; I daresay the gentlemen would like to wipe their faces."

"There is iodine and adhesive tape in the medicine cupboard," said Ohm Robertson.

"Excellent. You'll need a doctor for that nose, I'm afraid, Kemp. Still, we'll make you as presentable as we can . . . All the same, you seem to have hurt Oettle more than he hurt you. I am quite surprised, really! . . . Meanwhile, let us have a little drink for the road."

I looked at Oaks. He looked back at me and nodded helplessly.

If he had made any other sort of gesture I was prepared to jump Oettle on his blind side as soon as Lalouette was out of the room, and go for his pistol—and I would have used it, too. And then, suddenly, I remembered the elegant whalebone and kangaroo-hide life-preserver in my breast pocket, and found myself giggling in a silly helpless kind of way. "I owe you a penny," I said to Oaks.

He replied, with a wry smile: "I was thinking of that myself. I forgot, too, to tell you the truth . . . but it does my heart good to see what you did to the Jerry over there. 'Red ruin from eyebrow to chin,' as Hazlitt said—Now *what* fight was it he was covering?" and he clasped his head in his sinewy hands and squeezed it hard.

"The brandy is in the blue 'Poison' bottle," said Ohm Robertson.

"I think I have something rather better here," said Chatterton, taking out a capacious but slender silver flask. "An Armagnac of 1859." He poured two generous measures and handed one to Oaks and the other to me. "Drink it up," he said, pouring for himself into the silver cup that screwed to the neck of the flask; "this will make you feel better. Here's to our better understanding. Happy landings!"

Oaks and I drank. The Armagnac stung my cut mouth and brought tears to my eyes. And in these tears everything suddenly began to swim. I tried to speak, but my cheeks and lips were too heavy to move. I saw Chatterton smiling as he emptied his little silver cup on to the carpet. Then he became fantastically long, ridiculously attenuated, like his own reflection in a Hall of Mirrors . . . and after that he began to spin, drawing himself out into a fine wire, which began to twang on a deep mysterious note which got into my head and vibrated until it shook me out of the world. . . .

. . . When I opened my eyes again I could still hear something like that noise in my head; only now I was part of it—I was, in fact, the genesis of it, the vibrant wire. And oh, but I was deathly sick! I felt about me before opening my eyes, and found that I was lying upon something soft that adapted itself to my slightest touch, like a cloud. Then, half-opening my eyes, I saw that I lay in a voluptuously cushioned, luxuriously curtained place, and I thought of Monte Cristo—but then I saw Chatterton. I believe I felt him, too, because I was aware of a kind of coldness above the ball of the thumb where he might have been feeling my pulse. But his face was turned away from me. He was looking over his left shoulder, not smiling now; restrained but angry, very angry.

He was saying: "Powell! What the devil are you doing here?"

Then I heard the voice of Chatterton's "man Powell", whom George Oaks knew as Mungo-Mitchell; but now it was heavy with insolence. It said: "What should I be doing here, Chatterton?"—he laid a special emphasis on his consonants, so that *Chattterrtttonnn* sounded like some especially vicious term of abuse—"what should I be doing here?"

"They let you go?"

"No, they did nott. I wentt."

"Mungo," said Chatterton, "if you did anything rash, you're an idiot!"

"I didd do something rash, and I am nott an idiott, *Chattterrtttonnn*. You don'tt imagine for one momentt, I hope, thatt I proposedd to stand trial with my recordd?" Here Mungo-Mitchell laughed through his teeth. "Oh no. In for a penny, in for a poundd, old man. Swing one, swing all, what? I wentt to be chargedd like a little lamb, asked for a cigarette—it was at Martell Street Station—hit the bobby, made a dash for itt, divedd into the crowdd, and got away—bought an evening paper, walked slowly to the nearest Underground station, hopped a train in the rush hour for Cockfosters, got out at Finsbury Parkk, and made my way here by easy stages. Do you mindd, *Chattterrtttonnn*?"

"I think you are crazy," said Chatterton.

"I think nott, don't you see. I wasn'tt going to be leftt in the lurch. In for a penny, in for a poundd."

"You might have been followed, you fool!"

"I am nott a fool, and I was nott followed. Be a little more polite, *Chattterrtttonnn*."

Chatterton was silent for a couple of seconds. I saw something like a frame of piano wire stretching the skin of his lean throat while little hammers seemed to beat at temple and jaw.

Then he said: "Very well, Powell. Get into your uniform."

"I'm tired of wearing menials' uniforms, *Chattterrtttonnn*."

Everything vibrated faster. A long way behind me, something rumbled and slammed. Hearing this, Chatterton smiled again; the wires fell back into his throat, and the hammers ceased their beating under his face. He sighed pleasurably and, in a voice that made me shudder, quiet as it was, said: "Into your uniform, this instant, Powell!"

"At once, sir."

I must have made some sudden sound, or movement, then, because Chatterton turned his head sharply before I had time to close my eyes again. "My word!" he said, pleasantly, "you can take it, Kemp, can't you?"

"Where am I?" I asked.

"You're in Lord Kadmeel's private plane, Kemp.... Oh, Doctor!"

A white-smocked man with a stethoscope round his neck filled his place at the parting of the curtains; cool fingers explored my wrist and my eyelids. "Some of our guests get airsick, you know, or otherwise need medical attention, Kemp," I heard Chatterton say. "Keep him quiet, Doctor, will you please?"

Something pushed rather than pricked at the inside of my arm, and the engines roared as the night rushed down on me again.

This time it must have been morphine, because when I awoke again I felt myself smoothly sliding up out of a black pit in Time. My mouth was very dry, but I was too drowsily preoccupied with the tails of strange dreams that were scuttling back into their holes in the basement of my consciousness. I groped, found a deeply upholstered ledge, and hauled myself into a sitting position. There was a curtained window on my left. Looking out I saw a vivid sky and caught a dazzling flash of sunlight on a silver wing. Then a restrained voice said: "Coffee, sir?" and Chatterton's "man Powell" stood at my elbow, dressed in white now, like a steward, offering a large tray richly laid with massive silver covers. "I did not wish to disturb you, sir," he said, "so I took the liberty of bringing you some devilled kidneys, and some Virginia ham, and eggs. But if there is anything else you prefer—"

"—A cigarette?" I said, gulping orange juice.

"Virginian? Turkish? Egyptian, sir?" He offered a silver box of three compartments.

"Where's Oaks?" I asked.

"Mr. Oaks has breakfasted, sir, and is dressing. He was inquiring after you. If you will ring when you have finished, sir, I will prepare your shower, if you will tell me how you prefer it. Your clothes are being pressed, and I have laid out a fresh shirt, underwear and socks. Also a bathrobe. Will that be all, sir?"

"Thank you," I said, stupidly.

"Thank *you*, sir."

He went away, and then, discovering that I was hungry, I ate ravenously, and climbed out of bed. The sheets, I noticed, were of dark green silk. A pair of dark green slippers were placed heel to heel at an angle of forty-five degrees on the dense carpet, and there was a robe of the same colour at the foot of the bed. I found myself standing, half-stupefied with astonishment, in a small but most luxuriously appointed chamber, carpeted, curtained, upholstered, and painted all in dark green and silver. One felt rather than heard the engines, much as one feels rather than hears the purring of a sleepy, satisfied cat. The bathroom fittings were of solid silver. I shaved, showered, and dried myself with a dark green towel. Powell was waiting for me, standing like a graven image, pointing to my clothes which were carefully laid out on the bed, which had been skilfully made up in my brief absence.

"You will find all your money and things in their proper pockets, sir," he said, "only I took the liberty of putting away a certain . . . instrument, which I found in your left-hand inside breast pocket. I was sure you wouldn't need it." The mask of the valet slipped; he uncovered three teeth in a mean smile and, in the voice I had heard him use before the plane took off, he asked: "Where d'you buy your coshes? Swaine andd Adeney, or Cogswell andd Harrison? I have mine made upp for me by a fellow calledd Sim." Then, with horridly simulated obsequiousness: "Shall I brush your hair for you, sir?"

"Get out of here," I said.

"Yes, sir. Thank you, sir."

I dressed. There was a silver-edged panel in the wall that

had the appearance of a little door. I pushed it tentatively, and it turned on a pivot, swinging into view a well-stocked cocktail bar, from which I helped myself to a whisky and soda, after which, glass in hand, I parted the curtains through which Powell had passed on his way out. They covered a door. The door was locked. There was nothing to do, then, but sit in an easy chair and wait; which I did. Half an hour passed before the door opened again, and Chatterton came in.

"You know," he said, "even if I hadn't liked you and George in the first place I couldn't help liking you now. Do you know, that was a devilish clever trick of yours?"

"What was?" I asked.

He chuckled. "Ah, deep, deep! I tell you, no other two men in two million would have had the presence of mind to keep their pistol and their blackjack in their pockets, confronted by guns as you were last night. You know, that was deucedly clever of you and George, Kemp! Your assumption was, of course, that we'd assume that if you had had weapons, you'd have tried to use them: *ergo* we wouldn't bother to search you later on. And we wouldn't have, either, you know. Only the Kad hates a sloppy appearance, d'you see, and we generally get people tidied up a bit before we present 'em. Otherwise we'd never have dreamed of going over your pockets. Dashed smart! I respect you for that. You know, I really believe we *are* going to get along together, once you begin to see eye to eye with us, what?"

I could only laugh, somewhat bitterly, at the memory of an advantage forgotten; but Chatterton misconstrued my laugh. He said: "Oh no, really, if it had just been a matter of hauling you along, we'd never have twigged that little ruse. Only the Kad likes everything just so, and his word is law . . . well, more or less. . . . Now let's go and get George, shall we?"

He opened the door and led me through a corridor into a dark green lounge curiously panelled with pale green glass behind which, at cunningly-measured distances, lay exquisitely-painted panoramas of strange seas and beautiful landfalls. Standing in the centre of this room, and slowly turning, a man might imagine that Satan had taken him to the top of a high mountain, and was showing him all the kingdoms of the earth . . . until he put out his hand to touch the middle distance, and felt a window, and saw through it to the heart of the illusion.

George Oaks was there, looking remarkably spruce, with a knife-edge crease in his trousers and a glowing polish on his shoes, smoking a cigarette and drinking a bottle of Bass. As soon as he saw me he said, with some indignation: "Albert, while I was asleep, they actually gave me a haircut!" Then he came close to me, holding up the long beer-glass, and his eyes, holding mine, were deadly serious as he said: "Will you do as I do, Albert? A Bass?"

I took his meaning, and said, easily: "Why, of course, I'll do as you do, George."

"You couldn't do better," he said, with an almost imperceptible wink, and turned to press a button. An attendant appeared immediately. "Mr. Kemp will do as I do. A Bass, without."

"Without, sir?"

"Without chloral hydrate. . . . Well, Chatterton, what now?"

"Well, now you drink your beer, and then you come and see Lord Kadmeel, George," said Chatterton.

"But where the devil *are* we?" I asked.

"Oh, somewhere close to the coast of Labrador, I fancy," said Chatterton, easily; and, smiling at my exclamation of astonishment, he added: "This is the Kad's own extra-special Stratoliner, you know, and you've been bye-byes a dozen hours or more, don't you see. We'll land fairly soon, I think."

"Up in the north of Quebec, where you took Kurt Brevis, eh?" said George Oaks.

"Perhaps," said Chatterton.

George Oaks said: "He played you for a sucker, didn't he?"

"Oh no, George, not in the long run he didn't. All's well that ends well, you know."

"Chatterton," said George Oaks, "only the God can see the end. Meanwhile, haven't you observed that all along the line His hand has been against you?"

"As I see it, quite the reverse," said Chatterton. "We must go into this at our leisure."

"I'll tell you in the Condemned Cell, if I live, Chatterton."

"Very necessary saving clause, that, George," said Chatterton.

A bell tingled very musically—a silver bell, no doubt. Chatterton said: "The Lord Kadmeel will see you now. Come along."

And so he led us into the presence of Lord Kadmeel, the Chief of the Sciocrats.

Over-insistence on a colour, like the perpetual repetition of a single note, drives some men mad. As I stepped into Lord Kadmeel's saloon, I caught myself gritting my teeth, and saying to myself: *Now, some more dark green!* And, surely enough, there it was, that same succulent decor picked out with silver. Only here large glass tanks were built into the walls, and in these tanks swam a fantastic diversity of brilliantly coloured and oddly shaped tropical fishes. Lord Kadmeel was contemplating four sea-horses in a tank by themselves. When the door closed, he turned to confront us—a large, sullen, fat man in a smoking-jacket of dark-green brocade. Then he put his hands behind him, and said, in a slow thick voice which made me think of the sluggish bubbling of boiling porridge: "They can sit down, Chatterton."

"Won't you have a pew, George? Kemp?" said Chatterton.

We sat.

"They may smoke if they like," said Lord Kadmeel.

George Oaks said to Chatterton: "Tell your master that Albert Kemp and George Oaks, having knocked about the world a little, will make shift to understand him without the aid of an interpreter, however wretchedly he mishandles the King's English. Make it clear to him that if he has anything to say to us, he will say it direct, or not at all. Construe!"

"Better humour them, I think, sir," said Chatterton.

Lord Kadmeel said: "I don't see why I should—but, well, if you like. It can't make any difference, ultimately . . ." Then to us: "You have given us some trouble. *I* believe, more trouble than you are worth. It remains to be seen. If you prove to be more trouble than you are worth, you'll be written off. Do you understand?"

George Oaks said: "I wish you would look at me if you are talking to me, instead of watching your reflection in that fish tank. Understand you? I'd understand you better if you cleared your throat. Say what you have to say. Come to the point."

"The point," said Lord Kadmeel, "the point is this. Firstly: Chatterton is convinced that you are in possession of some information which may be useful to Us. We have means of extracting information—means which We do not hesitate to use. Why should We hesitate? But Chatterton is opposed to Our using these means except as a last resort because . . . Secondly: Chatterton has a remarkably high opinion of your ability in general. By 'ability' I mean, of course, your potential usefulness to Us. He argues, not without reason, that if We were to have recourse to . . . compulsion, you could not possibly afterwards be of any service to Us. By the time We had finished with you, you would only be a charge upon Us if We kept you alive; so that, naturally, We should in that case have you destroyed. Chatterton is of the opinion that once Our intentions, together with the inevitability of their fulfilment, are made clear to you, you will become one with Us. The decision rests with you. You will give Us, fully and freely, all information in your possession which may be in any way of service to Us. If you do not give to Us fully and freely, We will take from you by inches. If you are for Us, you live in comfort and with dignity. If you are against Us, you die. And if you withhold one crumb of the truth from Us, you will pray for death. I hope Chatterton may be right. He generally is. . . . They can go now, Chatterton. Take them away."

He turned back to the sea-horses, and Chatterton conducted us back to the panoramic room, and when we were seated, with full glasses in our hands, he said: "Well, George? Well, Kemp? What do you think?"

Now George Oaks put on an air of resignation, and said: "You have us here, twenty thousand feet above the open sea, and you say 'What do you think?' What would you think, if you were me?"

"You didn't talk like that to the Kad, did you, though, George?"

"I don't like him. He got me the sack for riding in his private lift. Besides, one has one's dignity. Eh, Albert?"

"I don't like him either," I said.

"Oh, but, my dear fellows, you don't have to *like* the Kad! I mean to say, how could one? You'll never see him, anyway. It's just a question of being sensible, that's all. You don't have to like, say, your Troop Sergeant-Major, but you've jolly well got to ride with him for your own sake, and everybody else's, haven't you? Likes and dislikes don't signify. I quite like a whole lot of Turks, for instance, but that didn't stop my killing quite a few of them in Mesopotamia. And I can assure you that while I've had the pleasure of knocking over a number of Prussians in my time, some of my best friends were Jerries; and I've never disliked any of the men I've killed one tenth as much as a fellow in my mess called Braithwaite, for the privilege of cutting whose throat I would have given ten years of my life . . . And he saved my life, in the end! And do you know, because he saved my life I hated him worse than ever. . . . Let's not talk of likes and dislikes. Let's take the long view, George, shall we? Emotion aside, like sensible people; let's be adult. Friendship . . . likes . . . dislikes . . . love-of-country . . . really, now, you and I have lived long enough to know these catch-phrases for what they are worth. You surely must know, George, that if the End is good, it justifies the Means?"

"Perfectly," said George Oaks. "There is only one snag. From where a man starts, it is not given to him to see the End. The Ultimate is always a dream. The End is never better than a hope. The only facts within your control are the Means, Chatterton. And your vision—you being only a man—is so limited that every Means must be in itself an End. And so, poor man, you follow a broken thread in a dark maze, and are lost. Lenin, for instance, imagined that he could see a noble End; and out of his Means came Stalin—and where, then, was the glory and the dream? Again———"

"———There isn't all the time in the world, George," said Chatterton, gently. "The metaphysics, or whatever you call it, can wait. You will meet all kinds of Thinkers where we are going, and can argue away to your heart's content. Let's take things in their proper order, shall we? I want to tell you this: first and foremost, I must have everything you know. You must open your heart, George, you really must, you know."

"Say I do tell all I know, what then?" asked George Oaks.

"Why, then, after a certain probationary period, you and Kemp become one of Us, and you are in clover."

"And if I don't open my heart?"

"Believe me, George," said Chatterton, "you will, you will! But, as the Kad said, if you don't talk willingly, and We have to compel you to talk, you'll be not much use to man or beast afterwards, so that We'd put you to sleep, eventually, if only for your own sake, you know. Oh, don't misunderstand me, George— We don't go in for thumb-screws, and racks, and strappados, and rubber truncheons, and what not, unless a case particularly calls for that kind of questioning. (It would astonish you, by the way, to see the figures: imaginative men hold out like the very devil against common or garden medieval torture; whereas they spill their guts at the touch of a needle.) No, no, We have a brilliant German neurologist who deals with these matters. He is tabulating his findings, and—this stuff is too deep for me, of course —is working on a quite ponderous treatise provisionally entitled 'Human Endurance and its Limits' . . . For goodness sake, George, do let us see eye to eye!"

George Oaks was busy with his left thumb, profoundly engrossed as only a nail-biter can be. Chatterton turned to me, idly rolling the stem of his glass between his long fingers. "Really, you know, Kemp, it would interest you too—you being a writer, and a student of human reactions, and all that kind of thing. Dr. Treit would fascinate you. He is one of the fellows that started to tabulate, among other things, human resistance to extremes of heat and cold, you know, in some concentration camp or other in Poland. Quite a character, Kemp—right up your street—just your pigeon. Purely scientific, you know—actually measures screams of agony in decibels, I believe, and makes graphs. Relaxes with the *lieder* of Schubert; tears run down his cheeks. Oh, I promise you, We can provide you with some unique material. Dr. Treit works, for instance, with a psychologist, Dr. Scarlatti, who is putting together some kind of rigmarole about 'Sanity in Relation to Applied Fear'. . . . You don't say much, Kemp, but that doesn't fool me, you know. You are as deep as the sea. Now do reason with George; you might save Us quite a bit of trouble, and yourself quite literally a *Hell* of a lot of unpleasantness."

I said: "Granting that. I still don't see, for example, what use I could be to you and your Sciocrats. I'm an old-fashioned storyteller, with old-fashioned moral values. I can't see any place or use for me in your new world. I don't see where I come into it. I don't fit into your scheme of things at all."

Chatterton looked hard at me for a second or two, then smiled; and with engaging frankness said: "Intelligent of you, Kemp! I'll be open with you, old fellow. To tell you the truth: if it comes to your fitting into Our scheme of things, well, you don't, and you can't. Your usefulness to Us is of an immediate nature, you know."

I laughed. "You can't get blood out of a stone," I said. "You can't get information out of me, because I haven't got any."

Chatterton replied: "I'm inclined to believe you, Kemp. I shouldn't be surprised if, on inquiry, We get nothing out of you, because you have nothing to give. But George, here, *has* something to give, I'm sure; and you are his friend, you know. So— since you force me to put it brutally—if the worst comes to the worst, we'll have to work on you in George's presence. Get the idea? I hate to be like this, but needs must . . . Needless to say, if you fellows see reason, nobody will get hurt. Savvy, George?"

George Oaks said: "Forgive me, old friend, for getting you into this."

I said: "Wouldn't have missed it for the world." What else could I say?

"After all, you know, inside another year, the world—as it will stand then—will have to accept the accomplished fact, and jolly well like it," said Chatterton.

Then he began to talk rapidly, and for the first time I saw something like animation in his set, sardonic face. The game now, he told us, was entirely in the hands of the Sciocrats. They held the grand slam. The Kadmeel Bathysphere had completed its survey of the great rocky barriers under the northern Atlantic Ocean and the Bering Straits. While the old gentlemen of the Geographical Societies had been chirping their applause, and Rear-Admiral Elm, who was nominally in charge of the expeditions, had been made an F.R.S., Kadmeel's men had been sounding the sunken mountain ranges for certain delicate spots. At a hundred points, stupendous masses of rock—billions of tons of it—were kept securely in position by their own weight, and the weight of the water above. At one place, for example, a few hundred miles off the North American coast, there was a rock formation comparable in extent, if not in height, to the Alps, which was kept in place by a species of natural keystone, which one well-placed atom bomb would knock out. Two more bombs, and the whole mass would totter; and then the pressure of the water would send it thundering down. It was clearly ascertained, beyond argument, that one hundred and fifty atomic mines of a certain magnitude were all that the Sciocrats needed to blast the sunken mountain ranges so that the hot waters of the Gulf Stream would rush to the polar ice . . .

Then, with sparkling eyes, Chatterton made articulate his savage visions of the moment when the hot water of the Equator met the bitter polar ice. Then, ah then, Kadmeel should indeed cut loose the foaming white horses of Poseidon, the Thunderer, and set free the thirty-two Winds of God! Hot air would strike cold air, and spin away in such whirlwinds as this earth had never seen since the Lord God Almighty divided the land from the waters; and roaring down under the lash of these winds would come the irresistible, the pitiless sea. Nothing that the combined civilisations of the world might do could possibly save them.

Grinning with glee, he drew a dreadful picture of the crashing of great cities, dwelling lingeringly on the destruction of New York—the panic flight of millions, mad with fear before a two-hundred-mile-an-hour hurricane—the wall of green water five hundred feet high falling with the weight of a mountain upon Manhattan—and, at last, a sullen, heaving waste of waters broken here and there by the battered upper part of a sodden skyscraper . . . Philadelphia, Washington, and Boston would be completely inundated. All centres of government, and of heavy industry, would be washed away. The mad winds would scream inland, destroying everything. Chatterton saw the vast deserts of Utah, and Arizona, and California, picked up like so many shovelsful of loose sand, and hurled upon the cities of the west, obliterating them, while the great rivers, now arms of the sea, burst their banks, and turned the fertile valleys into brackish lakes. And over all, the rolling thunder, the jagged lightning, and the pelting hail.

England would practically cease to exist. Chatterton was rather sorry about this, but it simply could not be helped. Of the whole of Europe, indeed, little would remain; only the mountains and the uplands, rocky, stripped naked by tempests, and cold, cold, bitterly cold! The south of Russia, "Russia's breadbasket", together with the Russian industrial centres, would lie fathoms deep. Flood and storm would thrash the life out of the north and central Russian cities, because the great snow wildernesses of the Siberias would melt and inundate the south and the west. The jungles and the plains of South America would go to the fishes. Australia would become a lagoon . . .

And when, at last, the turbulent waters, having found their level, subsided, there would be a new world ready to hand—a manœuvrable world of some few score million able-bodied survivors. They *had* to be the cream of the population, didn't we see? Otherwise they wouldn't survive, would they? A nice, not-unwieldly population, naked, clinging to the rocks and crying for bread. Now here was where the Sciocrats stepped in. Having planned this situation, of course, they were in a position to deal with it. In many different places—in the Rocky Mountains, Canada, the Andes, the Himalayas, the Apennines, etcetera, the Sciocrats had prepared immense strongholds in which were stored fabulous supplies of food, clothing, medical equipment, and, of course, arms and ammunition, tools of all sorts, seeds, and so forth. For years now, Chatterton reminded us, the newspapers had periodically been trying to inquire into the circumstances in which countless millions of tons of wheat had mysteriously disappeared from the markets of the world. He could solve that mystery, he said, with a laugh . . . But why did we look so shocked? The Sciocrats were simply hastening a natural evolutionary process. The Great Wash was bound to occur in the course of nature, only gradually, in about five or six hundred years.

Five or six hundred years hence, everybody now living would be dead and forgotten, anyway . . . And the way things were going, it was more than likely that in a couple of hundred years Mankind would lapse again into complete barbarism. Actually, the Sciocrats proposed to save humanity from another Dark Age, and now that they had Kurt Brevis's Megatopic Silicon Bomb, nothing in the world could stop them. A dozen great plants, operating ostensibly for the manufacture of rayon and nylon fibres in various parts of the world, would go into production immediately.

He concluded: "We have uranium, of course. The Kad, among others, is under contract to supply the stuff to the United Nations. There's plenty of it, I may say, that the United Nations do not know about on the Kad's land in Canada. But it's tedious stuff, uranium, you know; and slow, devilish slow. However, all's well that ends well, George. What say you, Kemp?"

We said nothing. Chatterton rose. "Well, my lads, I shan't bore you any more for now. I daresay you'd like to talk things over quietly. I'll leave you to it. Help yourself to anything you want, and if you can't find it, just ring for it. Toodle-oo!"

And he left the room. The door locked itself behind him.

"Courage, Albert," said George Oaks, when we were alone.

"I'll need it," said I. Then, in a whisper: "I hope they left those buttons on that fancy suit of yours." I was thinking now —quite calmly, to my pleasurable surprise—of cyanide.

He whispered back: "They took only the gun. I can't see how they overlooked those buttons—they pass only a casual glance; and that valet pressed the suit, and thoroughly too——" He stopped then, snapped his fingers, and clutched at his temples. "—I have an idea," he whispered between his teeth, "a mad idea, a wild idea. . . . God give me strength, Who gave me my photographic memory! . . . Or have I drunk it away? . . . No, no! The *helix*, by the God, the *helix!* . . . Albert, do as I do, do as I say: all hope depends on it! In a second I'm going to ring for Chatterton's 'man Powell'. I'll talk to him. You stand behind him. Then, when I give you the signal, clap me a Nelson on him, get his head down, and hold him fast. Your cue is the word 'Back'! Now . . ."

He pressed the bell-push, and Chatterton's man came in, carefully closing the door behind him, and said, with that simper of his which so brazenly invited the back of one's hand: "You rang, sir?"

"You might mix us a Stinger," said George Oaks.

The man bowed, and busied himself with a bottle of brandy and a flask of white crème de menthe.

Oaks went on: "You're a little of everything, aren't you, Mungo? You must have quite a quick eye, or you could never have learned to measure out your jiggers as you do from the customer's side of a cocktail bar. Clever fellow, Mungo."

"My name is nott Mungo. If you happen to recognise me, and wish to address me by my real name, call me Mungo-Mitchell, will you? . . . Your cocktails, gentlemen. Will thatt be all?"

"Not quite," said George Oaks. "Mungo-Mitchell! I know all about Mungo-Mitchell. The grandfather made a fortune dealing in woollen rags, which he tore up and re-processed into shoddy cloth. Hence, his nickname 'Mungo', which is a slang word for tailors' cuttings. Nickname stuck so hard that his wife, the grandmother, hooked it on to the surname with a hyphen. . . . Any rags, bottles, or bones, Mungo? Now, now, take it easy! Better get a curved spine humping a ragbag in Bradford than a *bloody back* in Pentonville——"

——And on the word, my hands went up under the man's armpits, and came down clasped at the nape of his neck, so that, taken off his guard, he crouched helpless in my grip, hissing with agony. "Good, good!" whispered George Oaks, "hold him a second." He pulled up the white jacket, and snatched loose the shirt and under-vest. I saw the man's back, china-white, wiry, absolutely unblemished. "Let him be, Albert."

The man straightened himself with difficulty, fighting for breath and grimacing with pain. "Tuck your shirt in, my son," George Oaks whispered, smiling and rubbing his hands in an ecstasy of quiet delight. "No, Glory Be, I still co-ordinate and turn over! . . . It wasn't that I recognised you, Mungo, old man; it was that, all of a sudden, I did *not* recognise you. I was in court for my paper when Mungo-Mitchell was charged in the Mayfair Jewellery Case. His profile was towards me part of the time; I noted the helix of his right ear. Yours didn't fit what I remembered, so, to check, I had to have a look at your back. Mungo-Mitchell got the 'Cat', and the 'Cat' leaves unmistakable marks. Your back is like a baby's, Praise Be to the God! Now, tell me—if you aren't Mungo-Mitchell, who the devil are you?"

The man called Mungo-Mitchell said: "Drink your cocktails while I mix another. I'll have one too, I think. . . . What the devil have you done with my neck?——"

He spoke, now, in quite a different voice, in a plain, unaf-fected accent. "—There's no need to whisper, by the way; you're in one of the Kad's private salons; it isn't wired for sound, and there are no peep-holes. . . .

"Who the devil am I? Never mind . . .

"As for Mungo-Mitchell, he's still 'inside' on account of a matter touching security, and I had plenty of opportunity to study him. He was, as I daresay you know, at school with Chat-terton; Chatterton's fag at Longchester. When Mungo-Mitchell was in the Third Form, Chatterton was a prefect; Chatterton was his tin god. Given a superficial resemblance to Mungo-Mitchell, plus data, and I—well, it wasn't at all difficult, after twenty-odd years, to establish identity——"

He spoke hurriedly, now. "—I'm sorry you're here, but at the same time I'm glad. Remember, my life's in your hands. Take your cue from me, and we'll talk when we get the chance. Mean-while, remember. The wind is up. Chatterton knows that there's somebody he has good cause to be afraid of. He thinks, now, that he's got that man—meaning you. For God's sake, let him think so. I'm sorry, but that's how it's got to be."

He turned to me. "I'm afraid you'll be the first to get it, Mr. Kemp, but if it comes to that I'll try to see to it that you don't know what's happening to you. Bear up. It's only a matter of time now."

Then, in as long as it takes for a lock to click, he changed. As the door slid open, and Chatterton strode in, the man clenched his fist on a cocktail glass so that it broke between his fingers, and stood, quivering, gibbering with rage, while George Oaks, pro-vocatively smiling, sang, admirably imitating a huckster's voice: "Mungo! Mungo! Mungo-o-o-o! Pot o' geranyums for a pair o' ol' trousis! Any rags, bo'lls, or bo'ones! Mungo-o-o-o!"

The man threw the broken glass to the floor and, turning to Chatterton, cried passionately: "Whatt have you been saying to them aboutt me?"

"What's up?" asked Chatterton.

George Oaks said: "Oh, I went into Mungo's genealogical tree, that's all."

Chatterton laughed, and said: "Poor old Mungo. We used to give you hell about it at Longchester, didn't we?"

"Lett me hitt him, Chatterton! I wantt to hitt him!"

"Try Mr. Kemp," said Chatterton—whereupon, turning suddenly, the man called Mungo-Mitchell seemed to fly rather than leap at me, and hit me with such a concentration of fury that I fell back into a chair. The end was ridiculous. Half-sitting, half-lying, I caught him between my knees in what they call a "scissors", and squeezed him until he collapsed gasping, buzzing and writhing like a knocked-down wasp, while Chatterton, still shaking with silent laughter, said: "Now tidy up, and get out. . . . You'll have lunch in about a quarter of an hour—dinner-time for me, of course; but you breakfasted rather late. We land in a couple of hours or so."

Carrying the broken glass, Mungo-Mitchell (as I will call him) left the room. "He's all right, really, you know," said Chatterton. "Bit of an inferiority complex, perhaps—sensitive, and all that. Considering his background, didn't have much chance, you know. But loyal; loyal as hell; trust him with my life, and yours too, George. Hope he didn't bother you, Kemp. Glad you put him in his place. Do him good. Mentally, he's still in the Third Form at Longchester. I used to lick him with an ash-plant when he burned my toast, or pinched my marmalade. . . . Want any books to read? Play chess, backgammon, cards? . . . No? . . . Then I'll leave you to it. Don't forget to ring if you want anything. And do think matters over carefully, won't you? Be seeing you. Ta-ta for now!"

After lunch we looked out of the window. Now we could see a kind of velvety, dark-green downland . . . but they were not downs, they were high, almost mountainous uplands, overgrown with fir, spruce, and maple trees. . . . We were coming down. A blinding white zig-zag appeared, and a great shining blot: a river and a lake; but it was as if a crucible had cracked, spilling molten steel. Soon, on a high plateau, far below, I saw something like a broken game of dominoes. The pieces became great oblong buildings. A runway came slapping up like a driving-belt, and we were in Lord Kadmeel's Canadian stronghold.

Part Ten

Chatterton sniffed the air as he walked with us to our quarters. "Distinctly autumnal," he said. "You'll love it when the maple trees turn red. The winters, of course, are devilish cold, but don't worry, we'll keep you snug. . . . Ah, here we are. Not much to look at from the outside, is it?" He was waving his hand towards a kind of gargantuan dish-cover of glass and grey metal. It looked like some contrivance by means of which a zoologist might observe the habits of imprisoned beetles. Some such thought occurred to George Oaks, for he said: "I see the slide, Chatterton. Where's the bloody microscope?"

"Microscope? Oh, ha-ha, oh yes . . . Oh, it looks a bit public, but it isn't at all. It's an improved model of the Iwerks 'Utopia Dwelling'. Pull a lever, and you are curtained off. Press a button, and all the dust and ashes are whisked away through vents in the walls and ceilings and floors. You want coffee at such-and-such a time? Set a dial, and up she pops, piping hot. Not that you'll need even to press a button, you know, because I've delegated a couple of efficient men to look after you." Chatterton smiled. "My man Powell, George; and your friend Oettle, Kemp. I believe you'll find that Oettle, a single-minded man, Kemp, has one ambition —to have a crack at you when you can't take him by surprise. I'm afraid you hurt his feelings, you know. Oh, that reminds me, gratters on a jolly good show. However, Oettle won't bother you if you behave yourself. No point in your doing otherwise, you know."

He touched a spring, and a panel opened, and then we were inside. Floors, walls, and furniture were all—oh, how I loathed that colour!—dark green. The very bindings of the books on the shelves were dark green stamped with silver.

"Airy lounge," said Chatterton, "cosy dining-room, two bedrooms, excellent bath, and usual etceteras. Quarters for two servants—they'll sleep on the premises, you know, but it's quite all right—they have a separate bathroom. They'll give you a

menu every morning, and you just tick off anything you happen
to fancy for lunch and dinner; the Kad's own chef will prepare
it—he's Grabo, you know, late of Lichen's, Berlin—so you
may repose every confidence in him. His refrigerators are well
stocked, I assure you . . . As for clothes, a word to Powell will get
you anything you want. Better stock up, George; you'll be with
us quite a time . . . you too, Kemp, let us hope. Our tailor here
has a remarkable gadget. Singer of Rome invented it. Too costly
for practical commercial use, of course, but we have it. You step
into a sort of Iron Maiden, only instead of spikes there are tens
of thousands of little rods that slide back where they touch you,
and so record every nook and cranny of your bally outline. Too
damned perfect for my liking, but it'll turn you out as if you'd
been poured into your clothes in a matter of hours. . . . Just
make yourself at home. . . .

"Oh yes; important thing: you are going to receive a signal
honour tonight. Some of the Council want to look at you!"

"And who the hell are they?" asked George Oaks.

Chatterton laughed. "Oh, why don't you come off it?" he
said. "You'll have to be frank with us in the end, you know, so
why act dumb? . . . However, to humour you: six of the Council
are here, or will be tonight, and the one who particularly wants
to say how-d'ye-do to you is the Maharajah of Pur. Also present
will be Mr. Tarrytowne; Romagna, of Italy; M. Janvier Simplon
of France; and Van Weenen of South Africa."

"And the rest?" asked George Oaks, watching Chatterton's
face. Chatterton smiled and shook his head.

"Of course, of course!" cried Oaks, snapping his fingers.

Chatterton said: "Do stop acting dumb, George; it's an awful
bore, and such a waste of time."

He touched a button. Mungo-Mitchell and Oettle appeared
behind him. He said to them: "See that Mr. Oaks and Mr. Kemp
are comfortable," and to us: "Better make up your minds not
to be uncooperative, you know. A little dickybird tells me that
things are going to happen in a Dickens of a hurry now. You will
be all cleaned up by ten o'clock, won't you? Good-bye, now."

He turned on his heel and went out.

Oettle stood motionless, looking at me.

I said: "Headache better?"

He said nothing, but Mungo-Mitchell giggled, and said: "Show the gentlemen your operation, Karl."

Oettle lifted his great chin, and we saw that the centre of his throat was horribly scarred and curiously sunken. "Three of his prisoners triedd to kill him with a knife," said Mungo-Mitchell. "He has no larynx. Dumb . . . Tea, gentlemennn? Or, perhaps, a cocktail? May I suggestt dinner for seven-thirty this evening, since you have an appointmentt att ten? . . . Oh yes, Karl, wouldd you mindd fetching menus andd wine lists?"

With a last slow look at me, Oettle left the room. I heard his heavy tread on the concrete path.

Then Mungo-Mitchell said: "These houses *are* wired for sound, I warn you. I've disconnected, for a few minutes . . . Oh damn the luck, and blast your photographic eyes, Oaks! You, of all the men in the world, have to be in court when Mungo-Mitchell goes up for trial!"

"Does that matter so very much?" asked Oaks.

"Yes, it does. They know there's one man in the world, somewhere, whom they have reason to fear. Chatterton is comfortably convinced, at present, that that man is you, Oaks. That was all right with me, because I calculated on their taking a few days before getting to work on Kemp, and afterwards on you. And even if you had had to go through the questioning then, it would still have been all right—in the interests of the Job, I mean—because what you didn't know you couldn't talk about. But now you do know one thing—that I am not Mungo-Mitchell—and knowing, believe me, eventually you'll tell; and when you tell, they'll know that *I* am the man they want. And that will be the end of me and the Job. Why didn't I tell you this on the plane? Because I've only just heard that the Council are having a look at you tonight. That means they'll get to work on you very soon now. Now, for God's sake, temporise, procrastinate, use your wits, play for time. A few days will see us through, with luck. Meanwhile, in case—*just in case*—eat very light tonight; eat very, very light. You, Kemp, especially."

"Why?" I asked.

But then Oettle's step sounded outside, and Mungo-Mitchell darted to the bar and all in one movement took out two tumblers and a bottle, so that when Oettle came in with menu and wine-list (bound in dark-green leather) he was meticulously measuring Scotch whisky, and simpering: "Soda, sir?"

"Water," said Oaks, sullenly, taking the menu. "What do you fancy for dinner, Albert?"

I said: "My nose hurts like the devil, and I've got a headache. An omelette is all I want."

"I shan't be hungry until much later," said Oaks. "I'll have the same for now. And see that mine is moist, Mungo—just about as moist as your grandfather's rags were when he damped them down to tip the scales another couple of pounds—in other words, not as dry as it appears on the surface. But see that there's something cold for supper about midnight."

"Wine, sir?"

"Hock. Ask the cellar-man for something decent. Don't use your own discretion. I trust you with filthy cocktails, nothing more. And one other thing: try and let us see as little of you as possible, will you? And that goes for your boy-friend, too. You both reek of the gaols. Scram!"

I gulped my drink, and mixed another, for my throat had become suddenly dry and tight. "I wonder what happens now," I said.

Tipping a wink in the direction of the curved wall, and touching one of his ears, Oaks said: "Question us, I suppose. Chatterton sounded as if he meant business."

"You don't seriously believe he means to torture us, do you?" I asked.

"I don't know, old friend. Why not? The Russians do it every day. Whenever they bring up for trial a prisoner who's too big for secret disposal, why, do you think, that prisoner invariably pleads guilty—even an iron man like Cardinal Minszenty, for example, who is beyond the ordinary tremors of the flesh and the spirit, and believes in Hell, to boot?"

I said: "All right. I can understand their torturing a man to make him say, in a public statement, exactly what they want him to say. But what's the use of torturing us if we don't know what they want us to tell them? You might as well, say, twist a Scotsman's arm to make him talk Greek."

"Just so, Albert, old friend," said George Oaks, gently. "But suppose you were convinced that this Scotsman really could talk Greek and was holding out on you?"

I knew, almost telepathically, how he wanted me to react to this, and my voice really broke as I cried: "But damn it all, what do I know? Nothing, nothing! Damn you, I believe you knew about Monty Cello all along, when you dragged me off to the Savoy! And that 'Regent Lambert' man he was supposed to get in touch with—he or Kurt Brevis—by God, George, I've got it now! *You are Regent Lambert!*"

George Oaks winked at me, but his voice faltered a little as he said: "Now . . . don't be silly, Albert. If it were as you say, why should I drag you into it? Where would you come into the picture?"

"I'll tell you where," I said. "You knew I loved and trusted you. You knew I'd follow you to the ends of the earth. You wanted a man with a strong arm, a loyal heart and a thick head—that's why I fitted into your picture!" I threw down my glass, and stepped very close to him, standing over him, so that he could whisper if need be.

And whisper he did: "*Strangle me.*" Then, aloud: "Albert! Alb——"

I took him by the throat, not very hard, and shook him, shouting: "You got me into this mess—you've got to get me out of it!"

And then my arms were pinned to my sides. Oettle had me from behind. Not drugged now with delight of battle, I was appalled by the strength of the man. Still, I butted him in the face with the back of my head before I submitted and became limp; whereupon he tossed me on to a settee. Mungo-Mitchell was there, too. He said: "Oh dear! No trouble, I hope?"

George Oaks gasped: "Nothing, nothing."

I said: "Sorry, George. Lost my temper. Nerves."

"Give us another drink, Mungo, and get to hell out of here . . . Calm, calm, Albert . . . It'll all come right in the end."

"I'm sorry, George."

When we were alone again, he winked at me, and we sat in silence after that, waiting for time to pass. But time seemed to have stopped. George Oaks was deep in thought, and I was in the clutch of cold, naked Fear.

Chatterton came in at nine o'clock, dressed, now, in a dinner-suit; only the double-breasted jacket was dark green, with velvet lapels. He noticed my look of exacerbated distaste, and said: "Bit on the bizarre side, perhaps, but the Kad finds the colour sooth-ing, so We all wear it for the evening—all except old Pur; he won't come out of those off-white rompers of his. . . . Dinner all right? Let's have some brandy—don't look at me like that, George; I'll drink some too, this time. . . . I hear that you birds have been having a bit of a row."

"Who said so?" asked George Oaks.

"Oh, Powell told me. What a fire-eater you are, Kemp! You made Oettle's nose bleed again. But there seems to be electricity in the air this evening. Eve of the Battle, and all that, you know. I tell you, the Big Boys are like so many over-trained bantam-weights in the dressing-room five minutes before a champion-ship fight. They were practically scratching each other's eyes out at dinner, and H.R.H. the Maharajah of Pur went into such a pet that he didn't eat his lentils. Can you imagine it? Revenues, ten million pounds per annum; hereditary reserve in gold and precious stones, incalculable. He has drawn on his Reserves to the extent of three hundred million pounds in the past three years, to my certain knowledge, and has scarcely scratched the surface of his capital. And he lives on lentils and sour milk! . . . Tarrytowne nearly lost his temper, too, but he managed to get through the best part of a young turkey. . . ."

He handed us great brandy-bubbles filled with fragrance. "Ah!" said George Oaks, inhaling, "this is the breath the God breathed into the grape! . . . What was it all about?"

"Question of manpower; nothing more. Some kind of argu-ment is inevitable, of course. You see, every one of the Council has, in the name of the Council, absolute control over a given area, where his particular stronghold is situated. Lord Kadmeel, for example, has Western Europe and Canada. Tarrytowne has the lower half of the North American Continent dominated by the Rockies. Pur has the northern half of what will be left of India—which will be the best part of India. Van Weenen (you know, the Diamond Syndicate) has all Africa south of the Equator; while the froggy, Simplon, has Africa north of the Equator: the whole of the Sahara will be under water, of course, and the 'Dark Heart' of the Continent will be a huge inland sea . . .

"Well, to cut a long story short—now that We come to the point of actually shifting our carefully selected (you might say, highly exclusive) population groups, there comes the inevitable palaver, you know. You understand how it is.

"The Maharajah of Pur, for example, complains that, when the waters subside, he will find himself with too many peasants and soldiers, as opposed to Kadmeel's and Tarrytowne's skilled technicians, artisans, and heavy-industry men. He wants Us to start immediately on a system of Decanting desirable couples— in effect, swapping bits of population. It can't be done, of course —it would attract too much attention.

"The wisest course is the course We are at present pursuing, and have been pursuing these past five years: to skim Our cream-of-the-cream of the population, teaspoonful by teaspoonful, into cold storage in Our Walled Cities—*you* know of them as hush-hush factories—and rely upon them, and the weapons at Our disposal, *plus* the prevailing chaos against which We'll be fore-armed. When the survivors of Our little cataclysm come crawling up Our slopes like so many flies out of a milk-pot, We'll be quite numerous enough and strong enough to dry 'em off, or chuck 'em back, at Our leisure . . .

"We don't need a very densely populated world, you know." Chatterton sipped his brandy.

"And so We start a clean, new breed of men. Any swapping will have to be done after the Flood. . . . There'll have to be quite extensive sorting out by a process of elimination, even of the survivors, you know. We'll be able to get along very nicely indeed with a world population of not more than ten millions. Because, don't you see, it will take a little time for the New Continents to dry off and grow fertile . . .

"And, in the meantime, Our Selected Population will be

breeding, naturally—but not breeding indiscriminately, need-less to say. We'll check and double-check 'em from conception to birth; pick 'em like pups. No runts, no scrubs—only the cream-of-the-cream. That's what Nature does, in the last analysis, isn't it?"

George Oaks said: "All resolved, eh?"

"Oh, yes," said Chatterton. "We have Our little differences, naturally. But We realise that it's all for one, and one for all, now. . . . One allows, naturally, for little idiosyncrasies. Pur, for instance, has a bias in favour of his country's gods. Two gen-erations of the very Decanting he proposes will soon wash all that nonsense away; because, don't you see, under the Sciocrats, every man, in his own right, will be in his way a God."

"What for?" asked George Oaks.

Chatterton ignored this. "Idiosyncrasies . . ." he said, with a short laugh. "Romagna, for example, wants to revive the old Roman Games, but on a modern scale. . . . There was nearly quite a scandal, once; he had two blindfold men walk a race over a course dotted with electrified studs; killed 'em both. Has an idea for a chess game between two masters, on a field with living pieces; every piece taken, to be killed on the spot; pawns armed with spears, knights with axes, the rest with swords; losing king to take poison. One indulges such fancies, what? A lot less bloody and vastly more amusing than a World War, don't you think? . . .

"However; the way things are, We're going to have to hustle you fellows, I'm afraid. Pur is particularly keen on looking you over, George. The others are, too. They expect to see a kind of Superman, like the one in the comics, or something. And do you know, I'm really half inclined to believe that you must be. We'll find out soon enough, won't We—eh, Kemp?"

I said: "You can torture me, Chatterton, but you can't make me tell what I don't know."

"No, Kemp, but good old Treit with his Limit of Human En-durance Test will certainly make you tell all you do know, you know . . . I'm afraid it'll be rather harrowing for you, George, if you force Us to it. However, one more brandy and a cigarette, and then we'll be off. What say?"

"All right," said George Oaks. "Only one thing: what Albert says is true. He knows nothing, nothing at all. He's in this affair by sheer chance."

"I'm not denying it, old fellow. But there's no harm in trying, is there? One never knows, does one—eh, George? . . . Besides, in a manner of speaking—you being Kemp's close friend—the very contemplation of his suffering ought, spiritually, to constitute quite a severe Form of Persuasion for you . . . without permanently injuring you for Us, as I'm afraid poor Kemp may be injured. Do you follow? Well, here's hoping it won't come to that. . . ."

Chatterton looked at his watch. "Not quite time, yet," he said. "Feel like a little walk?"

So we went out. At a respectful distance, Oettle and Mungo-Mitchell walked behind us.

Beyond the high circular wall that ringed this, the inviolably secret centre of the place, towered the disturbingly strange shapes of mysterious edifices ghostly in the moonlight. Here five leprous giants huddled in a ring about a titanic hookah, through the test tubes of which they seemed to be sucking green smoke; there twenty cubical colossi crouched before a dreadful mosque, domed with darkness, and with minarets tipped with flame. Beyond steamed four fantastic Turkish coffee-pots, with twisted handles, straddled by pot-bellied things with spidery tripod legs. And they all simpered and muttered, bubbled and chuckled, murmured and whispered together.

"That's the Research Plant," said Chatterton. " 'Industrial Research' as We call it. We've got half a dozen uranium mines tucked away back there, but We're all set to go into production on Silicon. There's a further ring of common or garden factory sheds beyond that; then the railway. It goes in concentric circles, as you might say; and for your information, this inner circle, and the one beyond, can only be got into, or out of, each by a single gateway."

"Where do you get your power?" asked George Oaks.

"Mainly, water from the mountain," said Chatterton. "It supplies Us with about four-fifths of what We need. Also, which is important, it feeds the Cooling System day and night. Do you know, even in the dryest weather Our little mountain torrent never fails; and in the hottest part of the summer is only a matter of a few degrees above zero. A blessing, that, because, as you must know, even if you're making harmless necessary nitrocellulose, there is a stage at which a sudden rise in temperature might easily spoil it—with very damaging results . . . I say nothing of what might happen to the Experimental Plant in such an eventuality. But it's out of the question, of course. Thermostatic controls switch on auxiliary refrigerators at a rise of one-quarter of a degree in temperature, and Bob's your uncle."

"Precarious," George Oaks suggested.

"Not a bit of it. Safe as Oak Ridge. . . . Here we are, troops. After you."

We passed through a corridor done with dark green carpet. Dark green guards opened dark green doors, and bowed us into a dark green ante-room. Chatterton said a word to a pale watchful man in a Sciocratic dinner-jacket, who said: "They are expecting you at ten precisely." He looked at his watch, and must have been counting seconds, for, after a long half minute, he nodded, and said: "Now!"

And as he said it, great double doors slid apart, and suddenly the ante-room was one with another, far greater room, dimly lighted, and so sparsely furnished that the dark green tables at the far end had the appearance of tables cleared at twilight after a dreary garden party on a funereal lawn. I say, tables—there were a dozen or fourteen of them. Obviously, every Member of the Council of the Sciocrats was head of his own table, at which he sat alone. Only six were present now, including Kadmeel, all dressed in green dinner-jackets, with the exception of a little old man in washed-out grey cotton clothes—a high-collared jacket, long as a nightshirt, long, narrow, wrinkled trousers, and a grey felt fez. This, of course, was the Maharajah of Pur, the richest prince in the world.

I did not like the cold, implacable arrogance of Tarrytowne's face; I detested the mock-innocent mouth and cruel languorous eyes of the Italian, Romagna; I hated the cynical fat face of the Frenchman, Simplon, with its topsy-turvy smile; and I wanted to hit the face of Van Weenen, just to see whether or no it was made of wood. But the face of the Maharajah of Pur filled me with indescribable loathing. Imagine a napkin which has been used to mop up spilled coffee, haphazardly thrown down, having accidentally pleated and wrinkled itself into an expression of senile lechery. In the fold that looks like the mouth, place three or four Brazil-nuts for teeth. Over the shadows, under the corrugated part that may be a forehead, hang a pair of gold-rimmed spectacles with half lenses. Such was the Maharajah of Pur. And his voice, when it came, seemed to come through wet linen.

He said: "Which iss the man? The big one, or the little one?"

Chatterton pointed to George Oaks.

The Maharajah said, hissing and whistling: "Ssmall ssnakess are ssometimess the mosst dangerouss. The krait iss more dangerouss than the cobra, because it iss more difficult to ssee. Sso, thiss iss the fellow who will have ssomething to ssay to Uss?" Chatterton nodded; and he went on: "You will be ssorry that you tried to pit your witss against Uss, ssir. I am very pleased to ssee you. I wass mosst curiouss. You are a very clever man, and when We are ssatisfied that you are truly ssorry, then you will be permitted, perhapss, to sserve Uss. Only firsst, you must be made to feel truly ssorry, sso that through repentance you will come to love Uss. You will be proud to be Our sservant."

With some impatience, Tarrytowne said: "Might I suggest that We haven't much time for philosophy right now, Pur? We are waiting for what can be gotten out of this fellow. I have a hundred and twenty-five agents standing by for a possible change of orders."

Lord Kadmeel said: "I agree with Tarrytowne. Arrangements may have to be altered. We do not know how much this man knows, or how much his employers may know. I propose that he be Questioned immediately."

"I second that," said Tarrytowne.

"Yes, but I should like to be present at the Questioning," said Romagna. "Is there any objection?"

Nobody replied. Van Weenen shrugged. Lord Kadmeel said: "Then you are to go to work without delay, Chatterton."

"I submit," said Chatterton, "that I be allowed to proceed

along the lines already suggested—that is, that the First Part of the Questioning consist in the application of Question Number One to the man Kemp, here, in Oaks's presence, Oaks being potentially too valuable a man to spoil."

Lord Kadmeel said: "You are always right, Chatterton. Proceed as you think fit. Take them away."

"When will you begin?" asked Romagna.

Chatterton replied: "In about an hour or so. I will see that you are duly informed."

I heard Romagna mutter: "He looks as if he might put up a stout resistance, the big fellow."

Then the doors slid together, cutting us off from the Council, and we were in the ante-room again. I saw tall men, now, standing against the walls. "Better come quietly," said Chatterton.

Walking like a man in a nightmare, I went with Oaks back to our quarters. Chatterton walked behind us now, with Mungo-Mitchell and Oettle. I knew then what the Ancients meant when they told of the Virtue going out of strong men: I was no longer angry, I was not even afraid . . . only heavily hopeless, so that when we reached our house I sat in a dull torpor, looking at my feet, counting the eyelet-holes in my shoes, unable to add them up.

Chatterton said: "Sorry, Kemp, but that's how it's got to be. Well, you still have about three-quarters of an hour to think it over. Powell, give the gentlemen some brandy. . . . You were speaking before (somebody overheard you and told me) of the Mysteries of Russia—the unlikeliest people betraying their friends, and pleading guilty to the most impossible offences, and so forth. Well, it may or may not surprise you to know that one of the very highest-ranking Russkies in the world is one of Us. They—and, incidentally, We—have three degrees of Persuasion, you know (I wonder why these things always seem to go in threes?), of which you, Kemp, are going, tonight, to get Number One, the mildest. . .

"The process isn't terribly blood-curdling to describe. Treit shoots some stuff into your frontal sinuses, that's all. I'm no bio-chemist, so I can't go into details, but it's something that sets up the kind of itching that you get with hay fever, only multiplied about ten thousand times, if you can imagine that. It starts in the forehead over the eyes, and, in about five hours, extends to the inner lining of the whole skull, so that you'd tear yourself to pieces if We let you. Simple as all that.

"The effects wear off in about eight hours. Even a very strong man generally breaks by about the fourth hour—can't become unconscious, you see. And after that, the memory of it being always with him, he'll say and do just about anything that's required of him. It takes quite a superman to hold out against Number One. Still, some do—in which case We apply Number Two; and that is rather disgusting. I only know, personally, one man—an Englishman, I'm proud to say—who got through Number Two. Then he went quite off his rocker, but We sifted what We needed to know out of his ravings before We put him to sleep.

"Number Three I've never seen applied, but I believe it's something quite out of this world. *How*ever . . . See you presently. Don't try anything desperate—it won't do the least bit of good, you know. . . . Oettle, come with me. Powell, don't leave the room."

"Yes, sir," said Mungo-Mitchell, grinning like a demon. "Oh, if you please, sir—may I watch, just this once?"

"Why, yes, Powell; I think you've deserved it."

"Thank you very much indeedd, sir!"

When Chatterton and Oettle were gone, he turned to us and, in a whisper that was quick, clear, yet faint, like the crackling of burnt paper, said: "Oaks! That stuff in the bottom fly-button of your trousers; the pills in the thin glass capsules—what is it?"

"Cyanide."

"Thank God! Get it out . . . Kemp, listen. Take this——" he handed me something like a little glassy imitation pearl—"keep it in your mouth, between your gum and your cheek, as far back as you can—that's it, right in the slack of the cheek. Now, when they strap you down in a kind of barber's chair, and push a kind of thin syringe with a curved nozzle up your nose, get that capsule between your teeth, bite hard, and swallow with all your might. It won't hurt—one pang, like a stab to the heart—you're unconscious before your nerves can register it. Oaks, you take one and do likewise."

"Why wait?" I asked.

"Brother!" whispered Mungo-Mitchell, with terrible intensity, "I'm not exactly a religious man, but I believe that Presumption of God's Mercy lies less heavy on the soul than Despair. I presume on God's Mercy—I make allowance for a miracle."

The feel of that glass bead between my gum and the big biting-muscle of my lower jaw gave me a kind of gallows-courage, and I whispered to Oaks: "You two talk the same language."

Oaks said, aloud: "We are men, Albert, old friend. All true men are brothers. We need no language in the Last Ditch. Therefore, I make no more apologies to you."

"George," I said, "no apologies are needed between you and me. All in all, I have a great deal to be grateful for."

I was thinking of the pill in my cheek, I believe, but he said: "Wow, but there will be something to talk about when we touch the Happy Isles and meet the great Achilles whom we knew!"—and squeezed my hand.

Mungo-Mitchell said, with a snigger: "Wouldd the gentleman care for a little something to moisten his lips? His throat sounds awfully dry." And he whispered: "*Keep mouth moist—save saliva for swallowing*."

"Brandy," I said.

As I was drinking it, Chatterton returned, followed by Oettle, who was carrying a folded white woollen garment over one arm; after him came a man in white, pushing—horror of horrors!—a hospital stretcher on wheels.

They led me into a bedroom, stripped me naked, and helped me into a kind of sack, a sack in five parts into which my limbs and my torso snugly fitted. A framework of metal kept my legs apart at an angle of about thirty degrees, my back immovable, and my arms almost at right angles to my body.

"The itching hits the armpits, also, you see," said Chatterton, as if in explanation, as they made everything fast with stout leather straps.

Oettle and the man in white lifted me on to the stretcher, and wheeled me through the lounge. I saw that Mungo-Mitchell had changed his houseboy's coat for a dark green mess-jacket with silver buttons. I heard George Oaks cry: "Courage, old friend!" —and then I was looking up at the stars.

I tried, tentatively, to move my arms and legs, but it was as if they were steel-stayed masts, and my will a mere squall—if I had been filled with the strength of a gale I could not have budged them. Then I lay limp. I tried to think noble thoughts, but could only say silently, over and over again: *Forgive us our trespasses* . . . *Forgive us our trespasses* . . . Yet I could not find it in my heart to forgive them who, in trespassing against me, trespassed against all I hold sacred. I caught one glimpse of the North Star, silent, white, and beautiful, and then I was travelling through a dully-shining white passage illuminated by livid fluorescent tubes, and so into a hot, dry, white room.

I was taken hold of, and lifted on to a kind of operating table. Cold sweat was trickling between my shoulder-blades, now, and from my armpits over my ribs . . . The wool, too, tickled my naked skin . . . This, in itself, was agony; I was happy that I was to be spared Question Number One.

I sucked the little glass bubble in between two strong molars. I had kept my mouth moist. I was ready. Someone tightened straps over my chest and above my knees, and pressed a lever; and then I was reclining, stiffly, at an angle of about sixty degrees to the floor. A pursy, heavy-mouthed, round-shouldered man was looking at me through thick bifocals. He was got up like a Park Avenue specialist, but he had the odour of a Turkish cigarette that has come loose in a lady's handbag.

"Clamp," he said; and an arc of padded metal came down upon my forehead, imprisoning my head. He picked up an instrument like a pair of scissors only it terminated in a hollow, truncated cone, which he inserted into my nose. But my nose still ached abominably from my fight with Oettle, and I cried out. Reflector on forehead, the pursy man stooped, scrutinised, and said: "Ze septub is broked. Ze bebrades badly idflabed—ve bust abbroach ze siduses srough ze sroat"—which I interpreted as: "The septum is broken. The membranes badly inflamed—we must approach the sinuses through the throat."

In that instant, with the capsule between my teeth, I made

ready to bite—but even as I began to close my jaws, a great rubber plug was thrust between my back teeth on the other side, and something cold and hard was exploring the upper part of my throat behind the palate.

I gagged, retching and coughing uncontrollably, and in that convulsion I felt the little glass capsule that contained my death and the lives of a billion better men flying away between my lips. My horror was such that I scarcely felt the long, curved nozzle of the syringe feeling its way through the sensitive passages behind my nose. I could see, at a distance, the face of George Oaks, green and appalled. Mungo-Mitchell, was standing beside him, grinning tightly. Near them stood Chatterton, coolly alert, with Romagna, whose mouth was puckered as if he was going to whistle.

George Oaks had seen the falling of the pill, I knew, because I saw his eyes following something that seemed to come to rest in an angle of the wall not far from where he stood. Mungo-Mitchell saw it, too, because even in that ghastly light his face changed colour. But the others, unaware and unexpectant, had seen nothing.

I felt a sickening fullness of fog between and behind the eyes. The pursy man withdrew the syringe, and said: "Zere is dothig to do budt vaidt, gedtlemed"—while I lay there, wondering whether I might find strength to bite off my tongue so that I could not talk. True, they could make me write, eventually; still, by that means I might gain time.

I prayed, silently: "Lord, one of Your saints bit off his own tongue to save himself from temptation: give me courage to do the same to save the world!"

Meanwhile, my eyes were on Oaks. He was gazing, with anguish, at Mungo-Mitchell. Chatterton and Romagna came forward to look at me. "Well, you're for it, now, you know, old fellow," said Chatterton. "What say, Dr. Treit?"

"He vill holdt oudt to ze bitter edt, zis vud, budt id fife hours he vill talk."

Romagna said: "I hope so, yet I cannot help hoping not. Oh, I would so like to see Number Three in operation!"

I saw Mungo-Mitchell turning to George Oaks. His right

hand disappeared under the skirt of his mess-jacket and came back into sight gripping a heavy blue pistol. Then, silently, they sprang forward together. A voice I had not heard before cried out in alarm, and Chatterton turned, just too late, as the barrel of Mungo-Mitchell's pistol crashed against the side of his head. He must have been very light; I scarcely heard him fall.

But before he had hit the ground, George Oaks's sinewy arms were about Romagna's throat, and his knee was in the small of his fat green back. Romagna went over backwards, and out of my field of vision, and Mungo-Mitchell, with grim death in his face, was covering Treit with his pistol, saying, between his teeth: "Unstrap that man, quick!"

The straps and the clamp fell loose. Tremulous hands fumbled at the buckles at my back, and I writhed free of the steel-stayed sack, and stood naked in that stark and grisly place of torment, with murder in my heart. Treit was sweating with fear. His assistant, a bald, burly, serious-looking young man started, in outraged tones, to say: "Now see here, I'll have you know———"

"—Shut him up," said Mungo-Mitchell, and so I did, with a right-hand punch that lifted him three inches from the floor, and sent him sliding into a corner.

"Keep Treit quiet," Mungo-Mitchell said to me, and turned to George Oaks, who was straightening himself over the inert form of Romagna.

"Oaks, strip him—quick, quick!" George Oaks's fingers flew to buttons and studs, while Mungo-Mitchell turned Chatterton over with his foot and, stooping, touched a bloody patch above the ear. Chatterton lay still, with his eyes half open.

"Well, you've had it, for one," said Mungo-Mitchell.

He handed me Romagna's dark green dinner suit. "Kemp, put this on, quick! . . . Shirt, collar, tie, and all . . . Treit, lend a hand —get this pig strapped down, or by God I'll beat your head to a jelly! Oaks, lend a hand!"

Romagna, half-strangled, was gasping himself back to consciousness. He was beginning to groan by the time the straps were buckled about him. I was dressed in his trousers, pumps, and shirt, and marvelling at the sureness of my hand as I knotted his tie about my neck, when he opened his eyes in an incredulous stare; and then an explosive puff of outraged astonishment blew his mouth into the shape of a scallop at the rim of a pie.

Mungo-Mitchell said to him: "Scream all you like, Romagna. You've heard screams in here before. This is a torture-chamber, sound-proof—remember? Even if you could make yourself heard, the guards outside have strict orders not to move . . . on their lives! So scream, if you like."

"What is the meaning of this?" said Romagna.

"This," said Mungo-Mitchell—I have never heard anything quite like his voice just then, stretched by hate to a fraction of a turn of breaking point—"this. You've seen Question Number One, and so have I. You've seen Question Number Two, and so have I—God keep it out of my dreams! But you've never seen Question Number Three in action. No. It has never been used before. It is going to be used now, Romagna, and you are going to feel it."

"No," said Romagna, "no, no!"

"Treit, prepare Question Number Three," said Mungo-Mitchell.

Sweating and trembling, Treit stammered: "For *hib?* Sir, blease, I dare dot! I dare dot!"

"Oaks," said Mungo-Mitchell, "to the right of the glass cupboard over there is a smaller steel cupboard. It is unlocked. Open it. You will see three drawers labelled 1, 2, and 3. Open Number 3. You will find some plastic tubes, apparently full of cotton wool. Bring me one. Also, a standard hypodermic syringe out of the glass cupboard. Hurry."

I was seeing through a fine haze, now, but my hearing was acute, too acute—the steel cupboard seemed to scream in my ears as it opened, and to box them when it closed . . . and my eyeballs felt dry and granular in their orbits . . . and between my teeth there was something like ground glass. . . . Still, I watched, telling myself that the ants in my ears and nostrils and armpits were not real. . .

Mungo-Mitchell had unstoppered the tube and pulled out its contents. On the palm of his hand I saw a topaz-coloured ampule in a nest of white cotton wool. I saw him nip off the tip of the ampule with a pair of tweezers; then, with infinite care, he drew its contents through the fine needle up into the barrel of the syringe, which he held very carefully between the first and second fingers of his right hand, while with his left he threw the empty ampule far away. I felt a hand on my arm, and heard George Oaks whispering: "Courage, old friend, we'll beat them yet" and, looking, saw that he held the pistol now, and that Mungo-Mitchell was tearing away Romagna's silk undershirt. The noise of its tearing was like the crackle of an electric storm.

"Intravenous, intramuscular, or subcutaneous?" asked Mungo-Mitchell, holding the syringe poised.

Romagna began to scream: "Chatterton! Chatterton! Chatterton!"

I picked up the limp body of Chatterton, and held it dangling where Romagna could see it, laughing, while Oaks said: "He is dead, he is the lucky one . . . Drop it, Albert. Mungo, let him have it!"

Then Treit (he could not stop himself) blurted: "It is *dot* idtravedous—it is subcutadeous!"

"No, no, for the love of God!" cried Romagna. "What do you want of me? Mercy!" I saw his large, swimming, blue eyes set like jellies as his look met mine. "The big one!" he screamed. "His eyes are red like blood—I tell you, he will rend, tear! Let me go!"

Mungo-Mitchell touched him with the hollow needle, and squeezed up a pinch of the skin of his upper arm; whereupon Romagna fell deathly still, whimpering: "What do you want of me?"

"The Password," said Mungo-Mitchell.

"That needle—take it away!"

"The Password!"

"The word for tonight is *Quid Si Coelum Ruat?* . . . For God's sake, take away that needle!"

Mungo-Mitchell's hand jerked; the needle disappeared under the skin of Romagna's arm. "If you're lying, think again," he said; but at the prick of the needle the Italian screamed like a horse in a fire, and I saw his biceps contract convulsively under the fat. Mungo-Mitchell stood back, looking blankly at the hypodermic syringe. The plunger was down; the barrel was empty;

and on the point of the needle hung one last transparent drop of clear amber liquid. He let the syringe fall to the floor.

Romagna sobbed: "Don't do it! Not that! Take away the needle—anything but the needle! I have not lied to you—*Quid Si Coelum Ruat?*—It is Latin for 'What If the Heavens Fall?'—It was I who chose it for tonight, I swear it! I will tell you everything, anything, only don't prick me with that needle!"

Mungo-Mitchell said to us: "Straighten your clothes. Follow me. Walk slowly. Kemp, shuffle your feet, walk with a slouch. This is madness; but we must take a chance." He picked up a white telephone, and cut the flex with a pair of surgical scissors, saying to Treit: "Make all the noise you please. You are locked in for five hours, now."

We left the room. The last I saw of Treit was his back. He was shaking his half-conscious assistant, saying: "Vake up, vake up, O'Fladdigad, add get your dotebook!"

Then the door locked behind us.

"Oaks, when I engage Oettle in talk, walk straight out. Kemp, stay close to me. Cover your face with your handkerchief, Kemp—mop it as if you were sweating. Now———"

My slouch and my gait were not simulated; I was moving with the dragging sag of a man without hope. The guards sprang stiffly to attention, staring straight to their front at their first glimpse of me, and I shambled into the moonlight.

Mungo-Mitchell said to Oettle: "Stand by, Oettle. No one to come in, or go out, for five hours. Nothing doing till then—Major Chatterton's strict instructions. Oh—I put in a word for you. Major Chatterton says you may come and look, about five a.m., when His Excellency and Oaks and I return. Compensation for your broken head—reward for being a good boy. Meanwhile, don't leave the gate."

I heard the guards' feet shuffle on the concrete as they stood easy, and then the three of us were walking at a leisurely pace through the shadows.

"What now?" asked George Oaks.

"What now?" said Mungo-Mitchell, with bitter mockery. "We die now, that's what now."

Conclusion

I began to say that I was sorry that I had lost my capsule, that I couldn't help it. But Mungo-Mitchell cut me short. "It wouldn't have helped much, in the long run," he said. "If you and Oaks had taken your poison, their suspicion would naturally have concentrated itself on me. I had charge of you. And if I managed to kill myself before they 'Questioned' me —why, that very fact would give them most of the answers. No, perhaps it's better this way."

"But we must die, anyway?" asked George Oaks.

"Yes, I believe so—but at least we'll die to some purpose. My evidence against these people is only half complete. I have scarcely enough for the tiniest international action, now. My case is hollow as a rotten nut. I can't call a raid for forty-eight hours, by which time every shred of evidence will be hidden over a dozen frontiers. There's only one thing left to do—send the whole damned works sky-high, ourselves and all. God give us strength to do it!"

"We are game, aren't we, Albert?" said George Oaks. "But how . . . ?"

I said: "Whatever it is, for pity's sake, let's do it soon—I tell you, I'm smeared with honey and crucified on an anthill!"

Mungo-Mitchell said: "My poor friend, you have nearly five hours before the agony really starts. What you feel now is nothing but a gentle hint of what's to come. . . . Here's the First Gate. Do you remember the Password?" I nodded.

Two trim sentries saluted me, and stood like statues in my path. "*Quid Si Coelum Ruat?*" I said. They stepped aside. High steel doors parted, and I led the way through them. The doors came together behind us with a gentle thud, and we were in the Second Circle, among the monstrous shapes that loomed over the murmuring sheds and shops. I realised then that Kadmeel's domain was terraced, built in circular steps on the plateau.

We climbed (I counted them) a hundred and twenty steps.

At the sixty-ninth, I remember, all the strength drained out of me, and I paused, whimpering that I was exhausted. Mungo-Mitchell said: "You begin to feel a catching in your chest? You can take your breath in, but you can't get it out? . . . Then we must hurry, hurry! You must bear up, Kemp, you must bear up!"

A quarter of an hour of walking took us to the Second Gate. "*Quid . . . Si . . . Coelum . . . Ruat . . . ?*" I wheezed. And again heels clicked; pistons sighed in cylinders; and doors opened.

I heard Mungo-Mitchell say: "His Excellency has an attack of asthma and wants fresh air. Let me have an open car. A jeep will do." And I stood, struggling for mouthfuls of air, dripping with sweat and tears until strong hands helped me on to a hard, cool seat, and an engine started, and I felt cool wind. I knew then how it must be to die of thirst at the brink of a pool; I would have given my right arm for half a breath of that wind; but now my lungs, having in one spasm emptied themselves, refused to expand again . . . and out of a million runways in the convolutions of my brain the frightened ants were crawling into my eyes.

I said, with idiotic resignation: "I'm bearing up. Only if it gets any worse, quite simply, I'll go mad."

"It will get worse and worse yet, Kemp, and the trouble is, you won't go mad," said Mungo-Mitchell. "Now hold yourself together, for God's sake, while your sense of honour, and loyalty, and decency lasts—which will only be for a little while now, Kemp!—Hold yourself, while I tell you what we have to do."

I managed to say: "Whatever it is, make it soon—soon!"

Mungo-Mitchell said: "It is a chance in millions, but we have got to fight for it. We have nothing to lose. We are as good as dead——"

"—Though we are ringed with spears, And the last hope gone, Romans stand firm, Albert, the Roman dead look on. Eh? Before the breath of life blows back to Him Who gave, Burn clear, brave hearts, and fight our pathway to the grave," said George Oaks.

"Chatterton told you that the power that supplies Kadmeel's place comes from the mountain in the form of water," said Mungo-Mitchell. "That is so. Kadmeel has harnessed a fall, dammed a torrent, and piped off a spring. The dam and the cataract provide electricity for the Plant. The perpetual cooling and washing systems are dependent upon the spring—it comes out of the rock, and is never warmer than seven degrees Centigrade. Up near the waterfall is the central powerhouse and the pumping-station. Well, as I see it now, we have to smash that power station."

George Oaks said: "Well and good, Mungo. You have, of course, a cache of dynamite?"

Mungo-Mitchell said: "No; all these things were to come, of course. Meanwhile, I was playing a lone hand—and you, with your sharp eyes, forced my hand . . . Yet again, perhaps, it's fortunate that you exposed yourself to me as you did, when you jumped me on the plane. Otherwise, there wouldn't have been this millionth chance. . . . No, there's no dynamite. There's only the three of us, and one pistol. But—a power-station! Lord! An educated woman can stop a power-station with a hairpin. Any of us could do it with his naked hands, if he knew which terminals to grab—if he were game! . . . I have eight high-velocity, forty-five-calibre cartridges in my pistol———"

George Oaks interrupted: "—Of which one or two, properly placed, would be as effective as a bobby-pin, or a human body, properly placed, to make a short-circuit in any power-station. Now, Mungo, you will listen to me. Stop the jeep for a minute: I want to be heard clearly, and once and for all."

The jeep stopped. George Oaks went on: "Mungo, The God knows that Albert and I are all for the counsel of desperation, and the millionth chance. The God knows, furthermore, that we throw ourselves upon His mercy, only when the light of reason fails us—and not until then. Mungo, your counsel of desperation is unenlightened."

A great owl screeched in the blackness of the trees, and in my agony I thought of Monty Cello on another Road. Mungo-Mitchell said, soberly: "How do you mean?"

George Oaks said: "First of all, there is desperation *and* desperation. Your desperation, Mungo, is nothing but despair."

"Say your say, Oaks, and let's get on!"

"All right, Mungo. Take first and foremost the business of busting the power-station. I grant you that, heavily guarded though it is, one of the three of us strong and desperate men could burst in, and burn himself between two terminals to short-circuit the electricity supply—or fire a pistol—or throw a wrench at a control board. But to what purpose? And for how long operative? Chatterton talked, down there, of auxiliary power sources, thermostatically controlled, and automatically sensitive to a fraction of a degree rise in temperature. I am telling you, Mungo, that it is not through the power-station that we must expend ourselves."

"Then *where*?" asked Mungo-Mitchell.

George Oaks said: "Let the power-station go full blast, feeding the works below. Our desperation is best expended on the cooling system. You've told me that the cold spring is piped off down into the plateau partly for cooling—but it must be mainly for the washing away of radio-active debris. The devil knows the inwardness of it; but I can tell you one thing, and that's this: in any atomic energy plant, where washing water doesn't flow, and flow fast, life stops."

"That is right," said Mungo-Mitchell.

"Now," said George Oaks, "there must, therefore, be an underground pipeline from the spring to the plateau."

"Yes," said Mungo-Mitchell, "there *is* a pipe four feet in diameter that runs three miles down from the mountain."

"Four feet? That's a big pipe," said George Oaks.

Mungo-Mitchell said: "It takes the spring floods."

"Good again," said George Oaks, "but we're early autumn now, are we not? Excellent! That pipe will be carrying scarcely two feet of water, surely?"

"For about two miles," said Mungo-Mitchell. "After that, the gauge narrows. The water goes in at high pressure, below, and there some of it is involved in a hydraulic pressure system for the freezing of air——"

"—In other words," said George Oaks, "this four-foot pipe must fork suddenly into two narrower pipes, one carrying water for washing, and the other for hydraulic pressure?"

"That's the idea," said Mungo-Mitchell. "But come to the point!"

"I am at the point," said George Oaks, rubbing his hands, and I saw his eyes shining in the moonlight. "I am at the point of intersection of three pipes. Mungo, I spit on your death, and your desperation! Can you lead me to the nearest manhole that lets into the great water-pipe?"

"Less than five hundred yards from here," said Mungo-Mitchell. "We had better walk."

I said, with something like gaiety: "Glory be! I feel better!"

"You can breathe now? You don't itch so much?"

"Why, no," I said. "It's passing."

"In that case," said he, "brace yourself, Kemp—your agony is just beginning to come on you." He took from a compartment in the jeep one of those heavy double-headed spanners that are cut to fit six different sizes of nut. "If we are to open the manhole," he said, handing it to George Oaks, "this will be handy. Hurry, now. Kemp, here, will be screaming crazy in a little while."

As we walked, George Oaks said: "You know, I was the runt of the family. My father and my brother were all six feet tall. All the girls used to laugh at me. I mailed a ten-shilling postal-order to a man who advertised an appliance to increase one's height, to be sent in a plain wrapper . . . I used to pray for a few extra inches. I asked the God why He had made me so little, out of the snippets left over from my tall brothers. Well, now I know. This is the end for which the God stamped me small—here is the key-hole for which I was cut! . . . From this base metal may be filed a Key . . . Eh, Albert?'

"What are you going to do?" I asked.

Mungo-Mitchell laid a hand on my shoulder, and said: "Let him be."

George Oaks was on his knees, now, working with the span-ner at the bolts which held fast a sunken circular plate of steel at the side of the road. In less than a minute, he had flung aside five of them. "Up with the manhole cover, Albert," he said, and I lifted it out, and dragged it to one side. The black hole which now lay open at our feet was little more than two feet in diam-eter, and from out of it came a noise of rushing water; and then I thought of the well in my garden, and the sick horror of George Oaks, shivering in the hot summerhouse at the very recollection of it; and I cried: "No, George, no—turn about's fair play! My turn this time——"

But he said: "—No, Albert, this is work for a little man. Thanks, Designer Infinite, for cutting me in miniature!"

He had been busy with his buttons; and now three of the plastic capsules of metallic potassium lay on his palm. "No," he said, "this is my show, without argument."

I knew that his whole soul shuddered away from the pit of shadows at his feet, but he looked steadfastly down at it with a face of stone. Then he put a finger in his mouth, and I thought that he was going to bite the nail; but he fished out his little bead of cyanide. Automatically, I held my hand out for it. He pushed my hand aside, gently, and politely wiping the capsule upon his neck-tie, gave it to Mungo-Mitchell, saying: "He knows more than you, Albert. He has priority. . .

"And now," he said, "this is what I am going to do. I am going down that pipe, past where it narrows, to the very intersection. Then, I am going to puncture my capsules of potassium and send them off, two into the feed-pipe of the cooling system, and one into the other pipe."

Mungo-Mitchell said: "The cooling system is the left-hand pipe. The wash pipe is on the right. That is a devil of a long chance, Oaks!"

"I know. A chance in millions, Mungo, but the only one. There are countless factors against it, but if I can wash just one pellet of potassium to where it will explode somewhere in the coils of any of the coolers, all their thermostatic auxiliaries won't switch on in time to save them. If that misses, a potassium explosion in the radio-active sludge may not. And in any case I shall have cut off the water."

"Cut off the water? With what?" asked Mungo-Mitchell.

"With *this*," said George Oaks, passing a hand over his body. "It stands to reason. I can go *down* the mountain *with* the water, but not *up* the mountain against the water. And the pressure of two miles of water in a four-foot pipe should tamp me into the fork, and give the plumbers a headache . . . because, don't you see, it will take a living, alert, intelligent foreign body to pass the Filters, and get far enough down to block the fork. Give me the wrench. . . . One thing, Mungo—have you a torch?"

Mungo-Mitchell handed him a little metal flashlight, such as doctors carry clipped in their breast pockets. "Thank the God for that!" said George Oaks, kissing it. "Albert, good-bye. It's all right! I have been living on borrowed time since Passchendaele. . . . *This* is what it was for. Put back the cover after me, and drive like the wrath of God over the mountain."

Before he disappeared, he smiled at me out of the pit, and said: "I will make my own peace with the God; but burn a candle for poor Monty Cello."

And then the manhole cover was back in position, and Mungo-Mitchell was half dragging me to the jeep, muttering: "There is a Man!"

I was crying, brokenly: "George! George!"

Mungo-Mitchell said: "There is still time. We'll take the mountain road. But first——" He fumbled under his tunic, and pulled out his belt. "——Better let me fasten your hands behind you. Your next spasm ought to be due any time now." I let him do as he wished. I looked up into the sky, and my eyes, hot and dry now, seemed to have sunk back and back in their sockets, so that I saw the stars too brilliant as through two tubes . . . And I thought of a little pencil of light stabbing the darkness underground between a bitter torrent and an arched darkness while George Oaks went to his glorious Doom singing; I knew that he must be singing, and that he would be comforted by the tremendous reverberations of his voice in the great pipe . . . I remembered his voice in the well . . .

. . . Then we were on a narrow road, and I could see below and beyond a chaos of black and white and green triangular dots —moon-lit mountain forest. About then, even in my agony, I felt that a certain sound was missing from Chaos. The jeep had stopped. (I learned, later, that we had been driving for nearly three hours.)

Mungo-Mitchell said: "No more petrol. We walk." And I begged him, for pity's sake, to shoot me in the head, through the ears, where the fiery itching was. When he would not, I wrenched my hands loose, and rushed him, trying to get the pistol; but he knocked me down with it, and when I—all too soon—came to, my wrists were strapped again, and my ankles also were tied with Romagna's braces. I was lying, writhing, in a little clearing. Mungo-Mitchell was sitting near me, limp and spent.

"This is about all, for the present," he said, "I have broken my ankle. The alarm will have been out this past hour, certainly. The helicopters will be up; they'll spot the jeep, and beat the mountain for us . . . We tried, God knows. But Oaks didn't make it; it was too much to expect; the odds were too long against it. Nothing to do but sit it out now."

He looked to the magazine of his pistol, balanced it in his hand, and said: "Eight cartridges. Seven for them; one for you; and the pill for me . . . *But what the devil's that?* It can't be dawn so soon!"

My face was set in the direction in which he was pointing. Over the great shaggy hump of the mountain down which we had so tortuously climbed, the sky was full of light. As we looked, the light grew brighter—unbearably bright—then sickly opalescent. It was a feverish, diseased, crawling, tingling, rotten kind of light—a cancerous light. It hung over the world for a moment, and then, as if to shade itself from that evil glare, the earth beneath put up three black umbrellas on one fantastic shaft. The umbrellas were sucked away. The light, in its anger, became red. And then the very concussion of the noise that followed, even from all those miles of distance, knocked me senseless.

. . . Shakily, at first, like a bubble in muddy water, I came up out of a deep black well of sleep . . . grew lighter, rose, pleasantly rocking, into a murmuring twilight, through which I sped, between the clutching fingers of grey dreams, into a film of luminescence, and so into the broad light of another day.

I was lying, propped at an easy angle, on a hospital cot, at the foot of which a nurse was sitting, turning the pages of an illustrated magazine. "Where am I?" I asked.

She dropped the magazine, and said: "Hello, there!" and reached for a thermometer.

"Where the devil am I?"

"You're in the hospital. Just take it easy."

"But *where* in hospital?"

"In Montreal, of course." She slipped the thermometer into

my mouth, saying: "That's fine; now you keep still," and went
to the door. When she returned a couple of minutes later, someone was walking rather heavily behind her. She caught the thermometer—it fell out of my mouth, and bounced on the edge of
the bed—as I cried: "Inspector Halfacre!"

Obedient to his gesture, the nurse went out again, and then
he sat beside me and said: "Thought I'd look in and see how you
were, Mr. Kemp. Feeling better? You look like a hundred per
cent."

"How did I get here?" I asked.

"You were flown in. You were suffering from . . . some form
of poisoning, I believe. You've been under one kind of anæs-
thetic and another, and after that just naturally asleep, for forty-
eight hours or more."

"Where's Mungo-Mitchell?" I asked.

"Who?"

"*Mungo-Mitchell!*" I cried.

"I seem to remember the name," said Halfacre with a blank
face. "Mayfair boy, wasn't he? Something to do with a jewellery job, wasn't that it? Not in my department. What makes you
ask?"

"You know very well who I mean," I said. "Not the *real*
Mungo-Mitchell; the other one—Chatterton's 'man Powell'."

"Just take it easy," said Halfacre, and he handed me a paper
bag. "I brought you a few grapes."

"All right," I said. "The man who brought me in—I think he
had a broken ankle. Where is he?"

"Well, Mr. Kemp, I don't know anything about anybody
with broken ankles. I'll inquire around the hospital, if you like.
The Royal Canadian Mounted Police brought you in, by plane,
I believe."

"From where?" I asked.

"From somewhere up in the Gaspé Peninsula, I'm told. . . .
Mr. Kemp, if I were you, I shouldn't bother my head about it any
more. You're alive and well. Count your blessings, Mr. Kemp."

His face was set like a plaster cast, but I said to him: "Halfacre,
if you won't talk, you won't. Only one thing——"

"——George Oaks? He is dead and gone," said Halfacre.

I said: "Yes . . . And that horrible light over the mountain? And Kadmeel's Place . . . ?"

"There isn't any Kadmeel's Place, Mr. Kemp."

I persisted: "Then George got through . . . ?"

"I shouldn't be surprised," said Halfacre. ". . . Come on, now, pull yourself together, Mr. Kemp. You're an old soldier, aren't you? Soldiers don't cry: do they now?"

I took the handkerchief he offered me, and blew my nose. "I wasn't crying," I said.

"I know; you're shaky, and a bit weak, but you'll be all right again tomorrow, and it'll all seem like a dream."

"But there are other Walled Cities in the world," I said.

"Mr. Kemp," said Halfacre, very gravely, "if there are, you can write them off as dreams too, now. You must rest a bit; the doctor says you can get up tomorrow. The day after, I'm flying home, when I've finished with my little bit of business here. And I took the liberty of booking you a place on the plane. See you tomorrow. So long, Mr. Kemp."

"So long, Inspector."

"Oh . . . And, Mr. Kemp, perhaps you feel that somebody owes you at least a 'Thank you'. Well, officially there is nothing to thank you for. Write it off, Mr. Kemp; write it off."

The day after next, we flew home to England; Halfacre to Parliament Street, and I to Sussex.

In the Piebald Horse two drenched farmers cursed the weather, as farmers have been cursing it in Sussex these two thousand years. Titmouse cursed the hop-pickers who had stolen twenty-eight pint glasses on Saturday night. He told me his odd-jobs man's wife had gone astray with a fishmonger. "Mr. Oaks gorn?" he asked.

"That's right," I said.

"Back soon, Oy 'ope?" Titmouse said. I shrugged noncommittally, and he went on: "Dat's a jolly liddle gendleman. Oy wish there were more loike Mr. Oaks, sir."

"So do I," I said.

"Ah," said Titmouse, flattering me with his confidence, and lowering his voice as he kept an eye on the grumbling farmers. "Winter draws on, Mr. Kemp, sir, and if it wasn't for moy licence

Oy might as well close th' eaowse. The loikes o' them 'll sit two eaours over a point o' bitter. What's moy profit eaout of a point o' bitter? One penny! Then they must play their liddle game o' darts, an' there's th' upkeep o' the board, an' money eaout o' pocket for chalk . . . Oy ask you, sir, is it worth it? Why eaout o' the locals Oy barely pay moy electric loight bill. Naouw, wi' gendlemen loike Mr. Oaks it's 'Double Whisky', an' 'Set 'em up all reaound' . . . Well, dat's de way o' the world, Oy suppose— The rich pays for de poor, loike. 'Somebody else 'll 'ave to suffer,' as the man said when 'e picked up a two-bob bit in the gutter, eh? —Going, Mr. Kemp?"

I went out into the mist of the Valley, feeling dreadfully lonely, and went home.

THE END

London,
 September, 1951

RECENT AND FORTHCOMING TITLES FROM
VALANCOURT BOOKS